Book 1 of the *Plug and Claim* Duology
Featuring Kira and Nathaniel

DARCY FAYTON

Contents

Book 1 of the *Plug and Claim* Duology
Featuring Kira and Nathaniel

DARCY FAYTON

Welcome! This is Book 1 of the *Plug and Claim Duology,* a very spicy enemies-to-lovers MF paranormal fantasy dark romance with a love story.

How dark is the story? The duology is an emotional roller coaster. It is dark, but features moments of light-heartedness, humour, and sweetness. Efforts have been made to minimise violence and gore. Most characters, including our morally grey male lead, have both flaws and redeeming qualities. Readers unfamiliar with dark romance books are especially advised to proceed with caution. Readers who *are* familiar with the dark romance genre may find this duology to be less dark (3/5 darkness scale) than they are expecting but still very spicy (5/5).

Before you begin reading, please note:

- This story is intended for an 18+ audience.

- This book ends on a cliffhanger, with a satisfying happily ever after in the sequel, *Plug and Tame*.

- This story was written with the intent of providing escapism. However, it contains elements that may be triggering for some readers.

- **Themes explored in both books include:** BDSM, D/S, pet play, CNC, dubcon, kidnap, virginity trope (central to plot), bondage, anal play, plugging, gagging, humiliation, degradation, praise, vampire feeding, grooming, gore, self-defence with blade weapons, and sex scenes involving other characters. The sequel also features breath play, other woman drama (not cheating), SA (one active scene in finale, not with MMC), and a flashback scene describing death of children. This list is not exhaustive; reader discretion is advised.

- This is a work of fiction. It is not a BDSM handbook. For useful information on BDSM lifestyle including safe play practices and health, please reach out to a safe online or local BDSM community.

- The story is predominantly written in British English with minor exceptions, leading to variations in spelling and expressions (eg. realise, sceptical, burnt, vice).

MY CONTACT DETAILS:

instagram @darcyfaytonauthor
email darcyfayton@gmail.com

Author website + newsletter signup: linktr.ee/darcyfayton
Add this book to your Goodreads shelf

Thank you in advance for reading *Plug and Claim*, I hope you enjoy the story as much as I did writing it.
—Darcy

Get on your knees, pet. It's time to play.

CHAPTER 1

Wolf in Sheep's Clothing

KIRA

IT WAS KIRA'S LAST night in the cottage. Someone in the village had discovered her secret, and now, the vampires were coming for her.

Sitting at the candlelit table, Kira warmed her hands on the cup of camomile tea, soaking up the small comfort as she braced herself for what was to come.

Would they feed on her before they took her away?

Probably.

Would they force themselves on her at the same time?

Perhaps take turns violating her right here on the kitchen table? She hoped not, but vampires were cruel. Thinking ahead, she'd added extra milk to her tea to cool it; if they spilt it while assaulting her, at least it wouldn't scald her. It was a ridiculous thing to think about at a time like this, but she had nothing to do now except wait, and think of ridiculous things to pass the time.

Yesterday, after years of hiding in the quiet village of Nordokk pretending to be one of the humans, the villagers had seen her shift into her wolf form and reported her to the vampire authorities.

Now, she needed only to wait. The vampires would come for her soon.

She glanced out the cottage window. The recruiting officers always came at night, and now that twilight had succumbed to pitch black, it was only a matter of time before they arrived. Even in her human form, her night vision was superior to a human's, and she could see into every shadow of the bushes and fence posts lining the dirt road.

Unless they come via the back garden.

Staring out of the windows was making her increasingly nervous, and she forced herself to look down at her tea and find a place of calmness. The camomile tea leaves floated across the surface. They were meant to help calm her, but she called bullshit.

How could she be calm when the enemy was fast approaching? When in a matter of minutes, she might feel sharp teeth sink into her neck, firm bodies pressed against her, rough hands spreading her legs...

She shuddered as she dismissed the thought. It would not help to imagine the worst. There was every possibility that they wouldn't touch her at all—not until she arrived at Volmasque Academy, anyway.

The academy had been established by Henrikk, the Vampire King, to train wolf shifters to become obedient pets, and vampires to be their masters, all under the guise of fostering harmonious wolf-vampire relations.

Vampires ruled over the population, the majority of which comprised of humans and wolf shifters. Humans were largely left alone, allowed to lead their lives peacefully like cattle—until the vampires grew hungry. But vampire attacks on humans were rare. Despite their disdain for wolves, vampires preferred to feed on them instead of humans. Some believed it was because they preferred the taste of wolf blood, whilst others claimed vampires derived more power from wolf blood. It made little difference to Kira—vampires could suck a dick for all she cared. She would never let one of those parasites suck her blood, not willingly.

They had tried to take her when she turned eighteen, and Kira had almost let them. She'd been planning revenge for as long as she could remember, but in the lead up to her eighteenth birthday, she'd allowed her foster father, Byron, to talk her out of it. They'd subsequently spent the last twelve months hiding in the vast mountain woods. But no longer. Hiding in the shadows was no life.

She tapped her fingernails against her cup anxiously.

How much longer?

A minute?

Two?

The vampires couldn't be far away. She could feel it in the dread that seeped into the cottage like smoke, rolling in under the door and through the open windows.

Suddenly, she sensed it. Someone was outside. She felt it all the way in the pit of her stomach.

All was quiet, but all was not well.

She heard movement outside—a single set of footsteps.

Every hair stood on end as Kira stayed perfectly still, feigning that she was unaware of the stranger's presence as she lifted the teacup to her lips. She heard the crunch of pebbles as the stranger approached, and then silence. She could feel eyes on her, and her throat was tight as she swallowed the liquid, gulping too loudly. Her cup rattled as she set it back down on the saucer. The footsteps resumed, striking the wood ominously as the stranger crossed the porch.

A deep, masculine tune met her ears.

He's fucking humming?

Kira watched the door warily. Would he break it down? Her gaze slid to the windows. Or smash the glass in?

Slowly, she looked up at the wooden beams and thatched roof.

Maybe he'll get creative and drop down on me.

She flinched as a knock came at the door.

She had not expected him to knock. The polite gesture was

surprising, and a mockery in light of what he wanted to do to her.

Feed. Fuck. Tease.

Brainwash her until she obeyed. Quite possibly in that order.

The knock came again on the front door.

Kira rose to her feet. There was no point in delaying the inevitable. Whoever was on the other side of that door would take her away. She'd returned to the cottage knowing this would happen, but there was no avoiding destiny.

Her feet felt like lead as she walked to the door. There was a very real possibility that she would never see the tiny, peaceful cottage she'd grown up in again. It was too late to say goodbye.

Her hands were clammy as she turned the handle. She was as ready as she would ever be for the vampires.

But were they ready for her?

The enemy was on her doorstep. Had she been in wolf form, her hackles would have been raised. Taking a steadying breath, she wiped the animosity from her face, and adopted an expression of polite confusion as she prepared to welcome her captor.

The vampires thought they had discovered her secret—but although she was indeed a creature of darkness like them, she was not the one they expected.

They thought she was a wolf shifter hiding amongst the humans, but they were wrong. She was so much more.

They thought she was a sweet, pliable wolf who would become a good student and integrate into their academy—wrong again.

Little did they know that she had no intention of falling into line. She was not there to be groomed and dominated by vampires.

She was there to start a rebellion.

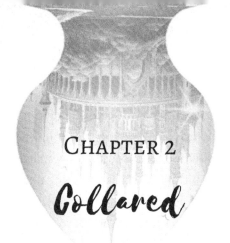

CHAPTER 2

Collared

KIRA

SLOWLY, THE DOOR CREAKED open. The first thing Kira noticed was the vampire's eyes—a piercing bright blue that captured her and did not let go. He was tall and impeccably dressed, with a black suit and a dark wool coat that had a sharp collar and tails trailing down to his calves. A few strands of his icy blond hair, which was loosely combed to one side, had escaped and fallen across his forehead.

"Good evening," he said, his voice deceptively pleasant. "I've come to extend an invitation for you to join our illustrious ranks at Volmasque Academy."

Of course you have.

Kira repressed a snort as she peered past the vampire's shoulder into the dark yard. He was alone.

The vampire raised an eyebrow. "Expecting someone else?"

"No, I wasn't expecting anyone," she lied.

"Well, then, I hope you will consider joining us. I presume you already know about our academy...and the expectation that you attend."

"Expectation? I thought you said it was an invitation," she said wryly, unable to help herself.

Even if her foster parents, Mary and Byron, had not told her about the academy, it would have been difficult not to learn about its existence. Everyone in the village spoke of it in hushed whispers. It was a point of fascination for the humans, who lived in fear of both vampires and wolf shifters, despite attempting to coexist with them.

His eyes narrowed as he smiled. "Don't play with me. You and I both know that all wolves are required to attend Volmasque Academy from their eighteenth birthday."

Kira crossed her arms. "I'm nineteen."

"I'm well aware."

"Too bad I missed the cutoff date."

His voice grew dark and ominous. "We will find a way to insert you."

The way he said it made her shiver, his cool words rippling across her skin like water in a stony creek.

"You have been avoiding me," he continued. "I have been searching for you all year."

Kira shrugged. "I was gone fishing."

The vampire did not smile, his words slow and drawn out. "Your value, has only increased."

She scarcely dared to breathe under his intense gaze. He didn't just look at her. His eyes struck her like a whip, making her muscles coil and her knees weak. It was as if he was pushing her down to a place beneath him, somewhere near his feet, paralysing her heart.

"I await your answer," the vampire said.

She regarded him coolly. "I'm not going."

The mild politeness on the vampire's face vanished, and his voice sharpened like chiselled ice. "I implore you to reconsider."

Alarm bells were ringing in her head, but she soothed them. She had nothing to fear from the vampire's threats because her goal wasn't to evade capture—it was to make him think she was reluctant to go.

It was not an accident that the villagers had seen her shift in Nordokk's town square. She'd done so on purpose for the briefest of seconds, knowing the villagers would report her to the authorities.

Still, it was not the abduction she'd been prepared for. He was meant to grab her and haul her away to the academy, and she was meant to kick and scream and put on a good show. But the vampire was surprisingly patient, as if he wanted nothing more than to stand on her porch talking to her. It made the situation trickier to navigate. His watchful gaze was creeping her out.

Kira lifted her chin. "I politely decline your invitation."

The vampire's eyes flashed. "You do *not* want to disobey me."

His words gripped her as if he'd seized her by the shoulders, and her mind cycled through the possibilities of what he could do to her if she provoked him.

Fuck it.

"Why?" she taunted. "Are you going to suck my blood?"

The vampire laughed, a surprisingly pleasant sound that melted his icy demeanour. Somehow, it made him even more frightening as he stepped up onto the doorstep, and she suddenly realised his full height as he towered over her. "But we've only just met, Kirabelle."

"It's Kira," she said, shrinking back from the vampire. "I prefer Kira."

The vampire took another step closer until they were toe to toe, their bodies inches from touching. "Well, *Kira*...unless you want me to feed off you, I see no reason for the delay. Your education at Volmasque Academy awaits."

"It can wait all it likes because I'm. Not. Going." She slammed the door shut.

The vampire caught it just before it closed and shoved it open, the tremendous force sending her stumbling backwards.

She managed to stay on her feet and ran for the cottage's back door, but he was faster. Cruel hands seized her hair painfully and jerked her back. Before she could react, he spun her around to face him, pinning her to the wall with his arms.

She screamed, forgetting in her momentary terror that this was what she wanted—that her capture and abduction was part of the plan.

"Calm yourself," he said, releasing one of her shoulders and unbuttoning his coat. "Or I will do it for you."

Is he undressing?

Fear coiled and she lunged forward, using his momentary distraction to bite him, her human teeth clamping down on his wrist.

The vampire hissed in pain and snatched his hand back, shoving her back against the wall.

They both panted as they glared at each other, not from exertion but...exhilaration?

"Feisty," he chuckled, his eyes shining with approval. "You have a nasty bite."

"That was nothing," she retorted, noting with disappointment that her teeth hadn't broken skin. His hand was red from bite marks, but there was no blood. Did vampires even bleed? She'd never thought to ask.

"It would be in your best interest to come peacefully," the vampire said, reaching inside his coat. He produced a thick, black strap of leather with steel buckles, from which dangled a thinner strap that had a smooth round ball at its centre. The ball was perfectly round, about the size of a plum, and was smooth and bright red.

"What the fuck is *that*?" Kira cried.

"A collar and gag. I will muzzle you if necessary. So, tell me. Is it necessary?"

Kira couldn't speak. The sight of the leather and steel was a horrific sight. She lunged forward, trying to push past him, but he was ready for her, and he slammed her against the wall, knocking the breath from her lungs.

"Last chance, pet. I will not ask again. Will you be good for me?"

The word 'pet' caused rage to surge through her, and a deep, angry snarl tore from her throat. "I am *not* your pet! Do not call me that!"

The vampire used that opportunity to shove the ball gag inside her mouth. She threw her head back, but it banged against the wall, and the cold object filled her mouth and muffled her protests. She struggled, but his fingers were fast and nimble, and his hard body pressed her against the wall as he roughly fastened the strap behind her neck. The collar was wide enough to cover her throat, and as he tightened it, she felt the leather constrict her breathing.

Panic surged through her as she lost her ability to speak or to even breathe properly. She tried to shout, but her words were incomprehensible.

Suddenly, it was quiet in the cottage. The only noise was Kira's wheezing as she was forced to breathe through her nose, and the pounding of blood in her ears.

What the hell had just happened?

The ball gag pressed heavily on her tongue, forcing her lips to stretch around it. She hated the thought of how she looked wearing it.

Meanwhile, the bastard just stood there, watching her.

Slowly, she lifted her gaze to meet his.

He stared back calmly, his head tilted as if to gauge her reaction. His apathy only added to her humiliation.

"There," he pronounced, running his thumb across her cheek, "isn't that better?"

Fuck you! she tried to yell, but she could not speak. The gag had robbed her of any autonomy she might have had.

"Are you going to behave?"

Kira managed to free her arm and threw a punch at his face. She missed.

"Don't make me tie your hands, too."

She flinched as he reached to touch her face, but his fingers were gentle, gliding along the thin straps that ran from the gag and dug into her cheeks.

She grimaced and turned her head away, refusing to look at him. It was the only thing she still had control over.

He let out a low chuckle.

She waited for him to release her, but the seconds stretched, and her contempt for him grew the longer his body remained against hers. He was tall and lean, and even through his shirt, she could feel his warm, hard torso where it compressed her breasts. She'd wrongly assumed that vampires were cold-blooded, assuming that's what he is. Her gaze darted to his mouth. His lips were parted in a subtle smile, and the tips of two fangs were visible.

Definitely a vampire.

With a shocked gasp, she became aware of a firm hardness pressing against the top of her thigh. Nausea crept through her at the realisation that the vampire was erect. He *enjoyed* doing this to her, and it was repulsive.

"You know...you are not what I expected," he murmured, his touch trailing along her jawline back to her cheek.

Kira swallowed.

Neither are you.

She'd expected a rough brute...not this elegantly dressed gentleman who balanced cruelty and manners with ease. She didn't know what to make of him.

He was beautiful in the same way a dream was beautiful before it transformed into a nightmare—ominous and clouded with darkness.

"Not what I expected at all," he repeated, still caressing her face. "But soon, you will obey, just like the rest of them. You will sit and stay...and drink from a water bowl. You will even fetch."

Without warning, he released her and walked away, leaving her standing by the wall, gagged and trembling.

"Go to your room and pack," he said idly. "You have five minutes. Oh, and Kira..." He turned back, his icy gaze chilling her to the bone. "Do not remove that collar."

Kira's eyes were blurry with tears as she disappeared into her bedroom and slammed the door. Her hands went immediately to the collar, trying desperately to undo the buckles, but the leather was taut and her fingers were clammy and slipped off the intricate straps.

This is all wrong.

The collar was a violation she was not prepared for, and for a wolf shifter, it was the ultimate act of humiliation. It robbed her of her humanity, symbolising that to him, she was little more than a dog.

There were many terrible things a vampire could do to a wolf. Mary and Byron had only hinted at them, telling her as much as she needed to know without going into explicit detail, but Kira had heard enough rumours from the villagers to guess. Even so, she'd hoped to avoid *this,* the inhumane punishment of being collared.

Kira caught sight of her reflection in the mirror and choked back a sob. The woman staring back at her was on the brink of defeat. It was so different to how she saw herself that she hastily wiped her eyes. She would not give the vampire the satisfaction of seeing her crumble.

Mary and Byron had tried to warn her that vampires were cruel. Well, this one had gotten under her skin within seconds, and she feared he'd left a permanent mark on her psyche.

She'd been ready to fight, ready to resist capture. But nothing could have prepared her for *him,* nor the collar he strapped around her throat.

This was no ordinary vampire. He was a monster.

CHAPTER 3

Predator and Prey

KIRA

THE GAG WAS LARGE and uncomfortable inside Kira's mouth. It made her breathing harsh and ragged as she tried to calm the panic seeping through her.

The vampire had said five minutes, but she'd been here at least ten by now. To her relief, he hadn't barged into her room. Still, it was not wise to keep him waiting. If this contraption was his first preference for reprimand, she did not want to find out what the more severe punishments were.

As the precious minutes passed, her heart rate calmed, and she was able to think clearly once more.

This is fine.

I'm fine.

Objectively speaking, nothing significant had happened. The vampire hadn't hurt her, and the fact that he was an insufferable jerk was not in the least bit surprising. If anything, the plan was going perfectly: she'd acted like prey, and he'd taken the bait not knowing she was a predator lying in wait. Resisting the urge to shift into her true form, however...now, that was the hard part.

Tearing apart the vampire was not conducive to that plan;

she had to get to Volmasque Academy. To avoid suspicion, she had to appear unwilling. Which meant letting this arrogant, conceited—admittedly handsome—asshole drag her to the school. That was the plan.

And yet, she felt utterly helpless. Try as she might, Kira couldn't overcome the effect the collar had on her. The collar's physical constriction around her neck was suffocating, but the gag was even more encroaching, invading her subconscious until all she could think of was the vampire and the power he held over her.

You will sit and stay...and drink from a water bowl. You will even fetch.

Kira wiped away an angry tear. He was wrong. She was not his pet. She was his death, and she would come for him soon.

Inside her closet was her travel bag, but she had no idea what to pack. The fact that he was even allowing her that opportunity astonished her, and she wondered if it was a trick. Her gaze roved over her belongings, looking upon them in a new light now that she had a chance to take them.

However, the most precious items had already been removed—journals and paintings that alluded to her past, which had been thrown out a year ago when they'd left the cottage. In fact, the entire cottage was carefully curated to suggest that she'd lived an ordinary, lonesome life away from other wolf shifters.

But the locket was here, hidden in the desk in a secret compartment, and the temptation to retrieve it was high. It was her only link to her past; to the night of the Revolution when rogue vampires overran Wintermaw Keep, home of the Royal Wolf family. They had slaughtered every last shifter they could find and claimed the Keep as their own. According to Mary and Byron, who had been working in the Keep as guards, Kira had been wearing the locket on that bloody night fifteen years ago when they found her sleeping in the servants' wing. They'd rescued her from the castle and raised her as one of their own.

The identity of her birth parents remained a mystery. Byron and Mary were the only parents she had ever known. Try as she might, she'd been unable to recall her four-year-old self's memories of loving parents—if they'd ever even existed.

But she remembered the other children. She had an old memory of playing with them in a sunlit meadow. It grieved her to think that they'd perished, and of the terror they must have felt as she slept through that night's horrors.

Kira broke out of her reverie and glanced at the clock. Fifteen minutes. The vampire was being generous to let her linger this long—or perhaps, he would punish her when she left her room.

Just another minute...

It was difficult to say goodbye. The cottage was the only home she could remember. Nordokk was a sleepy village a few hours by carriage from the Capital, a sprawling city that contained Volmasque Academy at its centre. On the far side of the city was Wintermaw Keep, where the Vampire King now resided, ruling over the fragmented lands and controlling the wolf shifter population with increasingly strict rules.

Kira had never seen any of it in person, not even the Capital, an ancient wolf city which had transformed in recent years into a central hub for vampires looking for an easy meal.

Kira glanced at her window. It was large enough to fit through if she decided to escape.

I can still change my mind.

A year on the run hadn't been so bad. Hunting for food and cooking it over the campfire. There had been a tranquillity to it. At least until she'd woken to the sound of logging. She'd been distressed to discover that the vampires were gathering timber for their multi-storey mansions and had commissioned miles of woodland to be decimated. The sight of the wood stumps was what had finally convinced her to return to her original plan. Someone had to do something, and it may as well be her. The vampires had taken her family from her, and their harsh laws had stripped away her freedom. She wouldn't let them take her home, too.

Wintermaw Keep was where her journey would end—it was unlikely she would walk away alive. Byron and Mary both knew it, though they never said it, and their tearful embraces of goodbye yesterday had confirmed it.

Her hand hovered over the desk, brushing the coarse texture of the timber Byron had shaped himself. The stocky man with salt-and-pepper hair had encouraged her painting. He and Mary had given up the cottage's only bedroom for her. Byron always referred to her room as her 'art studio', and he'd tried to convince her to carve out a new life for herself.

Except Kira had never been able to let go of the past. She did not want to spend her entire life hiding her wolf form and the dark secrets that clung to her heart. There had to be something better.

The walls were bare. The paintings that she'd made of her dreams of a new revolution were gone, as were the nails that had held them, but she remembered exactly where each canvas had been and the bloody scene each one had depicted. The wooden box of paints still sat in the corner, and she half considered taking them. Byron had been full of excitement when he came home from the market with a set of tin paint tubes. It had been his last attempt to sway Kira from her pursuit of revenge.

She ran her hands over the paint tubes. All of them were full and untouched, except for the red one, which was rolled up and nearly empty. Revenge only needed one colour. And, as Byron had informed her, black was not a colour.

In the end, she took nothing except a small silk bag of coins. She would leave the happy reminders of her life at the cottage behind. Maybe, if she survived, she would be back one day to claim it.

Worry gnawed at her as she crept to the door. Would the vampire be mad she'd taken so long?

Tentatively, she opened the door and peeked out. The cottage was deserted. She glanced at an empty space where, until just a few days ago, Byron and Mary's bed had been. The couple had moved it out of the cottage in preparation for Kira's demonstration, stripping the cottage of any evidence they'd ever lived there.

It hurt to think that even after she was gone, Byron and Mary would not be back. They were both unregistered wolf shifters, and staying here was too risky. Despite their good standing in the community, the humans would not hesitate to report them. The lure of immunity from feeding, which was what the vampires offered in exchange for reporting illegal wolves, was too great.

It was why she'd insisted that they not stay for her capture.

"Promise me, you'll leave," Kira had begged, her voice shaking as she tried to hold back tears. "Go somewhere far away. I don't want them to take you, too."

Unlike humans, who could work normal jobs like farming, all adult wolves were allocated roles by the Vampire Council. Most were assigned to be donors and were required to present to vampire households every week for the purpose of being fed upon. Sometimes, the vampires solicited other services.

Kira exhaled through her nostrils. She was thankful every day that the two old wolves had escaped that fate, and that to this day, she'd never had the misfortune of being fed upon either.

She lingered a moment longer, trying to picture the bed that had been there. One of her happy childhood memories was of playing hide-and-seek beneath the sheets with Mary and Byron. The old couple had humoured her as she peeked out giggling, pretending they couldn't find her. She pushed the cherished memory deep down, protecting it from the outside world. Steeling her nerves, she went outside.

The vampire was waiting on the back porch, looking at Byron's beloved garden.

Her heart squeezed.

How dare he stand there as if he owns the place?

She hated the sight of him. She hated his chiselled face, and his commanding presence, and the predatory grace of his movements as he turned to face her. His expression gave nothing away as he regarded her, but lurking behind his mask, she sensed something seductive and dangerous, and she felt drawn to him like a moth to a flame.

A part of her dared hope he would remove the gag. Her jaw strained against the gag's intrusion, and despite her efforts to suppress it, a trickle of saliva escaped from the corner of her mouth, and she knew he could see it.

"It's nice to see you like this," he said, a smile tugging at his lips, "*quiet.*"

Never mind.

Kira threw him her dirtiest glare.

Asshole.

The vampire laughed. "Don't look so affronted. I have other ways to keep you quiet."

Kira didn't want to know what those other ways were. She followed him to the front of the house, hurrying to keep up with his steps. A carriage awaited them in the country lane. It was harnessed with a pair of horses, whose black coats were as glossy as the carriage body. She was relieved to see there was no driver.

At least I'll be alone for the journey.

It would allow her momentary respite from the blond vampire while he drove. She walked begrudgingly to the carriage.

He opened the carriage door and offered her a hand up. She promptly refused both, raising her eyebrows at him. Really? He was being chivalrous *now?*

Holding her head high, Kira stepped into the cabin and sank down on the upholstered seat. She let out a long breath of relief through her nose, the tension in her shoulders easing.

Her heart fell when the vampire climbed in after her, sliding onto the seat opposite and folding his long legs.

He caught sight of her disappointed expression and explained, "The carriage is enchanted. It will drive itself."

When she continued to stare at him, he smiled. "We don't have to talk."

She stared out the window silently, hating him and hating the gag that prevented her from giving him an earful.

Asshole.

CHAPTER 4

Carriage Ride with a Wolf

NATHANIEL

NATHANIEL WASN'T SURE WHAT he'd expected, but it wasn't this. He'd taken one look at her peasant clothes and calm demeanour and considered his work half done. The last thing he'd expected was for her to bite him. He couldn't help but be impressed.

He stared at Kira, and she stared out the window, refusing to so much as look at him as the carriage trundled down the country lane.

For his part, he could not look away. She was not only beautiful, but a force of nature, and he was completely and utterly captivated by her. Most wolves had brown skin, but Kira's was a shade darker, an exquisite bronze that seemed to glow even in the dim carriage. Luscious brown hair pooled around her shoulders, thick and slightly wavy, and her amber eyes were riveting, with shimmering flecks of gold that he could get lost in. The few times she deemed to look at him, their fierceness gripped him, inviting him in even when the rest of her clearly despised him.

He couldn't blame her. She had every reason to hate him and his kind. But the carriage ride was a good opportunity for them to become better acquainted—and it did not require speaking. He had so many questions for her, but for now, he was content to watch her.

Before he'd gagged her, her full lips had formed the perfect pout. He did not know her well enough to discern if this was an expression of defiance, or if they naturally rested that way, but it was unnervingly sexy.

Now, with her lips stretched and taut around the ball gag...well. There were no words to describe what it did to him to see her mouth stuffed and stretched, and the sight of the drool shining on her chin made him ache and burn.

He was just as helpless as Kira.

If only she knew.

He was tempted to see how far he could push her. She was not the type of wolf to submit easily, and he relished that challenge. But although the thought of making her bend over his lap sent heat rushing to his loins, it was not worth the risk—Kira was the type of wolf to bite first and ask questions later.

No, this was not the time for wetting his cock. He sensed that behind Kira's fierce mask, she was scared and confused, and, as everyone knew, the kindest way to handle a scared animal was with a firm hand.

Judging by how quickly she'd submitted, the collar and gag were the right course of action, but they would lose their effectiveness over time. She was in shock, and understandably so after he'd caught her off guard in her own home. It almost felt like cheating. She wouldn't be so easily subdued next time.

Kira shot him a resentful look before returning to look out the window.

She'd hated it when he laughed at her earlier.

"Don't look so affronted," he'd teased. *"I have other ways to keep you quiet."*

Like filling your mouth with my cock.

An hour passed, then two. Nearly five hours now, according to his pocket watch.

His earlier arousal had dissipated, mostly because he could tell she was growing uncomfortable from wearing the gag for so long. She was struggling to swallow properly, and her saliva flowed freely, dripping a puddle onto her lap and creating a wet patch down the length of her skirt. She was stubborn, making no move to wipe it, not even when he passed her a handkerchief.

Nathaniel drummed his fingers on his knee. He'd made his point—almost. He would wait another tantalising thirty minutes before he removed the gag, just to ensure the message had sunk in. Until there was no doubt in Kira's mind that *he* was in control.

When they reached the smoother roads leading to the Capital, he cleared his throat.

"Very good, Kira. That concludes our lesson. I think you deserve a break."

The gold of her irises brightened with hope.

Reading her unspoken question, he inclined his head. "Yes, I'll remove the gag for you."

Kira turned in her seat so he could reach the back of her neck more easily.

He didn't move. "Oh, no, Kira, that won't do."

She glanced at him in confusion.

"Kneel before me."

Her eyes clouded with anger, sending lethal daggers his way. He waited for her to comply...but she did not.

His tongue eased over the tip of his fangs. They throbbed, craving to sink into her tender neck. Her defiance whet his appetite like nothing else.

"Come now," he said lightly, nodding at the carriage floor between their seats. "This does not have to be difficult. Kneel, and I will remove the gag."

She looked as if she'd sooner chew broken glass than obey him. It would make it all the more satisfying when she did eventually comply.

"Kneel, or don't kneel," he said, placing his hands behind his head and smiling like an arrogant prick. "But if you do not, I'm afraid the gag remains."

A part of him was disappointed she hadn't shifted into a wolf in order to try and escape yet. There was nothing more beautiful, in his opinion, than a female wolf.

More beautiful than Gloria, the vampiress he'd been pursuing to satisfy his father's orders. That courtship was painfully drawn out—Gloria had kept him chasing her for several years, and his patience was wearing thin.

Movement caught his eye. Kira had shifted ever so slightly in her seat.

His breathing stopped.

She's considering it.

His pulse thrummed with anticipation. She would kneel before him and stare up with those soul-gripping brown eyes, and then, he would be ensnared.

He watched in amazement as Kira slowly raised both her hands and gave him the middle finger.

Laughter erupted from his chest, echoing in the cabin.

She was *perfect*.

She stared out the window again, and he stared at her, hungrily this time, with his cock straining against his trousers. There was so much he could do to her, secluded inside the carriage, but there was one thing he desired above all else: her submission.

He leant back comfortably against the seat.

There was plenty of time. When they arrived at Volmasque, she would be on her knees looking up at him. He would make sure of it.

CHAPTER 5

Carriage Ride with an Asshole

KIRA

THE LUXURIOUS CABIN WAS more spacious than any carriage she'd been in, but its appeal was diminished by the vampire's presence, and it was infinitely small given that she had to share it with someone as manipulative as *him*.

The vampire whose name she still didn't know. He hadn't bothered to introduce himself, and she hadn't asked what his name was when she'd had the chance. She'd gone ahead and assigned him one anyway.

Dick.

Despite the tension in the carriage, she stole fleeting glimpses of the interior when she thought the vampire wasn't looking. Lavish, sheer drapes adorned the windows, the polished mahogany seats were gilded with gold, and the cushions were soft and finely upholstered. The vampire looked like he belonged in this setting, regal and elegant, and her gaze had strayed a little too long on his long arms and legs when he first climbed into the carriage.

A secret part of her had felt a jolt of attraction, but it had since been erased by his smug smile and the intensity of his gaze.

Behind the vampire, the back wall of the carriage was nearly all clear glass, and it provided a stunning view of the starry sky above the dark countryside. It was too bad he was here with her—the carriage ride might have been a pleasant one otherwise.

The only source of light inside the cabin was the soft orange and purple glow of wall sconces, which bore no candles. Instead, the tiny glass bulbs glowed of their own accord. The only other place she'd seen magic before was at an antique shop in Nordokk that had acquired a table lamp that lit up the room with a bright white light. In contrast, the sconces in the carriage were clearly designed more for ambience, and it made the vampire's features a little harder to distinguish in the darkness.

Good.

It was bad enough he'd been staring at her unblinkingly for hours on end.

Because that's what it had felt like. *Hours.* Which didn't make sense. Volmasque Academy was in the middle of the Capital, and the city was only an hour and a half away by coach, potentially less with the swift pace of the horses.

A small coffee table held refreshments, but even if she hadn't been gagged, she was anything but hungry, and neither she nor the vampire had touched the food or wine.

"Kneel, or don't kneel," he had said, placing his hands behind his head. "But if you do not, I'm afraid the gag remains."

And so, the collar remained. His cocksuredness rubbed her the wrong way, and he was dreaming if he thought she would ever kneel for him.

She only had to put up with the gag and collar until they arrived at the academy—surely he would remove it then? There couldn't be much longer left in the journey. She just had to endure a little longer. It was getting difficult to ignore the growing ache in her jaw muscles.

Kira tried to distract herself with memories of happier times, but her thoughts kept drifting back to how the vampire had held her against the wall in the cottage. Physically, wolves were usually stronger than vampires, but he had the advantage of being male—something that had been all too clear when she felt the press of his hard cock. She supposed she was lucky he hadn't forced himself on her, but it was too early to count her blessings—she had no idea what he had in store for her.

That was the problem with vampires. It wasn't just that they were parasites living off other living creatures. They liked to play with their food. And that was what he was doing now, playing with her, messing with her mind, trying to convince her that kneeling before him was in her own best self-interest.

He can get fucked.

Another long minute passed, and her frustration grew. The physical discomfort of the gag had long surpassed her emotional qualms. The foreign object invaded her mouth, and she tried to find a semblance of comfort by adjusting the position of her lips and tongue around it, but the suffocating grip of the collar made movement impossible.

What do I value more? My dignity? Or breathing?

The sensation grew worse with each passing minute, and her resolve, which had burnt brightly earlier, was faltering. She tried to adjust the position of her jaws again, but it was no use, and the movement of her head caused her dribbling saliva to land slick across her hands.

The vampire tilted his head expectantly. He had not uttered another word, and his silence made one thing absolutely clear: there would be no concessions, and no exceptions. His command had been simple, and he expected her to obey.

Kneel, and I will remove your gag.

Those had been his words.

She hoped he couldn't read her mind, or else he would have witnessed her intense desire to transform into a wolf and attack him. In her fantasy, she mauled him as the dark silhouette of Wintermaw Keep burnt with flames, along with the vampires inside it.

They would all burn—starting with him for daring to assault her in her own home. Intentional or otherwise, his arousal had disturbed her.

But what was even more disturbing was the heat pooling in her core, and the throbbing ache at the apex of her thighs. She'd never felt physical desire so intensely, and she didn't know what it meant. Alarmed, she buried the sensation deep.

Several more minutes passed. Kira's neck became cramped from gazing out the window beside her, so she took a break to stretch it. Saliva slopped as she rolled her head from side to side, but her physical comfort took precedence over her pride.

That was when she realised how tired she felt. She reluctantly let her gaze meet the vampire's.

There was no pity in his expression. His cold amusement had vanished as well. In its place was something that resembled admiration.

Odd.

Dismay swept through her as she looked through the window behind him. In the far distance, the inky blackness was tinged with grey. Dawn approached.

Her eyes widened as realisation hit her. They truly had been riding for hours, and he had no intention of stopping the carriage until she complied with his demand.

"Yes, we've been going in circles," he said matter-of-factly. "The city is just beyond the crest of this hill. We've been circling the Eastern Lake—I was wondering when you'd notice."

An angry, muffled snarl erupted from her as she launched herself at him, claws bared, but the vampire was ready for her, and he grabbed her wrists and tugged her closer.

She had put everything into lunging forward, expecting that he would try to block her attack. She was not prepared for him to pull her *closer*, and as she fell forward, he positioned her so she sat astride him with her legs splayed.

"*Farghhhhhhh!*" she screamed, the swear word unrecognisable as she wrenched her arms free and hit him.

He chuckled, unfazed by her attack, and grabbed her hips, pulling her even closer until she was left in no doubt of what he wanted. His hardness was prominent through his trousers, with what she suspected was the head of his cock pressed into her thigh.

She went still, too afraid to move or do anything that would increase that contact. But slowly, the vampire rocked his hips upward, the movement gradual but deliberate. It brought his rigid length closer to her mound, causing a strange desire, forbidden and intoxicating, to flare in her core as he rubbed himself against her.

"Is this what you want?" he murmured.

"No!" Kira cried, but the word was garbled. She tried to pull her hips away, but the vampire's grip dug into her ass cheeks painfully, and he held her in place as he ground himself against her again.

Disgust and failure washed over her as he repeated the motion, and the tingle of pleasure she felt left her feeling exhausted and confused. She hung her head, letting it drop onto his shoulder as the last of the fight left her.

He had won.

She couldn't take one more minute with the gag, or of this humiliation.

"Had enough?" he murmured. Still clasping her hips, his fingers grazed her ass as his warm breath tickled her ear. "Kneel before me, pet. Show me how obedient you are."

His words were like venom, and Kira shook her head angrily even as a choked sob escaped her. She had dribbled saliva onto his shoulder, and it glimmered in the dim light, decorating the dark fabric of his coat. He followed her gaze but made no move to wipe it away.

"You're stunning," he whispered. "I so wish to tame you."

Go to hell.

"The choice is yours, pet. You may continue to wear the gag if you prefer. Or you can kneel."

Kira huffed. This was not a choice—more like coercion, but she was too damn tired to play this game anymore. Her mind had somehow even rationalised what he was asking of her. Was kneeling really worse than what she was doing now? Sitting on the vampire's lap with his hands on her ass and his cock poised? The only thing preventing him from penetration was the taut fabric of their clothes and—she hoped—their self-restraint.

The vampire whispered in her ear. "While you are deciding, pet, let me warn you...if we continue much longer like this with you straddling me, it will end with my cock deep inside you. So, think carefully...and choose."

The threat of his words instilled fear in her, and she shoved off him. He didn't try to stop her as she rose to stand on shaky legs before him. Beneath her feet was an ornate rug in a floral pattern. That was where he wanted her. On her knees, under his control, to be dominated however he saw fit. To surrender would break her spirit—but physically, she was at her breaking point.

The vampire tossed a thin cushion at her feet. "For your knees."

Fucker, she thought, kicking it aside.

I will kneel, but not on your terms.

Squeezing her eyes shut, she lowered herself down on one knee, and then the other, every inch of movement a betrayal to herself. Where was the strong Kira who'd vowed to avenge the wolves? The floor was hard and unforgiving beneath her knees, and she regretted having forgone the cushion.

The vampire drew a sharp breath, and she reluctantly opened her eyes, her face burning hot with humiliation.

He was watching her with a different intensity than he had before. His eyes were glazed with lust, his voice deep as he said, "good girl."

Kira hated the way his praise warmed her like sunlight, especially when she felt so defeated. Still, she allowed herself one final act of defiance. She raised her chin and narrowed her eyes at him. It was the best she could do, and she mustered every remaining scrap of willpower she had left to do it.

"Bow your head," the vampire commanded, each word stabbing her as he denied her that one little morsel of pride.

She shook her head, refusing to look away.

No.

Enough.

I did what you asked. Now take the collar off me.

His voice grew gentle. "Kira, I cannot reach the strap unless you lean closer and bow your head."

The tenderness in his voice surprised her, soothing her anguish, and his words made sense. Reluctantly, she obeyed and lowered her head.

Clever fingers worked the straps behind her head, and as the pressure eased, so too did the gag. The collar was still tight around her neck, but at least the gag wasn't cutting into her cheeks anymore.

Her jaw went slack, but she was too weak to spit the ball out. Before she could take a hold of it, he took hold of the loose leathers in front of her face and jerked it out.

She gasped for air, falling forward onto her palms as she adjusted to the gag's absence, wriggling her jaw, wetting her dry lips and swallowing several times. She could breathe normally again, and she hung her head as she savoured her freedom. Her hair was damp with drool, and her vision blurred, the rug's pattern of purples and pinks blending together.

"Very good, pet," said the vampire, the note of approval in his tone sending a shiver down her spine.

Her head snapped up. "I am *not* your pet."

She was not a dog, or a pet, or a plaything. She was *Kira*, and it was the only name she would accept from him.

"Oh?" said the vampire. "But look at how well you knelt for me. It took a little coaxing, but you gave in far more quickly than the others."

His words hit her like a slap across the face. What others?

No. He was riling her up on purpose. He had to be.

"Liar," she snarled, a wolfish growl rumbling in her chest.

His lips parted in surprise, and something menacing glimmered in his eyes as he leant forward in his seat. Their faces were inches apart, and she could see the faint blond shadow of his stubble. What would it feel like to run her hand along it? Rough?

"I wouldn't growl, if I were you," he warned.

Whatever.

"Why not?"

"Because," he continued, his voice deep and low like thunder, "it turns me on like you wouldn't imagine. So, unless you want this evening to finish with my cum all over your face, you'll desist at once."

Her jaw dropped, and she stared up at him in shock, scarcely able to believe her ears.

"Mm, yes," he said, trailing a long finger along her jawline and tipping her chin upwards, "that's exactly the 'O' face you'll make when it happens."

White-hot anger shattered her stupor.

"Asshole!" she cried, knocking his hand away as she leapt up. "You're disgusting!"

He shrugged. "I want what I want. And you, my dear, are not so different."

"I will *never* want that," she spat, only seconds away from transforming into her wolf form so she could tear him a new one.

Nathaniel smiled, and it was the first wide smile he'd given her. He had a nice smile, which might have been pleasant if he wasn't so damn smug. Her attention snapped to the long, curved canines that glinted in the lamplight. "Well...we shall see."

Kira bit back the urge to scream at him again. "What's your name?"

"Nathaniel," he said, pausing as if to gauge her reaction.

Kira had no idea who that was, but *he* seemed to think he was someone special.

"Is that so?" she asked in mock-astonishment, crossing her arms. "Well, you can *fuck right off,* Nathaniel."

The bastard still hadn't removed the collar.

CHAPTER 6

The Capital

NATHANIEL

"YOU DIDN'T REMOVE THE collar," Kira said. Her tone was accusatory, implying he'd promised to do so.

But he had made no such promise.

"I said I would remove the gag," Nathaniel said, pouring himself a glass of wine, "and I did."

"Bastard." She reached up behind her neck.

"Ah, ah, ah," he warned, holding up a finger. "I wouldn't do that, if I were you, or the next toy I use won't be in your mouth."

Kira froze, watching him as if to gauge if he was serious. Nathaniel held her stare, even though secretly it was an empty threat. He'd only brought the collar, but she didn't know that. He could improvise if he had to—the wine bottle would do.

Slowly, Kira lowered her hands to rest in her lap. "How much longer do I have to wear this thing?"

"Until I say," he said, plucking a grape from the tray and biting through the juicy flesh.

"How much longer?" she repeated.

There was a desperate edge to her voice, and after a moment of consideration, he conceded. "Just until we arrive."

Kira gave a tiny nod. She refused the food and wine he offered her but drank a glass of water thirstily.

He focused his attention on the platter of cheese and fruit, simply for the purpose of staring at something other than Kira; she had earned a moment of respite.

With the tension dispelled, her boldness soon returned.

"I thought vampires only drank blood," she said, nodding at the biscuit he was eating.

"I can subsist on food just fine."

"So, you're not going to bite me?"

"Bite you?"

"Yes, bite me. Feed off me. Isn't that what your kind do?"

His lips curled. "I hadn't planned to. However, if you are offering…"

"I am not offering!"

"Pity." *I might have said yes.* He drained his cup and set it down. "We'll arrive at the academy soon," he informed her. "The carriage will take us directly there."

"Will it, now?" she said bitterly. "It would have been nice if it had taken us *directly* to the academy in the first place."

"It would have, if you'd obeyed my order. Your noncompliance delayed what should have been a quick journey."

She sniffed. "You are loathsome."

"I'm sincere," he corrected, "and I have your best interests at heart."

"I *sincerely* doubt that."

"Truly, you have nothing to fear from me. The academy has recently introduced new rules to ensure the wellbeing of all its pupils, including shifters like yourself. As a student of the academy, you have certain rights, privileges, and protections. No one will touch you without your consent. As the chief security officer on campus, you have my protection."

"Fuck your protection. Do you really think gagging me was in my best interest?"

"It was for my own safety."

Kira was struck speechless, and he could see her deciphering the meaning behind his words. After all, he'd just acknowledged that she had the power to harm him. It was a mutual respect of a sort.

Kira lifted her chin. "Yes, well...it wasn't as if you didn't enjoy it. Gagging me, that is."

"I never said I didn't."

She huffed and looked out the window, and it was with some difficulty that his gaze slid past her.

They had arrived in the Capital. The sandstone city buildings were illuminated by burning torches and the early rays of sunrise. Despite the early hour, there were already people moving about the cobblestone streets.

"Is this your first time in the Capital?"

Kira nodded, muttering something that sounded like 'first time with an asshole like you,' as she craned her neck to peer at a man patrolling the streets.

"Vampire," she observed, her nostrils flaring as if she were sampling the air.

"A watchman of the city guard. You can tell by the red uniform. Speaking of which...you'll receive a school uniform at the academy. But I must ask, why did you not pack anything?"

She shrugged. "I didn't think my clothes would be suitable."

She was right. If her current attire was anything to go by, plain peasant clothes in faded colours and frayed edges, she would need a new wardrobe. There was nothing wrong with a respectable set of working clothes, but her ankle-length skirt and belted tunic was a far cry from the chic fashion observed by the academy's students.

"I can arrange for someone to take you shopping in the city," he offered.

They exchanged a small smile, and his heart skipped a beat as Kira leant forward.

"Nathaniel?" she whispered softly, sending an involuntary quiver through him as she shuffled closer.

"Yes, Kira?"

Her expression hardened. "Why don't you *fuck* off?"

He didn't bat an eyelid. "Why are you living alone in a cottage on the outskirts of town?"

Kira looked surprised by his question. "To get away from people. I like nature."

That was obviously not the whole truth. "And your parents?" he asked.

"I never knew them. I was raised by humans, but they abandoned me when they realised what I was." She paused, swallowing dramatically as she stared at her hands.

Nathaniel couldn't tell if she was genuinely upset or not, but either way, he didn't buy her story. The subtle tremble of her hands was—he was sure—just an act. He tilted his head at her. "What about the wolves who raised you?"

Kira's eyes widened for the briefest of seconds, and he could only imagine how her heart raced at the thought that he might know more than he let on.

She quickly recovered. "There were no other wolves."

He didn't press the point. Unlike the authority he served, he was not interested in hunting illegal wolf shifters. He cared about her. The academy wanted to rehabilitate her—but he had other plans.

"How old are you?" Kira asked suddenly.

"How old do you think I am?"

"I don't know. A century?"

"A century?" he asked in amusement.

"Two centuries? Your lot live forever, right?"

Her bored tone suggested she didn't care, but he knew better.

He was her captor, and it was natural she would want to discover everything there was to know about him. It was flattering.

"You are thinking of made vampires," he explained. "They are ageless and not truly alive. But the majority of vampires are born vampires, myself included. We age just as shifters and humans do."

"Glad you come with an expiry date," she muttered.

He ignored that. "As for made vampires, there are very few of them left, and none of them are at Volmasque. We lost our ability to turn humans into vampires when the witches became extinct."

"Wasn't the witches' extinction the vampires' fault?"

"A little clumsy on our part, yes. And rather inconvenient."

It was an understatement. Without witches, there was no magic, except for the scraps of enchanted items they'd left behind. With no way to create made vampires, the born vampires were under pressure to continue the legacy of their kind. But unlike wolves, vampires did not have many children, and the rising number of wolves was part of the reason the Revolution had been deemed necessary.

Fearing extinction, many vampires had rallied behind a ruthless vampire named Henrikk, who had annihilated not only the Wolf King, but their very own Vampire King as well. Under Henrikk's leadership, the rogue vampires had seized control of both kingdoms to rule all factions. As for the extermination of the witches, that was a result of Henrikk and his followers hunting down the covens one by one and getting a little too carried away. As the new self-proclaimed king, Henrikk had later publicly acknowledged his regret at the 'unfortunate accident', but there had been no witches left to receive the apology. The announcement, therefore, had been made purely because of the vampire nobles' frustration that there was no one left to enchant their newly built carriages and sulkies.

"I was born a vampire," Nathaniel explained, "to parents who are both vampires."

"So...you're less than a century old?"

"I'll be turning thirty in a few weeks."

Kira shrugged as if she'd lost interest in the topic, but he suspected she was mentally calculating the age difference between them. Nearly ten and a half years.

"What happens when we arrive at Volmasque?" she asked.

"You will join the first years for class. It's the middle of the semester, but I'm confident you'll catch up in no time."

"What about tonight?"

"Tonight?" he asked, his voice growing soft and hopeful as blood rushed to his groin.

Kira must have read his thoughts because she stammered, "I mean, where will I sleep?"

"In your own bed," he said, resisting the temptation to invite her to his. The carriage paused while the wrought iron gates creaked open. "Here we are. Welcome to Volmasque Academy."

Chapter 7

Volmasque Academy

KIRA

EVEN THOUGH THE SKY had lightened, a fog still blanketed the school grounds. The carriage glided along a pebbled drive lined with trees. The academy building was an imposing presence, with dark stonework, arches adorned with intricate carvings, and tall but narrow windows. Stone gargoyles perched upon ledges, and towering spires pierced the sky, bleeding sunlight onto the iron vanes.

Kira felt a sense of trepidation as the driverless carriage pulled to a stop. Taking a deep breath, she faced the vampire.

"Will you take the collar off now?"

"Not yet," he said, opening the door for her. "Ladies first."

She might have strangled him had he not been an enemy capable of killing her, and had she not been overwhelmed by the strange new environment. Still, while violence may not have been the answer, it was time to make a stand.

She crossed her arms. "I'm not getting out until you remove the collar."

"Really?" Nathaniel said. "Well, then I suppose you're not getting out at all, are you?"

She narrowed her eyes at him. "Fine. Close the door on your way out."

To her annoyance, he pulled the door shut and settled himself lengthwise on his seat. He put his feet up on the table, crushing the rare cheeses beneath his polished shoes.

"What are you doing?" she demanded.

"Enjoying your company."

A streak of sunlight breached the cabin, warming her forearm. It gave her an idea. "Tell me," she asked, shuffling closer to the door, ready to put herself between it and the vampire to trap him, "do vampires burn in the sun?"

His eyes tracked her movement with interest. "You're thinking of 'made' vampires—undead vessels brought alive by magic. But I was born a vampire. Born vampires such as myself have many of the strengths of made vampires—and almost none of the weaknesses. I can subsist without blood, feel the sun on my skin, and enter private residences without an invitation."

The last one Kira had learnt the hard way.

"Coffins?" she asked.

He looked amused. "I don't believe any of us sleep in coffins anymore."

"Wooden stakes?"

"As you prefer. But there are a whole variety of ways you could end my life, and I'm sure you could be more creative than that."

Kira absorbed the information like a sponge. "Can you see your reflection in the mirror?"

His eyes flared, and he leant forward, invading her space. "Why so curious about my weaknesses and sleeping arrangements?"

Her breathing hitched. "I was just curious."

"Well, for the record. I sleep in a very comfortable bed facing a very large mirror, and if you are ever so fortunate as to be bent over it, you will see my reflection clearly behind yours."

His words shocked Kira into silence, but only for a moment. "Well, at least something will be large."

Nathaniel's lip curled in response and placed a relaxed arm over the back of his seat.

It was not at all the reaction she'd expected.

"Fine," she sighed, climbing out of the carriage. She was sick of the cramped space, and she couldn't stand his company for a minute longer.

She barely had a chance to glance up at the academy's dark silhouette before Nathaniel appeared beside her, standing too close as he said, "Follow me."

He set off up the stone steps.

Kira hesitated before following him, hurrying to keep up with the stride of his long legs as he took the steps two at a time.

The entrance doors creaked open of their own accord, and Nathaniel's shoes clicked on the marble floors of an elegant foyer with tall ceilings and ornate decorations.

She was embarrassed by the collar and the prominent ball gag dangling from it, but to her relief, the hall was empty.

A muffled sound caught her attention. Nathaniel heard it too, and he veered towards the grand stairs, beside which were two figures panting in the shadows.

As they drew near, Kira was horrified to discover a female wolf shifter with dishevelled strawberry blonde hair, who was completely naked as a male vampire rutted her from behind. Kira froze in her tracks, her chest tightening in shock as her gaze swept over the couple. Her first instinct was to help the female wolf, but she seemed to be enjoying herself.

The shifter was in human form, except for her fluffy wolf tail, which was raised high to grant the vampire easier access as he penetrated her. Worst of all, her eyes were shut and she panted softly as she clutched the wall.

The vampire looked close to Nathaniel's age, perhaps a little older, because despite his smooth face, his brown hair and short beard were streaked with grey. He was a slightly shorter than Nathaniel, but he radiated dominance as he gripped the wolf by the hips and thrust into her.

Kira wanted to flee, but Nathaniel snatched her wrist and pulled her along with him, ignoring her protests. He stopped before the fornicating couple.

"Headmaster Arken," he greeted.

Headmaster?

The vampire looked up, blinking in surprise behind his fogged-up spectacles. He wore a long, purple nightrobe and little else, and as he turned towards them, Kira caught sight of his bare chest, rippling with muscles. Coarse hairs trailed down over his abdomen, leading to—she quickly averted her eyes. She'd seen too much, and if this was truly the headmaster of the academy, they were all fucked.

"Ah, Nathaniel," he greeted, while still thrusting against the naked wolf. "Good evening. How can I help?"

Kira was not prepared for his casualness, but she found the female wolf's lack of embarrassment even stranger. The wolf hardly glanced at them, her face red with exertion and her head lolling as if lost in the moment.

"I'd like to speak with Susie," Nathaniel said, indicating the female wolf. "I've brought our new student, Kira."

"Ah, of course," Headmaster Arken said, giving Kira a nod. "One moment, if you please." He increased his pace, his breathing growing heavier as he thrust hard into the wolf, their moans growing louder.

Kira tried to pull out of Nathaniel's grasp, but his grip tightened on her wrist like iron.

"I want you to see this," he murmured as the sound of skin slapping on skin grew louder.

"You are fucked up," she hissed.

"This is how things are at the academy."

She bit back a response.

Things will be changing...very soon.

The headmaster groaned loudly in time with his thrusts, each sound punctuated by the wolf's shrill cries, until finally, he gave a final shout and collapsed forward, both of them slumping against the side of the stairs. After a few seconds, the headmaster straightened, pulled out of the wolf, and gave her a soft slap on the ass.

"Well done, dear," he said. "That was very good. Now, why don't you get dressed and help the gentleman and this student...Kira was it?"

She didn't reply, but Susie nodded and reached for her clothes.

"Yes, sir."

Fucking whipped, thought Kira. How could Susie look at the headmaster with those sappy eyes...

And why was he patting her head as if she were a dog?

Without bothering to tie his robe, Headmaster Arken turned to face them, the part in his robe displaying his nakedness, including his dripping cock.

She averted her eyes once again, but still saw the cheerful nod he gave them in her peripheral vision as he ascended the stairs.

Susie finished buttoning her blouse and smiled brightly at Kira. "Hi, I'm Susie, your Residential Adviser. Welcome to Volmasque."

Kira eyed her extended hand, shaking it with reluctance. "Thanks."

"Did you just arrive? Oh, I should give you a tour—"

"Later," said Nathaniel, the single word spoken gently. "Just her room key, if you will."

"Right, of course," Susie said, sweeping back her loose hair. "You'll want to get settled in."

Instead of taking the grand stairs up, Susie led them through a narrow door, disappearing inside a small office before returning with a key.

Kira accepted it in surprise. "I get a key?"

"Yes, new rules. As of last year, all students have the right to privacy."

"That's...good," Kira said uncertainly, wondering what the catch was.

"You have Susie to thank for that," Nathaniel explained. "She's advocated to improve lives for shifter students."

Kira couldn't tell if Nathaniel was bothered by this, but Susie's chest rose with pride, mingling with a shy smile.

"All students, not just wolves," Susie corrected. Then, as if the floodgates had opened, she took Kira by the arms as a flurry of words burst from her. "Any activities between students, including feeding, must be consensual, so don't let anyone take advantage of you, Kira. The doors are just a precaution. You deserve to be here just like everyone else!"

"Sure," Kira said, trying not to visualise what those other activities were, or that she was wearing a collar she had clearly not consented to. "Thanks...?"

"Shall I take you down?" Susie asked.

"No need," said Nathaniel. "I'll escort her."

"Of course. Kira, I'll come knock on your door before school and give you a tour, if you like?"

"Er, sure," Kira said, waving goodbye as Nathaniel led her to a stairwell. She hesitated, glancing back out at the foyer. She glimpsed trees swaying gently in a breeze through a window. Sighing, she followed Nathaniel down the winding stairs into darkness. "The dormitory is downstairs?"

"It was once a dungeon," Nathaniel said.

"Probably still is, knowing vampires."

He shot her a quizzical look. "It was a dungeon before vampires ever dwelt here, back when wolves ruled the kingdom. This was where the Wolf King, Bakker, kept his special prisoners—vampires, wolf spies, prisoners of war, and, of course, criminals. It was only after the Revolution that it became a school." When she didn't answer straight away, he gave her a sidelong look. "I'm sorry. Does that not suit your narrative for evil vampires?"

Kira huffed. "A dungeon for criminals is better than a school that turns wolves into sex slaves, so don't pretend you have the moral high ground."

Nathaniel laughed, the timbre grating on her nerves, mostly because of how unsettled it made her feel. His proximity didn't help, nor the way he spoke, as if there was a camaraderie between them—there was not.

They descended the winding steps, heading deeper and deeper underground. They passed several landings until they halted at one labelled *fifth floor*. The stairs continued down, but Nathaniel led her down a long, narrow corridor with greying carpet. Doors lined the walls on either side and wrought-iron wall sconces burnt with soft purple flames that she was sure were magical.

"This is your room," Nathaniel said, stopping before a door labelled *505*. "There are seven underground floors. The first five are all occupied by wolf shifter students. The ones below are reserved for vampires."

"How many students are there?"

"Nearly seven hundred."

Her eyes boggled. It was more than she'd expected. As Nathaniel unlocked the door, her mind raced with possibilities. There were seven floors, and only two of them were for vampires. It was a positive sign. The wolf shifters outnumbered the vampires by more than double, which meant that, just like the outside world, they had the advantage of numbers.

"After you," Nathaniel offered.

Kira cautiously entered her new room. It had a small bed, a

desk, a chair, a shelf, and, oddly enough, a pedestal sink. This far underground, there were no windows, and the only source of light was a glowing purple flame from a ceiling lamp, and an unlit candelabra. It was a plain room with nothing to like or dislike.

"Which floor do you live on?" Kira asked absently.

Nathaniel laughed. "Why, do you plan on paying me a visit? I can have a key cut for you, if you wish."

"What? No, I ..." she blinked furiously, realising he was joking.

"I'll leave you to settle in," Nathaniel said, but he made no move to leave as he leant in the doorway. "Before I go, a word of caution. Many things have changed in recent years, courtesy of Susie, but at Volmasque Academy, an open door is an open invitation."

Her stomach twisted. "Can you be more specific?"

"Of course. Unless you want to be fed on, I suggest you lock your door."

"Will the lock keep you out?"

Nathaniel's smile slipped. "No. Not if I really wanted to be inside."

The air thrummed with tension as they faced off, her insides coiling unpleasantly at the thought of what he was insinuating, at least until she realised... *He's teasing me again.* The tug of his lips gave it away.

"Then what's the point of locking my door?" she whispered into the silence.

"It might bring you a lovely, false sense of security."

"Great." She rolled her eyes. His meaning was clear: while progress had been made at the academy, few things had changed, and it was still a dangerous place for anyone who wasn't a vampire.

"It bears repeating," Nathaniel said, his humour vanishing, "that unless you *want* one of the vampires to feed from you, or to do other things to you, it is best you keep your door closed in the evenings. It will save you from some rather awkward conversations...and from unwanted visitors. Understood?"

She nodded.

"Good. Now, come here."

She didn't budge.

He arched an eyebrow. "Don't you want me to remove the collar?"

Well, yes, but...

Kira sighed, her legs feeling like lead as she dragged them forward across the small room to where he stood in the doorway.

"Turn around." It was a harsh command, and she could tell by his tone that he would not accept anything less than full obedience.

Resigning herself to the situation, she turned. There was a long pause in which she dreaded he would make her kneel.

Another second dragged by, and she became certain he was considering it.

Please no.

She could not submit a second time. She was barely holding herself together as it was. And this was supposed to be *her* room, her only sanctuary in this parasite-infested hellhole.

Her thoughts stilled as his hands brushed her hair aside, sweeping it over her shoulder so he could undo the collar. His touch was agonisingly gentle, a contrast to the collar's tightness, and she did not hate the brush of his fingertips against her skin as much as she ought to have.

The collar fell away, and her hands flew to her neck, massaging it in relief. Feeling his eyes on her, she turned to face him.

Nathaniel was quiet, his expression inscrutable as his gaze roved her neck. He seemed reluctant to leave, and the longer he hesitated, the hotter the tension became. The air simmered with it, making the room feel too small, as if there was not enough air.

They were standing too close, but her feet felt glued to the floor. She couldn't move away, could not move a single muscle as her heart pounded in her chest. The collar dangled in his hands, and he looked very much like he wanted to put it back around her.

Fucking move, she yelled at herself, finally getting her feet to cooperate as she took three quick steps back. Was the vampire turned on? She was too afraid to look, her eyes locked on his, but heat flared in her core, the low throb of desire beating like a drum.

Nathaniel snapped out of it first. "Susie will be here in approximately two and a half hours. Try to get some sleep." He turned to leave.

"Nathaniel, wait," she called after him.

He turned back, his head cocked to one side. What did he see when he looked at her? A damsel in distress? "Yes?"

She kept her voice cool. "If you ever dare put a collar on me again, I will rip your fucking heart out."

He nodded solemnly and began to leave.

Kira felt a small burst of triumph, at least until he turned back and said, "The next time I collar you will be because you beg me to."

White-hot anger blinded her, and she wished she'd packed something hard so she could throw it at him. "There will not be a next time!" she shouted after him as he left. The sound of his quiet footsteps faded.

He'd left the door wide open. Kira stared at it for a long moment before slamming it shut. She fumbled with the key as she slid it into place, the sound of metal grating on metal making her feel more secure, even if that safety was only an illusion.

It annoyed her that he'd left it open after warning her to leave it closed, and she couldn't help but wonder why. Was he toying with her? Or giving her a choice?

Nathaniel's earlier words echoed in her mind.

Unless you want to be fed on...

She shivered. Why would anyone *want* to be fed on by a vampire?

CHAPTER 8

The Poplarin Pack

KIRA

GET SOME SLEEP, NATHANIEL had said.

What a ridiculous notion.

It was a strange room with a strange bed, and the best thing that could be said about it was that she didn't have to share with anyone else. It was about the size of her room at the cottage, but without so much as a hairbrush to fill it with, it felt empty.

I probably should have packed a few things.

Still, the room's bareness complemented her goal to reinvent herself. She was no longer the wolf who'd lain dozing on the deck on a spring afternoon while the sun warmed her fur. Nor was she the woman who'd laughed as she tried to deep fry pastry with Mary, whose short, curly red hair had been dusted with icing sugar.

This was a new Kira.

She would guard her secrets close to her heart and lie in wait for the right opportunity to strike. If it meant sacrificing her pride and dignity to play the part of a nervous student, so be it. She would become whatever they wanted her to be. The perfect pupil. An obedient wolf. And as much as it made her cringe—a good pet. These façades would mask what she really was: a snake in the grass.

Nathaniel had thought she was easy prey—at least until she'd bitten him. Then again, he'd come prepared with a collar. It was almost flattering that he considered her to be a formidable adversary.

Oh for fuck's sake. Who cares what that parasite thinks? We're not frenemies.

Kira kicked off the sheets in frustration. Hopefully, she would be seeing very little of him at the academy.

Still, she wished she'd taken the opportunity to ask Nathaniel more about his kind. He'd been forthcoming enough in answering her questions, at least once he finally removed the gag, and she knew too little about vampires. Mary and Byron had told her all about the made vampires—their strengths, their weaknesses. The way they burnt beneath the sun, and could not see their reflection in the mirror, and were prone to garlic poisoning. The made vampires felt no pain, making them terrifying opponents in battle, and they lived forever unless staked.

But she'd known nothing of born vampires until this morning. If most of Nathaniel's kind were born vampires, then she would learn everything she could about them. She'd already learnt that he was hot-blooded; she could still feel the warmth of his body as he'd pressed her against the cottage wall, the heat and lust emanating from him like dark, stormy clouds.

Kira went to the brass pedestal sink and splashed water on her face and neck to refresh herself. Using her fingers, she attempted to tame her dark brown hair. Mary had fondly described her locks as chestnut-coloured, glossy, and thick. She had also called Kira beautiful, commenting on her naturally brown skin and full lips, but those descriptions felt misplaced for someone destined to be a killer.

Which was what she needed to be to restore balance in the world. In their greed for power, the vampires had annihilated the witches, and enslaved the wolf shifters. It seemed the world would be better off without vampires, and her vision for balance involved wiping them out of existence.

A soft knock came at her door.

"Hullo? Kira? Are you awake?"

The female voice sounded friendly enough, and Kira opened the door to find Susie smiling at her. She looked less flustered than when they'd first met a few hours ago, her yellow eyes calm and inquisitive, and her strawberry-blonde hair was neatly braided. She was portly like Mary had been, but much closer to Kira's age, and she looked far too cheerful for the ominous backdrop of the stone-walled corridor with green flames. She wore a navy blazer, white blouse and a pleated red skirt that was almost too short. Her wolf tail was still present, causing the skirt to flutter as it wagged gently.

Despite their unusual manner of meeting, Kira was glad to see a friendly face, especially one that wasn't a certain blond-haired vampire.

"Good morning, how did you sleep?"

"Err, fine." There was no point explaining that she hadn't slept a wink.

"I'm sorry about a few hours ago," Susie said, biting her plump lip. "Must have been strange for you to see me and the headmaster like that."

It was not a topic Kira wanted to know more about, but she had to ask... "Does he do that often? The headmaster? Take students and...have sex with them?" The words were coming out weirdly, making the situation even more awkward, but Susie listened earnestly.

"I'm the only one he does *that* with," Susie giggled. "He singled me out, a long time ago."

"As in...you had no choice?"

"Well, it's complicated. Things were different back when I first started. I'm a third year now, but when I was in first year, vampires had free rein of the academy. And Arken was accustomed to having his pick of the students to feed on."

"And he chose you?"

"Well, sort of. But we're together now, and it's all consensual."

Kira frowned as she tried to untangle Susie's seemingly contradictory statements. The wolf was beaming at her expectantly, so she said, "I'm, err, happy for you, if you're happy."

"Thank you. I am. Now, I'm supposed to give you a tour, but classes are starting soon. Do you mind if we just get your breakfast and uniform sorted? We can meet up again at lunch to do the tour. There're always three classes in the morning, an hour-long lunch break, and then three more classes in the afternoon. Sound good?"

"Sounds good," she said, repeating Susie's own words back to her. Mirroring was a manipulation tactic Byron had taught her. It involved copying the gestures, speech and opinions of another person. Susie was an easy target, bubbly and accepting, but it was a habit Kira needed to start practising, especially after her dismal efforts with the vampire, who'd pissed her off too much for her to even try manipulating him. She hadn't even adhered to her plan of appearing docile and weak—it was something else she would have to work on.

"Fantastic! Ready to go?" Susie peered past Kira's shoulder and frowned. "Hold on. Where are your things?"

"I don't have any."

"Why not? Did you leave them at home?" Susie asked, trying to shuffle past Kira into her room.

"It's complicated," Kira deflected, using Susie's own words against her. There was nothing in the room that was hers, but even so, she valued her privacy and didn't want anyone snooping around. She stepped into the corridor and locked the door. "Is there a place where I could buy a few things?"

Susie's face brightened. "Sure. We can go shopping after school!"

Wherever Susie planned to take her, Kira feared from her excited reaction that it was a little more than the small general store in Nordokk that she'd frequented with Byron and Mary.

"By the way," Susie said, her brow furrowed in concentration as she leant into Kira's personal space, "how's your neck? Nathaniel didn't bite you, did he?"

"Err..."

"Because we've asked the vampires to stop preying on first years before they've even had a chance to join a pack. It's been disrupting pack dynamics. Although, there's not much we can do if students ask to be bitten, but I mean, come on, at least let them settle in at the academy and have a chance, you know what I mean?"

Kira felt uncomfortable as Susie examined her neck for bite marks. "My neck is fine."

"And he didn't hurt you?"

Yes, he hurt me.

The words were on the tip of her tongue, but she hesitated to say them. Nathaniel had made the trip to the academy needlessly unpleasant. Had he angered her? Humiliated her? Signed his own death warrant? 'Yes' to all those things—but he had not hurt her. She shook her head.

Susie exhaled in relief. "Good. It's best you stay away from him."

"Why?"

"Because he's dangerous."

Kira had already gathered as much. "How dangerous, exactly?"

Susie offered her a too-cheerful smile and gestured at her wolf tail. "You're probably wondering why I have a wolf tail."

Kira blinked at the abrupt change in subject. "Actually, I *was* wondering that."

"I was born like this," Susie said simply. "I can't morph at all."

"Oh." Kira struggled to think of what to say. Wolf shifters were capable of half-morphing, but she'd never met or heard of one who was stuck between human and wolf form. "I'm so sorry."

"Don't be sorry!" This time, Susie offered her a genuine smile. "It makes me who I am, and I've embraced it. Besides, Arken likes it."

"The...headmaster?"

"Yes. And—" She cut off as students began emerging from rooms. "Actually, never mind, I'll tell you later."

Kira was the only one not in uniform, and it made her feel self-conscious as she followed Susie down the corridor.

The students all wore the same navy blazers with red trim on the lapels and pockets, but otherwise, the men and women's uniforms varied. The male wolves wore navy trousers and red neckties, whilst the females like Susie wore black thigh-high socks, red tartan skirts that were short and pleated, and red bows at the neck.

As much as Kira despised the academy, she had to admit that the uniforms were striking and sophisticated. Meanwhile, her own lack of uniform instantly made her an outsider. The simple flowery blouse, long skirt and sturdy boots she had on were more suitable for visiting the market or walking forest trails, not for impressing peers and teachers at an academic institution.

The students shot her curious looks on the stairwell, which she tried to ignore as she ascended the steps with Susie.

"We'll have to eat breakfast quickly if we want to get you a uniform before class starts," Susie was saying.

"We can skip breakfast," Kira said immediately. The last thing she needed was to have the whole school ogle her simple clothes while she ate. In the past, she would not have cared what others thought, but that would have to change if she hoped to be their leader. She only had one chance to make a first impression, to prove she was one of them, which meant she needed a uniform, and fast. "Let's just do the uniform."

"Oh...but I haven't eaten yet," Susie said. Her internal battle was obvious as she weighed the options—to eat breakfast, or be obliging to the newcomer?

"Maybe we could get my uniform first, and then find something to eat?" Kira pleaded. To enter the cafeteria like this would be social suicide.

"Sure, that will work."

Kira squinted her eyes as they emerged from underground.

"This is the foyer," Susie said, waving her hand around the large, imposing space.

Kira hadn't had a chance to look at it properly when Nathaniel led her through it last night, and she paused to gaze up at the high ceilings where tall windows of stained glass let in streams of morning light. Above, a wrought-iron chandelier flickered with candlelight, and the grand staircase was made of polished wood and covered in red carpet—a colour that the vampires seemed fond of, because it was everywhere in the heavy drapes, banners, wallpaper and decorations. To the right of the staircase was a black marble fireplace dancing with purple flames, around which gathered a group of students. Some of them stretched out on dark furniture, others stood confidently, and a couple lay by the fireside in their wolf form. It was obvious at a glance that they were a pack.

Kira stared openly, appraising the pack. Every member radiated confidence, as if they had nothing to fear from the vampires.

Kira's heart beat a little faster when one of the female wolves detached from the group, her yellow eyes giving Kira the once-over as she approached. She was the same height as Kira, but whilst Kira was slender, the woman was skinny, with a narrow face and angled cheekbones.

"Who is this?" she drawled, flicking her black twin plaits behind her as if she had better places to be. "Aren't you going to introduce us, Suzanna?"

Susie's smile flickered out. "This is Kira," she said in a strained voice. "Kira, this is—"

"Chelsea," said the female student airily, her thin eyebrows arching in disdain as she looked down her nose at Kira. "Chelsea Poplarin, beta wolf of the Poplarin Pack."

Kira's eyes widened. This was it. An introduction to a pack. This was the sort of connection she needed to make if she hoped to rally the wolves to rise up against their oppressors. It was a lofty goal, but suddenly, it seemed within reach.

Except that Chelsea did not seem friendly. In fact, she sensed an undercurrent of hostility.

Kira squared her shoulders and met the challenge head-on. "Pleased to meet you."

Chelsea drew back, angling her body away. "I'm not so sure. You *reek.*"

Reek?

But she had washed last night, and these were fresh clothes, even if she'd spent the night in them.

"Have you not been bled yet?" Chelsea asked impatiently, wrinkling her nose.

Kira had no idea what she was talking about, but she didn't want to reveal her ignorance, so she changed tack. "I'd like to meet the rest of your pack."

"No. Absolutely not. Leave at once."

"Come on," Susie said, tugging on Kira's sleeve.

Kira stood her ground, feeling confused. Why was Chelsea suddenly so defensive? She'd been introducing herself only a moment ago. Adopting a polite but loud tone, she said, "I'd like to speak with your alpha."

Several sets of yellow eyes turned towards them.

"What are you doing?" Susie gasped as Chelsea's human lips drew back in a snarl.

"Forget it," Chelsea snapped. "You are meeting no one. You *are* no one."

"I'm not discussing this with a beta," Kira said. Unlike Chelsea, she had no rank. This was an obvious disadvantage, except in one aspect: without a rank, there was no protocol as to who, if anyone, she had to defer to. It was not her pack. *Yet.* Kira turned to face the pack, ignoring Chelsea to address them. "I wish to speak with your alpha, and no one else."

A hushed silence fell as the entire pack looked at her. It was a bold move, but Kira had met enough people like Chelsea to know there was no point negotiating.

Chelsea growled like a wolf. "Final warning."

Kira hesitated. She did not want to fight on her first day, not when her fighting experience was limited to the training she'd done with Byron. They'd covered hand-to-hand combat and trained with knives, but most of her combat training relied on her wolf form—and that was a secret she could not reveal.

But she wouldn't back down either.

Chelsea's aura pulsed with a golden glow, a sign that she was preparing to shift. "You think I won't?"

Kira smiled. "I dare you."

Apparently, Chelsea wasn't bluffing. Dense fur erupted across her face and body in a shimmer of gold light, and she emerged in wolf form, pointed ears lowered and sharp teeth bared as she pounced.

Kira dodged, shifting her weight on other back foot. As the wolf sailed past, she kicked it in the midriff.

Chelsea yelped and whirled around, razor-sharp teeth bared threateningly.

Kira backed away. She didn't have a knife, but she knew where a wolf's weak spots were, including the tail. Pulling that could cause serious injury, and she would avoid grabbing it unless she absolutely had to.

It depended how dirty Chelsea wanted to fight.

A crowd was gathering around them as Chelsea lunged for her foot, barrelling forward.

Kira stayed light on her feet, leaping up in a smooth jump that brought her back down on Chelsea's back. She managed two swift punches before the wolf threw her off.

Kira rolled as she fell, the manoeuvre not quite as smooth as she practiced as her shoulder clipped the edge of a pillar painfully.

She was back on her feet in an instant, but not quickly enough. Suddenly, the wolf hit her hard in the chest, sending her flying backwards. There was no time to shift, or to even brace herself as she fell against the hard marble floor, her head cracking against the tiles as the heavy wolf landed on her. She cried out in alarm, angling her head away from Chelsea's gnashing teeth.

"Enough," said a deep voice, calm but commanding.

Chelsea's weight lifted off her immediately. By the time Kira pushed herself up into a sitting position, the skinny woman was already back in human form, sauntering away in victory with her pigtails swaying in time to her hips and pleated skirt.

Kira swallowed and gazed up at her saviour—a large, broad-shouldered student with a square face and chin. He was older, probably a seventh-year student, and he was easy on the eyes, with sandy hair, a relaxed expression, broad shoulders and bulging muscles to spare.

"You have my attention," he said, gazing down at her. "Kira, was it?"

"Yes."

"Kira," he repeated with a smile, rolling the syllables as if savouring her name. "And are you all right, Kira?"

"F-fine," she said, hurrying to stand.

The male wolf was faster, scooping her up so quickly she gasped. He set her back on her feet. "Are you hurt?"

"No, not at all. Thank you."

"You're most welcome." He offered her a perfect white smile. "I apologise for the rude introduction. Chelsea thinks she runs the pack."

Kira gave a weak chuckle. "I take it, you're the alpha?"

His smile widened. "Mark," he said, extending a broad hand, one that swallowed her own slender one as he grasped it.

"Kira," she said, feeling the heat rise in her cheeks.

This was what an alpha should be. Strong, calm, and dependable, a protector who kept the peace—not an instigator of fights like Chelsea.

Mark leant into the handshake, and she heard him sniff softly, drawing in her scent. It made her feel naked, and when he finally pulled away, her cheeks were burning.

"Welcome, Kira," he said softly, his gaze lingering on hers. "What a pleasure to meet you."

"It's a pleasure to meet you too," she breathed, captivated by his presence. In contrast to his large physique and high rank, Mark had a quiet, soothing voice. She wondered how he sounded when he howled. Would it leave her breathless, just like now?

"Kira, we have to go," Susie said, tugging on her arm.

Mark smiled, acknowledging Susie as well. "I best not hold either of you up. Kira, I do hope we can...speak again soon."

"I hope so too," she said, reluctantly allowing Susie to steer her into a corridor. "So, that was Mark?" she asked wistfully.

Susie rolled her eyes. "Yes. Mark Poplarin. He's Chelsea's second cousin and the leader of the Populars."

"Populars?"

Susie laughed; her good humour returned now that they were far away from Chelsea. "Technically, it's the Poplarin Pack, but everyone calls them the Populars because they think they're top shit."

"Mark didn't seem so bad," Kira said.

"He's not so bad," Susie agreed, "but you should see him when there are vampires around."

"Is he fierce?"

"Well, sort of. But he loses his swagger pretty quick."

Not surprising, Kira thought. *He'd have to take any threat to his pack seriously.*

"What pack are you in, Susie?" Kira asked as they rounded a corner.

"It's called the Ark, I founded it when I was in first year. Are you interested?"

"Um—"

"I think you'd love it; everyone is really friendly and we have a book club meeting every week. Would you like me to introduce you? There's no initiation, anyone is welcome to join."

"Sure..." Kira lied, hiding her grimace. Ordinarily, a group of friendly people who liked reading would have appealed to her. And the invite touched her. But measured up to her thirst for revenge, the thought of joining Susie's pack of misfits was mortifying. She needed soldiers, not read-a-longs.

In another life, she thought regretfully.

"Makeover time!" Susie squealed, pulling her into a sunlit room full of built-in wardrobes and mirrors.

Sure. More like conformity time.

CHAPTER 9

White Socks

KIRA

SUSIE THREW A PILE of clothes at her. "Try these on."

Kira weighed the clothes in her hands. Conformity was not as heavy as she'd expected. In fact, the uniform had an elegance she'd been unprepared for, and Susie swore that the sparkling gemstones decorating the blazer's buttons and cufflinks were real rubies.

Here goes nothing.

Twenty minutes later, Kira stood before the mirror, staring at her reflection as she adjusted the red bow at her neck.

I look good, she thought in surprise.

None of her clothes had ever been this flattering, not even the lace dress she'd worn to the country dance last summer. She'd nearly lost her virginity that night but had decided at the last minute that the mayor's arrogant son was not worth the trouble.

Kira smoothed the academy blazer, which was particularly impressive. It fit her perfectly, with sleek lines and structured shoulders that were not in the least bit tight, and she liked the sense of regality it lent her.

The short red skirt, however...

"Can we go longer?" Kira pleaded, tugging the hem down, which only reached halfway down her thighs.

"Like I said, that's as long as they go," Susie said with an apologetic shrug. "It's way longer than mine."

It was of small consolation; Susie's was barely decent.

"It doesn't even reach my knees," Kira complained.

"It's not meant to."

"But—"

"Just give it a chance. You look good. Any longer and you'd look like a prude."

Kira poked her tongue out at Susie's reflection and couldn't help but smile when the woman repeated the gesture. It was the sort of thing she and Mary would do when they argued—acknowledge the disagreement and move on.

Susie helped tuck the bright red bow beneath her blouse's collar.

"There," Susie proclaimed, "Now you're one of us. Well, nearly..." She pulled out a drawer and threw Kira a pair of long white socks.

"White?" Kira asked, frowning at the socks. "But...everyone else was wearing black."

Susie shook her head. "No, only the *wolves* wear black. The vampires wear red. But you're special—you get to wear white."

Kira froze. Was Susie implying that she was neither a wolf shifter, nor a vampire? Did she *know*?

The woman laughed. "You should see your face! You poor thing. Relax." She rubbed Kira's arm. "There's nothing wrong with being a virgin."

Kira nearly jumped out of her skin at the word. She was sure she'd misheard. "Excuse me. A *what?*"

"A virgin," Susie said lightly.

"What...how...?"

"How do I know?" Susie asked, "Come on, even *I* can smell it."

Kira licked her lips, trying to process the information. She hadn't expected the wolves to be able to *smell* her V-status. No shifter she'd met had ever mentioned that she was a virgin... but then again, it wasn't exactly a polite thing to comment on. Apparently, the academy was a lot more open about these things.

"Is it...a bad smell?"

Susie laughed. "It's a *strong* smell. It's no wonder Mark was so smitten with you, or that Chelsea was so threatened by you..."

Kira's brain ground to a halt. "Mark was...smitten?"

"Oh yes! Couldn't you tell?"

"No..." It was unsettling that something so private would be so obvious to others. Byron and Mary had warned her that the students at Volmasque Academy were promiscuous, but they hadn't known there was a special dress code for virgins. Clearly, there were a lot of fucked up things at the academy that weren't public knowledge.

Her foster parents had done their best, but there was only so much intelligence they could gather when they were in hiding. They were paranoid, spending most of their time in the forest in their wolf form, not even trusting their own kind not to turn them in. The couple viewed their trips to the village as a necessary risk. They'd never stopped Kira from visiting Nordokk, though, for which she was thankful. She'd amassed a wealth of theories about the academy from the humans' speculations, including the misconception that vampires slept in coffins.

Great, now she was imagining Nathaniel's bed.

Kira gave her head a small shake to clear it and sank onto a chair.

"So...everyone will know I'm a virgin by the end of the day?"

"By lunchtime, more like," Susie said. "But relax, this is good news! The alphas will be *very* interested in the fact that you're still intact."

Kira held up the white socks apprehensively. Why wear the socks if the wolves could tell she was a virgin just by smelling her? Bile crept up her throat as a horrible thought to her. "Is it only wolves who can...smell that I'm a..."

"A virgin?" Susie finished.

Kira sighed. "Yes. That."

"Vampires have a shit-poor sense of smell, if that's what you're asking. On par with humans."

Good.

The less Nathaniel knew about her private affairs, the better.

"Most first year females have to change their socks by the end of orientation week," Susie said. "That's when everyone gets recruited into packs. But as it's the middle of the year, so you're going to stand out."

Kira groaned, unsure if that was a good thing. "Can't I just wear the black socks?"

"No. Not until you've had sex for the first time."

"This is disgusting. And sexist. The vampires are sick in the head for thinking up this stupid dress code."

Susie shot her a strange look. "Actually, the white socks were proposed by wolf shifter students on the student council. Every shifter student voted, and it was a unanimous decision. If anything, the staff were allowing us a concession."

So, we're the ones sick in the head?

It made her head spin. The apple truly was rotten from the inside out.

A bell clanged somewhere outside the room.

"First period is starting soon," Susie said anxiously. "Are you putting on the socks or not? Only, I want to get to the cafeteria before it closes..."

Kira was tempted to not wear any socks at all just to make a point—but she wasn't here to be a lone wolf or rebel.

"Yes, sorry, of course," Kira said, snapping out of her reverie. She pulled on a sock, rolling up the soft fabric until it nearly reached her mid-thigh. She hesitated before putting on the second. "Susie?"

"Yes, what is it?" Susie asked, waiting restlessly in the doorway.

"You said the alphas would be very interested in the fact that I'm a virgin. What does that mean, precisely?"

"It means that the packs will be practically fighting each other to convince you to join them."

Kira's eyes widened. "Really?"

"Oh, yes," Susie said. "It puts you in a very good position. You'll have your pick of the packs. But can I give you some advice? Don't rush this decision. Keep those mutts drooling for a while. Oh, and stay away from the Populars, they're full of bitches."

Kira snorted. "Sure." But as they hurried to breakfast, Kira's thoughts had already drifted to Mark's barrel chest and easy smile.

They hurriedly ate their food at the edge of the cafeteria in a window seat overlooking the grounds. The sky had turned grey, but the sight of the lush, green lawns and hedges had a calming effect on her—just like Mark had.

He and the Populars were all she could think about as she spooned yoghurt and berries into her mouth. That was the sort of pack she needed to join—one where their omegas were worth more than another pack's alpha. If the Populars ruled the wolves, then it was where she needed to be if she hoped to have a chance of uniting all of the packs.

Kira glanced down at her long white socks. Would her virginity really give her first choice of what pack to join? The thought that anyone would take such interest in whether she'd had sex before or not was unnerving.

"I'll drop you off at your first class," Susie said, glancing at the timetable she'd given Kira. "Looks like you have potions, ick. Fair warning, wolves are always terrible at potions, so don't feel bad if you suck at it."

The classroom was on the ground floor.

"Last door on the end," Susie said. "I'll see you at lunch."

"Wait," Kira said. "I want to say thank you. And also, just for the record..."

Susie turned back. "Yes?"

"I think the whole white socks and virginity thing is really fucking stupid."

Susie laughed and patted her on the arm. "I know. But you may as well make the most of it."

Oh, I plan to.

It was bizarre to think that she was now a prize to be won. It would be interesting to see who the candidates were, even though she'd already made up her mind on who she wanted. There was only one alpha who was deserving enough to win her.

Smile, Mark. Enjoy your victory. You'll have exactly five seconds before I knock that crown off your head.

It was time for a new alpha to take charge.

CHAPTER 10

Potions Class

KIRA

KIRA SAT AT THE back of the classroom, hoping she would be less conspicuous when she failed to replicate the thick, orange sludge called 'Havagash' bubbling in the cauldron on Professor Parna's desk.

Kira stared down at the textbook the wispy-haired professor had lent her. He'd given her some helpful tips on how to achieve a pumpkin-soup-like consistency, but she didn't recognise half the ingredients on her desk.

"Don't look so worried," said a female vampire sitting at the desk beside her. She had disinterested eyes and a black bob with a very short fringe. "It's not that hard."

"It's not?" Kira asked. She couldn't tell from the vampiress' flat tone if she was being helpful or patronising.

"No, it's not. As long as you mash the sulphur to a fine enough powder, you'll be fine."

"Right," Kira said, pulling the mortar and pestle towards her. "And the sulphur is..."

"The yellow one. And don't add too much moonstone essence—you only need a drop. Otherwise, you'll be numb for weeks."

"Numb?"

The vampiress gave her a wicked smile that mimicked the wings of her eyeliner. "Oh yes. It numbs your mouth, and if you swallow it, your throat will go numb as well." She winked. "Popular with your lot in particular."

"With my lot? Why's that?" But she already knew. If the wolves had a reputation for being sexually active, she could only guess why a potion that numbed the throat would be helpful.

The vampiress clicked her tongue and grinned. "Honey, don't be shy!"

"I'm not," Kira answered, turning her attention back to the textbook. She skimmed the other pages—the more interesting potions had all been crossed out, presumably because they required real witch magic. She sighed and peered into the small cauldron on her desk. It looked like milky broth.

"I'm Victoria," said the vampiress, extending a dainty hand across the aisle.

"Kira," she said, shaking her hand. Her gaze lingered on Victoria's long nails, which were a bright shade of fuchsia.

"Like them?" Victoria asked, inspecting her nails.

"Yes, but...pink? Why didn't you choose—"

"Red?" Victoria made a disgusted face. "Ugh, I'm so over it. Have you seen this place? Give me *any* other colour." She glanced back at Kira, her gaze trailing down her body. "Speaking of colours...nice socks."

"Thanks," she muttered hesitantly.

"Wolf customs are so strange. Still, I don't suppose you'll be wearing white for long, will you, sweetie?"

Kira shrugged.

"Had any offers yet?"

"Not yet."

"Hmm." Victoria drummed her nails on the desk, then gave her a wink. "Well, perhaps *I'll* take you, then."

Kira froze. "Excuse me?"

"Oh, sweetie, won't you relax? I'm teasing. Not that you aren't cute. But you better join a pack soon—before one of the vampires claims you."

"*Claims* me?"

Victoria's eyes glinted. "No one's told you?"

"Told me what?"

"I suppose it's normally covered in orientation. But still, someone should have warned you..." she lifted her eyebrows conspiratorially and lowered her voice. "If you don't choose a pack, then sooner or later, a hungry vampire will choose *you*."

Kira gulped.

A vampire would choose her?

What about needing consent?

"And if I say no?"

"Oh, honey..." Victoria pouted and gave her a pitying look. "That's not how it works at all. We have ways of making you say yes."

She could scarcely breathe. "Mind control?"

Victoria laughed. "No. But I'm afraid it's one person's word against another's in these cases. Sad, isn't it?"

Kira understood perfectly. A vampire's word held more weight with the faculty than a wolf's did. She dropped her gaze, suddenly regretting the conversation. "Right, well...I need to focus on this." On the bright side, her potion looked orange now.

Victoria leant closer across the aisle and whispered, "Just so there's no confusion...if you let a vampire bite you before you join a pack, none of the packs will go near you."

Kira pretended to be busy, chopping something soft and slimy that she sincerely hoped was a vegetable. "Not even the alphas?"

"Especially not the alphas. They wouldn't dare, not if you belong to a vampire. It would be perceived as a challenge. The last alpha who stood up to a vampire was fed on and lost his status in his pack. I mean, that's not the official story, but there it is. Shame, isn't it?"

A nervousness settled in the pit of Kira's stomach, making her heart pound in her chest. She set down her knife, the chopping board before her a blur of yellow gooey pieces as she tried to formulate a plan to approach Mark after class. The sooner she made a move, the better.

"Ahem."

The male voice interrupted her thoughts, making her jump. She stared up at the tall vampire standing beside her desk. He was dressed like a teacher, with a pine green suit and a glen-check necktie that complimented his pale skin and icy blond hair, which was carefully combed to the side. A familiar, hateful eyebrow was arched expectantly at her.

Kira resisted the urge to touch her neck where the collar had been.

"Nathaniel, nice of you to finally join us," Victoria said, giving him the middle finger.

"Charmed, as always, Victoria," he replied, but he held Kira's gaze, his blue eyes drawing her in.

Before she could ask him what he wanted, his gaze drifted downwards, lingering on her legs.

On my socks, she realised, cringing as he raised his other eyebrow as well. Nathaniel had just realised she was a virgin. She didn't know why, but it unnerved her to no end.

Well, he can join the other creeps who think that increases my value.

She was half tempted to flip him a rude gesture as well, but instead, she crossed her arms. "Yes? Got something to say?"

To the only girl in the whole school wearing white socks?

Nathaniel's gaze flickered back up to hers. "Yes, I do, actually. That's my seat."

She blanched. "Pardon?"

He bent down close to her and spoke in a slow, measured tone, his warm breath tickling her ear as he enunciated every syllable. "You're. Sitting. In. My. Chair."

The heat rose in her face as she realised Nathaniel hadn't been looking at her socks at all, but at the chair she was sitting on.

"She's sitting there now," Victoria said slyly, licking her lips as she looked between the two of them.

"That's right," Kira said confidently. "I'm sitting here now."

"You would be wise to move," Nathaniel stated. "Unless you wish to share with me. I have no qualms about you sitting on my lap..."

"I have plenty of qualms about that," Kira said, rising abruptly and tucking the textbook against her chest. Too mortified to look at him, she took the only other desk that was free—the one that was directly in front of Nathaniel's.

She slapped the textbook down and stared at the empty cauldron before her. She was missing a knife, but she was too embarrassed to go and ask for a new one.

What the hell do I do now?

Unable to stand the suspense, or the sound of Victoria laughing, she slowly turned in her chair. Nathaniel was looking at her, his arm outstretched as he held out the knife handle-first, offering it to her.

She eyed it suspiciously.

"Oh, believe me," he said, "I'm fully aware that handing you any kind of weapon could be a fatal error on my part."

Kira huffed and took the knife. "Your error is thinking I need a weapon to end your life."

Victoria erupted into a fresh burst of cackling, but Kira didn't so much as spare her a glance. She was too mesmerised by Nathaniel's reaction, including the way he ran his tongue over the sharp point of a fang.

She hastily dropped her gaze, her eyes narrowing as she took in his pale green suit. He wasn't wearing a uniform. "I thought you were the chief security officer."

"I'm also a student—"

"He's not," Victoria interjected.

"I'm a postgraduate researcher," Nathaniel insisted.

"Bullshit, no one believes you," Victoria said.

"They *might* if you didn't contradict me." Nathaniel didn't seem annoyed, however, and he never once took his eyes off Kira.

I should focus on making my potion...

Alarm bells were ringing, but her curiosity got the better of her, and she remained half-turned in her chair, transfixed by the vampire. What was a postgraduate researcher—or whatever—doing in a potions class for first years?

"I didn't realise that was your chair," she said suspiciously.

"It's not," he replied.

"He doesn't even take this class," Victoria commented.

Kira's chair scraped as she turned to face the vampire head-on. "Then *why* did you make me get up if it's not even your chair?"

"I wanted to see if you would do as you were told."

Anger struck her like lightning, derailing the last bit of patience she had left. "Dick!" she cried, causing several students to turn and stare.

"Mm, she's feisty," Victoria said approvingly. "Watch out, Nathaniel. This wolf has fangs."

"I'm well aware." Nathaniel's eyes twinkled, and the corners of his lips held the hint of a smile.

Danger, her insides screamed. The urge to run and hide was strong, but her fighting spirit was stronger. Her lips drew back in a snarl, and she wished she could shift, right here, right now, and put him in his place.

If only.

The sudden clang of school bells signalled the end of class and saved her from doing something so incredibly stupid as revealing her true form.

"Bye, pumpkin," Victoria called fondly as Kira stormed out of the classroom.

She was halfway to her next class when she stopped abruptly in the middle of the corridor, hanging her head as she remembered the textbook in her hands. She'd forgotten to give it back.

Exhaling a long sigh, she returned to the potions classroom, dragging her feet in the hope that the two vampires would be long gone by the time she arrived.

Thankfully, the classroom was deserted except for Professor Parna. The portly professor adjusted his spectacles in confusion when she approached his desk. "Ah, Kirabelle, you've returned it, just lovely."

"Actually, sir, it's just Kira."

"Just Kira? Oh, I see, it's a modern thing. But you know, Kirabelle is such a distinguished name. A traditional Old Wolfe name, I believe?"

"I wouldn't know, sir," she said.

"Actually, a colleague of mine was telling me—Professor Sawyer, the History teacher, have you met her yet? Lovely woman. She was telling me—and now, it's just a myth, of course. But fascinating, I think. Truly, for before the Revolution, there apparently was a K—"

"Sorry, sir," Kira said, backing towards the door, "but I'll be late for class."

"Just a moment, Kira," he said, forcing her to turn back. "I must ask. How did you find your first potions class? I saw you getting along rather well with the prince."

Her heart skipped a beat, then jarred to a grinding halt as the professor's meaning sank in.

"The...*prince?*" she asked through gritted teeth.

Tell me I misheard. Because if he means Nathaniel, I'm sure he meant to say 'prick'.

"Why, yes. The tall, blond-haired gentleman with whom you were speaking. He looks so much like his father...I've taught him since he was your age, you know. Excellent student. One of our brightest. I do appreciate that he still pops by from time to time to humour this old professor..."

"Who did you say he was?" Kira asked weakly.

"Why, he's the Vampire King's son, of course. Son of Henrikk. Next in line for the throne. Crown Prince Nathaniel."

Kira groaned and turned away.

You have got to be fucking kidding me.

CHAPTER 11
The Forbidden Corridor

KIRA

Susie was right—the male wolves could not get enough of her scent, and it made moving between classes increasingly difficult as the day wore on. Lunchtime was the worst. Her presence generated a thick crowd of admirers vying for her attention, preventing her and Susie from reaching the cafeteria window.

When Kira commented that she only wanted lunch, a dozen wolves immediately volunteered to fetch her some, and a fight broke out between two betas from the same pack to decide who would receive that honour.

"They're mad," Kira said as she and Susie were forced to flee the cafeteria without food. "Absolutely crazy."

"That's primal instinct for you," Susie said. "But this is worse than orientation week! At least we had multiple females for them to chase. Now, it's just you."

"Fantastic," Kira muttered, glancing over her shoulder at the fifty or so men following behind. The desire on their faces was unnerving, and some had lost all self-control and shifted into wolf form.

Susie tried to give her a tour of the academy grounds, but the open space was worse, with males approaching them from all directions.

"Perhaps, we can go someplace private?" an alpha asked her.

"Perhaps another time," Kira replied. She couldn't focus on the tour, and she was treading a fine line between politely rebuffing the advances and snapping at them to keep their hands to themselves.

"You're rocking those white socks, sweetie," Victoria called when Susie and Kira passed by the water fountains. She was sitting on the edge of the stone basin, intertwined with another vampiress.

"Err, thanks," Kira said, trying to appear as if she wasn't unnerved by the fact that the group of men behind her were all sporting rigid boners—wolves included.

She and Susie retreated inside.

"This is the teachers' wing," Susie said when they reached the second floor, trying to make herself heard over the squabbling students.

The only benefit Kira perceived of the male wolves' presence was that it kept the vampires away. Even so, she was growing tired of the commotion of barking and snarling that followed in her wake.

They were on the second-floor corridor when Susie took a sharp turn and pulled her into a narrow passage. It was a dark corridor with no windows, and only a single door at the end. For a moment, Kira worried they had trapped themselves in a dead end, but to her surprise, no one followed them.

"Why did they stop?" she asked as Susie peered back out into the hallway.

"This area is forbidden to students," Susie explained. "Strictly out of bounds."

"Then why did you bring us here?"

"Because I knew they'd be too scared to follow us here."

"Aren't *you* scared?"

"A little." Susie let out a sigh of relief and slumped against the wall. "But I couldn't hear myself think, could you? Let's give it a few minutes. The bell will ring soon. Hopefully they'll go away."

Kira approached the plain door. It was painted dark grey with a simple brass knob. "Susie, where does this door lead?"

"Nowhere," Susie said quickly.

Kira was certain that she was lying. "Susie..." she pressed.

"Really, don't worry about it. It's just a cleaning closet."

Kira didn't believe her. "Then why is it out of bounds to students? If it's merely a cleaning closet, you won't mind if I have a look..."

She'd not taken two steps before Susie pulled her back.

"Okay, I lied. But please, don't go in there."

Kira's curiosity sparked. "Why not?" she asked, trying to step past. "What's in there?"

"Nothing you want to see," Susie said, blocking her way. "Trust me."

Now I definitely want to see it.

Kira was torn between the mysterious door and Susie's look of genuine concern. She was still trying to wheedle the answers out of her when the school bell rang, signalling the end of lunch.

Out in the corridor, the wolves were gone.

"Good," said Susie. "Let's go, before he catches us."

"Before who catches us?" Kira asked.

Susie wouldn't say. "I don't want you getting hurt. Let's just leave it at that."

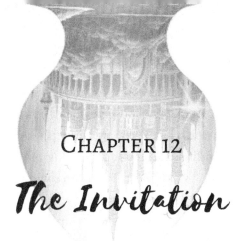

CHAPTER 12

The Invitation

KIRA

KIRA'S OTHER CLASSES WERE not nearly as interesting as potions had been. She'd had Literature and Maths in the morning, and after lunch, she endured a double period of music, which she enjoyed but wasn't any good at. The final hour of the day was Physical Education, and she relished the chance to run outside on the field, even if she'd had to borrow a sports uniform several sizes too large. After all the attention she'd drawn, it was a relief to wear something that wasn't form-hugging.

When the final bell rang, Kira waited for Susie on the front steps of the school. She was eager to see what was outside the academy. It would also be a relief to get away from the male wolves, who still hovered around her, extending invites to join their packs. She might have been flattered had she not been overwhelmed by their obvious erections.

"You won't regret joining our pack," a beta said, his eyes hopeful.

Kira offered him a strained smile. "I'll think about it."

She did not want to burn her bridges, but she was holding out for the only invite that mattered. To her disappointment, Mark was not amongst the admirers. The only time she'd seen him was when she glimpsed him in the cafeteria eating lunch with his pack.

As she waited outside the school entrance, she noticed a long, steel pike mounted vertically at the top of the steps. Despite the throng of students descending the steps and spilling out onto the lawns, she noticed that the crowd gave the weapon a wide berth. Kira soon discovered that the male wolves wouldn't go near it either, and that by standing beside it, she was granted a small reprieve from their attentions.

Her skin prickled, and she could have sworn she heard a low raspy whisper near her ear. She heard it again, and this time she was certain the haunted whisper had emanated from the pike. She backed away hastily, and soon lost sight of the weapon altogether as the male wolves huddled around her.

She was beginning to lose hope of hearing from the Poplarins when the crowd suddenly parted and Chelsea Poplarin appeared, wrinkling her pointed nose as she scanned the male wolves disdainfully. She rolled her eyes as she approached Kira, and said in a snide voice, "Enjoying yourself, I see?"

"I'd happily trade places."

"I'm sure you would," Chelsea said, stroking her sleek plaits. "But we can't all be me."

No argument here.

"What can I do for you?" Kira asked.

Chelsea sighed and handed her a crisp envelope. "Congratulations," she began in a flat, unhappy tone, "you have received an offer to join the Poplarin Pack."

Kira's face lit up. "What? Really? I—"

"In order to confirm your membership," Chelsea continued, talking over her, "you are required to attend an initiation ceremony after school tomorrow in the gym."

"Initiation?"

"A *secret* initiation. Tell no one. Attendance is compulsory if you wish to join our ranks. Non-attendance will result in your invitation being withdrawn. Is that understood?"

"Yes," Kira said, eagerly opening the letter and scanning the beautiful calligraphy. The invitation had been signed by Mark himself. "I'll be there."

"Fine." Chelsea hesitated, scowling to herself as if she'd just remembered something. "And one more thing. To prove your loyalty to the pack, you must bring a physical item from the vampire hunter's room to the initiation."

"A physical item?" Kira asked, frowning down at the letter. "Where does it say—"

"It's not in the letter," Chelsea said impatiently. "Membership to the Poplarin Pack is *very* exclusive, and we don't allow just anyone in. Mark only accepts the best, and he expects you to use your initiative."

"Right. So...what kind of item am I looking for?"

Chelsea rolled her eyes. "Something small enough that you can carry it. Something that's obviously the hunter's. I will warn you, though, this mission could be dangerous. If you don't feel up to it..."

She's hoping I'll back out.

Kira rolled her shoulders back. "I'll do it. But...Chelsea, who is the vampire hunter? Does he actually kill vampires?"

Chelsea smirked. "Oh, yes. But he's no one you can't handle. Besides, he won't be in his office tomorrow afternoon. He'll be out hunting. Now, do you know where his office is?"

Kira's eyes widened as Chelsea described the grey door in the dark corridor on the second floor.

"Think you can find it?" Chelsea asked. "If you need me to show you—"

Kira shook her head, feeling determined. "No need. I know where it is."

"Excellent," Chelsea said, sounding almost cheerful. "See you tomorrow after school."

"See you," Kira said, watching her go. She reread the letter, her heart swelling at the word *Congratulations*. Had Mark handwritten it himself? Doubtful, but one could hope.

This was what she'd been waiting for. Gaining membership to a prominent pack was only a stepping stone to greater things. Less than a day ago, she'd been a nobody in a worn blouse and skirt, looking so much like a peasant she may as well have had straw in her hair, and the task had seemed daunting. Now, she was holding the rich parchment in her hands, savouring the victory that was only a day away.

"I'm here," Susie panted, hurrying down the steps and dispersing Kira's group of admirers. "Ready for shopping?"

"Ready," Kira said, folding the letter and stowing it in the inside pocket of her blazer.

They walked across the green lawn towards the school gates. Thankfully, the wolves could not follow them. Students needed special permission to leave the school grounds, and Susie kissed the permission slip she'd obtained from Headmaster Arken and grinned at Kira before handing it to the vampire guarding the booth.

As the gates opened, a familiar drawl made Kira tense.

"And where are the two of you off to?"

Kira smoothed her expression as she turned.

Nathaniel was standing in the booth's doorway, managing to look both bored and smug as he appraised them. His gaze flickered ever so briefly to the crowd of male wolves that had followed them hopefully to the gates. He arched one eyebrow questioningly.

Susie opened her mouth to explain, but Kira beat her to it.

"We have a letter from the headmaster granting us permission to leave the school grounds—and that's all you need to know, *Prince Nathaniel*."

Nathaniel remained silent as he tilted his head, his cool eyes unnerving as they stared unblinkingly at her.

"Well?" she prompted when he didn't respond. "Can we go to the city or not?"

His lips curled with amusement. "I'm not stopping you. That being said, if you're asking for my permission—"

"I'm not," Kira said firmly, annoyance flashing as she and Susie passed through the gates. They began to creak shut.

"Shall I let your admirers through as well?" Nathaniel called.

A hopeful cry emanated from the crowd of wolves.

Without turning back, Kira held up her middle finger in the air as they walked away, the gates clanging shut behind them. She could feel Nathaniel's gaze on her long after the whining of the wolves at the gate had ceased.

Susie laughed. "You don't seem afraid of Nathaniel."

"I'm not." With some distance between them and the gates, Kira finally chanced a glance behind her, and immediately wished she hadn't. Some of the wolves were staring after them with their faces pressed against the bars. If Nathaniel was still there, she couldn't see him.

"Maybe you should be," Susie suggested softly.

"Maybe," she conceded. "But not today."

Kira faced straight ahead. She wouldn't let Nathaniel ruin things. Not when she had an invitation from the Poplarins.

Her chest was full of butterflies as she ran her fingers over the parchment in her pocket. Joining the Poplarin Pack would set her on the path to making a real difference to the wolf race, not just at the academy, but throughout the kingdom.

She linked arms with Susie, and as their long hair and skirts rustled in the winter breeze, Kira allowed herself a rare, girlish squeal of excitement.

Everything was falling into place.

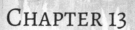

CHAPTER 13

A Shopping Revelation

KIRA

VOLMASQUE ACADEMY WAS IN the centre of the Capital, and Kira and Susie only had to walk a few blocks along the cobblestone streets to reach the shopping district. The sun was beginning to travel low in the sky, its golden rays painting the stone façades of the shops and boutiques with an ethereal glow and casting elongated shadows across the narrow streets.

Shopping with Susie was the most fun she'd ever had. For two precious hours, she felt normal, forgetting all about the academy and her quest for revenge. The scent of freshly baked bread mingled with the earthy fragrance of books, and Susie laughed as Kira drew her into an antique bookshop that doubled as a café.

"You definitely need to join my pack," Susie said. "But even if you don't, you're still welcome at our book club meetings."

Kira gave her a sincere smile. "Thank you."

"Now, come on. Let's buy your essentials first. We can come back later."

"Promise?" Kira asked, her mouth open as she stared at the coffee special—a tall concoction of cream and mint with wafers sticking out of it.

Using the bag of coins she'd brought from home, she purchased several sets of clothes to wear outside of school hours, a hooded cloak lined with fur for the colder nights, a hairbrush, a towel, and a set of satin pyjamas.

It was dark by the time they finished, but the streets were bathed in the golden glow of torches, and the soothing music of street musicians tempted them to stay longer. They sat on the concrete steps of Market Square, warming themselves by a burning brazier as they ate chocolate pudding.

It had never once occurred to Kira that she would make a genuine friend while she was at the academy, but as she and Susie chatted, she felt some of the empty loneliness inside of her ease, and she dared hope.

Their conversation took an ominous turn when she told Susie about the Poplarin's invitation. Rather than be happy for her, as Kira had expected, Susie looked concerned.

"You're not thinking of accepting it, are you?"

Kira glanced down guiltily. "I already have."

"Well, it doesn't matter. Don't go."

"Why not?"

"I think it's too much. I don't think you can handle it."

Kira frowned and set her cup of dessert down. "What do you mean?"

"Do you have any idea what the initiation involves?"

"Of course," Kira said as her stomach twisted unpleasantly. The initiation ceremony was something she'd purposefully avoided thinking about. "I appreciate your concern, Susie. But I know what I'm getting myself into."

"Do you?" Susie peered at her apprehensively.

"I mean, I think so." After a day of having male wolves drool after her and solicit her company, she'd pieced together what the initiation ceremony of each pack involved: submitting to the alpha.

Which meant she would have to have sex with Mark. It was a strange concept, given she had no experience, but if it had to be someone, she was glad it would be him. She shot Susie a shy smile. "Mark doesn't seem so bad. I'll be fine."

"Mark?" Susie groaned and put her face in her hands. "You think all you need to do is to have sex with Mark? Ugh...see, this is why I warned you stay away from the Populars."

"I don't understand."

"Of course not." Susie shook her head sadly. "I should have told you sooner."

"Told me what?"

"The Populars aren't just the most powerful pack in the school. They're also the largest."

"So?" That was the whole reason why she wanted to join. Get the Poplarins to follow her, and the other packs would fall in line.

"You don't understand. A pack that large doesn't have just *one* alpha. It has several."

Her jaw dropped. "*What?*"

"Kira...I really think you should change your mind about going. The initiation requires you to submit to *all* the alphas. And given that you've attracted so much interest, I highly doubt any of them will sit back and not want their turn. I mean, given you're a virgin and all."

Her stomach rolled with nausea, and her voice was barely a squeak as she forced herself to ask the question she was afraid to hear the answer to. "So...how many alphas are there?"

Two?

Three?

Four?

Susie gave her a pitying look. "Twelve."

CHAPTER 14

The Vampire Hunter

<u>KIRA</u>

KIRA LAY AWAKE THAT night, tossing and turning in her new bed as she wrestled with the dilemma of what to do. Submitting herself to Mark had seemed like a simple thing—daunting, but simple. The muscled, sandy-haired alpha wolf was physically attractive, and if first impressions were anything to go by, he was kind, thoughtful, and an alpha she could respect. There would be no shame in coupling with him.

If circumstances were different, would she still want to have sex with him?

Maybe.

Probably.

She'd assumed that Mark was the sole alpha of the Poplarins Pack, and that the sex would likely be awkward and uncomfortable. There was also the chance that it would be wonderful, and a part of her hoped it would be so. The worst-case scenario was that he would be rough with her, but she could handle pain if she had to. Regardless of what the initiation would be like, she'd calculated that the whole thing would only take a couple of minutes, and then it would all be over. It was a small price to pay to elevate her rank and further her mission.

But she'd been mistaken.

There was more than one alpha, and once Mark was finished, pulling his cock out of her, another would take his place, climbing on top of her and claiming her all over again. And when he was finished, the next one would be waiting.

Twelve alpha wolves, Susie had said.

How the hell was she supposed to lie there and subject herself to that...*experience*...*twelve times*?

The whole thing was starting to feel less like a sacrifice, and more like something akin to the degrading punishment Nathaniel had put her through.

At least *he* hadn't tried to share her.

Ugh.

Kira rolled over in her bed, pushing any thoughts of Nathaniel or the alphas out of her mind. She'd been around humans too long, and all the customs the wolves took for granted seemed wrong. The tiny bit of hope she'd had that she might actually enjoy the initiation had all but deserted her, leaving her feeling disgusted. Could she really go through with it?

She was sure her body wasn't built to take twelve alphas.

Was anyone's?

"You'll be exhausted...both physically and mentally," Susie had warned. "And the whole pack will be watching the entire time. Are you sure you want to go through that?"

Susie wanted her to back out of the ceremony, to settle for another pack, and as Kira finally drifted off to sleep, she was tempted to do just that.

They can all fuck off.

But when the morning came, Kira felt a fresh wave of optimism.

She'd showered in the shared bathroom on her floor and was feeling much more like herself. Her brown skin was dark against the fluffy white towel wrapped around her, and her wet hair fell across her face and leant a fierceness to her yellow eyes.

"I can do this," she said to her foggy reflection in the mirror. "This time tomorrow, I'll be part of the Poplarin Pack."

Despite her improved spirits, the school day ticked by so slowly it was excruciating, and the anticipation was killing her.

She still needed to break into the vampire hunter's room and steal something of his before the initiation, so she skipped her final class of the day, Physical Education, to do it.

Whilst her classmates were outside enjoying the sun, she was sneaking into the dark corridor and turning the knob of the plain door. She was surprised to find it unlocked.

The door creaked open.

A cold draft met her as she stepped inside. The room was deserted, and she took a moment to take in the bizarreness of it. It was lavishly furnished, with a tall-backed armchair behind a large, heavy-looking desk, and several upholstered chairs facing it. Large windows let in the grey winter light, and one window was open and banging eerily against the wall.

Behind the desk, several large animal pelts were mounted on display, and the floor of the office was covered in similar pelts with hardly an inch of the floorboards visible underneath. She recognised the deerskin one beneath her feet, a light brown with dappled white spots. Byron and Mary had one just like it in their cottage.

Well, they used to.

She didn't recognise what animal the others were from, which all had grey shaggy fur. She bent down and ran her hand along one of the rugs. The grey hairs were dense and coarse.

The room was thick with the musty smell of animal pelts, to the point that it smelled like death.

Bang.

She jumped and whirled around, but it was only the window

hitting the wall. Clicking her tongue at her own jumpiness, she went to secure it.

When she turned back to face the desk, she had the horrible sense she was being watched. Except there was no one there.

It's just nerves.

She sniffed the air cautiously, but all she could smell were the damn pelts filling her senses.

Wandering around the room, she examined bookshelves, rifled through boxes, and pulled out drawers. She needed something small that distinctly belonged to the vampire hunter, whoever he was. She half hoped there would be a letter or invoice with his name that would satisfy the pack's requirements.

Her heart skipped a beat when she spotted a small jewellery box on top of a cabinet. She opened the velvet case tentatively and drew a sharp breath at the sight of the gleaming ruby ring, surrounded by sparkling diamonds. The engagement ring was magnificent, the blood-red stone large and oval-shaped as it dominated the gold band. She snapped the box shut and went to pocket it, but hesitated.

It would be despicable to take it. Truly awful. It was clearly intended for someone.

That was when she sensed movement behind her—a figure emerged from the shadows and moved swiftly towards her.

She shrieked, gold light dancing before her eyes as she began to shift, but the figure was on her in an instant. His cruel hands clamping over her wrists and shoving her against the wall.

"Nathaniel!" she gasped as she recognised the vampire. "What are you doing here?"

"What am *I* doing here?" he asked in disbelief. His voice was cold and edged with something sharp that took her a moment to recognise—it was fear. "What are *you* doing here?"

"I asked you first," she said, trying to push him back, but he held her firmly in place. "Aren't you worried the vampire hunter will catch you here?"

Nathaniel lips parted in confusion, and then... "Ah. You think *I'm* in danger. That's endearing. Let me educate you." He released her wrists and spun her around so she faced the desk, her back pressed flush against his chest. "I *am* the danger."

Kira's heart fell as the realisation hit her—Chelsea had tricked her. Somehow, she'd known Nathaniel would be here. "This is your office, isn't it?" she whispered.

"Yes."

"But...wait..." she shook her head. "How can you be the vampire hunter?"

Nathaniel's lip twitched, and some of the fear on his face faded. "Well, I suppose I *am* both a vampire and hunter." His hand trailed along her waist, the other covering her neck. "But I've never heard anyone call me the vampire hunter."

"Oh."

Chelsea, you fucking bitch.

"Yes—*oh*. Now, what are you doing in my office?"

She deflected. "If you don't kill vampires, then what do you hunt?"

He laughed harshly. "Look around you."

She did, scanning the office with its blood-red drapes, the dark-wood of the furniture and walls, the pelts...

Her heart sank as she finally recognised the pelts.

"No," she whispered, shaking her head.

"Oh yes," Nathaniel said, leaning close so his mouth was inches from her neck. "Are you familiar with the Wintermaw Revolution?"

Her blood turned cold.

It was the night the vampires had attacked the Keep—the same night Byron and Mary had rescued her. "No. You're lying. You're just trying to scare me."

"Maybe. But you are not nearly as scared as you should be."

Suddenly, his hand squeezed her throat, and she screeched in terror as his mouth pressed down on her neck. For a moment, she thought he was going to bite her, but instead, he licked her, his tongue hot and wet as it dragged from her collarbone up to the angle of jawline. She shuddered as he sucked her earlobe.

"Wh-what are you doing?"

Grasping her jaw, he lifted her chin until she was forced to stare at the display of pelts on the wall behind the desk.

A shocked whimper left her as she noticed the shape of the pelts. When she'd first entered the room, she'd been too busy making sure she was alone to look at them properly. Now, she absorbed every detail. The wall-mounted pelts were not grey like the others but tan-coloured, the fur almost golden where the light touched it. The paws were larger than the average wolf's with sharper claws. The majestic wolf heads had thick fur that could have rivalled a lion's mane in its regality. But their faces...

Kira's chest tightened. Their expressions had been recreated to look like they were suffering. Finally, the tails. She'd been blind not to spot them sooner. Each wolf had not one, but nine tails spread out in a fan-shape.

And beneath... more of the same, but smaller...

Puppies.

Her eyes welled with tears. She knew who those wolves—who those people—had been.

"Kira, meet the Royal Wolf family."

"No..."

"Oh yes. There wasn't room for all of them on the wall. But we got most of them. And the pelts beneath your feet are the guards, the servants, and the nobles that were slain that night. You trod on them when you entered, and if you are lucky enough that I let you leave here alive, then you will tread on them again on your way out."

She felt faint, and her knees buckled underneath her.

Nathaniel caught her, one arm around her middle, just beneath her breasts, whilst the other held her throat.

"No reply?" he asked, his breath warm against her cheek.

She shook her head, her eyes squeezed shut against her tears. She had been wrong. He wasn't just a monster. He was pure evil, and she had no quips, no comebacks, and no anger to offer him. She was more scared now than she'd ever been in her life, and she was completely at his mercy. Panic surged as he choked her, and she didn't dare move, not even to struggle. Her breathing was strained, and she began to feel faint as stars danced before her eyes.

Please, don't let it hurt.

Whatever he does to me...

Nathaniel's voice was loud in her ear. "Kira, I want you to listen to me very carefully. Are you listening?"

She made a small, wheezing sound of affirmation.

"If I catch you in my office again, you won't leave. I will mount you on my desk, and when I'm done with your cunt, I'll mount you on the wall with the others. Is that understood?"

When she didn't answer, he gave her a rough shake. "Is that understood?"

"Y-yes."

He released her.

She dropped to the ground, rasping for air, before picking herself up and bolting from the room.

It wasn't until she'd reached the school's gym, a large separate building on the grounds, that she realised she still had the jewellery box trapped in her fist. She didn't have the courage to return it, nor to ever step foot in that office again. It was a miracle she'd gotten away without the vampire biting her. She'd been fully prepared to never leave that office alive.

She flinched when the school bell echoed in the empty gym. The initiation would begin soon, but she couldn't think about that.

Her mind was consumed with fear of the cold, sinister side she'd discovered of Nathaniel. Up to this point, he'd been little more than an exceptionally frustrating vampire to her, and she'd hated him by default. But after discovering that he'd murdered the Royal Wolf family, and goodness knew how many others...

She couldn't breathe, she couldn't think.

By the time the Poplarin Pack arrived for the initiation, she was still trembling.

CHAPTER 15

The Shower Fantasy

NATHANIEL

NATHANIEL STOOD ALONE IN his office. There was a fine line between being alone, and loneliness, and he was somewhere in between. He had not needed the wolves' heightened sense of smell to detect Kira's fear. Her skin had been clammy with it, and he had tasted the saltiness of her sweat when he licked her neck. Her body had been so warm against his, her stiff shoulders unable to mask her involuntary shivers when he touched her, or the way her fingers trembled. His fangs throbbed, and he longed to sink them into her neck.

Oh, how sweet her blood would have tasted.

If only.

If only, instead of making empty threats to scare her, he'd let himself do what he truly desired: to mount her on the desk. He wanted to hike her skirt up, spread her legs, pull her panties aside. He wanted to be on her, his body folded forward so he could watch her face as he pushed his cock into her tight, wet cunt.

Would she make little sounds of surprise as he fucked her? Or would she howl in outrage, hating him even as she loved how he made her feel? He was dying to find out, not only to satisfy his curiosity, but to feed the primal hunger that burnt within him whenever she was near.

Nathaniel had resolved to keep his distance, but she was pushing him to the brink of madness by entering the abomination he called an office.

He could no longer deny it—he wanted to fuck her, and badly. Maybe then, he'd finally be able to get her out of his mind, instead of lying awake at night with his balls aching. Jerking off hadn't helped.

He'd tried thinking of Gloria, his bride-to-be. Gloria hadn't said 'yes' yet, of course, but the match had been arranged since they were young and was designed to strengthen his father's rule by combining their bloodlines. Technically, it should have been *Princess Gloria*, but no one used her title anymore for fear of being overheard by Henrikk's spies—which usually resulted in a swift execution.

Henrikk had killed Gloria's parents, Vampire Queen Liddia and her first husband, the late Vampire King Dmitri. Despite Henrikk's iron-fisted rule, the old royals in his court quietly bemoaned the land of yesterday. Henrikk wanted their support, and badly. It was why he'd arranged the alliance between Nathaniel and Gloria. Their marriage would unite the vampires and put a stop to infighting. For who could contest the marriage between Prince Nathaniel, son of the usurper king, and Princess Gloria, who was—as every vampire knew—the rightful heir to the throne?

Any children they had would be undisputed heirs, and Henrikk could then be satisfied in securing his legacy and ensuring a stable rule.

Princess or not, Gloria despised Nathaniel for obvious reasons, but he could not bring her parents back any more than he could have stopped his father from slaughtering them.

When it came to the arranged marriage, he was just as trapped as Gloria was. She was wise enough to know this because she played her part well. She always offering him smiles and curtsies, and she never let her contempt show, even if he did sense it simmering underneath her polite veneer. Gloria's revenge was slow, quiet, and ongoing. She had punished Nathaniel and his father by dragging out the courtship all these years, always emanating interest without ever giving him a firm 'yes'.

Nathaniel understood the source of her anger, but it was a game he was beginning to tire of. There had even been a time that he felt something for her, a delusion he'd held about their union mending the wounds of the past. But he'd soon discovered that the real Gloria had no interest in healing anything, nor making the world better—she was stuck in the past, and her venom was primed for anyone who tried to take her pain away.

Fantasising about Gloria did nothing for him, and he only thought of her to try and take his mind off Kira.

It didn't work. He could still feel her warm presence pressed into him, and the way her hair tickled his face.

Except that she was gone.

There was nothing left for him here in this façade he called an office. It was designed for intimidation, and little more. Surrounded by death, he only came here to store old records, and did as much of his work as was practical in his suite downstairs.

Whether he was a student was debatable, but after graduating, he'd continued to live in the vampire dorms. Shutting the office door without locking it, he returned downstairs to the seventh floor. His suite was vastly larger than Kira's room, and contained a lavish king bed, several sitting areas, a desk, wardrobe, and an ensuite.

He stripped off and stood in his shower, shivering as cold water beat down his back. It did nothing to douse his desire. If anything, it beat away all other thoughts, leaving only Kira at the forefront of his mind.

Finally, he gave in. He turned the hot water on, letting the warmth soak his skin until the room was full of steam, and he was hidden amongst it.

But he could not hide from himself, nor his dark desire of all the things he wanted to do to the female wolf.

With his head bent against the tiles and his eyes closed, he stroked his cock, letting out a low moan as he pictured the wild anger on Kira's face when he'd gagged her. It was a beautiful thing, and she'd been fiercer than he'd dared hope, the way a wolf ought to be. He thought of the blush that reddened her face as he made her kneel, bringing her eye level with his groin and at the perfect height for him to undo his belt and trousers and let her perfect mouth taste him.

The shower grew unbearably hot, but he didn't adjust the tap. He was so close. He slammed one arm against the tiles above his head, leaning forward and panting heavily as his other hand worked his heavy cock with fast, deliberate strokes. Sensations rippled and pulsed through him as his orgasm grew.

All it took was imagining that it was her hand, not his, jerking him off, to cause his orgasm to erupt through him. His abs clenched, and he gave a deep groan as he fisted his cock and blew his load on the tiled wall. His movements slowed as he milked the last of the cum from his cock, a hollowness taking form.

If only she were here with me.

It had felt good in the moment, but without her, it was meaningless.

He remained in the shower for several minutes longer, eyes squeezed shut as he pictured drawing the wolf close, kissing her cheek and tracing the length of her throat with his fangs.

His breathing gradually calmed, and his clarity of thought returned.

What am I doing?

Lust was one thing, but there were a dozen reasons why he shouldn't be thinking of Kira in a romantic sense. The pressure on him to woo and marry Gloria was only one of them.

But the ten-year age gap between him and Kira didn't bother him. She seemed older than nineteen. And for all that the white socks claimed of innocence, he knew she thought of killing him more than any other wolf he'd ever met.

And that was hot.

No, it wasn't the age difference that bothered him. It was the fact that he was thinking of her, even after he'd spilt his seed all over the wall. And the longer he stood here thinking of her, the more his blood boiled, and it had nothing to do with the hot water searing his skin.

Having sex with a wolf was not unusual for vampires, especially during feeding time. Thanks to the academy, the new generation of wolves were all but domesticated, accepting both without any qualms.

Even Susie's efforts to secure shifter rights at the academy had made little difference in the grand scheme of things. When the lights went out and the dorms grew quiet, hungry vampires prowled the corridors. No vampire had ever had to break a lock to enter a wolf's room—there were too many wolves who willingly left their doors open.

Wolves liked sex, plain and simple, and were not shy about it. Some packs even had orgies. But there was no one who could fuck quite like a vampire.

Wanting to have sex with Kira was considered normal by society.

Any kind of romantic feelings, however, were ludicrous.

Frowned upon.

Forbidden.

As his father would say, *you may play with your food, but you must throw the leftovers out.*

When it came to Kira, even playing with his food seemed dangerous.

Nathaniel had done all he could to scare her away from his office.

He sincerely hoped she would not be reckless enough to return.

Although, I will have to retrieve Gloria's engagement ring at some stage.

He changed and exited into the vampires' common room, a large open area shared by the two lowest levels of the dorms, floors six and seven. A staircase connected the two levels, which led up to an interior balcony that overlooked the common room.

Compared to the wolf dorms, which had drab door-lined corridors, the vampire dorms contained large suites, and the common room was equally as grand, boasting fine furniture and decorations. The common room was technically for the use of all students, but no wolf ever dared come here. He and the other vampires had the luxurious space all to themselves.

He sank into his favourite armchair by the fire, shifting to the flames. The heat failed to melt the image of Kira from his mind. It wasn't just that she was a pretty wolf. It was her sharp tongue, her fearlessness, and the blazing determination that threatened to engulf him if he stood too near.

And yet, he'd intentionally made her fear him, making him the opposite of what she truly needed. Behind her tough exterior, there were two wolves: one who was fierce and protective, and another who was timid and shy. They both needed someone to guide them, to fight with them, to help them succeed.

I could be that person for her.

But Kira was not his. He had to remind himself that she could *never* be his, not truly.

Despite this, he had a fantasy that she might one day show him her wolf form. There was something special about when a female wolf shifted. Except for battles, females were far less likely to shift than their male counterparts, and Nathaniel knew why. It was an intimate transformation, and it was considered a great honour when a female deigned a male worthy enough to shift for.

Fuck.

Now he really wanted to see Kira's wolf form. There was no chance of that ever happening, especially not after what a brute he'd been in his office. As if the horrors of the slain wolves were not enough, he'd driven the point home by being cruel.

I will mount you on the wall.

He had purposefully let her misunderstand his meaning.

Yes, he would mount her on the wall—but not in the grotesque way. He wanted to be on top of her, to slide his cock into her and mount her anywhere and everywhere. On the wall, on the table, on the floor...it didn't matter, so long as she writhed beneath his touch as he finished inside her.

"I know who you're thinking of," Victoria said playfully, her voice echoing down from the balcony.

Nathaniel sighed and gazed up to where she was leaning over the railing. He hadn't heard her emerge from her room.

"I could hear you brooding even with the door closed," she said with a dramatic sigh. Her heels clicked as she walked down the steps. She took a running leap into the armchair across from him, crossed her legs, and shot him a wicked smile. "You're thinking of Kira."

"No."

"Oh yes, you are," Victoria insisted. "I called it the moment I saw you two in potions."

There was no point denying it a second time.

Victoria's smile widened, revealing her fangs. "You're going to fuck her, aren't you?"

"No."

"So, you've already fucked her?"

Nathaniel sighed. "No. No one is fucking anyone—especially not Kira."

"As in, you're not fucking Kira? Or Kira isn't fucking someone who isn't you?"

The implication hit hard, driving deep as he imagined Kira with someone else. "Neither."

"Oh? I wouldn't be so sure. Those packs will snap her up pretty quickly."

He didn't answer. It was something he'd known would happen sooner or later, but he was trying very hard not to think about it.

"Can you imagine the thought of her belonging to someone else?" Victoria pressed.

His jaw clenched as anger sparked, causing a surge of protectiveness to rush through his veins. He pushed the emotions back and forced himself to shrug for Victoria's benefit. He wasn't supposed to care about Kira, not when he had someone else to pursue—Gloria with her thick blonde ringlets, false smile and cool blue eyes. So different from Kira's burning amber eyes, free-flowing hair and hot temper.

Try as he might, his heart beat only for Kira.

Victoria stroked her chin thoughtfully. "I wonder which alpha will have the honour of taking her virginity?"

He didn't know, and he tried very hard not to think about it as he stared into the flames. "Drop it, Vic. You're disrespecting Gloria."

"Whatever, Gloria is old news," Victoria said, putting her feet up on his knees as if he were a footstool. "You need fresh blood—literally. Someone with a beating heart."

He smiled at that. Gloria's heart, if she had one, was muffled by her callousness and self-centred nature. Ten years ago, when their courtship began, he'd mistakenly thought that these made good qualities for a queen. Now that he was twenty-nine, on the cusp of his thirtieth birthday, he had a feeling she would use him for breeding and dispose of him when she was done with him.

Victoria kicked off her shoes and wriggled her toes back and forth. They were painted a horrible, happy shade of yellow. "Like them?"

He arched an eyebrow. "Very nice."

Victoria wriggled them in satisfaction before giving him a sidelong look. "Now, back to Kira..."

"Can we not?"

"I just can't help but wonder—do you think she'll be all right after the initiation?"

Nathaniel tensed.

Of course, there would be an initiation.

He'd known there would be, but the activities of the wolves were none of his concern, not even if they were against school rules. And yet, he felt a sharp fear pierce him. "Why wouldn't she be all right?"

"Oh, I'm sure it's nothing," Victoria said, giving a lengthy sigh before continuing. "I'm just not quite sure that Kira will enjoy the initiation as much as the alphas will."

Her words hung in the air.

"Alphas?" he asked, every muscle in his body tensing as hot anger flared.

"That's right, plural." She shook her head with a smile. "That Kira of yours is so ambitious—she somehow got an invite to the Populars pack. Poor thing will be exhausted after tonight after taking so many dicks, I hear there are twelve alphas lining up to—"

Victoria's words cut off as he sprang out of his chair, causing her feet to slide off him.

"Rude," Victoria said, but she was smiling in triumph as he rounded on her.

"Where?" he asked urgently.

"In the gym," she said, adding with a wink, "centre stage. But what you really should have asked me was *when* the initiation's starting."

His eyes narrowed. "Well? *When?*"

Victoria rose leisurely and moved to stand before him. She walked her fingers up along his arm, taking far too much pleasure in seeing him on edge. "Hm, let me see if I recall..." Her fingers came to a rest on his shoulder. "If memory serves, it should be starting right about now...in fact, I think it's already started."

Victoria's high-pitched laughter followed him as he tore from the room.

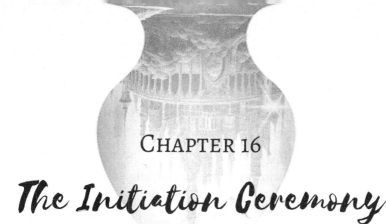

CHAPTER 16

The Initiation Ceremony

KIRA

THE BASKETBALL POUNDED ON the polished court. The sound made Kira wince. The Poplarin Pack were throwing hoops, which was a front to disguise what they were really doing here. Initiation ceremonies involving sex, fighting or blood rites were strictly forbidden by school rules.

Chelsea was the first to approach her.

"Surprised to see me?" Kira asked, crossing her arms. She was not afraid of confrontation, and she dealt out her accusations with calm force. "You knew the hunter would be in his office. You wanted him to bite me so I wouldn't be able to join your pack."

Chelsea shrugged. "So what? It's your fault for being gullible."

Kira bared her teeth. "I'll soon be a part of this pack. And I will remember your deception."

Chelsea's eyes widened. "*You* will be the lowest ranking member, and you *will* respect me."

Kira smiled. "I will not be an omega for long."

Before Chelsea could reply, Kira handed her the jewellery box.

Chelsea stared at it but didn't take it. "What is *that*?"

"An item of the hunter's," Kira said casually. "Just like you asked.

Or was that requirement made up as well?"

Chelsea's eyes widened. "Put that away! Are you crazy? What if he comes looking for it?"

"Then I'll be happy to tell him who gave the order to steal it."

Kira had no intention of doing such a thing, but it was worth it to see Chelsea's fearful reaction.

"Put it away," Chelsea hissed, her voice edged with panic. "*Now!*"

Kira took her time pocketing the box in the inside pocket of her blazer.

Chelsea took hold of her shoulder and steered her up the steps to the stage overlooking the gym. "For your sake, and the sake of the pack, you need to return that. We don't need Nathaniel targeting us again."

"Nathaniel, huh? What happened to 'the hunter'?"

"Shh, not here." Chelsea pulled her behind the heavy, closed curtains of the stage.

Kira had a brief glimpse of stage props and furniture before the curtain fell back into place, plummeting them into darkness. She could hardly make out Chelsea's silhouette standing before her.

"Nathaniel has a history of targeting packs and abducting female wolves," Chelsea whispered, her voice growing high-pitched. "He took two from our pack last year. First Ana, and then Haley. He fed from them and made them sleep in his room. Shortly afterwards they disappeared."

"What do you mean, disappeared?

"We never saw them again. I knew Ana's parents—they were devastated when she went missing. There were investigations, too, but nothing came of it. They never found the bodies. But we all know he killed them—probably buried them out of town in the woods. Piece of shit gets away with it just because he's a vampire."

"Probably doesn't hurt that he's the prince," Kira pointed out.

"No prince of ours," Chelsea spat.

Her comment sparked Kira's interest. Perhaps, there was hope for the wolves after all. "No prince of ours," she agreed, mirroring Chelsea's words. "What I don't understand is, didn't Ana and Haley have the pack's protection? How could a vampire claim them?"

"He didn't claim them. But they let him feed on them. They left their doors open, as some wolves do. Our theory is he got excited and drained them by accident, and then discarded their bodies. In the morning, Ana's door was left wide open, and she was missing. Same thing happened to Haley some time after that."

"Why would a wolf let a vampire feed on them?" Kira asked. "Doesn't it hurt?"

Chelsea fell silent. Just when Kira thought she wasn't going to answer, she said, "Yes, it can hurt. But vampires also have a way of making it feel pleasurable, if they want to."

Kira didn't ask Chelsea if she'd ever let a vampire feed on her.

The answer was obvious.

Chelsea's voice was shaking with anger when she next spoke. "Want some advice? *Never* let a vampire feed on you. Never leave the door open. You don't know what kind of monster you'll let in. Yes, it can feel good, but they can make us suffer too, if they want to. Bastards."

"Bastards," repeated Kira, surprised at the sympathy she felt for Chelsea, and surprising herself even more when she placed her hand on the woman's shoulder. "They're the real enemies, Chelsea. We'll make them pay."

Whatever they did to you, they will pay.

Chelsea huffed. "Vampires always get away with it. The council always decides in their favour, it's a joke."

Kira laughed under her breath. "They won't get away with it if they're dead."

Even in the darkness, she could make out the way Chelsea tilted her head to the side. "Maybe you're not so bad. But stay away from the prince. He's a sick fuck."

"No problem," Kira said. "As soon as I return the ring—"

"Just give me the box."

Kira frowned. "I thought you didn't want it."

"It's my fault. I didn't want you joining the pack, but I shouldn't have sent you there."

No, you shouldn't have, Kira thought.

Not when you know he abducts our females.

She had very mixed feelings about Chelsea, but she needed followers, not rivals, and Chelsea might have been a bitch, but she was a formidable one.

"You were right," Chelsea continued. "The vampires are the real enemy. I forgot that. I'll return the ring."

"Are you sure?"

"Yes. I'll go when it's safe and just leave it outside his office."

Kira hesitated before passing her the jewellery box. "I can help."

Chelsea snorted. "You'll be in no state to walk after the initiation. And the sooner this is returned, the better."

"I...w-won't be able to walk?"

Fuck.

What the hell were they going to do to her?

"You'll be fine," Chelsea said, her tone becoming crisp and business-like as she tucked a strand of hair behind Kira's ear. "In a few hours, you'll be one of us. Which means that from now on, we are your pack, and you can count on me."

Kira pressed her lips together. She did not trust Chelsea further than she could throw her bony ass, but at least she had a tentative ally.

A sliver of light appeared on the stage as Chelsea peered out through the curtains at the pack assembled on the court. She faced back to Kira. "All the alphas are here. The initiation is starting."

Kira's heart lurched, her confidence vanishing as the air left her lungs.

"You should probably sit," Chelsea said.

"Okay," she said, trying not to panic. "Where?"

The simple chairs and table did not look comfortable for the ordeal ahead, and the floor was hard and dusty.

Chelsea seemed to take pity on her because she pointed to the back of the stage. "There's a gym mat there."

"Thanks," Kira muttered, slowly lowering herself onto the firm mat. It was better than nothing.

"Ready?" Chelsea asked.

Kira opened her mouth, but no words came out. A lump had formed in her throat, and she didn't dare speak.

Was she really going to cry?

Pull your shit together.

Chelsea hovered near the curtains. "Kira?"

She didn't reply.

Chelsea hesitated before walking over and crouching down beside her. "You know what to expect, right?"

Kira hugged herself. "Sort of. Yes. No."

"Since you're a virgin, they'll stay in their human form, so there won't be any knotting, if that's any consolation."

Fuck me.

It hadn't even occurred to her that they could turn into wolves to have sex with her.

Fuckkk.

"Hey, relax." Chelsea reached forward and undid the buttons of her shirt.

"Wh-what are you doing?"

"Mark likes breasts. Unless you want to lose any buttons, you want this open. And take off your blazer."

"Right." Kira felt a chill as she shrugged out of her blazer. "Any other advice?"

"Make some sounds."

"Sounds?"

Chelsea shrugged. "If they think you're enjoying it, it will hurry things along."

"Right." It did not bode well. "But I might enjoy it, right?"

Chelsea sounded sceptical. "The first time can be painful. But you'll probably have Mark first, and he's all right."

"Really?" That made the prospect of what was about to happen a little less daunting. At least her first would be someone she knew.

"Yes. Since he invited you, he decides who gets a turn, and in what order. He'll probably be gentler as it's your first time."

Kira hoped so.

"Also," Chelsea continued, "I'm not sure if you're aware, but one of the alphas is female, and it's not clear whether she'll opt out or...have a turn. So, just be prepared for that."

Kira did not know how to be prepared for that. She jumped when Chelsea placed a hand on her shoulder.

"You'll be fine. Just lie there and pretend you're somewhere else." Chelsea rose. "Good luck. I hope it's quick."

"Chelsea, wait."

"Yes?"

Kira took a deep breath.

I can't believe I'm saying this.

"Thank you."

"Don't mention it. Your black socks will be waiting for you when they're done."

Black socks.

Just like what the other wolf shifters wore. Another small step forward.

Suddenly, the curtains shifted as a colossal form passed through the parting, letting in a beam of light before they fell closed again.

"It's starting," Chelsea said, squeezing her shoulder. "Good luck."

Chelsea's quick footsteps crossed the stage and faded.

Kira was all alone with the alpha. She hugged herself tighter as heavy footsteps moved towards her. She was shaking again. It was a different kind of fear to when she'd been in Nathaniel's office. She had feared for her life then. Now, she was simply scared of the unknown. The anticipation was getting to her.

"Kira?"

Her heart leapt at the sound of the deep, male voice.

"Mark," she said, her fear easing slightly.

"I'm glad you're here," Mark said. "Are you ready?"

She heard him unbuckling his trousers.

"I, err..."

She was distracted by another person passing through the curtain—it was a muscled alpha, even larger than Mark. The curtains fell closed, but only briefly, and then a third alpha passed through.

And then another.

And then another.

Her vision danced with flashes of daylight as one by one, the twelve alphas passed through the curtain and formed a semi-circle around her. They talked in low, rough voices, and all she could make out were their shadowy figures. The sound of belts clinking and the rustle of clothes dropping to the ground unnerved her. In the faint light, she could have sworn that one of them had his cock out and was stroking it.

Panic flooded her system as her heart pounded hard.

"I'll go first," Mark announced, dropping to his knees.

"Wait," Kira gasped. "I feel faint."

She tried to stand, but Mark placed a gentle hand on her chest and pushed her back onto the mat.

"It's all right, just lie back."

"But—"

"Shh, it's all right, I'll be gentle," he soothed, forcing her to lie down until she felt the cool, firm mat on her back through her thin blouse. She flinched when she felt his hand between her knees, trying to push them apart. "Spread your legs, darling. Come on, now, we haven't got all day."

The sound of clothing being shed and the soft panting of the other alphas made her skin crawl. Taking a shaky breath, she slowly parted her legs.

"That's it," Mark coaxed, climbing atop her, his weight heavy, "there you go, that's it."

Her body was stiff, every muscle tense as she braced herself. She recoiled as she felt his large fingers pulled aside her panties.

The alphas murmured excitedly.

"Hold on," said a voice.

Kira's head whipped towards the newcomer, hope filling her as a candle flared to life, but it was only one of the alphas. He placed the candle near her head, the bright flickering light interfering with her night vision. Except for Mark, who was right on top of her, she was effectively blind.

"I want to see her face when Mark puts it in," the alpha said with a grin as he retreated.

Bile crept up Kira's throat as the naked head of Mark's cock touched the lips of her pussy.

"Here we go," he grunted, pushing himself against her.

Kira gritted her teeth, wincing as he pushed.

It didn't seem to work.

He pushed again, but he kept meeting resistance. She grimaced at each attempt.

"Relax, will you?" he said, readjusting his position and forcing himself forward again.

"Sorry, I'm trying," Kira said, trying to adjust her position as well.

"Hold still," Mark reprimanded. He forced his cock against the lips of her pussy again, but he failed to enter her.

Kira bit her lip. The friction was uncomfortable, and it made her fearful for what the actual sex would be like.

After a minute of trying, Mark sighed in exasperation.

"Can't get it up, Mark?" someone taunted.

"Shut up. She's dry as a fucking bone," Mark complained.

There was a scatter of laughter from the dark silhouettes of the other alphas.

"Dry? I can fix that," said a female voice, moving to take Mark's place.

"Wh-what are you doing?" Kira stammered.

The woman ignored her, ducking beneath Kira's short skirt.

Kira gave a small shriek when the woman's tongue touched her pussy, and it took all her self-control not to flee as the woman repeated the motion, her wet tongue foreign as it explored her folds. Nausea roiled within her, and she inched her body as far away as she could, but the female wolf advanced, her tongue dipping inside her.

The wolves around them made appreciative sounds, and one voice she didn't recognise said, "Two female wolves is so fucking hot."

"Going to blow my load any second," said another. "Want it on your face, Kira?"

"Yeah, she does," someone snickered.

Kira's fists were clenched so tight her fingernails had almost certainly drawn blood, and she was just about to scream 'stop' when the woman sprang to her feet.

"That's more than enough for me," she said dismissively. "Got her nice and wet for you, Mark. And that's my part done."

"Cheers, love," he said, kneeling back down in front of Kira as the female alpha left the stage. "Hope you're ready this time, Kirabelle."

"It's just Kira," she whispered, but if Mark heard her, he didn't acknowledge her response as he lowered his weight over her again.

He froze when the sound of commotion from the basketball court met their ears.

"Kira?" Susie shouted, "Are you in there?"

"You can't be in here," someone protested.

"*Kira!* Are you up there?"

Kira whimpered and opened her mouth to yell back, but a large hand covered her mouth.

"Shh," Mark warned.

The sounds of a struggle could be heard as the pack tried to make Susie leave.

"*Kira!* I know you're up there! Listen, you don't have to go through with it. You're allowed to change your mind! You can say *no!*"

Kira closed her eyes to the darkness as tears welled in her eyes.

Susie's cries became strangled, and Kira could imagine her being hauled away.

"You can join *any* other pack, Kira!" Susie shouted. "You have nothing to prove!"

Yes I do.

Her heart ached. Susie didn't understand.

She had to do this.

It was a small sacrifice on the path to ascending the pack's hierarchy. Yes, there were twelve alphas, but that would make it all the more impressive when she challenged them all for sole leadership of the pack.

A tear rolled down her face, and she wondered if Mark felt it on his hand, which was still clamped over her mouth. She had no intention of backing out of the initiation, but the fact that Mark was denying her the right to speak was almost as bad as the gag Nathaniel had placed on her.

"Kira!" Susie shouted, and then the gym doors slammed shut, cutting her voice off.

Mark removed his hand from her mouth. "Sorry about that. We don't usually get interruptions."

Before she could reply, she felt his cock pushing against her again, and the revulsion she'd felt earlier was back.

"No," she said, trying to shuffle away, but Mark held her in place.

"Hold still, love. This won't take long. At least let me get it in there once."

The head of his cock parted her lips, and she braced herself for the pain that was about to come.

"Here we go," Mark said. "Take my cock, baby."

Chapter 17

Claimed

Kira

Before Mark could penetrate her, bright lights flooded the stage, illuminating every alpha. They didn't seem so impressive in the stark white light, especially not with their trousers down and erect cocks swinging as they whirled around in confusion.

"What the fuck is it this time?" Mark asked in annoyance, leaping to his feet.

"Sorry, am I interrupting anything?" asked a smooth, sinister voice that Kira recognised only too well.

"Nathaniel?" she exclaimed, propping herself up on her elbows.

He was standing at the edge of the stage. When she spoke, his gaze snapped to meet hers. She gulped, withering beneath his hard expression, which carried a strange emotion she couldn't decipher.

Horrified to realise her skirt had been pushed up to expose her parted legs, Kira quickly sat up and smoothed her skirt down. She made to stand, but Nathaniel shook his head.

"Stay seated, Kira."

She didn't know why she obeyed—whether it was the way he'd threatened to kill her in his office, or the fearful way the alphas regarded him now—but she stayed seated on the mat.

Why the fuck am I relieved to see him?

He's the last person I should want to see right now.

"What the hell are you doing here?" Mark demanded, his trousers done up again and his expression stern as he faced Nathaniel.

"I've come to claim what is mine," Nathaniel replied, his eyes hardly leaving Kira's. "And you would be wise to leave."

Mark moved so he stood between her and the vampire, and she felt a note of gratitude and pride.

She'd been right—he was everything an alpha should be.

"You can't have her," Mark growled. "She is ours. We've just initiated her."

Nathaniel's lip twitched. "Liar."

"I'm not lying," Mark said, puffing out his chest. "Kira belongs to the Poplarin Pack."

"Then you won't mind if I bite her—just a little."

He took a step forward.

All the wolves tensed, growling. But to Kira's shock, they retreated, almost clearing the path between her and Nathaniel as he advanced. Even Mark looked unsure as Nathaniel took another step forward.

"Stop. Let Kira decide who she wants," Mark said. "It's only fair."

Nathaniel paused, tilting his head as a smile spread across his face. "Oh, no, I don't think I will."

"You're just afraid she won't choose you," Mark said, his voice edged with nervousness.

"Perhaps," Nathaniel agreed, regarding Kira with a calculating expression, "so I'm taking the choice out of the equation."

His eyes darkened, paralysing her as he advanced. She looked at Mark pleadingly.

"Mark?"

Why wasn't he moving?

At the sound of her voice, Mark came to life. "Stop," he growled.

Nathaniel halted. He was just as tall as Mark, but leaner in physique, and he regarded Mark with polite surprise. "Are you still here? Very well. I'll give you one last opportunity to fight for her. If your precious virgin means so much to you...prove it. And if you win, I promise I'll leave her alone."

"If I fight you, you'll be dead," Mark said.

"*If* you fight me?" Nathaniel asked. "I must say, I'm disappointed. I didn't expect you to give her up so easily."

His words were like a slap across Kira's face. Seeing Mark hesitate hurt even more.

"Well?" Nathaniel asked. "I'm waiting."

When Mark still didn't move, Nathaniel laughed softly. "All bark and no bite, aren't you?"

Without warning, Mark pounced, shifting so quickly that Kira nearly missed it. Dark fur and fangs erupted, and a large, muscled wolf landed on Nathaniel.

The vampire was ready for him, hissing as he dodged the attack, his sharp fangs bared as he leapt at the wolf's throat.

Before the vampire could bite him, Mark twisted in the air and closed his powerful jaws over Nathaniel's head.

Kira gasped, waiting for blood, but Nathaniel caught the wolf's jaws in his hands and held them open with a strength she would not have expected. His face contorted with effort as he shoved Mark away.

The wolf pounced again. Nathaniel threw a punch at its head, aimed right at the wolf's snout. At the last second, Mark's jaws opened.

Kira winced as Mark's jaws snapped shut on Nathaniel's arm, but the wolf's mouth sprang open almost instantly and Mark fell back, howling and making a raspy retching sound. Nathaniel had punched Mark in the back of the throat.

"Had enough?" Nathaniel asked coolly, wiping drool against his trousers.

Mark snarled in between raspy breaths.

Nathaniel turned slowly in one spot. "Anyone else?"

Most of the alphas had shifted. They were a terrifying sight with hackles raised and sharp fangs bared, their menacing growls rumbling like crashing waves around the stage.

And yet, none of them stepped forward to fight.

"Well?" Nathaniel queried, surveying the wolves. "*Anyone?* I don't mind fighting you all at the same time if you want to even the odds."

No one stepped forward.

Kira's heart fell in disbelief, and a seething rage crept in. These fuckers were lined up to take her virginity, but none were brave enough to fight for her, not even when they outnumbered the vampire.

"Well, then," Nathaniel said, stepping onto the gym mat, "to the victor, the spoils..."

Kira leant away, but she stilled when she felt his hand on her head. It rested there, calm, protective, possessive. She should have hated it, but it made the inner turmoil within her calm, like a boiling pot taken off the heat. Oddly enough, she felt safe.

Except that *he* was the real danger.

"Well, that was remarkably easy," Nathaniel quipped.

Kira used that opportunity to seize his arm and jerk herself to her feet, punching Nathaniel's cheek.

He went down, falling backwards onto the mat, but his hand tightened in her hair and wrenched her down with him.

Kira fell in a sprawling heap on top of him. She couldn't shift, not when she didn't want anyone to see her true form, but she was more powerful than a human, and she pulled her fist back to hit Nathaniel again.

She gasped as he caught her fist, and he flashed her a triumphant smile before he rolled them so he was on top.

Before she could tell him to get off her, he climbed off, pulling her towards him by the hair until she was half-sitting up. She cried out in pain.

"On your knees," Nathaniel said, his icy voice gripping her just as forcefully as his hand fisting her hair. "Now."

Whimpering, Kira shuffled her legs so she was on her knees.

"Good girl," Nathaniel purred, rising to his feet. He retained a hold of her hair, but the tension eased.

She drew a shaky breath.

The alpha wolves were still watching.

None of them had moved.

"Don't just stand there!" she yelled. "Help me! I'm a wolf, just like you!"

"Ah, but you're not a pack member," Nathaniel said, staring down at her. "They're under no obligation."

"I know they're under no obligation," Kira snapped, her anger directed just as much at the wolves as it was at the vampire, "But we're kin! What about honour? And decency?"

She bristled as Nathaniel chuckled.

"I think you're confusing wolves with vampires."

Kira shot him a dirty look. "I don't think so."

Nathaniel shrugged. "Maybe not."

His smile faded, and a deadly silence stretched as he stared down at her. His expression grew dark and hungry, and it made her blood run cold. Too late, she realised what he was going to do.

"I have to ask, pet, just out of curiosity," Nathaniel began, his tone dangerous and soft as velvet, "if I had asked nicely before, would you have chosen me over Mark?"

The nickname caused white-hot anger to flare inside her. "Never," she spat.

Nathaniel smiled. "That's what I suspected."

Pain exploded as he seized a fistful of her hair, jerked her head back so her neck was arched, and pressed his mouth to her throat. Sharp pain shot through her as his fangs pierced her skin.

She screamed as terror seized her, and she tried to break free, but his grip was firm and her struggles were futile.

His teeth... all she could think about were those curved teeth embedded in her flesh.

And then, as quickly as it had come, the pain was gone.

She was aware of his mouth on her neck, his teeth sunk in her flesh, but it no longer hurt.

Instead, she felt bliss as he held her in his arms. He lapped at her neck, groaning softly as drank.

A warm euphoria filled her, reminding her of warm spring days spent in the sun, with the grass beneath her paws and the scent of flowers in the air.

Nathaniel was here, in her mind, his thoughts almost close enough to see. Could he see hers?

Yes, he whispered, so quietly she didn't know if she'd imagined it.

She felt a note of panic, but he wasn't trying to read her thoughts. He was there; close and intimate as he fed from her, but he made no move to encroach on her privacy.

She was conscious of Nathaniel crouched beside her as she lay on the mat, and she placed her hands on his arms to steady them both. She braced herself for his reaction, expecting him to emanate disgust or contempt to her touch. Instead, he seemed pleasantly surprised.

Her own jumble of emotions was far less controlled as fear, disgust, and curiosity swirled around her. There was something else hidden underneath which she hoped he couldn't sense: a deeper longing for his closeness, and a happy pleasure that was sweet and tantalising.

The softness of his lips on her neck was a contrast to the harsh grip on her hair, but even that was loosening, until eventually, he released her hair and simply held her.

Like a fool, she'd melted in his arms. The fight in her gone as he sapped her energy away.

The minutes passed.

How much blood had he taken?

She could feel his hunger, and it was overwhelming. Somehow, he'd bewitched her senses, because she desired nothing more than to give him what he needed, to let him lap at the blood flowing from her throat for as long as he wanted to.

The outside world was forgotten, and the two of them were alone in this secret place, sharing in this euphoria.

Time seemed to lose meaning, but she suddenly became aware that her body felt weak, and her head had lolled to one side.

Something wasn't right.

Horror shook her as she realised her life was ebbing away. The fucker was going to drain her, just like he had with the other female wolves Chelsea had warned her about.

No, no, no.

Suddenly, Nathaniel released her, and their connection was broken.

Fear jolted Kira back to her senses, and she jerked away from Nathaniel. He didn't try to stop her as she scampered away from him.

A thin sheen of blood was visible on his chin, and he was looking at her in awe.

"Please don't stand," he said, looking dazed, "I fear I have taken too much."

Kira ignored him, kicking him as she stood abruptly. The stage swayed dangerously, and he caught her as she fell.

"You're a monster," she snarled as he held her in his arms. Her voice sounded pitifully weak.

"I don't deny it," Nathaniel said, "and I'm sorry that I took too much blood. But at least *I* didn't leave you."

"What?"

"See for yourself."

Kira managed to lift her head and gazed blearily around her.

Nathaniel rotated slowly on the spot, showing her the empty stage, then walked through the part in the curtains. Her heart shattered to realise that both the stage and the gym were empty. The pack had fled. Abandoning her to the mercy of the vampire, letting him feed on her even though she'd been mere seconds away from being one of them.

"They abandoned me," she whispered, angry tears flowing down her face.

"There, there," Nathaniel said, his breath warm in her ear, making her shudder. "I will never abandon you, pet. You will always belong to me."

CHAPTER 18

Drained

NATHANIEL

NATHANIEL CARRIED KIRA IN his arms across the grounds and back to her dorm.

There was no sign of the Poplarin Pack, but there were other students about. They all stared as he passed. The vampires looked mildly surprised, whilst the wolves glared at him in horror when they saw Kira's limp form. She'd passed out almost instantly from blood loss.

Guilt stabbed at him.

He'd taken too much.

Condemning whispers filled the corridors as the wolf packs followed him, albeit at a safe distance.

He deserved their condemnation.

He'd abused his privileged position. Not only had he bitten one of their own without consent, but as far as they knew, he'd drained her within an inch of her life.

But there was nothing they could do. That was his right as a vampire, regardless of whether he was a prince or not, and regardless of the new protections Susie had fought for. They should have protected Kira, but the academy answered to the real world outside its walls. The society his father had created favoured vampires to a disproportionate degree and rendered the wolf shifters as second-class citizens. As for the humans, they were hardly mentioned at all in their laws.

Although the law gave him the right to drain a wolf, it was not *morally* right, and as he glanced down at Kira for the hundredth time, he felt another pang of guilt. She was fierce and had dared challenge him when Mark had admitted defeat. The rest of the pack hadn't even tried. They were followers, not leaders.

But not Kira. Nathaniel admired her for the way she'd stood up to him. She was so strong.

Look at her now.

A knot of guilt formed in the pit of his stomach. It wasn't fair that he'd taken so much, and left her so little.

She'd given her blood so willingly. He hadn't expected that. He'd only meant to bite her, to taste her briefly before he withdrew his fangs. Her eager offering of her blood, her soul, herself, had astounded him as much as it had surprised her.

He should have refused.

He should have ended things before they'd begun.

But beneath her prickly exterior, she was as sweet as her blood, like a nectar that coated his tongue and refreshed his soul. Perhaps she hadn't known what she was doing, but she'd teased his heart and made it ache.

Now, he ached with shame.

Yes, he was a monster. But he would never hurt her again. Not unless she begged him to.

He was surprised to find Susie in Kira's room when he arrived.

"Susie," he greeted, elbowing the door open and crossing the room to the small bed.

Susie paled when she saw Kira's unconscious form and rushed to her side. Grabbing Kira's limp hand, she appeared to check for a pulse before rounding on him, her normally friendly face turned ashen.

"What did you do?" she shouted.

"I drank her blood, but unfortunately, I took too much—"

"You *think?*

It was a testament to how much Susie cared for Kira that she dared berate him, especially with curious students jostling each other in the corridor outside, vying for a peek.

"Why?" Susie said sadly. "Kira was my friend."

"She still is," Nathaniel said, assuming a calm tone to mask his regret. "She'll be fine, I promise. I took too much, but I haven't drained her. Compared to the activities that you and Arken—"

"That is between me and the headmaster," she snapped, before shaking her head in disbelief. "How could you do this, Nathaniel? You, of all vampires!" Hurt crossed her features. "Get out!"

Guilt stabbed at him over and over. He had intended to stay with Kira, at least until she woke, but that was no longer an option, not with Susie giving him an earful at the top of her lungs. Even so, he hesitated.

He wanted to stay with Kira.

"As her Residential Adviser, I'm ordering you to get out!" Susie shouted, more sternly this time.

As the R.A., Susie's authority didn't mean shit, but Nathaniel respected her enough that he retreated. Besides, in a few hours, Kira would be fine. She was a fighter, and when he'd laid her down on the bed, he could feel her pulse beating stronger than ever. He'd even felt the faint brush of thought fragments floating towards him, as if she were trying to reach him across their severed link.

Had there been any risk to Kira's health, he could never have left her side. But with Susie watching over her like a fierce guard dog, and Kira's vital signs normal, he let himself out.

Just before he shut the door, he stole a glance at Kira. She lay on her side, her expression peaceful with eyes shut and lips slightly apart. He didn't need his sharp vision to see the two small fang wounds that now adorned her neck. He frowned as he spotted a small package on the bedside table. It was a pair of folded socks.

Someone had gone to the trouble of bringing them here—probably one of the Poplarins.

Talk about fucked up priorities.

And they call me a monster.

He wondered how Kira would react to her new socks, proclaiming her new status.

They weren't white.

But they weren't black either.

They were red.

CHAPTER 19

Lingering Taste

<u>NATHANIEL</u>

FROM NOW ON, I'LL leave Kira alone.

That was the thought Nathaniel was trying to drum through his skull as he wandered the corridors late at night. He couldn't sleep, not until he was sure Kira was all right. Besides, her blood had filled him with energy, and sleep was impossible with the exhilarating rush of strength coursing through his veins. He was ready to run a mile, climb a mountain, and fuck everyone on it.

Except he only wanted Kira.

The second her blood had coated his lips, it was like a hurricane had swept through him. Demolishing all his careful planning and leaving behind only her, locked into place at the forefront of his mind. Her blood had revitalised him, but it was not enough to satisfy his new yearning, and he wandered the darkened corridors half-starved and burning for her. He'd been with women before—both vampires and wolves—but no one like her. She had an inner fire that tested him, a way of challenging him that was both genuinely curious and unflinchingly defiant. It was a push and pull, and he wasn't sure which one excited him more.

Nathaniel passed the fifth landing several times, pausing to listen to her gentle breathing through the door.

He straightened when the door swung open.

Susie appeared and shot him a reproachful look.

"Is she awake?" he asked.

Susie exhaled disapprovingly as she shut the door and locked it. "Yes. Now, go away."

He walked away, but halted mid-step when Susie spoke again. "Don't you dare, Nathaniel."

He didn't pretend not to know what Susie meant, and he forced himself to walk away. Of course he wouldn't. Would he?

And yet, as he took the stairs down, he couldn't help but think of how simple it would be to wait until Susie was gone and return to Kira's room. She would be too weak to get out of bed, but he could let himself into her room and stay by her bedside.

But she would not welcome him. Not after what he'd done, and not ever.

She already despised him.

And yet, if she accepted him...he would take his time and claim her properly, pleasuring her until the hate in her eyes transformed into reverence. The mere thought made his breathing ragged.

How glorious it would feel to be the one to conquer her.

Crazed fantasies dogged him with every step he took downstairs, his hardened cock growing increasingly painful the further he was from her. It was nothing compared to the ache in his chest. He needed to be with her, and he didn't know why it hurt so much to walk away.

I'm not thinking straight.

There was something different about Kira. The taste of her blood had magnified his desires, and he felt as wretched as if he'd been torn from his mate, desperate to return to her, to cling to her, to penetrate her. But it was no excuse.

He would not force himself upon her.

He was not his father.

Instead, he returned to the common room, a monumental task that left him on edge and stricken with grief. Victoria was at the table playing cards, laughing loudly with her friends. Spotting him, she opened her mouth to say something, but he threw her a cold look that snapped her mouth shut.

He stalked over to the fireside and sank into his usual armchair.

I have to leave Kira alone...for both our sakes.

While unsurprising, he was disappointed that no one besides Susie had come to Kira's aid. It confirmed what he'd feared: that things at the academy had not truly changed. Which meant that the only thing standing between Kira and the long list of things he could do to her, was his own self-restraint. No one would stop him. He could bury his cock in any wolf, and bury them in the ground, and the only consequence would be a tedious investigation. He'd learnt that after he'd dealt with Haley and Ana.

It gave him all the more reason to check himself. He was not a tyrant who was ruled by lust and impulse, or at least, it was not who he wanted to be.

His mental connection to Kira had opened his eyes to something new. He had claimed her out of selfishness because he wanted her, and because the thought of anyone else having her was intolerable. But in that moment that his teeth had pierced her skin, her pureness had shattered the icy wall he'd built around his heart as if it had never been.

And she had no idea.

He had refrained from intruding on her thoughts, but her emotions had been laid bare, and they had betrayed her own longing for connection.

But it was not his love she desired. Besides, there could be no future for them. And yet, he feared he would break her heart anyway, for he was prepared to do many things to her.

I cannot. I will not.

Nathaniel drew a long breath, then let it out, closing his eyes against the fire's warmth. His mind was set. He would stay away from Kira for her own good at least until he could fortify his will and become the unfeeling creature he needed to be.

He only hoped Kira would have the sense to stay away.

Sensing his tiredness, the enchanted armchair drew him closer, the cushion softening invitingly, and he dozed, his thoughts returning to that wonderful forbidden place that only existed for him and Kira. He relived the sweet taste of her blood, and her soft, involuntary moans that made his cock throb. She had been soft and warm in his arms, and if he focused on that memory, he could almost feel her now.

Strong, but fragile.

Dangerous, but vulnerable.

Stubborn...

But she'd made no protest as he drank from her. Yes, he'd physically held her down, but most people—whether willing donors or victims—shut him out of their mind. Kira hadn't shut him out. Instead, she'd opened to him, and he'd been so taken aback, so mesmerised, that he'd fed for far longer than he'd intended.

The memory left him as giddy as if *he* were one who'd lost blood.

He startled awake sometime later when the card table erupted in cheers as someone won a hand.

Nathaniel felt a gentle pressure squeeze his hands. As he glanced down at the armrests, he saw that the carved vines had curled and intertwined between his fingers. He had never thought of himself as lonely before, but he wished in that moment that it was Kira's hand he was holding.

CHAPTER 20

Outcast

KIRA

WORDS COULD NOT DESCRIBE Kira's fury when she awoke the next day. Nathaniel had ruined her initiation and any prospects she might have had of fulfilling her goal at Volmasque Academy.

The other wolves wouldn't speak to her. Not Mark, not Chelsea, and not even the omegas of the lowliest pack. They all gave her a wide berth in the cafeteria as if she were diseased.

All except Susie, who had been there when she woke, and hadn't left her side as she made the arduous walk to her first class.

The red socks turned heads wherever she went. It was the colour of vampires, and yet it was her colour now, too, because after last night, she now belonged to one.

She'd been tempted not to wear them, but it wouldn't have made a difference. Word had already spread about how Nathaniel had interrupted her initiation and claimed her as his own, although the Poplarins had managed to frame it in a way that put them in a more positive light. According to them, Kira was naïve and had let the vampire trick her into biting her, and this was quickly becoming a cautionary tale for other first years. Even so, tension filled the air, greatening the divide between the vampires and shifter students.

And then there was her.

The anomaly.

The one that did not belong.

To be pitied, avoided, shunned.

At least the white socks had made her popular and given her bargaining power. The red socks made her an outcast. Susie assured her that she was not the first wolf shifter who'd been claimed by a vampire, but that was hardly reassuring.

Apparently, vampires could 'claim' a victim by biting them on the throat. A bite anywhere else—wrist, inner thigh, and other, more intimate regions—meant nothing.

Nathaniel could not have made his bite marks more obvious. Try as she might, even her thick hair failed to hide them. She spent the same amount of time touching the bite marks as she did adjusting her hair to cover them.

The wolf students stared in horror, whilst the vampires seemed as apathetic as ever. No one wanted anything to do with her. Apparently, Nathaniel's claim on her diminished her in everyone's eyes.

Screw them all.

Kira kicked up tufts of grass on the wet lawn in frustration. She hadn't had the courage to face class this morning, especially not potions class where Nathaniel might be waiting.

Without entering the classroom, she'd spun on her heel and fled the building. It had taken all her inner strength not to break out into a run as she power walked through the corridors and out the front doors, ignoring the clang of bells signalling the start of first period.

To her surprise, Susie wordlessly followed her as she crossed the dewy lawn, the frosty grass crunching beneath her stomping feet.

"You don't have to miss class because of me, you know," Kira said.

"I'm your friend," Susie replied, "and I'm here for you."

Kira was touched by Susie's words, and the tears she'd been

fighting to hold back flooded her vision.

"Why don't we sit down?" Susie said quickly, guiding her to sit at the foot of a leafy tree. They perched themselves on the roots, which were damp from the morning rain.

"I *hate* these stupid socks," Kira said, kicking at her shins. It left a brown streak on the blood-red fabric. "Can't I just take them off?"

"You could," Susie said, "but it wouldn't change what you are."

"And what is *that*, exactly?" she asked, even though she already knew. She'd heard it whispered in the corridors, but the worst was when one of Poplarin's alpha wolves who'd lined up to have sex with her yesterday had yelled it after her in the corridor: *Kira the vampire's whore.*

The memory of the insult made her wince.

No one cared that she was still a virgin. A bitter part of her thought her socks should at least have red and white stripes, like a fucking candy cane.

"Fucker," she shrieked out loud, making Susie jump. "I'm going to fucking kill Nathaniel!"

"Be careful around him," Susie said, eyes wide with alarm. "You don't know what he's capable of."

"Yes, I do," Kira said, covering her face with her hands. "I know about the wolves he killed—Haley and Ana. He fed on them, then dumped their bodies somewhere no one would find them."

And he killed and mounted the royal family, she thought, but didn't feel like admitting to Susie that she'd gone to his office against her advice.

"He did more than that," Susie said, her voice full of concern. "Kira, you need to prepare yourself—and you need to be careful. Without a pack, there's no one who can stop him except you."

Kira frowned. "What are you on about?"

"I'm talking about Haley, and Ana. You weren't here, you didn't see. Nathaniel didn't just feed on them. They were his...well, I don't know how to say this gently. They were his sex slaves."

Kira's eyes widened. Chelsea had said Nathaniel made the wolves sleep in his room, but she hadn't fully considered the implications. "As in...?"

"He made them wear collars to class. Humiliated them. And he had...*intercourse* with them."

"Whatever he did has to be pretty fucked up if you're using words like 'intercourse'," Kira scoffed.

"He did things to them—unnatural things. And I'm worried because I don't want the same thing to happen to you."

Kira sighed. "I know. I'm sorry. I appreciate everything you're doing for me. I just need to figure a way out of this mess."

They sat quietly under the tree, watching the pigeons wander the nearby courtyard.

Kira eventually broke the silence. "Thanks for being here for me, Susie."

Susie nodded solemnly. "Anytime. Hopefully, Nathaniel will leave you alone now that he's fed on you."

Kira chewed on that.

Leave me alone?

She doubted Nathaniel would leave her alone.

Maybe I won't leave him alone, either.

An idea flickered to life, a way to stop him. It might not improve her status, but it would stop him fucking up her life any further.

Kira sprang to her feet.

"Where are you going?" Susie called, hurrying after her.

"The potions classroom," she said, jaw set.

"But...potions class will be over by now."

Kira smiled.

Good.

She only needed the paring knife.

She was going to make Nathaniel pay for everything he'd done to her—and to the other female wolves he'd taken advantage of.

"Susie, do you think you can help distract Professor Parna for me?"

Susie's eyes gleamed. "Consider it done."

CHAPTER 21

Teach Me

NATHANIEL

NATHANIEL HAD TOSSED AND turned in his bed, torn between concern for Kira and his insatiable lust. It would have been wrong to jerk off when she was lying, barely conscious, in her own bed just a few floors above him.

Not until I'm entirely certain she's recovered.

He was too worked up to sleep. He'd never wanted to fuck something so badly. Human form, or wolf form, he had to have her, if only to get it out of his system.

Common sense prevailed—but only just, and as the hours ticked by, he was only ever a mere heartbeat away from springing out of bed.

By the time morning came, his carnal lust had mellowed, and he entered the common room feeling irritable. He slumped in the dining chair beside Victoria.

"So?" she asked, combing her immaculate fringe with her long bright nails. "Did you end up fucking her?"

It was none of her business, but Victoria seemed to read the answer on his face, because she clicked her tongue sympathetically.

"That's a shame. Maybe next time?"

Nathaniel didn't bother enlightening her with how'd he'd

quashed the Poplarin's initiation ceremony. Gossip travelled quickly, some stories more accurate than others, and the whole academy would know what had happened mid-morning. Let Victoria decide which juicy version she preferred. His only concern was how it would impact Kira, but it was too late to worry about her reputation now.

She was his.

Nathaniel left soon after and went upstairs to his office. He didn't have the patience to play 'student' today. He had more important work to do—like deciding what the hell he would do when his father arrived in a few weeks for their annual meeting.

Every year, Henrikk, the Vampire King, demanded a report on the number of targets Nathaniel had located. His role as security officer was little more than a front to disguise his real job at the academy: weeding out the last of the royal wolf bloodline.

So far, Nathaniel had yet to meet his quota, which was anything above zero. His father did not tolerate zero.

And although Nathaniel hadn't captured any shifters yet, he had something special in mind to placate his father. Something that the King desired even more than a wolf with royal blood: two of them.

Nathaniel sighed and halted his pacing to stare out of the open windows at the grounds below. The lawns were empty, the only sign of life the grey mottled pigeons cooing on the roof eaves opposite him. He smiled. It was such a simple thing, but he'd always loved their soothing calls. He wondered if Kira did too.

He remained in his office until late afternoon. He forced himself to work, but he was uninspired. As the hours passed, his anticipation grew, until he was forced to admit that he wasn't hiding in his office after all.

He was waiting.

And hoping.

He stopped breathing when a soft knock came at the door.

Could it be?

No one ever came to his office at this time of day except his father, who was not due for several more weeks, and the only other visitors were students who snuck in during the small hours to gawk at the horror show of pelts on display.

He straightened his tie and stood. "Come in," he said,

The door creaked opened. His insides froze at the sight of Kira, fidgeting shyly as she stood in the doorway. Her lips were full and glistening in a soft pout, her expression was grim, and her chocolate-brown hair luscious as it fell across her shoulders. It can't have been just the amalgamation of their blood in his system—she was stunning.

Her long, supple legs had looked beautiful in white, but in red, she was fucking hot. Nathaniel sucked in air through his teeth as an image flashed in his mind of her legs wrapped around his head.

If I could be so lucky.

He banished the thought as he met Kira's gaze, giving away nothing of the damp smack of skin that filled his ears.

She spoke first. "Nathaniel." The single, husky word was like water for a parched throat. He would have knelt to hear her say it again.

"And...to what, do I owe this pleasure?" He fixed Kira with a steely look, feigning disinterest, but his words had betrayed him, each syllable soft and drawn out, as if he could move inside her simply by speaking.

"You claimed me," Kira said, nodding down at her red socks. "Apparently, I belong to you now."

He didn't so much as incline his head—Kira was merely stating the facts.

"They're calling me...the vampire's whore," she continued.

"Actually, I prefer the term *slut*."

Kira flinched, her eyes flashing with anger for the briefest of moments before she bowed her head.

"Yes," she said, so softly he hardly heard it. "I'm your...slut. So, here I am."

"Indeed." Nathaniel tilted his head at her, trying to make sense of her sudden meekness. "But you were not summoned."

Kira bit her lip. "I know that, but...I wanted to see you. I couldn't wait. After last night...after that connection we shared, I...I know you felt it too."

He had, but he would never admit that. "You should leave." It was almost an order, but he was too transfixed on Kira, too hopeful that she would stay to shut that door completely.

Kira frowned as she played with the sleeves of her blazer—was she nervous, or was the movement contrived?

Finally, she spoke, her voice as gentle as a feather touch. "I had to see you."

His breathing hitched. "Oh, did you now?"

What is she up to?

His voice grew low in warning. "Let me remind you...the last time you were in my office, you nearly didn't make it out of here alive. The last time you *saw* me, I took my fill of your blood and then I took some more. So, explain to me—*why* are you here?"

Kira licked her lips shyly, and the sight of that seemingly innocent gesture from those seductive lips caused hot flames to roar to life within him. His cock was already straining against his pants, and the growing suspicion that she was manipulating him only served to turn him on more.

But was she manipulating him?

It was difficult to tell. As a vampire, he was an excellent manipulator, but feeding had frazzled his judgement, especially when it came to her. Which was why, with Kira's blood still fresh in his veins, it would have been wiser to send her away.

Still staring at the floor, Kira said, "I want to learn how to serve you, Nathaniel."

A thrill ran through him even as alarm bells rang in his mind. He had to send her away. Now.

But before he could speak, her amber eyes flickered up to meet his, and she spoke the words that led to his downfall. "Teach me?"

His heart stopped as all the blood rushed to his cock. A part of him wanted to believe that it was true—that her submission was real. "And what is it you wish to learn?"

Her eyelashes fluttered innocently. "I'll let you decide on the subject matter."

Holy hell.

He was right. She *was* playing him. But what was she hoping to achieve?

Who cares?

His lip curved as he regarded Kira. She wanted to play?

Let's play.

"Very well," he said, sitting behind his desk and pouring himself a glass of rum. "Prove it."

It was Kira's move—he would not force her to do anything sexual unless she initiated it first.

And he would not kill her—not unless she killed him first.

He gestured at the floor expectantly "Kneel for me, slut."

CHAPTER 22

The Vampire's Slut

KIRA

THERE WAS NO POINT asking Nathaniel to 'unclaim' her—even if that was possible—he wouldn't let her go. That monster had a reason for claiming her, but she had no intention of keeping him alive for long enough to find out exactly what that was.

There was no point in begging either—he would not sympathise with her plight. He was not kind, and while she'd seen another side to him while he'd fed from her, it had been mitigated by the fact that the bastard had fucking *fed from her.* Plus, she'd woken the next day with a splitting headache, but it was nothing a little revenge wouldn't fix. She'd felt nothing but grim satisfaction as she stole the paring knife from Professor Parna's cupboard and tucked it into the waistband of her skirt.

Now, she stood before Nathaniel, pretending to be a shy maiden, when deep down, her anger and heat for him boiled. She wanted nothing more than to shout and scream at him, to berate him for how royally he'd fucked up her life, but the next few minutes had to be perfect. So, she became what he wanted.

Eager and submissive.

Kira kept her smile in place as Nathaniel sank gracefully into his armchair, his long legs stretched out, exuding elegance. His shoulders were relaxed, his smile lazy, and his fingers were lithe and elegant as he balanced a glass of liquor on his knee. "Very well. Prove it."

Kira hesitated. She knew what he wanted. It was obvious, and by now, Susie had told her everything there was to know about what the vampire would expect from her.

Nathaniel gestured at the pelt-covered floor, motioning to where he wanted her. "Kneel for me, slut."

She hesitated, her gaze travelling down his shirt, taking in his wide shoulders, slim athletic frame, and tapered waist. When he moved, the loose fabric gathered in some places, and clung to others, hinting at powerful muscles. A ridiculous part of her wanted to unbutton his shirt and confirm her theory. From the way he was staring at her, he probably would have let her.

Instead, she lowered her gaze to his belted trousers, where the dark fabric stretched over muscled thighs. There was something very sexy about his long, lean legs and the masculine power exuded by his polished shoes. She stole one more glance at his face—narrow features, chiselled nose, discerning eyes and side-swept blond hair. He was very handsome—for a vampire. Her gaze returned to his chest. That was where she would plant the knife.

And then her gaze dropped lower. In order to distract the vampire until he let his guard down, she would need to do the unthinkable. Susie's descriptions on what to do had raised more questions than answers, but she had a general sense of what to do. Still, nothing could have prepared her for this moment. Bile crept up her throat as she imagined placing his cock in her mouth. There were other ways, but none that would lure him to let down his guard in quite the same way.

If Nathaniel enjoyed it as Susie had promised he would, she would have the perfect opportunity to strike. Of course, Susie hadn't known she planned to kill Nathaniel. She still hadn't worked out the strange unspoken tension that seemed to exist between Susie, Headmaster Arken, and Nathaniel.

Not that it mattered in the grand scheme of things. She was about to eliminate a vampire, and good riddance. After all, Nathaniel had ruined her chances of joining a pack, and overnight, she'd gone being the school's most desired virgin to the unwanted one. Because of him, her great plans to lead a revolution were in shambles.

But she could still hit the vampires where it hurt. She would kill their precious vampire prince and avenge Ana and Haley for what he'd done to them. For what he'd nearly done to her when he'd nearly drained her.

"Well?" Nathaniel asked, raising his eyebrows. There was the faintest hint of a smirk in his otherwise expressionless face. "I'm waiting."

Yes, I know what you want.

She resisted the urge to touch the knife at her waist as she slowly lowered herself onto her knees, glancing down to ensure the edge of her blazer still hid the hilt.

Silence stretched in the room; the tension thick enough to cut.

"Good," Nathaniel finally said, taking a sip from his glass.

Kira resisted the urge to smile. She wasn't finished yet. Without waiting to be asked, she began crawling forward on her hands and knees. The pelts softened the hard floor, and Kira tried not to think about the wolves they'd once belonged to. She knew they would forgive her for treading on them now; this was retribution, and the vampire's blood would soon flow down and soak their fur.

Kira drew closer to the vampire, rounding the desk as she crawled. Nathaniel repositioned himself in his chair, and she could have sworn she heard him draw a sharp breath.

She couldn't bring herself to look at his face—she wouldn't be able to follow through if she saw the look of smug satisfaction there.

She stopped and sat back on her heels, her body tense with nerves as she knelt, trying to fight off her trepidation. Ironically, the prospect of seducing Nathaniel terrified her more than killing him did. As silly as it was, she could not stand the humiliation of him rejecting her.

Come on, Kira.

Despite her fears, there was a strange appeal to what she was about to do. Susie's enthusiasm for the act had certainly drawn her curiosity, Kira wanted to see what kind of hold she would have over Nathaniel.

"Good girl," Nathaniel breathed, his impressive length visible against the straining fabric of his pants.

If this was the effect she'd had on him just by crawling towards him, he was in for a surprise. He didn't give her another order—he didn't have to. She was already shifting forward, reaching for his belt.

Nathaniel tensed, but he made no move to stop her as she seized the strap. The dark leather was supple, and the soft clinking of metal made a subtle echo as her trembling fingers worked.

Still, Nathaniel said nothing, staring at her with hawk-like precision.

Kira couldn't bear to look at him. Her breathing was shallow, as was his, the anticipation thick in the air. They were crossing a line at an accelerating speed, and it suddenly hit her that no one was coming to intervene.

This was it.

In a matter of minutes, her lips would be on the enemy's cock.

She parted his pants, revealing dark underwear and a thick erection that stretched for miles. Tentatively, she slipped her hand inside his underwear...and gasped. It was one thing to see his arousal silhouetted against his clothes, but it was another to see it in all its glory, to feel his rock-hard cock twitching beneath her touch. His shaft felt smooth, like velvet, beneath her fingertips, and she trailed her fingers up and down, marvelling at the throbbing veins. Nathaniel surrendered to her touch, but when she leant forward, her lips parting as they drew near his cock, he seized her chin and lifted it.

She kept her gaze cast down.

"Kira, look at me."

Nathaniel's voice was hard, and she didn't dare refuse him. She met his icy gaze, which bore into her, making her insides squirm.

"Yes?" she whispered.

"If you bite me, I will whip your back open. Is that understood?"

She glared at him, her pride overriding her fear. "Yes. There's no need for threats."

His grasp on her chin tightened painfully. "Isn't there?"

When she continued to glare at him, he said, "*If* you bite me, I will whip your back open, *and* I will ensure Byron and Mary watch."

His words made her blood went cold. "H-how—"

"How do I know about the wolves who raised you?" He snorted lightly. "I made it my business to find out."

Fear and anger shot through her as she tried to stand, but Nathaniel held her in place.

"If you've done anything to harm them—"

"Hush," he said. "I have no intention of hurting them. They're probably running wild in the woods, none the wiser. No one knows about them...except for me. It can be our little secret."

Fucker.

"Consider yourself warned. Now," he said, settling back in his chair, a move that made his hard, erect cock point up at the ceiling, "where were we?"

She'd never hated anyone more in her entire life. For Nathaniel to threaten her family while he had his dick in her face was beyond demeaning. How dare he blackmail her with Mary and Byron's safety? The blowjob, which had started as an offer on her part, had just become compulsory.

But she still had the knife.

Nothing's changed, she reassured herself. This would still end with Nathaniel's blood on the floor, and Mary and Byron would be safe.

Taking a deep breath, she swallowed her pride, and then, she swallowed him, leaning forward and taking his thick cock in her mouth. She opened wide, her jaw muscles immediately straining as her lips stretched around his girth.

Nathaniel tensed and made a soft sound of pleasure that was almost surprised.

Kira quickly realised she had no idea what she was doing, not really. She braced for a reprimand, but Nathaniel seemed content to let her explore.

And so she did, trying to gauge from his reactions if she was doing it right. She licked him up and down, glancing up to see his reaction as she rolled her tongue over the head of his cock.

His grip on her hair eased and he stroked her hair.

"Such a good girl," he said, and she couldn't help but feel a wave of accomplishment. "Show me how much you want it."

His cock felt large and foreign in her mouth, but as she dragged her lips along the shaft, a strange calmness came over her, and the room grew quiet except for the sound of her wet lips and the crackling fire.

Every time she took more of his cock in her mouth, she was rewarded by a soft groan, and she couldn't help but feel a rush of excitement each time he praised her.

Soon, Nathaniel's head tilted back, his eyes shut, his lips parted ever so slightly. He looked vulnerable. And he looked glorious.

It was almost a shame she had to kill him.

His breathing was fast and shallow, and he was none the wiser as she licked his cock. Slowly, she slid a hand off his thigh where she'd been resting it, but before she could reach down for her knife, his grip tightened in her hair and she whimpered.

With his cock still in her mouth, she glanced up fearfully, convinced he'd somehow realised she had a weapon.

But Nathaniel simply stroked her cheek with his thumb, his voice gentle. "Is this your first time, pet?"

Slowly, she drew away from him until he was no longer occupying her mouth. "Maybe," she admitted. "Why?"

"Because," he said, pulling her close by the hair so the head of his cock hit her lips, "it's called *sucking* cock for a reason."

"I know. That's what I'm doing—"

Her protest was cut short as he shoved his cock in her mouth mid-speech, garbling her words. She choked and glared up at him, trying to push herself off him, but he held her in place, his eyes cold and his fingers cruel as they grasped her hair.

"Keep your eyes on me," he commanded, pushing himself deeper into her mouth, "and suck."

She had no choice, not anymore, and she did as he asked, cursing him with every stroke, every lap of her tongue.

Fucking prick, asshole, monster.

Insulting him was the only way she survived his throaty groans of appreciation, as well as the confusing way the noises he made excited her entire being until she ached.

Fuck. What's wrong with me?

"You're a fast learner," Nathaniel mused. "I'm pleased."

Fuck. You.

She stared daggers at him, but that only seemed to excite the bastard more.

After a few minutes of her sucking, Nathaniel took over and began to move her the way he wanted, pushing his cock deeper and deeper until she couldn't breathe and tears formed at the corners of her eyes. When he hit the back of her throat, he let out a long, husky moan, holding her there and ignoring the way she tried to push herself off him. Her struggle grew more frantic.

She gagged violently, and he finally withdrew.

But he didn't pull out all the way. He rested the large head of his cock on her tongue, allowing her a few seconds to pant. She gasped for air as a combination of tears, saliva, and something gooey and salty that had to be from *him* coated her lips.

Yuck.

But, admittedly...not as bad as she'd expected.

"You are so beautiful," Nathaniel said, holding her in place as he went deeper again, pumping in and out. Every time she choked, he withdrew, but it was never long before he was going deeper again, pushing the boundaries of what she could handle.

It's a challenge, she realised dimly.

Now that she knew that she approached it with a new gusto, determined to prove that she didn't need him to direct her, not now that she knew what he wanted. He seemed to like it when she took him deep, and he seemed to like it even more when she failed and choked on it.

"Such a good pet," he groaned after she took him deeper than she could handle and pulled away retching.

It was the only time he let her pull away completely, but he never gave her more than a few seconds of respite.

"Back on my cock."

Kira didn't throw up, thank goodness, and her efforts earned her another warm pat on the head.

"You're doing so well," he purred, guiding her back to his cock. He stroked her hair in a way that made her melt. "I knew from the first time I met you that I wanted to fuck your throat. Open up and show me what else you can do."

An idea sparked in Kira's mind. Susie had told her the secret—take his shaft so deep in her throat that the tip of her tongue touched his balls. The goal seemed ridiculous and impossible. Taking even half of Nathaniel's cock was a challenge, and she was gagging whenever she got near three quarters of the way up his length.

But that didn't stop her trying.

The minutes stretched. Giving head was a million times more intensive than she could have imagined, and it demanded every ounce of effort and attention for her to service him like this. At least the bastard was enjoying himself, but it left her no room to think.

In fact, she'd nearly forgotten why she was sucking his cock to begin with.

The knife, she groaned internally, glancing up at Nathaniel.

Her heart leapt as she realised he'd closed his eyes again. His fingers were gentle as he stroked her hair, and she was tempted to close her eyes too and lose herself in the moment.

But this was it.

This was her chance to be rid of him once and for all. Could she get to the knife without him noticing?

CHAPTER 23

Finishing Him

KIRA

KIRA'S JAW MUSCLES WERE aching, but she doubled down on her efforts to suck his cock, squeezing his balls with one hand as she reached for the knife with the other. Her head continued to bob up and down as her fingers travelled down, feeling along her skirt's waistband for the knife's hilt.

Come on...where is it?

"I'm going to come," Nathaniel announced, saying the words she'd been dreading. "Needless to say, you will swallow."

Kira winced, her eyes flying open to meet his.

"Are you ready?" he asked.

She didn't bother answering—she obviously couldn't talk with his stupid, fat cock in her mouth.

"That was not rhetorical," Nathaniel said. "Answer me. Are. You. Ready?"

You've got to be fucking kidding me.

She was going to kill him, literally. Her hands fumbled for the knife more desperately now. Had it slipped through her skirt to the floor?

"Yes," she tried to say, but the bastard pushed his cock deeper on purpose, interrupting her answer. Her throat clenched, and nausea simmered somewhere between her stomach and throat.

"I can't hear you," he said sharply.

"Yssghh," she cried, the word a garbled mess, but Nathaniel seemed satisfied. His nostrils flared with triumph, and his eyes held no mercy as they bore into her, their scorching intensity intoxicating as they undressed and demeaned her. His unwavering gaze didn't just fuel her anger—it fuelled a dark desire that threatened to burn her up and melt her down into a steaming pool of giddiness.

"Very good, pet. Now, eyes on me as I finish in your mouth. And don't you dare spill a single drop."

Despair filled her.

She couldn't find the knife, and she was out of time. She needed to physically look down to find it. She tilted her head to the side, hoping he wouldn't notice as she glanced down.

Where was it?

"Looking for this?" Nathaniel asked.

Kira looked back up and froze. Nathaniel was holding her knife, and the tip was pointed inches from her face.

She gasped on his cock, his other hand preventing her from fleeing. When had he taken the knife? Was he going to cut her?

The knife moved, and she flinched, but Nathaniel only tossed it on the floor.

"You can have it back when we're finished," he said. "Understood?"

She nodded slowly.

"*Yes, sir,*" he corrected.

She didn't hesitate this time, repeating the words even though it didn't sound like anything with his cock in her mouth.

"Fuck," Nathaniel panted, regarding her with lust and appreciation. "I should have known you'd try to kill me. I nearly blew my load when you went for the knife."

The fact that he seemed aroused by that left Kira feeling more confused than ever.

"Continue," he commanded.

She was too defeated to do anything else as she resumed sucking his cock.

"That's it, pet. Take my cock like a good girl. Here we go..."

She had to get that knife. Now. But it was out of reach, and with Nathaniel on the verge of climax, she was panicking. Susie had given her one tip for this moment, and as gross as it sounded, it made sense: "The best thing to do is to keep him at the back of your throat when he comes, and swallow all of his semen straight away. That way, you'll hardly taste it."

As much as Kira detested the thought of any part of the vampire being inside her, that ship had already sailed, and if she was fast, she could strike as soon as he reached orgasm. Finishing what she'd started was a small price to pay to see him bleed. As Nathaniel's groans grew louder, she plunged her tired mouth down until his throbbing head hit the back of her throat. She gagged, her throat contracting in warning, but she held herself there, waiting to feel the gush of liquid as he released.

To her surprise, Nathaniel dragged her head back at the last second so that the heavy head of his cock rested right on her tongue.

"No cheating," he grunted as the first thick spurt of cum erupted in her mouth. "Taste it."

She made a sound of protest, but it was too late. His sticky seed flooded her mouth, coating her palate, tongue, and the insides of her cheeks. It was everywhere, and it was *in* her.

And it was all for nothing. Fresh tears sprang to her eyes, but her despair gave way to pure rage when she saw Nathaniel's face. He was regarding her with a triumphant, predatory expression, and all the while, thick spurts of cum were filling her mouth as he held her in place, pumping his seed into her.

He groaned loudly, the sound harsh and animalistic as the last spurt of his cum hit the back of her throat and slid down.

Finally, he went still.

"*Now* you can have it down your throat, pet," he said, pushing his full length down her throat. "Swallow my cum like a good girl."

She couldn't think, and she couldn't breathe, not with her mouth filled to the brim with cock and cum. She looked at him pleadingly, but he was too consumed with passion to stop, or maybe he just lacked compassion as he rocked back and forth, his cock twitching with the final waves of his orgasm.

Fucking vampire bastard.

"Do not make me ask again," Nathaniel warned. "Swallow."

How?!

His cock was still hard as iron, making it impossible to do anything, or to even breathe, and panic set in as she ran out of air, her nostrils barely drawing air.

Was this it?

Was she going to die choking on his fucking cock?

Nathaniel's expression softened. "You can do this, Kira. I wouldn't ask you otherwise. Do you understand?"

She gave a tiny nod.

"Good. Now, show me."

He didn't need to add 'or else'. His unspoken threat to expose Mary and Byron had taken all resistance out of the equation. She'd failed.

Fuckkk.

She attempted a partial swallow, her throat and jaw muscles tensing uncomfortably.

"That's it, there's a good girl," he coaxed, his words of encouragement rolling off her and causing heat to pool in her core. "You can do it. Show me how good you are."

Kira hated the sound of his voice, and yet, she found strength in it too. There was a part of her that longed for his praise, and it frightened her almost as much as the rapid beat of her heart as she met his blue eyes. They had softened, the once-icy irises glazed with pleasure.

He was beautiful.

Fucked in the head, but...beautiful.

It took a series of half swallows, but little by little, she was able to swallow most of his cum before she suddenly choked and fell back. His cock slipped out of her mouth as she landed on her ass, spluttering the last streams of gloopy cum onto the fur pelts at Nathaniel's feet.

She tensed and looked up at him, conscious of his sticky cum trailing from her chin.

He tilted his head at her, and she shrivelled at the note of disappointment in his tone. "Well, you get points for trying. But chin up, pet. I'll give you another chance to make it up to me." He nodded at the floor.

She bristled as she realised what he meant—he wanted her to lick it up off the ground. "You can't be serious," she said, her voice thick and mucousy.

His words were low and threatening. "You do *not* want to find out how serious I am."

She was about to tell him to go fuck himself when she spotted the knife out of the corner of her eye, lying on the floor less than three feet from her.

Retrieving the knife was doable— if she was fast—and after sucking off her mortal enemy, she would never be able to live with herself if she didn't at least *try*.

"Yes, sir." She bent forward, her head dipping to the floor. Her tongue flicked out to collect the strands of cum clinging to the grey pelts. Fur and semen stuck to her tongue, the coarse hairs tickling her nose as she bent even lower, her hand stretched out, groping for the knife.

Her heart leapt as she felt the hilt, her fingers closing over it.

Yes!

And then her hand was crushed by the heavy press of Nathaniel's shoe.

"Ow!" she cried, the knife falling out of her grasp as her hand sprang open. She lost her balance and fell face first into the sticky wolf pelt.

Nathaniel sighed. "Oh, Kira, what am I to do with you? For a moment, I dared believe your obedience was genuine."

His shoe lifted off her and she snatched her hand back, nursing her wrist as she shot him the dirtiest snarl she could muster.

"*Fuck, you.*"

"Oh no," he said, surprising her when he slid off the armchair and hoisted her onto it instead, ignoring the knife at their feet completely. He knelt before her, gazing up at her with hunger in his eyes. "It's your turn, my dear."

Chapter 24

Hate and Obey

NATHANIEL

THIS WAS NOT HOW Nathaniel had expected to spend his morning—in pure and total bliss.

He appreciated Kira's efforts; each time she gagged, her throat tightened deliciously around his cock, and when she pulled away to retch, it was like a symphony to his ears. Seeing her like this would be etched in his mind forever—teary eyes, flushed cheeks, and engorged red lips covered in drool and precum. It was heart-stopping, as was her expression as she gazed up at him. It was the perfect mix of anger and defeat as she panted with desire, and it made him want to do all kinds of things to her.

Once she'd drawn a few breaths, he motioned for her to resume, and the contemptuous look she shot him did not hide the gleam in her eyes as she took him in her mouth again. As she went down on him, he stroked her hair.

He had to remind her to look at him, and each time he did, her golden eyes radiated disdain, which turned him on even more than the sight of her lips stretched around his cock did.

At first, Nathaniel was patient, but after a while, he couldn't take it anymore—he *had* to throat fuck her.

His hold tightened on Kira's hair as he moved her the way he wanted. He did not take it easy on her, either, fucking her mouth as if she were a ragdoll and making her squeal as she tried to keep up with his demands.

Teach me, Kira had said.

Yes, he would be very glad to teach her. He would train her to obey, and to endure. He could already tell she was a good student—it was just a shame she wanted him dead, but he was too close to his orgasm to stop now.

And then, just as he was about to fill her mouth, she tried to cheat him—to swallow his cum quickly so she wouldn't have to taste it. Maybe she wasn't so inexperienced after all—or perhaps someone had tipped her off. Either way, he quickly called her out on it, rectifying the situation by holding her head where he wanted it, so she was primed to taste him.

And then he'd come hard, blowing his load in her mouth and groaning as he shuddered, holding her in place. It was a large load that kept on coming, and his body shook as he pumped her mouth full of cum.

Seeing her try to swallow it all while he was still buried down her throat filled him with pride. It was a commendable effort, even if she did choke and spit out half of it.

Now, his creamy seed glistened where it had spilled on the grey furs at his feet. He didn't mind—to say that he was comfortable would have been an understatement. He was slumped in his armchair in the privacy of his office whilst the most beautiful female wolf he'd ever seen sucked him off. To top it all off, she'd even tried to kill him—that was the highlight.

When he asked Kira to clean up the floor, he fully expected her to tell him to 'fuck off', especially with how he'd treated her. Therefore, he was taken aback when she lowered her head to the ground. He leant forward in his chair to get a better view, and he watched, captivated, as Kira's feminine pink tongue lapped at the spilt cum on the furs. He was pleased she'd obeyed, but also a little disappointed.

Where was the fight?

Where was the pushback?

Suddenly, out of the corner of his eye, he spotted Kira's hand inching towards the knife. He pressed his lips together to stop himself from smiling as her fingertips brushed the hilt.

Oh Kira.

He took care not to hurt her as he stepped on her wrist.

Her first reaction was to struggle, and it caused her to lose balance and fall face first onto the cum-covered pelt.

When she sat up, her face was shining with his cum, and a few stray wolf hairs were stuck to her cheek.

Oh fuck, yes.

She's a goddess.

He rose, scooped her up in his arms and placed her in his armchair. She was smaller than him, and she made the chair look like a throne.

"Good girl," he said, stroking her thighs as he knelt before her. "That concludes our first lesson."

Kira immediately reached to wipe her face.

"Don't," he commanded. "Leave it. I want to see you like this."

Kira's hand slowly lowered. "You're a sick bastard."

"You don't sound very grateful."

She scoffed in outrage. "Grateful? For what?"

She tried to stand, but he pushed her back down on the chair.

"Stop it!" she snapped. "You've had your fun, now let me go."

"Not just yet." Nathaniel said. "It's time for the reward."

"I don't want one," Kira said immediately. "I decline."

Nathaniel chuckled low, the sound a deep rumble in his chest. "What about *my* reward? You had the pleasure of sucking my cock, pet." His voice turned ice cold. "Now, you will do as you're told."

"The pleasure of sucking your cock?" she cried in outrage. "As if!"

He arched an eyebrow as he forced her legs apart and stroked her inner thighs. "Yes. *You* loved it. And here's the proof."

In one deft movement, his hand cupped her mound through her panties, which were soaked.

"So fucking wet," he growled, rubbing her through the fabric.

"Don't," she cried, drawing her knees up to hug them. "I don't want you taking my virginity."

Strangely, her words caused a pang of sorrow in him, but he brushed the feeling aside. "Don't worry. I will keep your maidenhood intact—I know how important it is to you wolves."

Kira looked relieved, but only for a moment, because then he whispered low in her ear. "Believe me, there are worse things I could do to you. The rest of you is *mine.*"

As Kira processed his words, he made his move. She still had her legs drawn up protectively, but that didn't matter. That only gave him better access to her pussy.

She shrieked when his hand slipped under her panties, making him hesitate.

"Tell me to stop," he growled.

She bit her lip but said nothing, her fearful gaze failing to hide her desire. She was wary, but curious, and he advanced, stroking her wet cunt—slowly, tenderly.

Kira shuddered, trying to shut her legs, but he was in the way.

"Tell me you don't want this, pet."

She didn't answer.

He removed his hand and rubbed her wet arousal across her cheek, trailing two fingers to the corner of her mouth as she stared at him in shock.

He leant close, his voice raspy. "Tell me it's someone else you're wet for."

Kira's fire was back, and it burnt brightly as she glared at him. "I *hate* you."

Nathaniel smiled, painting her lips with her wetness as he slipped two fingers into her warm pussy, hooking them upwards and drawing her closer until she was at the edge of her seat. "But you love how I make you feel."

She shook her head in refusal, her voice high-pitched. "No."

He dipped a third finger in, making her gasp as he eased all three in and out. "Oh yes, you do. And you're going to prove it to me right now when you come for me."

"No, I'm not," she insisted, panting as he rubbed her clit with the flat of his palm.

"Oh yes, you are." He pushed his fingers back in. "You, my dear, are going to come all over my hand like the good little slut you are."

"No," she gasped, but her eyes were out of focus, her breathing laboured.

Nathaniel leant into her space.

"Yes." He delivered the word in a deep, powerful voice.

Kira's head lolled forward. "This is...not what I want."

"Isn't it?" he whispered. "But why else would you be here?"

She lifted her chin slightly to meet his gaze. "I only came to your office...to kill you." There was a flicker of conviction in her eyes, but it vanished as he thrust his fingers in, hard and cruel. Her eyes fluttered shut as he repeated the motion, withdrawing to rub and stroke before forcing his fingers in again.

Damn, she felt exquisite. His hand was slick with her juices and the edge of his shirt cuff was dark and damp.

"Kill me?" he asked. "Somehow, I don't believe you. If you wanted to kill me, I'd already be dead."

"I tried," she protested, her words barely audible as she clutched his shoulders, holding on for dear life as he sped up, relishing her gasps of surprise.

"You tried? Oh, pet...if you'd put half as much effort into killing me as you did sucking my cock, we wouldn't be having this conversation."

Her body convulsed with anger, but he had her trapped. His eyes widened as he witnessed the storm building in her as her breasts rose with ragged breaths.

"Yes, pet. That's it..."

He half knelt, half stood, kissing her neck as he thrust his fingers into her again and again, making her cry out as the heavy chair shifted bit by bit.

God, how he wished it was his cock pounding into her right now.

And after all, why not? He rose to his feet, grabbed Kira by the hips and pulled her towards him, hovering over her as he aimed his erection at her entrance.

"No!" she yelled, her eyes wide with horror when she realised what he was doing. "Don't!"

He froze.

"You ruined my initiation," she went on. "I...I don't want you."

He ignored the way her comment stung. She was on the cusp of release, and one way or another, he was going to drive her over the edge.

He pushed her back against the chair and buried his fingers inside her. "You want revenge."

"Yes," she breathed, grabbing his wrist as if to stop him but making no move to push him away. As he moved in and out of her, her head tipped back in surrender.

"How's that working out?" he smiled.

Kira didn't return his smile. "You killed Hayley and Ana."

He paused. "It's my job to find and eliminate the last of the royal line."

"The nine tails," she breathed, her gaze darting to the wall behind his desk before staring at him in horror.

It almost made him feel guilty.

"Hayley and Ana were never found," she said, a flicker of hope in her eyes, as if she hoped his soul could be redeemed.

It was a flicker of hope he was about to crush. "I presented my father with a scarf made of their tails—eighteen in total. He's rather fond of wearing it."

Kira turned a shade of green, and it made her moans of pleasure all the more satisfying.

She was so close.

He leant close to whisper in her ear, easing his fingers in and out of her clit. "Barbara, my taxidermist, outdid herself."

Kira turned her head, bringing her face so close he felt the brush of her lips against his neck. "You deserve to die."

There was nothing he could say to that.

His face hardened as he drove her to the brink, and he revelled in the conflicted emotions on her face.

She thought him a monster, and yet, she was about to come for that monster.

It seemed poetic... or maybe just perverted.

"I have a secret to tell you," he hissed, relishing the tiny yelps she made each time he thrust his fingers in—a sound that had him hard and throbbing once more. "Are you ready? It's a secret that is going to send you right over the edge."

"Doubt it," she said with a strained voice.

Nathaniel grinned and nibbled her earlobe. "I know you *believe* that you want to kill me. But deep down, you know that you were never going to use the knife on me."

"Yes, I was!" Kira argued, jerking against him.

He held her down and doubled his efforts, rewarding her swollen folds with more strokes. "You're only here because you want me to fuck your greedy little cunt."

"No, that's not true! I told you, I don't—"

"Oh, but it *is* true. And I'm going to prove it to you."

Kira's jaw dropped in shock when he pressed the hilt of the knife into her hand.

"Wh-what are you doing?" she cried as he guided her hand so the point of the knife pressed sharply against his midriff.

"Proving that you'd rather keep me alive so I can pleasure you than kill me," he said. "But if I'm mistaken: kill me now. Either way, it'll be one hell of an orgasm for you."

"No," Kira moaned, "I won't..."

But it was too late. She'd reached the point of no return as he thrust his fingers deep into her sopping wet clit.

"That's it. Moan for me like a good little slut."

Kira seemed unable to resist, because she moaned as she rocked her clit against his hand, seeking his touch. Her forehead rested against his chest, her hips thrusting as she brought herself closer to the edge—one step closer to being his.

"Good girl. Now, *come for me,*" he commanded, each word harsh. "*Now.*"

Kira shrieked and wailed as she came hard, her eyes wide and unseeing as she tipped her head back. She seized his shoulders, her fingernails digging into his skin through his shirt, and all the while, she humped his hand, drenching it, her movements ferocious as she rode her orgasm to completion.

She finally stilled, trembling as she released him.

"Such a good girl." Nathaniel's gaze dropped to the knife, the point of which had snagged his shirt and torn it, a small patch of red welling on the fabric. It was a cut, nothing more. "Well, I suppose I should be flattered that I'm still alive."

Kira bared her teeth threateningly. "I *really* fucking hate you." But she released the knife, and it landed on the furs with a defeated thump.

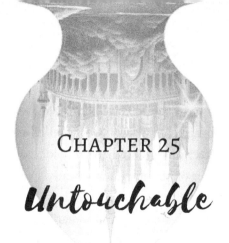

CHAPTER 25

Untouchable

KIRA

DROPPING THE KNIFE WAS like the nail in the coffin for Kira's plan.

What have I done?

She'd betrayed her own kind. He was a vampire, her mortal enemy, and the son of the king no less, and she'd just humiliated herself, and not just by performing a sexual act on him—no, that had been a means to an end, a way for her to get close enough to kill him.

But to lower her guard, and to let him touch her...and for her to feel pleasure at his hands...*and* to hold onto him like a lover as a climax shook her to the core...that was too much to bear.

And it was unforgivable. However begrudgingly, unintentionally, and briefly it might have been, the fact remained that she had lost control. And *that* was the ultimate submission. Not kneeling on the floor. Not undoing his trousers. Not even swallowing his seed...

But this: *her* cum on *his* hand. It was proof he'd won.

And the vampire knew it.

Kira's heart hammered in her chest as she met Nathaniel's gaze. He sank back to kneel before her, as if she were a queen, but he looked no less powerful than he had standing.

Was it possible to be powerful *and* submissive at the same time?

Doubt it.

And yet that was how she perceived him as he studied her from his lower vantage point. His expression was calculating and mysterious, his smile almost affectionate, and that just made it all the worse when he slid his fingers out of her pussy and smeared her own fluids across her face.

"Bastard," she hissed, slapping him so hard the sound rang in the room.

Nathaniel's smile didn't waver. "*You* are exceptional," he purred. His gaze lingered for another moment before he abruptly rose and moved to the window.

Kira stared after him in disbelief, his sudden absence chilling her like a draft. Over by the window, Nathaniel had his back to her. He was motionless as he stared outside.

Her gaze darted to the knife.

This was it.

One final chance at redemption. But as she crawled towards it, her fingers closing over the hilt, she sensed a trap.

Knife in hand, she rose to her feet...and faltered.

For some inexplicable reason, she couldn't bring herself to advance, to close the distance between them and plunge the knife into the vampire's back.

Her humiliation deepened as she realised the truth—that she didn't have the heart to kill him. Worse still, it seemed Nathaniel knew that too, or why else would he have turned his back to her, and left the weapon on the ground between them?

There was no way he'd forgotten about it—he'd made a point of stepping over it when he'd walked away.

Well, that's just bloody fantastic.

The fact that Nathaniel didn't consider her a threat struck her like a blow, ringing louder than when she'd slapped him. Her arm fell by her side, useless, the knife hanging limply in her hand.

Without turning, Nathaniel spoke calmly. "You can show yourself out, pet. I'll summon you if I need you."

You can shove your summons where the sun doesn't shine, Kira thought, but she didn't have the will to say it out loud.

Instead, she lurched towards the door. Her face felt sticky, her insides were aching where Nathaniel's fingers had plunged into her, and the room felt small and suffocating. She needed a chance to compose herself, or to curl up in a ball and hide from the world—whichever came first.

But she hesitated so she could ask the question weighing on her chest, the one that sent fear curling inside her. "Why did you claim me?"

That made him turn, his gaze locking with hers. "Perhaps, I like the thrill of the hunt."

"Except you didn't hunt me."

You just showed up and fucked everything up.

"You called me the hunter," he reminded her. "I hunt."

A chill ran down Kira's spine, and she tried very hard not to look at the deceased royal family mounted to the wall. But they were there, in her peripheral vision. "But...I'm not a nine tails."

"I know."

"So, why?"

He gave an indifferent shrug, but his eyes were empty, the emotion drained out of them. It was a killer's stare. "I want what I want."

She repressed a shudder.

"If it's any consolation," he continued, "the last thing I want is to kill you."

She huffed. "You may as well. I'd rather be dead than yours."

His lips flattened and he returned to stare out the window. "We shall see."

She turned to leave, but Nathaniel's voice made her stop.

"One more thing..."

"Yes?" she asked warily, addressing his back.

"Remember how I taste, darling pet."

His words made her excruciatingly aware of the way his semen clung like film to the back of her palate. Mortified, she fled, clutching the knife to her chest as she returned to her dorm room, ignoring the stares of passing students moving between classrooms.

I can't give up. I won't.

She showered in the bathroom on the fifth floor, running the water extra hot in an attempt to wash all traces of the vampire away. She felt better once she'd rinsed her mouth with water, and washed her face with frothy soap, but she couldn't forget the way his thick cum had tasted in her mouth. When her hands drifted down to wash herself, she stilled, her fingers caressing her clit. The place where Nathaniel's long, slender fingers had touched her—invaded her.

She wanted to be angry at him, to blame him for touching her against her will, but she would have been lying to herself.

She shut her eyes, her head falling back against the tiles as she stroked herself the way he had, exhaling through her nostrils.

The stall was full of steam, the hot water cathartic as it drummed against her skin. Her breathing grew ragged as the feelings building inside her intensified, and she moaned softly as she brought herself to a long, slow climax. She let out a long sigh of relief when she was done, blinking against the shower of water.

"There," she muttered to herself, leaning heavily against the tiled wall as her knees weakened. There was nothing special about Nathaniel, nor the way he'd made her feel. She could make herself feel good too.

She didn't need him.

So why had she fantasised about Nathaniel as she made herself come?

Why was the memory of his condescending smirk as he'd fingered her in his office the thing that drove her over the edge?

Kira spent the rest of the day in bed, cursing Nathaniel and trying not to feel sorry for herself. She needed to formulate a new plan, but her brain was frazzled and echoing with the last words he'd spoken.

Remember how I taste, darling pet.

It pissed her off—but not nearly as much as it should have.

Chapter 26

Rejection

Kira

The following day, Kira summoned the courage to attend class and face her peers, who were still too afraid to associate with her.

In the corridors, the wolf shifter students avoided her. Some went so far as to press themselves against lockers or duck into classrooms just to get away.

Not like I wanted to speak to them anyway, she thought, lifting her head higher. She allowed herself a hopeful smile when she spotted a familiar, hulking figure laughing with his friends.

"Mark," she greeted, trying to appear unfazed as she walked up to him in the middle of the corridor. She had half a mind to yell at him after his cowardice in the gym, but she pushed that feeling aside and forced a pleasant smile to her face. Shouting at him wouldn't get her anywhere. All she needed was for him to acknowledge her in front of the others, to show that there was nothing to be afraid of. Maybe then, people wouldn't avoid her like the plague. "I'm glad we bumped into each other."

"Kira!" Mark said, startling. "How are you?"

"I'm good."

"That's good," Mark said, glancing around before taking her by the shoulder and steering her into an empty classroom. "How are things with the vampire?"

"Not great," she said. "I need your help—can you talk to him?"

"Talk to him?" Mark repeated, rubbing his neck and looking uncomfortable. "What for?"

Is he really playing dumb?

She forced her polite smile to stay in place. "To convince him to relinquish his stupid claim over me."

"Ah, Kira...I'm afraid that's not how these things work."

"But it *could* be," Kira insisted. "If you challenged him—"

"Challenge? Kira, I'm sorry, but that's out of the question. I can't simply challenge him out of nowhere, not without a good reason."

"Aren't I a good enough reason?"

Mark grimaced. "Yes, of course you are. But...as an alpha, I can't be selfish. I'm responsible for the entire pack, and I need to think of what's good for everyone, rather than just the individual."

His words hung in the air, and the person she'd imagined him to be began to fade.

"Right," she muttered.

"I am sorry. I hope you understand."

"I do."

I understand all too well now.

Mark backed away—his friends had long scattered. "I'm afraid I've got to run. Look after yourself, won't you?"

He hurried around the corner and out of sight.

Kira watched him go, feeling angry and crestfallen at the same time.

To her surprise, Chelsea had lingered.

"Are you alright?"

"Yes, fine." Kira plucked at the top edge of her red socks in frustration. "Never better."

Chelsea frowned. "Has Nathaniel hurt you?"

She laughed bitterly. Had Nathaniel hurt her? His interference with her initiation had made her life at the academy miserable, and her heart ached from the way everyone was ignoring her. But otherwise... She shrugged. "Not really. No."

Chelsea nodded, and they stared at each other for a few moments longer, but there was nothing else to say.

"If there's anything I can do..." Chelsea began.

"Sure."

Chelsea gave her a small wave and left, leaving Kira feeling more alone than ever.

In contrast to the wolves, the vampires hardly paid her any attention at all, and Kira wasn't sure what was worse—the way the wolves went out of their way to avoid her, or the way the vampires drifted past indifferently, paying her so little attention she may as well have been invisible.

She'd hit rock bottom.

One moment, she'd been the most in-demand female in the entire school. Now, she was a social pariah. She was cut off from everything. To rebuild her reputation from scratch would take months if not years.

She needed a new plan. While she looked for an opportunity to present itself, she remained alert and on the lookout for Nathaniel, partly because she'd prepared the perfect combination of *fuck you* and *asshole* to berate him with. And partly because her gut feeling told her that when his summons finally came, she could use it to her advantage.

But the week passed uneventfully, and his summons never came. She was sure he would summon her on the weekend, but that, too, passed.

Kira grew increasingly agitated when another school week passed and Nathaniel still hadn't sent for her. She hadn't even seen him since the incident in his office.

Rather than feel relieved, Kira felt lost. The dreaded red socks made her an outsider, and even Susie's friendship wasn't enough to overcome the fact that no one else at the school so much as smiled at her. The wolves didn't want her, and the vampires certainly didn't. The polite greetings of professors didn't count.

As a second week passed, it became more and more obvious that Nathaniel didn't want her, either. And that stung. He'd ruined her reputation, then left her to pick up the pieces.

She hated to admit it, but she'd almost looked forward to Potions in the hope that she'd see him, but he hadn't showed up at all.

"Nathaniel? Yes, he's still around." Victoria shrugged when Kira summoned the nerve to ask her at the end of class. "Just moping about as per usual. It's sweet that you're worried about him."

"I'm not worried," she said quickly, even though a part of her had been. Except now that she knew he wasn't unwell or injured, she fucking hated his guts for ignoring her.

"It's such a waste for him to claim you and then ignore you," Victoria said sympathetically. "He's normally more attentive with the wolves he claims. Not sure why he's stonewalled you."

That made her feel a hundred times worse as she stared at the porridge-like contents of her cauldron. For the briefest of moments, she felt a primal pang of jealousy at the mention of other female wolves—but then she remembered that they'd wound up dead.

Be careful what you wish for, Kira.

Victoria's slender brows drew together when she caught sight of Kira's disappointment. "He's probably just busy."

Busy my ass.

She made to leave, but Victoria stopped her.

"Hey Kira, what are you doing tomorrow night?"

Kira hesitated. "Tomorrow night?"

"It's Friday! You should come to our dorm for drinks."

The invitation caught her off guard. Victoria was regarding her excitedly, and while Kira did not want to be anyone's pity project, the invitation seemed genuine.

"Come on, Kira, don't tell me you have other plans," Victoria prompted.

"I'll...think about it."

"Great! See you then." Victoria winked and gave her arm an affectionate squeeze. "Move along!" she chirped to a group of first-year wolves who were still standing outside the Potions classroom.

They scattered as Victoria strode past, but reassembled in a nearby alcove, talking in hushed voices. Curious, Kira pressed herself close to the wall and crept closer.

"My knees were so sore," a male student was saying. "If he expects us to do that again next week, I swear—"

"We don't have a choice," a female voice interrupted. "The sooner we do what he wants, the easier it will be. That's what the older students said."

"Rubbish. I'll tell Zott where to stick it."

Zott? Kira thought. *As in Professor Zott's Pet Obedience Class?*

"No, you won't," the female retorted. "Zott said he'll use whips next week, remember? He said that if he has to discipline us—"

"Nah. He's bluffing."

"He's not. My brother's in third year, remember? He still has the scars on his back."

"Shit."

An awkward silence fell, and Kira used that opportunity to slip away. She didn't take Professor Zott's class, and the last thing she needed was to remind the others of yet another reason why she was different.

When she arrived back at the dorm, Susie was waiting outside her room.

"Kira!" Susie cried pulling her into a tight hug. "Are you alright?

Are you hurt?"

"Hurt? No, I'm fine," Kira said.

"So it went alright?"

"What are you talking about?"

"Zott's induction of the first years. You had that before Potions, right? Gosh, I was an emotional wreck after my one last year. But I swear, if you just do as you're told, it gets easier. I've never been disciplined, not badly anyway, and—"

"Susie, wait, hold on. I don't take Zott's class."

Susie frowned. "Yes, you do. I saw it on your timetable on your first day."

Kira shook her head. "Headmaster Arken gave me a new timetable last week. He said there was a conflict with another subject."

Susie crossed her arms. "He did, did he?"

Kira had a strong feeling that the headmaster was going to be in trouble.

"Pet Obedience is compulsory for all shifter students, even the seventh years." Susie narrowed her eyes. "What *exactly* did Arken say?"

Kira shrugged. "He put me in the Accelerated Learning Program."

Susie blinked. "There's no such thing."

"Yes there is," Kira insisted. "I'm taking Woodworks with the fifth years. I'm making an oak filing cabinet—" She cut herself off as the realisation hit her. "Oh."

"Yes," Susie said, managing to cross her arms tighter. "*Oh*. We don't have an Accelerated Learning Program. Especially not for *Woodworks*."

"Shit." Kira hadn't questioned it. She'd been too busy trying to keep up with the older students who were already midway through their woodwork assignments. Fortunately, the wolves in that class were less concerned about Kira's *claimed* status than the younger students were, and they'd been friendly enough that the class had quickly become her favourite. Combat skills weren't the only thing she'd learnt from Byron and Mary, and with a little help from her new classmates, she'd learnt to use joinery tools with relative ease.

Had she been an ordinary student, she might have been proud of those achievements. But her feeling of satisfaction came from having convinced the majority of the fifth years to her cause. It was not enough, but it was a start.

Susie frowned at her. "I don't understand. Why would Arken take you out of Zott's class and put you in woodworks?"

"Not Arken," Kira corrected as a realisation dawned on her. She ran her hand through her hair irritably. "Nathaniel."

"Nathaniel?"

"He must have tampered with my timetable. He probably asked Arken to transfer me to another class. I don't know why."

I just know he won't stop messing with my life.

"I know why," Susie said, a small smile playing across her face. "And I can understand why Nathaniel wouldn't want his newly claimed pet to attend Professor Zott's class."

"I'm not his pet."

Susie shrugged. "Maybe not. But I guess he's protecting you anyway."

"No, that's not it," Kira muttered. "He doesn't care about my safety."

"He's possessive, then. Most vampires are."

Kira liked that even less.

Susie sighed and uncrossed her arms. "I'm going to *kill* Arken. He's as bad as Nathaniel."

Kira nearly asked what she meant by that, but then decided she'd rather not know. However, she *did* think it was high time she confided in Susie about her plan. Kira had wanted to tell her sooner, but Susie's close relationship with the headmaster had made her cautious.

Susie listened intently, a small frown playing between her gently curved eyebrows. "So...you're telling me that you want to upset the power balance between us and vampires?" Susie asked in awe.

Kira nodded. "Yes, I—"

Her answer cut off as Susie hugged her tight.

"Count me in."

That night, Kira lay wide awake in bed. She felt tired but wasn't in the least bit sleepy.

She groaned and fluffed up her feather pillow for the hundredth time. There was nothing wrong with her bed, and in fact, it was quite comfortable. And for some reason, ever since Nathaniel had fed from her, she'd slept like a log. But the last few nights she'd been on edge.

The puncture wounds on her neck had healed, wiping away the evidence that Nathaniel had ever bitten her, but that hadn't made a difference to how the students behaved around her. The isolation was getting to her, and she felt a deep hollowness. To be alone was one thing, but to feel lonely in a crowded corridor was much worse. What bothered her the most, however, was the feeling that she wasn't making any progress.

Nathaniel was at the root of all her troubles, and he was nowhere to be found. It was as if the interaction between them on the gym's stage had never been. As if it had all been a twisted, nightmarish, tantalising dream, where unknown fears had collided with strange pleasures.

Fucking stop it, she chastised herself, sitting bolt upright. She checked the clock on the wall. Its constant, gentle *tick-tock*s were reassuring, and the face glowed softly, illuminating the numbers: two in the morning.

Kira flopped back onto her bed. Against all reason, she needed to know the real reason why Nathaniel was ignoring her. Had he only claimed her so he could cut her off from any friends and support networks she might have had?

Was he really that that callous?

Or was he simply selfish as he'd implied? Acting on a whim without thinking of the consequences?

The emotions boiled inside her until the urge to lash out won over. She would make Nathaniel pay for his cruel disregard of her—even if it came at her own expense.

An idea began to form, and a calmness washed over her. Nathaniel had said to leave her door closed unless she wanted to be fed upon, and she'd kept it shut every single night.

Tonight, she would leave it open.

The prospect made her nervous. Was she exposing herself to danger? Would a vampire come and make her feel pain and pleasure like Nathaniel had? The mystery of it compelled her to at least see what went on at night for herself.

She sprang to her feet, shoved the bolt aside and flung her door open. The corridor was empty.

Here I am, she thought, peering out into the corridor.

Come and get me.

If Nathaniel didn't want her, then he wouldn't mind if anyone else fed on her, either.

Except that deep down, something told her that he *would* mind, very much, and that gave her all the incentive she needed to stand in the doorway and face whatever dark creature graced her doorstep tonight.

The corridor was deserted, but she'd heard the muffled sounds of footsteps and low voices through her door, just like she had every night, as well as the occasional creak of a door. The magical lights lining the walls glowed softly, painting the doors in a sickly hue.

But not all the doors were closed. At least one of them was open, because she could hear the faint sound of moans. A forbidden thrill vibrated through her core. Feeling brave, Kira crept down the corridor, her footsteps padding softly as excitement built in her chest. Near the end of her corridor, she reached an open door.

She'd memorised the names of everyone on the fifth floor. The female shifter who lived here was called Peach, and Kira was not at all surprised to see that her door was open. Peach had a reputation for being 'frequently available' for nightly feedings. For some reason, this had not diminished her rank amongst the wolves at all—she was a beta in one of the more notable packs.

Maybe that should be my strategy, Kira thought dryly as she peered into her room. There were three figures on the bed, their bodies bathed in a soft orange glow of candles.

It took Kira several long seconds to process what she was seeing. All three figures were naked. Peach was a gorgeous, curvy wolf, and she'd half-shifted so that she had a tail, pointed wolf ears, a black button nose, and a soft dusting of fur on her back. Everything else was human in shape, and it was both strange and sexy, especially with the way she was on all-fours on the bed.

Kira didn't have time to form a more concrete opinion on Peach's appearance, however, because she was almost immediately distracted by the muscled vampire that was gripping Peach's hips, driving his cock into her in a way that made small squeaks escape Peach's mouth.

The third figure was a mousy-haired vampire, who was tall and athletic, and the way he carried himself reminded her a little of Nathaniel. Or maybe it was just the fact that he had his cock buried in Peach's mouth that made Kira draw that connection.

I probably shouldn't be watching this...

Kira was about to move away when the muscly vampire who'd been taking Peach from behind suddenly threw himself forward so he was close to the wolf's neck, gripped her by the hair so he could bend her head back, and bit her neck.

Kira's eyes widened in shock, and heat pooled in her core. She was transfixed by the vampire, who kept rocking his hips against Peach, and the way the female wolf's eyes rolled back in seeming pleasure. The room was full of grunts and moans. Kira gulped, a curious part of her wanting to join the trio.

She shifted her weight, and that made the mousy-haired vampire's head snap up, his gaze locking on hers. He immediately pulled out of Peach's mouth and approached her, not bothering to cover himself even though he was fully naked. His rigid cock nearly touching her as he advanced, shepherding her out of the room wordlessly.

"Er, hi," Kira began, distracted by Peach and the other vampire, who were continued to feed and fuck undeterred by her presence. "I thought...I could maybe join?"

The vampire blinked at her.

"I left my door open," she added lamely. "I'm Kira, by the way. A first year—"

"I know who you are," the vampire said. "You are Nathaniel's."

"No, I'm not," she said, rolling her shoulders back. "I don't belong to anyone."

The vampire shook his head. "You belong to the prince. *You* are untouchable." His gaze travelled up and down wistfully, taking in her body, which was clad in nothing more than her satin singlet and night shorts. The craving in his eyes was undeniable.

Suddenly, he tensed, and as if shaking himself out of a stupor, he retreated into the room and slammed the door in her face.

Great.

Kira dragged her feet back to her room and sat on her bed to await the dawn. Shadowy figures moved through the corridors, and she could hear the occasional creak of a door, and the muffled sound of laughter and moans.

The vampire had said she was untouchable. What the hell did that mean?

She kept her door open all night—but no one came to visit her. Not even Nathaniel.

CHAPTER 27

Drinks with Vampires

KIRA

BY FRIDAY EVENING, KIRA was fed up with the entire academy giving her the cold shoulder. Which was why she decided at the last minute to take Victoria up on her offer and join her in the dorm that night for drinks. It would be interesting to see the vampires' dorm and see what she could glean about the enemy—and to finally put to rest the rumours she'd heard about a supposed indoor swimming pool deep beneath the school.

Figuring out what to wear to Victoria's party was a little more challenging. Even though she'd purchased several sets of clothes with Susie in town, she'd hardly worn any of them. She'd spent most of her time in her uniform, including her evenings where she went jogging outside on the school oval in her gym clothes. A secret part of her always hoped to see Nathaniel on the grounds. But she never did.

Kira eyed her satin pyjama set longingly. It was tempting just to stay in, but she wasn't ready to admit defeat. Since she couldn't change how the other students perceived her, she would have to adapt. Tonight would hopefully be an opportunity to learn more about the vampires. She didn't let her mind dwell on the possibility that she might see Nathaniel as well.

She considered the pile of clothes before her, and eventually chose a pair of slim, navy trousers that hugged her hips, a sparkly, white top made of a soft, silky fabric that she was now glad Susie had made her buy. It had a fitted bodice that put her small breasts to their best advantage, loose elegant sleeves that gathered at the cuffs, and a tight cinched waist, from which sheer curtain that was almost see-through draped down, flaring out to emphasise her hips and the curve of her ass.

She pulled her hair up in a loose ponytail that tumbled down her back, and finished the look with a pair of simple gold earrings.

It was playful, elegant, and—

"You can't wear those," Susie said when she caught sight of Kira's running shoes.

"It's either these or my school shoes," Kira shrugged.

But Susie was adamant, so they went to her room, where she pulled out half her wardrobe in search of an alternative.

"Here they are," she said brightly. "They were a size too big for me, but I fell in love when I saw them."

Kira was in love too. The ankle boots were made of a soft, crimson velvet that felt luxurious and had a short thick heel that was sturdy. They were so comfortable that Kira did something she'd never done before—she pranced around the room.

"So cute," Susie said. "Hold onto them."

"Thank you,' Kira said gratefully.

"Are you sure you wouldn't rather come to the library? We're reading a spooky story, and there'll be chocolate chip cookies."

Tonight, Susie and her pack were hosting a sleepover in the library instead of their usual book club meeting, and Kira was sad to be missing it.

"I wish I could, but I already told Victoria I'm going." And, if she was being honest with herself, the chances of seeing Nathaniel at Victoria's party were higher.

"That's all right," Susie said, hugging her. "Just be careful, okay?"

"I will. Have fun at the library."

Kira headed to the stairwell. It was strange to take the twisting stairs down instead of up, and she felt a rush of excitement as she descended past the fifth floor and entered vampire territory.

Officially, this part of the school was for all students, but that was bullshit. Most wolves had never seen it; they all knew it was strictly invite-only. Although, no one knew what would happen if they came here without one.

The steps continued for a long while, as if to give trespassing students plenty of opportunities to turn back. She didn't pass anyone, but the stairwell grew darker as the lamps grew less frequent, and she felt herself tensing.

She hoped Victoria would be there when she arrived. Had the vampiress even bothered to tell the others she was invited?

Her heart was beating fast, her footsteps echoing in the stairwell. As her trepidation grew, she half expected to come across a heavy door flanked by guards.

Not quite.

When the steps ended, she found herself in a small, dim antechamber flickering with torchlight. The walls were lined with tapestries, and the floor was covered in a thick crimson carpet that matched her shoes almost perfectly—she wasn't sure how she felt about that. Rusted suits of armour stood on either side of a tall arched opening, which led to a common room beyond.

Kira approached cautiously, sniffing as the scent of cooking reached her nostrils.

Rosemary?

Kira halted in the archway. She had promised herself to walk in confidently as if she owned the place, but who was she kidding? This was not her territory.

Still, she tried not to look awestruck as she took note of the dorm.

The large, open space was richly furnished just like the antechamber had been. The carpet was soft and plush beneath her feet, and several chandeliers flickered with candles, casting a soft golden glow around the room. On one side of the room, a large fireplace crackled with flames that transitioned from one colour to another, and there were several comfortable-looking armchairs and ottomans around it. In the dining area, a long table was flanked with high-backed chairs of carved wood, and an open stairwell led up to what she realised must be the sixth floor.

She glanced behind her. On either side of the archway from where she'd come, there were two separate corridors lined with doors, which presumably led to bedrooms. She couldn't help but wonder which one belonged to Nathaniel.

The common room was quiet, but there were several vampires in the adjoining dining area who looked over at her. Their sharp eyes and blank expressions unnerved her, but no one said anything, and after a few seconds, they returned their attention to their food.

A voice rang out from the kitchen on the far side of the dorm.

"Kira, there you are!" Victoria called cheerfully, her head popping up from behind the kitchen. She held up a tray. "Come try these. I just took them out of the oven."

"What are they?" Kira asked, crossing the common room as casually as she could.

"Snacks," Victoria said, setting a hot tray of crispy potato wedges onto the counter. She plucked a potato wedge from the tray with her long nails—orange with gold sparkles today—and dropped it in Kira's hand. "Careful, it's hot. But I suppose you don't mind that?"

It *was* hot, the steam rising off the freshly baked wedge, but wolves had a high tolerance for heat, and Kira bit into it with relish. It was delicious, both crispy on the outside and soft and fluffy as it melted in her mouth.

"Well?" Victoria asked.

"It's really good," Kira said, finishing it.

"Too much rosemary," complained a male vampire, who came to stand by Victoria's side. He tried to pick up a wedge before clicking his tongue and dropping it.

"It's hot, you idiot," Victoria said. "Kira, this is Felix, my boyfriend."

Kira startled when she recognised the mousy-haired vampire she'd seen the other night. She could tell he recognised her, but she was relieved that he didn't bring their meeting up.

"Nice to meet you, Felix."

"Pleased to meet you," he said with a brief smile. "Vic, you know I hate rosemary."

"You also hate cooking," Victoria retorted.

"Yes, but I *begged* you not to." He looked at Kira, clearly asking for her support. "I on-my-knees begged her. And she said she wouldn't add any."

"I didn't say I wouldn't add rosemary. I merely suggested that you *beg*."

"Bah." Felix kissed her on the cheek and began wiping the bench down, which in Kira's opinion was already clean.

All vampires were neat freaks.

Kira frowned as she recognised a familiar mellow scent. "Is that...garlic?"

"Secret ingredient," Victoria winked.

"But..." Kira looked between Felix and Victoria.

Understanding crossed Victoria's face and she laughed, rolling her eyes as she flicked her dark fringe aside. "Oh, Kira-Kira-Kira..." She tipped the wedges into a bowl and steered Kira towards the fireplace. "Have a seat, have a chip, and let me tell you a few things about vampires..."

Victoria perched herself onto a poofy ottoman, whilst Kira sank into a deep armchair, which was so comfortable that it was almost as if the cushion moved to accommodate her.

She gave a small yelp when the carved wooden armrests unfurled and wrapped themselves across her midriff, pulling her deeper so the cushion engulfed her.

"Ugh, don't mind those," Victoria said, leaning forward and slapping the armrests, which creaked in protest as they rapidly withdrew. "*Rude.*"

"Magic chair?" Kira asked weakly, unsure whether to stay seated or leap up.

"Magic *pain in the ass.* Don't worry, it should behave now. They just get a touchy-feely with strangers."

Kira rapped her knuckles on the armrests tentatively. Solid wood.

Felix sat on the stone hearth and indicated Kira's armchair. "That's Nathaniel's seat."

Kira made to rise, but Victoria held out her hand. "Stay," she commanded. "I insist. Besides, our revered prince isn't here, so who cares?"

Kira resisted the urge to ask where he was. Instead, she turned to Victoria. "You were going to tell me about vampires…?"

"Just a sec," the vampiress replied, indicating Felix who was pouring a golden-coloured liquor into three ornate crystal glasses.

Kira accepted hers cautiously.

"A toast," Victoria said, eyes agleam as she raised her glass, "to Kira."

"To me?"

"Baby, you're one of us now," Victoria smiled.

"You mean I'm a vampire?" Kira asked wryly, unsure whether she was flattered to be likened to her enemy.

"Not quite, but you know what I mean. You don't need anyone's permission to come to our dorm. Call it a perk of being claimed by one of us." She leant close and clinked her glass against Kira's and Felix's. "Cheers!"

"Cheers," Kira responded. Following the vampires' example, she sipped at hers. The alcohol had a slight fruity taste, but it was so strong that it stung her eyes and burnt the back of her throat, leaving her coughing.

Felix chuckled. "It's the good stuff."

"Sure is," Kira said, unable to help herself from laughing as she wiped a tear from the corner of her eye.

"Here," said Victoria, pouring water into her glass. "I've watered it down. But in return, you have to skull it."

"I never agreed to that," Kira muttered. But by now, several of Victoria's friends had joined them, and as they chanted, urging Kira to skull the drink, she caved. "Fuck it!" she exclaimed, tipping the glass and gulping the contents down in one go.

"*Yes!*" cried Victoria. "Go Kira! What a badass."

Someone clapped Kira on the back, and as the night wore on, she began to feel a strange sense of camaraderie with the vampires. She blamed the alcohol—a warm, hazy feeling had descended over her, and she sat contentedly, conversing with the vampires as they played cards.

"My room's up there," Victoria said, nodding at the balcony above them. "First door on the left."

"The one with the purple lilies painted on it," Felix added with an almost-straight face.

"If you ever need anything at all, come find me."

Kira thanked her, wondering if she would ever take her up on that offer. Befriending a vampire could be useful—she'd already learnt so much from Victoria. It turned out that born vampires rarely had children and had a knack for persuading others to do their bidding—although Victoria insisted it was just charisma. Unlike made vampires, garlic and sunlight didn't harm born vampires, and as Nathaniel had said, they could survive without blood, albeit in a weaker state.

"Here's another valuable thing you should know, Kira," Victoria tittered, slurring her words slightly. "Sex is always better during feeding—for both parties."

Kira wasn't convinced, but her limited encounters with Nathaniel weren't enough to base an opinion on. She had left his office feeling disappointed by her failed attempt to kill him, and angry at him for the obvious joy he'd taken in her humiliation. But the longer he ignored her, the more confused she became. She was angry, of course, but she also felt hurt, almost as if he'd betrayed her.

Except how could he betray her when they were nothing to each other?

She wanted desperately for Nathaniel to summon her, just so she could tell him to *fuck off*. She had no intention of seducing him ever again, although her plan to kill him was still very much on the table.

Whilst Kira didn't agree with Victoria's generalisation, it was clear from Susie's tales of academy life that some wolves truly *did* enjoy being fed upon. Kira had been surprised to learn of the arrangement between the sweet-tempered wolf and the headmaster. Arken had extended his protection to not only Susie, but her pack. By virtue of Arken's position and formidable reputation, neither wolves nor vampires dared hassle the pack, which had become a sanctuary for vulnerable wolves. The story was almost heart warming, but the things Arken expected from Susie in return chilled Kira's blood. It made her feel a little better about what Nathaniel had done to her.

Kira bit her lip as the memory of his arousal flashed in her mind. That had been nearly two weeks ago, and it was starting to feel like a bad dream.

A bad dream that had become a perverted fantasy that she'd been curious enough to revisit each night as she lay in bed touching herself. Thinking of him in that way brought her shame, but somehow, that feeling of shame was what pushed her over the edge every single time. To want him in any capacity was a failure on her part and accepting that failure allowed her to let go of all her fears and stress as she allowed the vampire in her dreams to dominate her.

It was bizarre, because she hated him more than ever, except that now, she relished hating him. Her body pulsed all the time, an aching thrum that yearned for his dangerous whispers. Her skin was covered in goosebumps all the time, craving his touches—the ones where he was heartbreakingly gentle, and the ones where he was demanding and rough.

She felt like a different person to Kira from two weeks ago. She was still hellbent on fighting the Vampire Kings' injustices against her kind, but she'd hit a snag in her plan. Belonging to the king's son could either help or ruin her plans, and she needed to find out which of those it was and fast.

Be patient, Kirabelle, Byron would have said. *Good things come to those who wait. The right opportunity will present itself.* It was one of Byron's many pearls of wisdom, one his wife would often contradict with: *And fortune favours the bold.*

The alcohol had restored some of Kira's boldness, so now she just needed an opportunity. But it was hard to focus on revenge when she was enjoying herself with Victoria and her friends. Their company was surprisingly pleasant, albeit a little unsettling, because even in their drunken state, they were quiet and reserved, showing little of their personalities. Victoria seemed to be the exception, alternating between bubbly cheerfulness and witty sarcasm.

As the night wore on, she noticed that the vampires were getting rowdier. Even Felix seemed more relaxed in her presence, and she suspected it was due to two parts alcohol, and one part Nathaniel's mysterious absence.

After her third glass of liquor, she finally had the courage to ask Victoria why they were afraid of Nathaniel.

"Afraid of Nathaniel?" Victoria snorted, but she kept her voice low as she glanced over her shoulder.

"You all avoid me or act differently. I assumed he was the reason why."

"We're not avoiding you. We just keep to ourselves, it's our way. But I doubt any vampire would ignore you if you said hello."

Kira chewed her lip. It was fair enough—she hadn't tried to speak to any of the vampires at school, apart from her brief interaction with Felix last night. But she had a feeling Victoria wasn't being entirely truthful.

The vampiress sighed. "The vampire hierarchy is simple. There isn't one. We don't have packs or covens. We have our families, and family honour is extremely important to us. I know *I* would do anything to make my family proud. The glue that binds all vampires together are our leaders. King Henrikk, and, if he had a wife, the Queen."

"And Nathaniel?" Kira asked. "You don't seem to care about pissing him off."

"Look, I'm not about to let him boss me around, but he *is* our prince. He bit you, staking his claim on you. For any other vampire to touch you without his permission would be perceived as a challenge. He could rightfully kill anyone who dares."

"Not if I kill them first," Kira smirked.

Victoria leant closer. "So, has Nathaniel fucked you yet?"

The change in subject caught Kira off guard, and she dropped her gaze self-consciously as she gave her head a small shake.

Victoria frowned. "Has he summoned you *at all*?"

"No."

"Want me to talk to him for you?"

Kira's eyes widened. "No. Definitely not."

"Suit yourself. But you should talk to him."

"Talk to who?" asked a familiar voice, making Kira flinch.

A cold breeze brushed her shoulder and she spun in her seat to stare at the tall figure who'd appeared beside her.

"Decided to join us, Prince Nathaniel?" Victoria teased.

"Maybe later," he replied.

Kira startled as a cold drop of liquid fell onto her forearm. Nathaniel's hair was dripping wet, and apart from a towel slung around his hips, he was naked. She had an unobstructed view of his chiselled body, each ab perfectly carved and gleaming with water. He moved slightly, and the firelight's flickering shadows etched his abs deeper, the sight causing her throat to go dry and her insides to throb.

Holy hell...

Her breathing stopped, and she tried to tear her gaze away, succeeding only in moving her gaze to the sculpted muscles of his arms and chest instead.

I shouldn't be staring.

Thanks to the armchair's tall back, Nathaniel hadn't spotted her yet, his focus on Victoria.

"And look who's here," the vampiress said, gesturing at Kira.

Her heart skipped a beat as Nathaniel glanced down to where she was sitting. His abs tensed, all eight of them, flexing in the firelight like a glorious attraction made just for her.

Time stopped.

Victoria gave a polite cough, breaking Kira's trance. Her gaze snapped up to Nathaniel's face, bracing herself for his smug smile, but mercifully, he didn't look amused. If anything, he looked startled to see her, and there was something haunted about his gaze as his blue eyes drew her in.

"Kira," he greeted.

She gave him a tiny nod of greeting, not trusting herself to speak.

He glanced down at the towel wrapped around his waist.

"I apologise for being underdressed. I've been swimming."

"I didn't ask," Kira said, blinking furiously as she tried to keep her gaze from drifting back down to his chest. "But I guess I can finally put the rumours of an underground pool to rest."

Nathaniel's lip twitched. "Would you like a tour?"

Her eyes widened.

Yes? No?

Maybe?

Be bold.

"Yes," she said, rising to her feet.

Nathaniel nodded, and he opened his mouth to say something, then hesitated, as if he were thinking better of it. He turned to Victoria and said, "You can do the honours, Vic," before leaving.

Kira's jaw dropped as Nathaniel sauntered away, the muscles of his broad shoulders and back flexing. She glared at him, hating the way his wet, blond hair trickled water down his neck and along the line of his back, past the dimples that were half-obscured by the towel.

She blinked rapidly as she noticed the striations on his back. Were they...scars?

"He's been acting strange ever since you arrived here," Victoria commented.

"Has he?" Kira asked absently, still standing and staring at the dark corridor Nathaniel had gone down.

"I think you're wearing him down." Victoria took a slow sip of her drink.

"I think he's just toying with me."

"Probably. You should go after him. Rip into him."

"I'll tear him a new one," she muttered, rising from her chair.

As she strode purposefully across the common room, she had the feeling that Nathaniel wanted her to follow.

As she roamed down the dark corridor, a small thrill of the unknown jolted through her, and she realised it didn't matter if he was playing games with her. She was ready to play along. More importantly, she was ready to strike a deal.

CHAPTER 28

The Deal

KIRA

KIRA STRODE AFTER NATHANIEL. He must have heard her footsteps, but he didn't turn to look until he'd reached the last door on the right, made of solid blackwood.

She halted in front of him with her arms crossed. He finally looked up.

"Yes?" he asked, tilting his head curiously as his keys jangled. "May I help you?"

Kira snorted. "Yes. For starters, fuck you." It felt good to get the insults out of the way.

Nathaniel raised an eyebrow. "I'll...take that under advisement." He unlocked his door and pushed it open, but he didn't enter. Instead, he licked his lips as he appraised her. "Was there anything else, Kira?"

"Yes, we need to talk."

His voice grew quiet. "Do we now?"

"Yes," she said, pushing past him as she marched into the room. "I'm here to make a deal."

"Well, I'm intrigued."

He followed her inside and shut the door.

She tried not to let that bother her. It was not the first time she'd been alone with him, but somehow, this felt more intimate.

Maybe his bedroom is not the best place for this conversation.

Kira peered around curiously. The room exuded an air of mystery and elegance. The centre of the room was dominated by a large bed. She held her breath, her spine tingling with the knowledge that she was mere feet from the place where he slept. The ebony frame was adorned with intricate carvings, and the covers and pillows looked luxurious with black-and-grey covers. Gulping, she wandered deeper into the room, resisting the urge to run her hand along the black satin on the bed. The walls were enveloped in dark, rich purples, and wall sconces flickered with the eerie glow of orange flames.

"Welcome," Nathaniel said softly from behind her.

She could feel his gaze boring into her back. Her shoulders tensed, the words she'd planned to say to him deserting her.

"Would you care to sit?"

"No, thank you," she said coolly, glancing at the sitting area Nathaniel pointed to. More dark furniture, a small fireplace where the fire had grown low. Beyond it, a door sat ajar, revealing an ensuite with a clawfoot bathtub, rainfall shower head, and marble countertops.

"Wow," she muttered, indicating the grand room. "This is..."

"Excessive," Nathaniel finished. "I know. All our rooms are like this."

"I guess it pays to be a vampire."

"Sometimes. It pays to be on the winning side of a civil war, anyway."

Kira bristled, unsure what he meant by that. She was tempted to pick a bone with him about it, but that was not why she'd come, and the luxury of the room distracted her. She tried hard not to stare, but she couldn't help it. Every aspect of the room, from the high ceilings to the polished tiles beneath her feet, added an overall mystique to the space. A mix of metallic wallpaper and embroidered tapestries adorned the walls. In the corner was a cosy nook with velvet cushions and a stack of books, which looked like it would be a good place to read.

Focus.

Kira spun back to face Nathaniel, but he'd disappeared behind a screen.

"What are you doing?" she called.

"Getting dressed," he replied. "Please, make yourself at home."

Before she could respond, a towel was flung over the top edge of the screen. She stared at it for several moments before averting her eyes, ignoring the heat flooding her face. Nathaniel was completely naked on the other side.

Why is this so much harder than going down on him was?

"So..." she began. "You haven't summoned me."

"I didn't say I would."

"You heavily implied that you would."

Nathaniel didn't immediately respond. She was right, and he knew it.

As the seconds ticked by, he drawled, "Did you *want* me to summon you?"

"What I want is for you to explain why you went out of your way to so-called *claim* me if you had no intention of doing anything..." she stopped herself just in time before she could add 'to me'. This was not how she'd rehearsed her speech at all.

Nathaniel peered over the top of the screen. "That sounds like you wanted me to summon you."

"No. That's *not* what I said." She began to pace the room, her voice carrying an edge. "You *ruined* any chance I had of fitting in. Do you have any idea how I feel?"

Silence met her ears. Even the rustling of clothes had stopped.

And then...

"I have an inkling." She heard him resume getting dressed. "I'm not oblivious to the effect my actions have had on you."

His voice was calm, and she didn't know what to make of that. It wasn't an apology, but he didn't sound indifferent either. It was simply an acknowledgement.

Kira sighed. "Since we're on the subject...why didn't you summon me?"

Nathaniel emerged, he was fully dressed in dark charcoal-grey pants, brown leather belt, and a crisp white shirt with a subtle herringbone pattern. He exuded sophistication and confidence as he stood straight, feet slightly apart as he rolled up his sleeves. The sight of his bare forearms had a similar effect on her to seeing him bare-chested had, especially now that she knew how defined his biceps were beneath his shirt.

He stopped before her. "I didn't summon you because I didn't have to."

"What does that mean?"

"I knew that you would come find me sooner or later. And I was curious how long that would take."

Kira narrowed her eyes. He was riling her up on purpose—probably to disguise the fact that he was lying through his teeth. "Bullshit."

Nathaniel didn't deny it. "Now," he said, seating himself on one end of a chaise and patting it for her to join him. "What is this deal you propose?"

Kira hesitated before seating herself on a chair instead. Nathaniel's lips curved, but she pretended not to notice as she sat tall with her hands clasped in a business-like manner.

"I believe we can make an agreement that would benefit both of us."

"Is that so? But I want for nothing...at least, nothing I don't already have." He looked pointedly at her.

Kira flushed. "You might have claimed me or whatever, but I'm not truly yours, and I never will be."

Nathaniel's eyes were piercing, but he remained silent.

"Unless..." she continued softly.

"Unless?" He sat back and crossed his legs.

"Unless you help me get what I want."

"And what is that?"

Kira rubbed her hands together. "I want to become a member of the Poplarin Pack...and I want to be its sole alpha."

"Really? How ambitious. And you expect me to help you achieve that lofty status?"

"Yes. I want you to unfuck the damage you've done to my reputation by unclaiming me."

Nathaniel stroked his chin thoughtfully. "While I'm sympathetic, there isn't a good enough incentive in the world for me to give you up."

His words struck her speechless, but she quickly recovered.

"Actually, there is. I know what you really want, Nathaniel."

"I doubt that."

His words were light, but she saw the nervous bob of his throat as he swallowed.

She was just his plaything, something to distract himself with while he put off doing what was expected of him: finding a queen. She reached into her pocket and placed the jewellery box on the coffee table beside them. Someone had left it in her locker the day after the initiation—so much for Chelsea's offer to return it.

Nathaniel stared at the jewellery box, making no move to take it.

"I know there is pressure on you to marry Gloria by your thirtieth birthday," Kira said. "Victoria told me," she added. "And I know that one day, she will be your queen."

"Not 'one day'," Nathaniel corrected. "That very day. The coronation will be held on my birthday. There is to be a party at

Wintermaw Keep."

"Wow." That was new information. "Well, you're going to need that ring, then." She lowered her voice, trying not to sound too smug as she continued. "I also know that despite your courtship, she has not said yes."

Nathaniel was deathly silent, and she suddenly felt cold under his icy stare.

"But we can help each other," she said, sliding off the armchair slowly until she was on her knees.

"How?" His voice was barely a whisper.

"I can help you win Gloria." Kira leant forward, her palms on the ground. "I can help make her jealous." Crawling forward until she was at Nathaniel's feet, she brushed the tops of his bare feet with her hands. They were covered in fine hairs, and she almost lost her train of thought as she stroked them. "You can prove to her that you brought an untameable wolf to heel."

She lifted her gaze, and her stomach did a somersault as she met Nathaniel's hard, hungry stare. His eyes were blazing with intensity, his focus on her unwavering as the icy shards of his irises sliced her. She spoke in a controlled tone. "And I will help convince her to say yes."

Nathaniel drew a breath, running the tip of his tongue over a sharp fang thoughtfully. "And in return, you want me to ensure the Poplarin Pack accepts you."

"Yes."

"Simply being a member won't give you alpha status."

Kira smiled. "I can handle that part by myself."

Nathaniel cupped her cheek. "My darling pet...so ambitious. Yes, I will help you become one of the Poplarins, but first..." His gaze hardened. "You will help me win Gloria's hand."

Kira nodded. "Fine. No problem."

Nathaniel's chest rumbled with a laugh so low that it reverberated through her core, slackening her muscles. If she hadn't already been kneeling, she would have had to sit down.

He placed a hand on top of her head, his fingers slid into her hair, where he patted and stroked her as if she were a dog. "I am looking forward to seeing this 'tameable wolf'. I have yet to see that side of you."

"Fucker!" she growled, jerking her head away, but his hand tightened painfully in her hair.

Nathaniel smirked. "Down, pet. I was merely joking."

She scowled at him, teeth bared, but he seemed content to wait.

When she finally dropped her gaze, he immediately relaxed his grip and resumed stroking her hair.

"I am not convinced you have what it takes to submit yourself to another," Nathaniel began. "Will you obey my every instruction and do as you're told?"

Kira swallowed hard, biting back an insult. "I will."

"Even in public? Will you do all I ask of you before others?"

Kira's stomach twisted. "Like who?"

"Anyone at all. Other students. Academics. Visiting students' parents. People in the city, should I take you out."

Take me out? Like a date?

Or like a dog on a leash?

She didn't have time to contemplate that, because her thoughts had snagged on his mention of 'parents'. "Even your father?"

Nathaniel's pupils dilated, signalling that she'd unearthed something critical. "Yes, pet. Perhaps, if you are good, I will trot you out before His Majesty as a prime example of wolf domestication."

His words stung like barbs, but she bit her tongue.

She suddenly became conscious of the fact that her head was lolling as he massaged her scalp. The touch felt incredible, evoking a flurry of pleasant sensations that warmed her, and she had a strange urge to drop her head in his lap.

"Very well," Nathaniel said, removing his hand from her head and rising to his feet.

She scrambled back onto her heels, the magic between them broken.

"I accept your proposal, pet."

"You do?"

"Yes." He walked to his desk, pulled open a drawer, and glanced back at her. "On one condition."

She crossed her arms. "And what's that?"

"You will demonstrate your willingness to obey me...right now."

Her breathing grew shallow—with anticipation, or dread, she wasn't sure.

"Come here." Nathaniel beckoned with a finger.

Kira's knees felt wobbly as she forced one foot in front of the other until she stood beside him at the large mahogany desk.

Nathaniel reached into the drawer and took out a jewellery case lined with black velvet.

"This is for you. Open it." He leant against the desk, watching as her shaky hands opened the case.

She gasped at the piece inside, nestled amongst satin. It was the largest gemstone that she'd ever seen, pink and heart-shaped, and it sparkled with light. The outer borders of the heart were made of steel, as was the rest of the piece, which was large, smooth and tapered.

"I hope you like it," Nathaniel said softly. "I had it custom made for you. Since you are mine, I thought it only fitting that you should wear one."

Kira had no words. She was entranced as she hefted the meticulously crafted object. It was exceedingly heavy, and unlike any kind of jewellery she'd seen before. It wasn't a necklace, or a bracelet, or a broach, and it definitely wasn't an earring. She didn't see how she could wear it in her hair, either. "Er, what is it, exactly?"

Nathaniel trailed a finger down the length of her back, travelling lower and lower until he cupped one of her ass cheeks.

She gasped as he squeezed, shivering as his warm breath tickled her ear.

"It's an anal plug."

"It's a *what?*"

"You heard me."

She froze as realisation slammed into her, and she dropped the case, sending the steel plug clattering across the floor.

"What the fuck?" she cried, rounding on Nathaniel in disbelief.

He hadn't moved, and he had the nerve to look unabashed. "Do you require further clarification?"

Kira squeezed her eyes shut. Susie had mentioned 'sex toys', but it had sounded so farfetched that she had all but filtered the conversation from her mind.

Now, she felt cheated. The beautiful jewellery box had caught her off guard. Not that she wanted him to be giving her jewellery, but the gesture had seemed romantic. For a moment, she'd thought she was glimpsing another side to Nathaniel. She hadn't expected the case to contain something so obscene—and she definitely hadn't expected the sick fuck to have an anal plug custom made for her.

Nathaniel rose to his feet and moved so close he was mere inches from her. He grasped her chin. "Just so there is no confusion: it's for your ass. Good, obedient little sluts wear them."

Kira snarled and slapped his hand away. "Forget it. I'm none of those things."

"Maybe not," Nathaniel agreed, caressing her face, "but you could be."

She hesitated before stepping out of his reach. "You make me sick."

"You make me hard. And I *know* I make you *very* wet."

"No, you don't."

Nathaniel smirked as if he knew she was lying. "The plug would make you even more wet."

"No." Her voice was firm, but it also carried a plea. "Not the plug."

"Why not?"

She raised her hands. "It's degrading."

"It's hot. And you'll love it."

"*You* wear it then."

Nathaniel barked in laughter. "Try it. I promise you'll like what I do to you while you wear it."

Her stomach rolled over, and her voice was shaky as she spoke. "No. I don't want that."

Nathaniel nodded slowly. "Very well. It's not compulsory."

Her shoulders relaxed. "Thank you."

"But without the plug, there is no deal."

"*What?*"

"That is my condition. I want you to wear it for the rest of tonight like a good little slut, and at any other time that I wish. It may take several days for me to secure a meeting with Gloria. Until then, I expect you to obey me. Do you understand?"

"Yeah, I understand," Kira said, her fists curling. "You're out of your fucking mind. You are not coming anywhere near my..." she licked her lips, searching for the right word, "my rear end."

Nathaniel laughed softly. "That's your prerogative."

She couldn't believe it. After all the concessions she had made...he wanted her to wear *that?* It was worse than the gag and collar. She knew he had dark desires, but she hadn't expected him to want to put an object inside her ass. It didn't seem right. Or sanitary. Her rear hole was an intimate part of her that even she hadn't touched, not like that, nor did she want to. It was outlandish.

She turned to leave, but Nathaniel's thundering voice made her freeze.

"Think carefully before leaving my room, Kira. The terms may not be so favourable tomorrow."

"Oh yeah? Well, I hope you find *these* terms favourable," she said, facing back and raising both hands to give him the most aggressive middle fingers she could muster. "Do *you* understand?"

Nathaniel's eyes glinted as he shook his head with a laugh. "Perfectly."

CHAPTER 29

Waiting for Her

NATHANIEL

WHILST NATHANIEL'S HOPES WEREN'T high, he allowed himself to hope, just a little, that Kira would accept his terms. That in a few minutes, her ass would be filled with the bulging steel plug. He wanted to see her face when he inserted it, wanted to comfort her through the pain, and revel in her pleasure. And he wanted to see the pink-coloured jewel sparkle so brightly between her ass cheeks that it blinded him.

But he was getting ahead of himself, because even though submitting had been Kira's idea, she seemed unable to swallow her pride. It was a quality that fascinated him, and he was curious how far he could bend her before she broke.

"You're out of your fucking mind," Kira said. "You are not coming anywhere near my...my rear end."

Yes, I am out of my fucking mind, he wanted to reply. *I'm out of my fucking mind waiting for you. I am in pain when you are far, and in pain when you are near and I cannot touch you. I need you close, and I need you forever. Most of all, I need you alive.*

But he couldn't tell Kira that. She would not understand. He could not say one word without the rest spilling out as well, so he did not speak them at all. Instead, he forced himself to laugh as if her protest amused him.

Kira scowled and left, slamming the door behind her.

He was alone, his bedroom quiet except for the soothing whispers of the low-burning fire. He crouched on the hearth and added two logs. The fireplace was magical and did not produce smoke, but it hungered for firewood all the same.

The flames leapt up to consume the logs, dancing and swirling, reminding him of the wildness of Kira's hair. She had worn it tied up tonight, but even that hairstyle had an unruliness to it. The updo, he'd noticed, had emphasised the graceful length of her neck.

He dusted his hands and swept the stringy wood bark from the hearth before settling into his armchair.

The hours ticked by as he waited for Kira's return. He knew she'd be back. Her pride was a temporary thing—her ambition was not.

He stifled several yawns as he waited. The jewellery box sat with the lid open on his desk, the plug returned safely to its bed of glossy satin. The steel gleamed, and the pink gem caught the glow of the fire and scattered rosy pink light around the room.

He'd packed away the ring. The ruby ring had special significance. It had belonged to Queen Liddia, the Vampire Queen—the woman his father had murdered in his quest for power. To present Gloria with the ring was fitting. She was to be his wife and future queen, after all.

Moreover, Gloria's mother was Queen Liddia, and her father Vampire King Dmitri, both now deceased. It was a fact many vampires knew but none dared speak of. It meant Gloria was a princess, the true heir to the throne.

And he, Crown Prince Nathaniel, was an imposter.

It was no wonder Gloria hated him. Years ago, when his father had given him the ring, Nathaniel had been confident that the return of her mother's ring would compel Gloria to accept his proposal. But the sight of her mother's ring had enraged her, severing any affection she may have felt for him.

"Your father murdered my mother and pulled this ring from her finger. How *dare* you present it to me now? It is not a bargaining chip. It is *mine*."

It was one of the few times he'd seen Gloria lose her cool. She'd been so upset that she'd refused the ring in its entirety, even though he knew deep down that she wanted it.

For the time being, he would safeguard the ring. Although he'd been content to let Kira hold onto it. He'd felt a sharp pang when she'd given it back.

The morning finally came and Kira still hadn't returned.

Nathaniel frowned. *I was sure that she would.*

He was wrong, and that did not happen often. The disappointment he felt at her absence cut him more than it should have. He glanced at the fire. It had grown low, and there was a chill in the room. He sighed and closed the lid of the jewellery box containing the plug. It was times like these he wished he had someone to curl up with by the fireside—and not just any someone. He closed his eyes and fantasised about the soft warmth of a female wolf curled up against him.

The faint sound of scuffling caught his attention, and his gaze snapped to the door a second before it banged open.

His heart leapt. Kira was back.

He gazed in wonderment as she stood in the doorway, glaring at him with blazing eyes. Her dark brown hair crashed around her shoulders as if it was angry with him as well.

As much as he'd liked her elegant party clothes, she'd changed into her school uniform, and he liked that even more. Especially given that it was a Saturday morning. There was something so incredibly alluring knowing she'd changed just for him, and he soaked in every detail.

Her navy blazer was impeccable and form-fitting, her white blouse crisp, the bow at her neck adorable, the short skirt delicious.

And the socks—he let out a low breath.

His arousal went from zero to a hundred almost immediately at the sight of them, and he resisted the urge to adjust his cock as it strained uncomfortably against his pants. The long red socks hugged her shapely calves and emphasised her full thighs. It pleased him to no end to realise that she wore those because of him—because she was his.

His lips curled. Red suited her more than she knew.

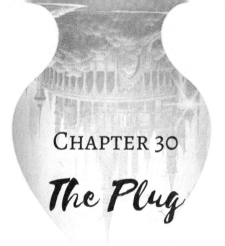

CHAPTER 30
The Plug

KIRA

KIRA HAD STORMED OUT of Nathaniel's room, but the plug wasn't the reason she'd left. Yes, his sick request was revolting, but it wasn't at the forefront of her mind as she bolted up the stairs, leaving the vampires' dorm behind.

Instead, her racing thoughts honed in on one tiny detail from her interaction with Nathaniel: the harsh way he'd reacted when he'd spoken of his father. As if he was trying to push her away from some truth by hurling barbed words at her. For the briefest of moments, a flash of contempt had crossed his features. She'd somehow known that it was not directed at her, but at his father.

There was another reason she'd left: the scent in Nathaniel's room was not at all what she'd expected. It was still dark, masculine, and musky, and it smelt *good*...and that was the problem. Instead of feeling repelled, like she should have, she'd wanted to move closer to him, to breathe in deeply.

Something about his room had felt right.

It was so unlike the smell of death in his office, and she suddenly couldn't reconcile the vampire who had slain her kin with the one standing before her. In fact, she couldn't make sense of him at all.

At times, he was domineering and twisted, and at others, she caught glimpses of a gentleman. And she couldn't forget the gentleness with which he'd brushed her mind when he'd fed from her. It was such a contrast from the cruel way he'd bitten her.

Her head was spinning. She hated him, but a treacherous part of her felt safe when he was near. It frightened her that she wanted to return to his bedroom more than she wanted to find something to use against him.

The memory of the way he'd stroked her hair eased into her mind. She wanted him to pet her like that again, lovingly, but she also wanted him to grip her hair, hold her down, and—

She slammed down on her thoughts, extinguishing the image that had appeared of him standing behind her naked, his towel fallen to the floor...

No. She did not want him. Could not.

And it suddenly occurred to her that she was running from herself more than from him.

Once in the foyer, Kira took the grand staircase up to his office. The academy was dark and deserted, and there was no one to stop her as she entered the forbidden corridor. She needed to investigate his office properly and find something that would help her renegotiate their deal. Wearing a plug was not what she considered 'favourable terms'.

She *really* didn't want the bastard putting anything in her ass.

She also needed to find out who, exactly, Gloria was, especially since she'd promised to play matchmaker.

Meanwhile, Nathaniel was back in his bedroom, waiting for her to return so he could plug her. They both knew it was inevitable.

How long would he wait?

All morning, I'll bet.

Nathaniel's office door was unlocked, just like last time. It was a bad sign as it implied there was nothing valuable or useful inside worth stealing.

It's almost like he wants people to come here.

Calling it 'the forbidden corridor' was just the icing on the cake to ensure that people do exactly that.

The room was cold and eerie in the moonlight. Alone with no one to see her true wolf form, Kira felt safe to morph. Golden light flashed for several seconds as she transformed.

It felt good to finally stretch her muscles. Her human form was fine, but shifting into her most natural form was like easing her feet out of a pair of shoes she'd worn for several days straight.

Immediately, her sense of sight, sound and smell increased, and she prowled the room, seeing it with new eyes.

The tan-coloured pelts of the royal family hung up on the wall behind Nathaniel's desk, their faces tortured and ghostly. The musty smell of death assaulted her senses. There was something else that irritated her, a faint whiff of something she hadn't been able to identify until now.

With her snout pressed close to the floor, she soon confirmed the source of the strange smell: old trees, plants, and magic.

This was the last place she'd expected to smell nature. It wasn't fresh, but it was alive like mould, as if magic had somehow preserved it. She dragged a pelt of a deceased wolf shifter aside with her teeth. Beneath it was another fur with the same bristly-grey fur.

No, not the same. Almost.

It reeked of magic, and she was convinced that it had never belonged to a real animal. It was an imitation of some kind. She searched the rest of the floor, unearthing more fake furs, putting them back the way she'd found them carefully to hide the evidence of her search. When she was done, she shifted back into human form and perched herself on the edge of Nathaniel's desk, frowning.

Besides the top layer of wolf pelts—of which there were a significant number in the large room—the ones underneath were all fake. As if Nathaniel had wanted to exaggerate the number of wolves that had been killed.

She sniffed disdainfully. It was not a surprise. History was written by the winners, and the vampires made sure everyone knew of the Revolution. But what *was* surprising was that someone had crafted fake pelts that were so life-like.

If the witches were wiped out during the Revolution, who had been left to make them?

A brief hope flickered alight in her chest as she approached the tan-coloured pelts on the wall, stroking the dappled white spots. Could it be that the royal wolf family was still alive? Her hope was quickly extinguished: these pelts were very real. The King, the Queen, the cubs. Other relations—aunts and uncles, perhaps. She let her head rest against the wall in disappointment, her grief renewed.

Despite the surge of negative emotions, Kira was glad she'd come. Charade or not, the room was a reminder of a vampire prince who was as ruthless as his father. Nathaniel had created this room to flaunt the murder of her kin. It was something she had to remember.

She checked the desk and shelves but found no personal effects of Gloria's. Nothing to indicate a long courtship, and it made her wonder if Nathaniel was serious about the relationship. Gloria didn't seem to be, not if she kept rejecting him.

Didn't she want to be the vampire queen?

Kira's heart ached as she left the office. For a moment, she'd allowed herself to hope that Nathaniel wasn't as bad as he seemed, and that his soul might be redeemable.

That *maybe*, he might actually care about her. But he only wanted to use her, and in all fairness, he'd never given her any indication otherwise. The person she'd hoped he was didn't exist—it was a naïve illusion she'd concocted, and she was angry at herself for romanticising his actions.

Without realising it, she'd let him in, just enough to touch her heart. But he did not deserve a place there—he had not earned it, and he never would.

By the time Kira returned to the foyer, the stress had gotten to her. Her breathing was short and sharp, and she stopped to take a break. She stared out of the window at the black night, trying to calm her breathing. She had to get these emotions out of her system. Otherwise, she would fail. She had to be as cold and heartless as Nathaniel.

The large grandfather clock near her ticked the hours by, the darkness outside softening to grey.

Without knowing how, she knew Nathaniel was still waiting for her.

Let him wait.

Angry tears ran down her face as she stared at the gardens outside. The academy had once been wolf territory. Had it been a happy place? Had the royal cubs ever frolicked on the lush grass, picking clovers?

Volmasque was not the home of the royal family—Wintermaw Keep was—but perhaps the royals had visited here?

Kira visualised the territories and places like a chessboard before her. Volmasque at the centre of the Capital, and on one side of the city, her little village of Nordokk where Byron and Mary had raised her. On the other, Wintermaw Keep, an elegant countryside estate. She knew what needed to be done to regain control of the Capital and surrounding territories.

But right now, she was just a pawn, to be used and pushed around by others.

But even a pawn could be dangerous if underestimated. Being close to the vampire prince, even as his 'pet', could give her the advantage she needed. It was time to do exactly what Nathaniel wanted of her: to become the docile, obedient sex slave he so obviously wanted.

Kira's breathing calmed, and the tightness in her chest eased. She felt numb, and that was good.

She was ready.

She took the stairwell, stopping in her room to change clothes before descending deeper into the underground dormitory's depths. She went through the quiet common room until she was standing before Nathaniel's door. Her arm did not feel like her own as she reached to knock on his door.

At the last moment, she changed her mind about knocking, and threw the door open instead. Nathaniel would be suspicious if she was *too* docile from the start, and it was a good excuse to glare at him now.

He looked up from where he sat in his armchair. "You wore your school uniform...are you aware it's Saturday?"

"I thought it would please you."

"It does. Very much." His expression grew stern, his voice edged with chips of ice. "Keeping me waiting, however, does *not* please me."

"I'm sure I can make it up to you," she said, entering the room and slamming the door behind her.

I'm sure you'll get over it.

He'd warned that the terms would be worse if she left, but she didn't dare ask what that meant. He wouldn't tell her until it suited him to do so.

Nathaniel stared at her expectantly, but she was already kneeling on the carpet in the spot he'd pointed to last night. There. Now, it was her turn to stare expectantly at *him*.

His lip curled and he snapped the jewellery box open. The steel plug gleamed, and Kira felt a sense of dread wash over her even as a tingle ran through her body as Nathaniel rose. "Let us begin."

She dropped her head, her heart fluttering as Nathaniel drew near. His feet entered her vision—elegant, black shoes, a glimpse of silk socks, and expensive slim-cut pants hemmed to sit on the top of his shoes. He hadn't changed since last night, and probably hadn't risen from the armchair at all while he waited for her.

"Look at me, Kira."

He was standing right in front of her, and she had to arch her neck back to meet his gaze. She swallowed. It was a vulnerable position, and she hated him, even as a part of her yearned for him to tell her what to do.

"This is your last chance to leave, pet," Nathaniel said. "If you stay, you will spend the entire weekend with me."

The entire fucking weekend?

She bit her lip to stay quiet.

"You will eat off the floor and sleep in my room and do exactly as I command. You will not leave this room until Monday morning, when you will leave with your ass plugged."

She cringed. "And then?"

"You will attend class as per usual and await further instructions from me."

A shuddery jolt travelled through her, rendering her breathless. "You expect me to wear it to *class?*"

"I expect you to do as I say." His cold eyes bore into hers. "I did warn you not to leave, Kira. Had you stayed last night, I might have let you enjoy the rest of your weekend as you deemed fit. As things stand, you will stay here and serve me as *I* deem fit."

"Do I have to share your bed?" she asked sulkily.

Nathaniel's eyes twinkled with amusement. "Pets sleep on the floor."

Bastard.

Although, the floor would be preferable to sharing with him.

"Now," Nathaniel said with a note of finality, "what is your decision?"

Her jaw muscles tensed, and she made him wait for her answer, even though they both knew she wouldn't back out, not now. She was in too deep for that.

"I agree to do as you say," she finally said, her voice thick.

"You will submit?"

"Yes."

"Say it."

Kira took a deep breath.

And then another.

Am I really doing this?

When she finally spoke, the words came far easier than they should have. "I will submit."

CHAPTER 31

Submission

KIRA

I WILL SUBMIT.

Kira couldn't believe she'd actually said those words out loud.

"Good girl," Nathaniel breathed.

He looked her up and down, his piercing gaze raking her body as if she were a piece of meat. Maybe that's what she was to him. She sincerely hoped he wouldn't try to drink her blood.

"Unbutton your blouse, Kira." His voice was calm and reasonable, as if he was used to being obeyed.

Still on her knees, she bowed her head and fumbled with the buttons. They'd never given her trouble until now, but her fingers were trembling.

When she was done, Nathaniel reached forward and parted her blouse, nodding in approval at her small round breasts. "From now on, when we are alone, you will call me *sir*. Is that understood?"

"Yes, sir," she mumbled.

"Good. Stand up and move to the desk."

She followed his command. The desk was completely bare except for a couple of crystal glass orbs that glowed, bathing the desk in red. She had a feeling Nathaniel had cleared the desk for this very purpose.

"Bend over it," he said quietly, "and lift up your skirt."

Kira obeyed. The tabletop had a rounded edge but still pressed uncomfortably into her stomach. She bent forward, supporting herself on one elbow as she reached behind to lift the short tartan skirt, exposing herself to him.

It was beyond humiliating.

Don't think about it, she told herself, trying to quell her nerves. She was afraid, but also nervous with anticipation as she felt cool air on her exposed buttocks.

Nathaniel exhaled slowly. "Simply beautiful."

Kira faced ahead, eyes unseeing, leaning her forearms on the desk and hoping the vampire would finish gawking and get on with it. She tensed when she felt his hands on her bottom, stroking and squeezing her cheeks. His hand slid beneath her blue lace panties deftly, pulling them aside.

She gasped when his fingers stroked her clit.

"Is that necessary?"

"Shh," he warned, "good pets don't speak unless spoken to."

Yeah, right.

A long minute passed as he stroked her, and she tried her best not to think about what was happening to her, or that it felt strangely good. After a string of nights filled with fantasies of Nathaniel touching her, she could no longer deny that she enjoyed it when he touched her there—but everything else was insufferable.

Her breathing grew shallow when Nathaniel's finger slid inside her pussy...or *fingers*, she realised as they curled inside her. The heat rose in her face as he moved them in and out, the sound of her wet folds squelching making her cringe. It was proof that on some level, her body was enjoying this, and now Nathaniel knew that as well.

"I don't see what this has to do with the plug," she protested, unable to stay silent any longer.

"I'm getting you ready." His damp fingers trailed up to her asshole, and she gasped when he rubbed it in circular motions, applying pressure. She felt him slide his fingers along her wet clit again, and then apply more of her fluids onto her ass, this time pressing a fingertip into her asshole.

"Oh!" she cried. "What the f—"

Pain sparked along her scalp as Nathaniel gripped her hair, jerking her head back. It forced her to look at him. "Quiet, or I will gag you. Do you understand?"

She pressed her lips together. "Yes...sir." The last part she added reluctantly, knowing he expected it.

He released her hair, and her head fell forwards. Tears had formed in the corners of her eyes from the painful tug of her hair, but that was nothing compared to what he did next: shoving his finger in deeper, invading her ass. The feeling was more uncomfortable than anything she'd ever endured.

"Fuck," she breathed, her voice almost a squeak. Her entire body tensed around Nathaniel's finger as it pushed in and out of her asshole.

"Yes, feel how tight you are. That's just the tip of my finger. Can you imagine if it was my cock?"

Kira winced. She did not want to imagine that. "You're not going to..." her face was burning, and she couldn't bring herself to finish the question.

Nathaniel laughed. "The plug is just the beginning. It will help prepare you for greater things." He removed his finger and slapped her ass. It stung and made her yelp.

"Get ready, pet," he crooned, and she could tell by his tone that it was time.

Bile crept up her throat. "Is...is the plug going to hurt?"

"Yes. It will hurt." A hand curled in her hair. "It will hurt, and if you ask me to stop, I won't. Not until I'm satisfied."

Suddenly, she felt the plug—large, smooth, and cold as he pressed it against her pussy, rubbing it until it was coated in her fluids.

Nathaniel folded forward so his chest warmed her back and pressed an unwanted kiss to the side of her neck. "It will hurt, slut, but you will love it. And it will be a constant reminder of who you belong to. Now, spread your legs."

Kira did as he said, shuffling her feet until they were a foot apart.

He spanked her, and she cried out in surprise and pain. "Wider," he said.

She spread her legs wider. Her bottom was exposed and in the air. Kira dared hope for a brief moment that the plug wouldn't hurt, that Nathaniel was just trying to scare her.

She was wrong.

She barely had time to collect herself before she felt the tapered point. It was cold, sharp, and unforgiving as it pressed on her sphincter, trying to force her apart.

"No," she whimpered, "it's too big."

"It's not. Just relax, pet. I've lubricated the plug. You can do this."

He pushed the plug in further, forcing her ass to stretch.

She cried out. "Please." The stretching force was almost searing, and if he pushed it in any further she felt like she would tear.

Nathaniel paused and leant close to her face. "Please, *what?*"

Kira avoided his gaze, shutting her eyes and shaking her head. It felt foreign, and wrong. This was not what nature had intended, and she was convinced her body was not designed for this. "It's too much."

"If you wish to leave, I won't stop you. You are free to go—there's the door. But if you leave now, you can forget about our deal."

Kira sniffed, her eyes brimming with tears as she clutched at the flat surface of the desk. "I hate you," she growled.

Nathaniel chuckled, and it made her hate him more. "What will it be, pet? Will you stay and play? Make me proud?" He tenderly stroked her back, her neck, her shoulders. His touch was so gentle it was unfair. "It is a lot, I know. But you have such a long way to go to being a well-trained pet."

Kira bit her lip as she deliberated. A part of her *wanted* to make him proud of her. She craned her neck to look behind her, taking in his cruel handsome features. Despite her loathing, an agonising ache throbbed as he locked eyes with her, his head tilted to one side expectantly.

"Well, pet?" He stroked her waist, rubbing soothing circles on her back. "Will you stay?"

"Yes, I'll stay." Surely, it couldn't get much worse? "Is the plug nearly in at least? Is there much more to go?"

"Oh, Kira..." Nathaniel's voice was half-amused, half-pitying. "This is just the tip. There is much more to go. But I promise you this: just when you think you can't handle any more pain, you will feel pleasure unlike anything you've ever experienced before."

Kira didn't care about that. She just didn't want him to fucking torture her. She sniffed and stared straight ahead. "Just do it."

Nathaniel eased the plug in, the pressure mounting until it was almost excruciating. She cried out as the toy stretched her, and her fingernails clawed at the smooth desk as pain exploded in her rear. She felt like a trapped animal, a victim at the mercy of a sadistic vampire, and panic rose in her as the pressure intensified. This was wrong. Nothing and no one should be doing *anything* to her ass. It wasn't natural.

"That's it, pet," Nathaniel said, stroking her back with one hand while the other pushed the plug. "Nearly there."

Just when she was about to scream for him to stop, the bulging toy sunk in fully, filling her inner cavity, and the horrible stretching sensation at her sphincter was gone.

She choked out a sound of relief, her body shaking as she lay across the desk. Her face was hot and teary, her body clammy as she adjusted to the plug, and she was panting, her breasts pressed against the tabletop. She couldn't believe it. The plug felt enormous inside her. It was heavy, but it no longer felt painful. In a way, it felt just right. As if it belonged there, fitting her perfectly. It was...fulfilling, and the cool sensation of the metal was pleasant.

And something else happened, something that kept her panting as the quiet minutes stretched.

Passion was exploding in her core, fiery and relentless. Something about the plug had hijacked her mind, and savage desire burnt through her, making her ache for more. Suddenly, the entire world melted away and there was nothing and no one in it except for her, Nathaniel, and the steel plug.

She'd entered the room as Kira, a wolf bent on revenge, but now she was rendered helpless as Nathaniel transformed her into something else. And yet, she didn't feel any less for it. In fact, she felt like he'd unlocked a part of her she hadn't known existed, allowing her to experience a state of bliss as she surrendered to him completely.

From the moment the plug had sunk in fully, her mind had turned into a frenzied mess of jelly. Nothing and no one existed out of this room. Her entire universe now revolved around the fact that Nathaniel had stuffed a large sex toy into her ass, and her clit was throbbing so much she was whining repeatedly like a dog.

"Well done, pet," Nathaniel said, his voice brimming with so much fondness and pride that it made her melt. "Such a good girl."

He stroked her bottom, and she yelped when he pressed on the plug. It was a small reminder of the pain she'd felt earlier when he'd inserted it. He pressed on it again, and she let out a soft moan. The tightness, the force...it was so big, it was like *he* was inside her. At least, that's how she imagined it would feel.

Nathaniel pressed on the plug a third time, and he cupped her pussy with his other hand, teasing her with gentle strokes.

She groaned, her head falling forward onto the desk with a small thud as pleasure rippled along her wet folds where his hand touched her. She craved his touch, and she could tell release was not far away.

What the fuck has he done to me?

Suddenly, Nathaniel's hand dropped and he walked around to the other side of the desk.

She watched in disbelief as he began to pull out papers and quills from the desk drawers, replacing them while he hummed to himself.

Meanwhile, she was still lying across the desk, her bum sticking in the air, her breasts splayed on the tabletop and rising and falling as she panted. "Is that it?"

"Hmm?" Nathaniel sank down in the armchair opposite her, staring at her blankly.

She shut her eyes for a moment as agonising aches pulsed in her. She was so close.

Fuck.

Her voice was strained as she asked, "What happens now?"

"You stay there until I command otherwise."

Kira gritted her teeth. Desire was dripping like acid, burning a hole in her core, and it made her want to scream with frustration. "You're...just going to leave me like this?"

"For the time being."

"And then what?"

Nathaniel tilted his head at her. "Ask the question, pet."

He wanted her to beg?

Fuck off.

"No."

Remaining seated, Nathaniel leant forward in his chair and grasped her chin.

"Ask."

"I...I thought you were going to...have sex with me," she finished lamely.

His lips curved in amusement. "Oh, my dear pet. I think you misunderstood our agreement. I never agreed to have sex with you.

Besides, I've already claimed you. I don't need to fuck you to make you mine."

CHAPTER 32

His Pet

NATHANIEL

NATHANIEL LICKED HIS THUMB as he paged through a novel. The epic adventure was far less interesting than the wolf in front of him, but it gave him something to do while he waited.

Kira needed to learn patience, or in failing that, obedience.

She was still bent over his desk, and he liked her like that. It took effort to read the story, especially with the delightful way Kira glared at him. She was radiating hate and lust, and he was dying to walk around and feel her sopping cunt.

In his peripheral vision, he saw her moving ever so slightly. She was discreetly rubbing her thighs together to try and alleviate her aching pussy. She thought he didn't notice—but he did.

Poor pet.

"Keep your legs spread," he commanded.

He would not prolong her suffering for much longer. He would see to her needs...eventually.

Right now, he was enjoying her reluctant submission, her angry defiance clashing with the humiliating pose he'd put her in. It was like her uniform had been designed to taunt him, and he'd never wanted to fuck anything so badly. He needed to feel her, taste her, to hear her moan.

Just like she'd moaned when he'd inserted the plug.

When it finally went in all the way, she'd reacted instantly as if lightning had struck her, the tension in her body slackening, her shoulders slumping, her eyes glazing as she turned docile. He loved the surprise on her face when the initial pain passed, and for the briefest glimmer of a moment, she had been completely his in every way.

With the plug in place, she was horny as fuck.

As was he. He loved seeing her turned on, loved seeing her pine for something that he could give her.

But not pining for me. I'm not the one she wants.

It was an important distinction. He ignored the twinge of regret in his chest at that thought. Mark did not deserve her, but neither did he. That wouldn't stop him from taking her, again and again. She was his, at least for a while, and he would make good use of her. His heart clenched at the thought that he would eventually have to let her go.

A soft mewl escaped Kira as she shifted her position ever so slightly, and his gaze snapped to her. His attention kept straying from the book, and no wonder. She was blushing so beautifully that it was visible on her bronze skin. Her cheeks glowed a dark rosy hue, and she was panting like a good little whore while she waited for him to give his next command.

Wolves always made the best pets.

Using her blue panties as a bookmark, Nathaniel snapped the book shut and set it aside.

He could tell Kira was growing uncomfortable, but he wanted to enjoy the sight of her splayed on his desk with her feet planted wide apart and her skirt hiked up for a few minutes longer.

Kira broke the silence first. It hadn't even been five minutes, but she couldn't seem to help herself.

"If you're not going to have sex with me," she grumbled, "then why are you making me wear a plug?"

"To remind you of who you belong to. And as I already mentioned...I have plans for your ass. The plug will ready you for what's to come. You'll thank me later."

"Doubtful," Kira huffed. She rose off the desk, but Nathaniel sprang forward, seizing her wrist.

"I didn't say you could move. Stay," he commanded.

Fear and rage flared in her eyes, but she stayed in place. Satisfied, Nathaniel nodded and stood, letting his chair scrape back.

"Before you get up, Kira," he began, pausing to savour the hopeful look in her eyes, "I want you to keep your palms on the desk, and slowly look behind you and look at yourself in the mirror."

Kira gasped.

Nathaniel walked around the desk so he could see her face, standing beside the tall, ornate mirror mounted on the wall. "Can you see what I can, pet?"

Kira's eyes widened when she caught sight of herself. Her ass in the air, perfect round cheeks glowing in the dawn light, the jewelled end of the plug flashing so bright it could have taken someone's eye out. He studied her face, relishing the exact moment she spotted the plug, the way her lips parted in surprise, and her chest rose as she drew a sharp breath, deepening her cleavage.

"I asked you a question," he prompted, tracing the gilded edge of the mirror. "Can you see how powerful you are?"

Confusion crossed her face. "I don't feel powerful."

Nathaniel smiled. "You could bring an entire kingdom to its knees." He stepped forward and helped her off the desk. She was shaky, relying on him for support as she regained her balance. He gently tipped her face up and held her gaze. "*You* are breathtakingly gorgeous. You've just about brought me to my knees."

Kira's eyes softened, causing his heart to leap. "If you ever *do* kneel before me," she murmured, licking her lips as he bent his head close, their faces mere inches apart, "you'll be missing your head."

He froze, his lips almost grazing hers. A smile spread across his face and he chuckled softly. "Do you always threaten to decapitate the men you court?"

That put her on the back foot, and she blinked several times. "I don't court men. Th-this isn't courting."

She pulled away. They were playing a game of chicken to see who would back out first. He couldn't tell who was winning, but he grabbed her hand and pulled her back against him. Her soft, slender figure pressed against his.

He walked to his armchair, pulling her with him, and sank into it, lifting her and wrapping her legs around him. It forced her to straddle him, her feet resting on the armrests while her skirt rode up, revealing all.

Kira's body was rigid, and he could tell she was panicking about what he intended next.

"Don't worry, pet," he said, brushing a thick lock of hair behind her ear, "I won't take your virginity. We'll need that to ensure the Poplarins accept you, don't we?"

Kira eyed him suspiciously before nodding. "Yes. That was our deal."

"And I will uphold my end of the bargain." He brushed her lower lip with his thumb. "But your hymen aside, I promise you will be anything but innocent by the time I'm done with you. Starting...right now."

Kira blanched. She could no doubt feel his raging erection. "What are you going to do?"

He smiled as he cradled her, holding her close and enjoying the feel of her in his arms. "Absolutely nothing. You're going to sit here quietly on my lap for the next hour. What you do in that time is up to you."

"That doesn't give me many options," Kira said coolly, looking regal and haughty as she sat straight-backed on his crotch.

"No," Nathaniel mused, "I suppose it doesn't."

His hand slid to her ass and tapped on the plug. She snarled in outrage, squirming in his grip.

"Cut that out!"

Nathaniel smiled. She was going to come all over his trousers.

All he had to do was wait.

CHAPTER 33

Humping a Vampire

KIRA

KIRA WAS IN AGONY, and it took every ounce of restraint not to grind her hips against the vampire's crotch.

He held her close, his proximity overwhelming her senses. His smoky scent, his sharp gaze, the feel of his hands on her, that condescending smirk, it was mesmerising.

And his boner.

Holy hell.

The rock-hard silhouette of his cock taunted her through his trousers. The prominent bulge agonisingly close to where she needed it, so close and yet so far. It made her arousal impossible to ignore, yet she felt nervous and giddy with his thick member primed and ready to shoot as it pressed against her clit.

The effects of the alcohol she'd had at the party were wearing off, and yet, she was intoxicated all over again as she sat astride Nathaniel. She was helpless, his sharp gaze peeling back her defences one layer at a time, unnerving her and making her body tingle with rippling chills.

Time stood still, and Kira felt her scowl slipping, her annoyance fading into the background as she absorbed the tension simmering between them. Nathaniel had a way of making her feel safe even when she was vulnerable. She still despised him, but she was no longer scared of him.

Maybe she should have been, but the fucking plug had overridden all logic. She couldn't think straight, and she squirmed feeling like an angsty ball of flames.

Nathaniel tapped on the plug again.

"What are you doing?" she gasped.

"Waiting," he purred. "Watching. Wanting."

She gulped at the smouldering desire in his hooded eyes, and for a flicker of a second, she almost felt something for the vampire.

Almost, because he had to go and fucking tap the plug again. He repeated the motion, firmly, cruelly, holding her gaze as he stoked the fire that was burning her insides with need. Her ass was stretched and full to the brim, the sensation causing her clit to throb. She desperately needed to stroke herself, or to have him touch it, or... or anything.

She didn't care who or what, she just couldn't take the anticipation anymore.

Nathaniel shuffled in his seat ever so slightly, and the movement put half an inch of space between his crotch and her pussy. The distance may as well have spanned miles for how it made her pine for him to move back closer. She felt a twinge of frustration as she realised that he'd moved away on purpose.

The thick bulge of his cock awaited her...

But was it worth her pride?

A whimper escaped her throat, and Nathaniel chuckled, stroking the back of her head as if to calm her. Which, strangely enough, helped put her at ease.

"It's all right, pet. Do what you need to do."

She shook her head.

I can't.

"Yes. Take what you want. It's your turn to use me."

Kira pressed her lips together.

Am I actually considering it?

An involuntary thrill ran through her as Nathaniel pulled her closer, crushing his hard chest against her breasts. She sighed softly. Her chin rested on his shoulder, giving her a view of the armchair's backrest. She honed in on the details—a brocade pattern in deep regal colours of midnight black and forest green, embroidered with metallic thread that glinted in the candlelight. The intricate, dark mahogany frame boasted ornate carvings of unbloomed roses, the twisting vines the perfect thing to distract her.

Maybe, I can pretend Nathaniel is someone else. Maybe, I can pretend he isn't here at all.

Her body moved before she'd made up her mind, her hips shifting forward, tilting as she closed that tiny, infinite distance. She let out a shaky moan as her aching pussy brushed the fabric of his trousers, shuddering as pleasant tremors rippled along her tender folds.

It felt so fucking good. But it was just a small taste of what she needed.

Abandoning her reservations, she pressed herself closer, rubbing her clit against his erection.

Fuck. Yes.

It would have been even better if he'd remove his trousers.

"Good girl," Nathaniel whispered as she rocked against him. "I knew you couldn't resist."

She didn't respond, trying to block his voice out as she focused on the armchair through her hazy vision.

Intricate wooden frame...

Rosebuds...

Twisted vine carvings that writhed, just as her core did, her pussy saturated with wet desire, the growing aches creeping steadily closer to an orgasm that promised to be euphoric.

Kira tried to be quiet, but she couldn't hold back the high-pitched whines that escaped her as she rubbed herself against Nathaniel's warm, hard body.

"I'm so proud of you," he whispered, his sultry voice penetrating her thoughts. "You're doing so well. Keep going."

She gripped him tightly, her fingernails sinking into his back like claws, clutching at him as if her life depended on him as she humped him.

I'm sorry, she told herself, apologising because she was about to pass the point of no return, and nothing and no one could stop her now. This was worse than when Nathaniel had fingered her and made her come. Now *she* was the one making herself come, proving that she wanted it.

"That's it," Nathaniel said, his voice raspy with desire. "Don't stop. Show me what a good little slut you are as you hump your master's leg."

Fuck.

Her movements intensified, causing the armchair to squeak as she rocked back and forth against his solid length.

She needed more.

More.

Nathaniel's eyes darkened, and as if he'd read her mind, he closed his hand over her throat, squeezing just enough to make her muscles scream *yes.*

Her vision grew blurry, her throat dry and breathing heavy as she approached nirvana.

Upholstered armchair.

Deep mahogany.

Thick solid wood.

Ivy vines...twisting, choking.

"Faster, slut," Nathaniel commanded, squeezing her airway. "And be silent."

A rose bud on the cusp of opening as thornless vines strangle it.

She was fucking delirious. She had to be, because she hated poetry.

Tears sprang to her eyes, rendering the room a wonderful swirling blur of stars as Nathaniel's rough voice rumbled in her ear.

"The time has come, slut. Ride my cock until you come."

Kira half-sobbed, half-moaned as the intense urgency gripping her body surged. The plug had heightened all sensations, and she was losing all control.

All the while, Nathaniel held her—he was the only thing keeping her grounded.

"You moan like an animal," he said softly. "Did you know that?"

"No," she gasped.

"You do, and I love it," he whispered, before his tone became dark and menacing. "And yet...I warned you to be quiet."

He grabbed her hips and pulled her close, thrusting his cock so it hit the exact spot she needed, causing her to cry out. She couldn't have been quiet even if she wanted to, and loud moans emanated from her lungs as Nathaniel drove against her, his lip curled and his eyes glinting as he watched her.

The tantalising hints of pleasure beckoned her, and the deep ache pulsing through her body grew increasingly unbearable.

She was nearly there.

Just when she was about to come, Nathaniel took hold of the plug and wrenched it out of her, causing pain to flash through her as the bulging toy stretched her sphincter wide.

"What the hell are you doing?" she cried angrily. She was right on the edge, needing only a few more soul-gripping moments to slide against his cock before she came...and he'd taken out the plug.

"Why? Because you're going to fucking come when I push it back in," Nathaniel growled, and the fierceness of his voice sent her spiralling over the brink.

A shriek erupted from her throat, and at the same time, Nathaniel followed through on his threat, shoving the plug back in. There was a moment of sharp pain as it stretched her tight ring of muscle, causing her entire body to spasm violently as it filled her again. He slapped her ass cheek, striking the plug and causing her entire body to shatter as she came all over him. She gasped and moaned as pleasure consumed her, leaving her weak and clammy as she twitched and jerked from the intense shudders jolting through her.

"Such a good girl," Nathaniel said, stroking her hair.

Kira shut her eyes to slits, enjoying the last waves of her orgasm as they rocked her body.

Her euphoria wore off far too quickly, leaving her to wonder if sacrificing her pride had been worth it.

Peering through her eyelashes, the chair's ivy carvings leapt out at her. The gothic craftsmanship had a haunting beauty, and carved into the top of the frame was a dark, royal crown, wrapped in thorny vines. It was a stark reminder of who Nathaniel was, not only in this room, but outside of it. He was the son of the ruthless king, who'd slaughtered the royal wolf family, along with hundreds of wolves, along with her family. And as the future king, Nathaniel was and always would be her enemy. She'd been a fool to forget it for even a second.

She'd ridden the vampire prince's cock and enjoyed it, and there would be no redemption for her.

She flinched when she felt Nathaniel's fingers caress her back. The sensation almost tickled, and now that her lust had abated, she recoiled from his touch.

"Can I get off your lap now?" she asked stiffly.

"Not yet," Nathaniel said. "We still have three-quarters of an hour to go."

"Fuck off." Kira sat bolt upright, trying to push herself off him, but he held her in place.

"Settle," Nathaniel warned, pulling open a desk drawer. "You're going to do that again, pet, but *this* time, you're going to be quiet, just like I commanded." He tossed a familiar jumble of black leather and fabric onto the desk. "I'll make sure of it."

She twisted on his lap staring in horror at the collar with the ball gag.

"No," she stammered, struggling as she tried to get away from him. "No way. I'm not wearing that."

"Yes, you are. And look..." He took hold of a silver name tag hanging from a chain link between his thumb and forefinger and angled it so the engraving flashed in the light. It read:

KIRA

"I had this added after we met," he said. "Do you like it?"

"What do you think?" she snapped.

He ignored her sarcasm. "It's double-sided, so that no one mistakes what you are."

She felt a deep pang of dread as Nathaniel turned the tag.

"Read it out loud for me, pet."

Kira shook with anger, her jaw tight as she read the capitalised word out loud—*SLUT.*

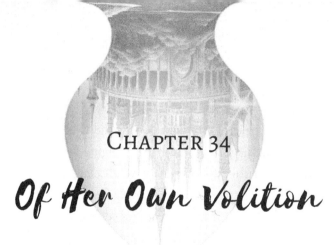

CHAPTER 34

Of Her Own Volition

NATHANIEL

THREE TIMES.

Kira had come on him three times in the space of an hour, twice while wearing the gag.

It wasn't a high number, but he preferred quality over quantity, and the desperate, tortured, euphoric look in Kira's eyes as she pleasured herself using his body made it worth it.

Hearing her muffled moans as she tried to breathe through the gag was heavenly. She could hate him all she wanted, but no one had forced her to ride him dry and make herself come. And if she hadn't been so loud the first time, he wouldn't have had to use the gag.

But that was all right. He liked reining her in.

Kira on the verge of climax was a sight to behold. It was the first time he'd seen her give up control like that, surrendering herself completely, not to him, but to the moment. It was temporary and fleeting, like a shooting star, and the transient beauty made it all the more meaningful. And he got to witness it: the glorious clash of conflicting emotions on her face, her eyes shining with victory before darkness dragged her down and swallowed her whole. He loved the way she held onto him as she came.

And her moans—*fucking hell*.

By the end of the hour, he was a wreck. There were several moments where he'd nearly come from the way she carried on. Somehow, he'd managed to hold back, clinging to his last shred of willpower as she rubbed her wet pussy all over him, her panties soaked and useless to stop the fluid seeping from her.

As predicted, the front of his trousers were glistening, and he'd made a point of showing Kira.

When the hour was up, he'd removed the gag and collar and commanded Kira to kneel on the floor in her 'spot'. She was still plugged, and the skin of her face and throat was lined with pink indentations where the gag and collar dug in.

Nathaniel stood before her, his crotch at eye level with her face. He could tell she was tired, and sensed she needed some time to be alone and collect her thoughts.

Soon.

"My poor pet, have you had enough?" He caressed her cheek. "Would you like to rest?"

She nodded tiredly. "Yes, sir."

She'd learnt in their brief time together that 'yes, sir' was the safest response.

"Can you remove the plug now?" she added hopefully.

"I'm afraid you'll have to be patient a little while longer, pet." He unbuckled his trousers, taking note of the way her face fell as he pulled his cock out. "It's my turn now. Eyes on me."

Finally, at long last, he fisted his cock stroking the engorged length.

Fuck. He needed this. Needed *more* than this, but at least he would finally get his release. With Kira's pussy off limits, he had few options. It was tempting to take her virgin ass like this, raw, but it would be brutal. She needed more time with the plug, and it was his responsibility to train her to take his size. Not only was he much larger than the plug, but a stationary toy was very different to putting up with the hard pounding he had in mind for her. The plug was the kindest way to introduce her to anal sex, but even so, it would not be easy for her when the time came.

As for her mouth...

Nathaniel didn't know why he held back asking her to suck him off, only that she looked exhausted, and he didn't want to force her right now. And he didn't want to *ask*. He was in the mood for something else.

It was quiet. Even the fireplace had burnt down to coals. The only sound in the room was of him jerking off. He was so damn close, and Kira was staring up at him, her brown eyes searching his soul, and it both aroused him and put him off.

It was too much.

"Keep your eyes lowered," he ordered, and she dropped her gaze. *Better.* Maybe he should have blindfolded her.

He fisted his cock, imagining how sore she must feel after the way he'd worked her ass with the plug. "Do you like wearing a plug for me, pet?"

Kira kept her eyes lowered. "No, sir."

It was the wrong answer, and they both knew it, and yet it turned him on to hear it.

Interesting.

"I'm going to come all over your face, Kira. Would you like that?"

"No, sir."

His cock throbbed at her defiance, and his movements intensified, the head aimed right at her face.

"Tell me what else you don't want, slut."

She lifted her gaze to look at him. "May I show you, sir?"

Her question took him aback, and he nodded. "You may."

His motions slowed as Kira shuffled closer, dipping her head beneath his cock, her hands holding his thighs for support as her warm, wet tongue found his balls.

Holy shit.

She licked them eagerly, lapping at them as if they were coated in honey, as if she couldn't get enough. He couldn't believe it.

Where had *this* Kira come from?

He nearly died when she took his balls in her mouth, somehow managing to fit them both at the same time. "Greedy pet," he murmured, petting her head.

Kira tried to take his cock in her mouth, but he didn't let her, gripping her hair tightly. He appreciated her initiative, and the fact that she'd licked his balls of her own volition pleased him greatly. But even through the maddening desire burning through him, he recognised that she was trying to take control away from him.

And that wouldn't do.

Not given the role he had to play.

She tried again to place her mouth on his cock, straightening as she knelt before him, but he dragged her down by the hair.

"Not in your mouth," he said, holding her in place as he jerked off in her face. "Like this. Open your mouth."

Kira looked unhappy about this, but she opened her mouth obediently, and that was all that mattered. It didn't even matter that she was looking at him with disapproval—it did her little good as he groaned deeply and came all over her face, spraying her cheeks, her eyes, and her forehead with spurts of creamy discharge. It clung to her hair and eyelashes, and it dripped down her chin. Somehow, he'd missed her mouth completely.

He swiped two fingers along her cheek and pushed them into her mouth, feeding her his seed.

"Suck," he instructed.

She obeyed, but he could see pure loathing sparkling in her eyes. But she couldn't fool him—there was something else in her expression that made his thundering heart jolt. Kira may have been trying to get the upper hand, but she enjoyed giving him pleasure just as much as he'd enjoyed pleasuring her, if only for the control it gave her.

It pleased him that she'd realised, at least on a subconscious level, that it was *she* who was in control.

It was going to be a long weekend—and it was only Saturday morning.

They hadn't even started.

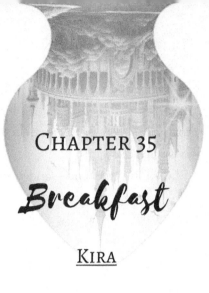

Chapter 35

Breakfast

KIRA

KIRA WAS ON HER knees. Her face was covered in cum, and she squinted through the sticky fluid at the vampire towering over her. He was silhouetted against the grey morning light of the window, and there was something impressive about the way he put away his cock and refastened his trousers, as if this was a business transaction that had concluded.

She reached up to wipe her face, but Nathaniel's brisk voice made her jump.

"Leave it."

Her jaw clenched, a retort on the tip of her tongue, but before she could snap at him, he added, "You look beautiful like that."

A silence passed between them. It wasn't tense, but it wasn't comfortable either. It was as if they'd crossed an invisible threshold together, and their relationship had changed. He kept calling her pet, as if she were an animal and he was her master, and in those dark euphoric moments where she lost herself to secret cravings she hadn't known she had, she believed that it was true.

Her mind was still groggy, but it was clearer than before when she'd sat astride Nathaniel. She loathed the power he held over her, but she also couldn't help but hold onto the morsels of praise and compliments he'd given her.

He was unlike any man—vampire, shifter, or human—that she'd ever met. She'd interacted with human males close to her age in her village, but Nathaniel was of a different calibre. When he said she was beautiful, she could tell it meant something more to him, that he was fascinated by her.

At least I amuse him.

She could also tell that he'd meant it when he'd threatened to take her from behind. How much longer before he acted on that threat? He'd implied it wouldn't be soon, but she was too sore to feel relieved. Not only was her clit throbbing, but after gagging her mouth and collaring her, he'd used the plug to fuck her asshole raw. Now she was aching everywhere.

On top of all that, he'd had the nerve to shove the plug back in, and he *still* hadn't removed it.

Sadistic fuck.

She was ready for their bargain to be over. And yet, a part of her was resigned to see this through. Nathaniel had a bizarre talent for making her feel good about herself, and degrading her, and it seemed the two were not mutually exclusive. It frightened her that he was teaching her things she hadn't known about herself.

Had those dark, disturbing fantasies always been a part of her? If so, maybe it would have been better if she'd never discovered them at all. Because now that the deed was done, what had been the point? She'd humped him like a bitch in heat, and now she was a tired, sticky mess. How on earth would she be able to face herself after the weekend?

Monday felt like an eternity away. She was already tired and it wasn't even nine o'clock yet. At least Nathaniel had removed the gag.

"You may stand," he said, offering her his hand.

She knocked it away, rising unsteadily. The window brightened as the sun came out, the light reflecting off the windowsill and blinding her for a brief moment. Suddenly, she registered its significance.

"You have a window," she said, dumbstruck.

"Indeed."

She walked over to it. Nathaniel made no move to stop her, and she stared out at the country lane lined with birch trees and thick woods in the distance.

"But...we're underground. How...?"

"It's not really a window. It shows another place. Magic," he added, as if that wasn't obvious.

"Right." She stared at the birch trees for a moment longer, watching the orange leaves flutter in the breeze. "There seems to be a lot of magic at Volmasque." She tried to keep her tone light-hearted as she ventured a risky question. "I don't suppose you know any witches?"

The atmosphere shifted.

He was standing close behind her, his gaze pressing on her back. "Officially, I must inform you that there are no witches left in existence."

Blah blah blah.

"And unofficially?"

"Unofficially, I cannot comment."

She gave him a funny look. Was he implying what she thought he was implying?

His face was blank, revealing nothing. Was he teasing her, or hinting at a secret? She truly hoped it was the latter, but he didn't say anything more on the subject.

Kira sighed and turned away from the window. "You're no fun."

He arched an eyebrow. "Aren't I? We were both having plenty of fun just a minute ago."

Kira scowled, and as her brow furrowed, she felt the skin stretch where his cum had dried over it in a film. *Ugh.* "Will you hurry up and take this plug out?"

"Soon, pet," he said, "but not yet."

He walked to the foot of the bed, where a thin, flat cushion had been laid out. "Come and sit here."

"No, thank you."

"I wasn't asking."

They stared at each other. To her surprise, Nathaniel broke the silence.

"I'll return soon. You may as well relax."

Kira scoffed. "Relax? While wearing a fucking plug?"

"Yes."

"Here, on the ground?"

"Where you belong, pet."

Her nostrils flared. "I belong in my own room." She wanted to shower, and to change out of these clothes. She'd been up all night, and she felt crummy.

When Nathaniel didn't speak, she sighed and dragged her feet to the mat and sank down onto it. "There. Happy?"

Nathaniel moved so fast she barely registered it, seizing her ankle and jerking it towards him.

"What are you—"

Cold metal clamped over her ankle, and she kicked out at him. But it was too late, and her leg came to an abrupt halt mid-kick as a chain clanked taut, jarring her muscles. He'd chained her to the foot of the damn bed.

"What the *fuck*?" she said loudly. "You can't chain me up."

Nathaniel set down a bowl of water at her feet. "Drink, if you're thirsty. With your mouth, not your hands."

She gaped at the ceramic dog bowl. It even had bones painted in a friendly circle around the outer edge. "What the actual fuck? I'm not drinking from this." She lashed out with her other foot, upsetting the bowl and spilling water on the ground.

Nathaniel watched the upset bowl roll across the room, trying to hide a smile. "You won't get a treat that way."

"Fuck. You!"

He shook his head, grinning now. "Oh, Kira. You have a wonderfully dirty mouth. Now, I'll be back soon. Stay on your mat until I return."

"Where the fuck would I go?" she growled, jerking the chain with her foot so it clanked.

Nathaniel ignored her, leaning close to whisper chilling words in her ear. "Do not remove the plug without my say-so. You will regret it."

He left, shutting the door behind him.

She was alone.

How long was he going to be gone for? He hadn't said.

She couldn't believe he'd chained her to the bed. It gave her no chance to search his bedroom, or to even contemplate sneaking upstairs back to her room.

As for the plug, it no longer felt comfortable. She was incredibly sore, the tender flesh irritated. But touching it even slightly made the feeling worse, as if she was disturbing an angry hornets' nest, and she grudgingly decided to leave it in place. She lay on the mat, curled up like a wolf as she stared glumly at the grey light on the carpet. Her gaze lifted to the window, where the sun had disappeared behind clouds, and she distracted herself by watching the distant birch trees. Was it a real place? Or an illusion? She let out several long sighs as she waited for Nathaniel.

He soon returned with a breakfast tray brimming with hot food, pastries, and orange juice. He set the tray down on his desk.

"What do you feel like?" he asked.

Kira eyed the food suspiciously. "Are you going to poison me? Or drug me so you can have your way with me?"

"I don't need to drug you to have my way with you."

She cringed.

Noticing her reaction, Nathaniel's brow furrowed. "Make no mistake, Kira. One day soon, regardless of whether you are in a pack or not, I'm going to find you, and I'm going to fuck you until you scream. And when it feels like too much, I'll fuck you some more. And you will be awake and lucid, enjoying every second of it. So, *no,* I have no intention of poisoning or drugging you."

Kira scowled. "A simple *no* would have sufficed."

"I feel like nothing is simple with you."

He'd said it as if it was a compliment, his gaze inquisitive. She didn't know what to say to that.

Nathaniel saved her from speaking, gesturing for her to turn around. "I'll remove the plug now."

"Finally," she muttered, but she felt nervous at the prospect, her skin crawling as Nathaniel drew closer.

"Keep your head turned towards me."

"Why?"

"Because," he said, crouching behind her and gripping the edges of the plug's jewelled end, "I want to see your face as I remove it."

"You are such a cunt—"

No sooner had she turned her head to face Nathaniel than he ripped the toy out of her. She screamed, but the pain, while sharp, was brief. The massive girth of the plug had grated her sore sphincter, but now that it was gone, she groaned in relief.

"Now," Nathaniel said, standing by the desk, "Breakfast is getting cold. What would you like to eat?"

Kira shut her eyes, resisting the urge to nurse her aching bottom. "I don't care. Just...give me a little bit of everything."

She wasn't hungry, but her request kept Nathaniel busy and his attention off her for just that little bit longer as he focused on preparing a plate for her.

He set it down on the wooden floorboards beside her mat, along with a glass of juice. "Enjoy."

At least there was a plate this time. Even so, she didn't touch the food, but she couldn't help but stare at the variety: muffins, flaky pastries, fresh fruit, sausages, fried mushrooms, and Eggs Benedict.

"Which one of your many servants made the eggs?" she asked snidely as Nathaniel prepared a plate for himself.

"I did."

She raised her eyebrows. She couldn't imagine the vampire prince doing something as domestic as cooking. "And the hollandaise sauce?"

"Also made by me."

"Really? How did you learn to cook?"

"I ordered my *many servants* to teach me."

He said this with a straight face, and it took Kira a moment to realise he was joking.

She was surprised when he sat down beside her on the hard boards, balancing his plate on one knee.

"What are you doing?" she asked.

"I'm having breakfast with you."

"Well...don't. I'd prefer to eat alone...and *unchained*."

Nathaniel's only response was to pass her a small white towel. It was wet.

"What's this?" she asked, taking it.

"To clean your face. But if you'd rather eat with your face covered in my—"

"I would rather you let me shower," she interrupted, patting her face generously with the damp towel. It was no replacement for a hot shower, and they both knew it. There was little she could do about where his cum had matted her hair, but she felt significantly better after wiping her face. "And you could unchain me."

"Soon." Nathaniel began eating, his movements smooth and refined. "Tell me something about yourself."

"Like what?" she asked, downing the glass of orange juice in one go. She was still thirsty.

Nathaniel refilled her glass from a jug. "Such as, what is your favourite food?"

Kira prodded an egg with her fork, splitting the yolk. She was not in the mood to make small talk. "I'll tell you what I don't like. *This.*"

"Eggs?"

"This Hollandaise sauce. It's too runny."

"Is it, now?"

"Yes."

It wasn't. The yellow sauce was rich and creamy, with a velvety texture that melted in her mouth.

"Hmm." Nathaniel chewed thoughtfully. "I'll have to practise."

"Don't bother for my sake. This—" she waved her hand at the plates of food "—will not be a regular thing."

"You don't like brunch?"

"I don't like you. Once you've held up your end of the bargain, you're never going to see me again."

He would be dead, buried six feet beneath the ground—but she would have to remember to get his hollandaise recipe first.

"Have you considered I might miss you?"

She froze, the fried mushrooms slipping off her fork. Her grip tightened on the utensil. "Have you considered I'm armed?"

His lip twitched and didn't answer, his calmness in the face of her threat irking her.

Whatever.

She focused on her food, taking her frustration out on a pastry which ended up being delicious.

"Victoria made the pastries," Nathaniel volunteered. "She's the one who taught me to cook, although, I must admit that eggs are the only food I know how to make."

Kira narrowed her eyes at him, trying to make sense of his weird attempt at small talk. She might have been more amiable, had he not chained her to the fucking bed. "Just eggs, huh?"

"Just eggs."

She pretended to dwell on this. "Do you do your own dishes?"

"Always."

He said *always* like he was professing love, his tone dark and sultry. *Yikes.*

"What about desserts?"

"I can make crème brûlée."

"Impressive," Kira said, keeping her tone even. "I'll be sure to let your future wife know."

She glanced up to see how her jab had landed, and was shocked to see Nathaniel's face fall, as if her remark had crushed him.

He's just feeling guilty that he's here with me when he should be out wooing Gloria.

When Nathaniel continued to appear dejected, she had a strong urge to cheer him up. But she was enjoying his discomfort too much, so instead, she asked him about Gloria. "Tell me about her."

Nathaniel hesitated; his fork suspended halfway to his mouth. He set it down on his plate. "Gloria is a vampire and heiress. She graduated when I did."

"So, she's the same age as you?".

"Yes."

"And your soon-to-be wife," she added, mostly to rub it in.

"Yes." He seemed to deliberate what to say, and it was the first time she'd seen him at a loss for words. "Gloria owns a club here in the Capital. You and I will visit there soon."

"We will?" Kira asked, swallowing the mouthful of buttered pastry.

"Yes. It will be the last time I propose to her."

"And what if she says 'no'?"

"She won't."

"How do you know? Will you woo her with chocolates and flowers?"

He smiled and lowered his eyes. "No. Those didn't work. Vampires like Gloria only respond to power. She is now the most powerful vampiress in the world. My father will not step down until I marry her and align her family with ours."

"I see," Kira said, mimicking Nathaniel's intrigued mannerisms. "What makes you so confident she'll agree to marry you? You've proposed before."

"Because I won't ask her. I will tell her and make her my wife."

A shiver ran down Kira's spine at his words. "How, exactly?"

A second later, she wished she hadn't asked. Nathaniel's face turned dark. It was like a storm had swept in, swallowing the brief interlude of light conversation they'd shared.

"My dear pet...over the coming days, I will show you *exactly* how a vampire prince claims his wife. In the meantime, your body will make for good practice."

He rose, retrieved the dog bowl that had rolled away earlier, and refilled it. "I highly recommend you drink while you can. I will have use of your body soon."

Kira stared glumly at the water bowl down at her feet. This time, she did not knock it away. Instead, she lowered her face to the water surface, and as Nathaniel seated himself at his desk, she began to lap at the water with her tongue.

CHAPTER 36

Naked

NATHANIEL

THE SOFT RHYTHMIC SOUND of Kira lapping up water soothed the tension in Nathaniel's shoulders as he sat at his desk. He was irritated—not at Kira—but simply at the circumstances. They were both caught up in a grand scheme larger than the both of them, and it saddened him that it left no room for anything else. Neither of them had a choice in what was to come, or the parts they had to play. It was a shame, because he was fond of her, more than he'd expected to be.

And he was not nearly as fond of Gloria, who did not share Kira's wholehearted passion, nor her steadfast moral compass.

Both women were ambitious, but unlike Gloria, Kira was selfless in her motivations, and her vision for a better world resonated with him. She made him believe that anything was possible—that maybe *he* could be different. And he wanted that in his life.

He wanted *her*, if only for a little while longer. To be near her, admiring her even as he tried to bend her to his will.

It was one of the reasons he was putting off the marriage proposal. He could have taken Kira to the club right now and used her to win Gloria's hand in marriage, but he was happy for an excuse to delay the inevitable for as long as possible.

He wanted more time with Kira.

Eventually, once Gloria was his, he would hold up his end of the bargain with Kira, even if he didn't like the terms—he would have to preserve her virginity so the Poplarin Pack would take her back. Even then, they would be reluctant, especially when she smelt of him...but Mark, in particular, would be unable to resist the lure of her virginity. The alpha had something of a reputation at the school for deflowering virgins and had even succeeded in extending his services to a couple of first year vampiresses who hadn't known any better.

Nathaniel exhaled through his nostrils. The thought of Mark and the other alphas being anywhere near Kira made him sick.

She's mine.

But as his, she deserved the best of what he could give her, and if she wanted to be a pack member, he would help ensure she achieved that goal. It was his fault the wolves had shunned her. He shouldn't have lost control and bitten her, and he felt sorry for that. Which was why he would make it up to her and ensure that she experienced that sense of belonging to a wolf pack.

He drummed his fingers on the desk. The room had become quiet. Kira was curled up at the foot of the bed, still in human form as she inspected the metal cuff around her ankle. He wondered if she'd ever morphed in the privacy of her dorm room.

Another thought snuck into his mind. Had she ever thought of *him* in the privacy of her bedroom?

His cock was hardening at the mere thought of her playing with herself, and a deep yearning pushed itself into his mind: he wanted to take her virginity himself. He wouldn't be gentle, either. To him, she wasn't just a quick lay like she was to Mark. She consumed him, and he would leave her in no doubt of that when he made her feel the full force of him.

He exhaled again, letting out a long breath he'd been holding. The anticipation was killing him, the urge to hold her down and penetrate her strong. The bed was right there. It was the perfect place to take her. He was ready to give her everything and unravel inside her. Would she fight him, or would she give in?

He wanted her to give in, to pull him close even as she wanted to push him away.

The sound of Kira drinking from the water bowl interrupted his thoughts. It was music to his ears.

His eyes had gone out of focus, but as he shook his head to clear it, Kira lifted her head and looked at him imploringly. She'd been ignoring him, but now that he had her attention—and she very much had his—he pushed his chair back and went to her. Crouching down, he unlocked the metal cuff around her ankle. She stayed still as he tossed the chain aside.

"Remove your clothes."

Kira tensed but obeyed. She'd already removed her blazer, and he noticed her blouse was still unbuttoned. She shrugged out of it, holding it out and dropping it at his feet pointedly with a withering look.

Hot.

The skirt was next, followed by her undergarments. Her breasts were the perfect size, the dark nipples striking him helpless, and he loved how they jiggled as she bent down to remove her red socks.

"Allow me," he said, crouching down and rolling down her socks. He bent his head to kiss her thigh, but then thought better of it—he didn't trust her not to knee him in the face.

He tossed the socks to join the pile of clothes and took a step back to admire her naked body. She stared back at him, and he was pleased to see the fire still burning brightly in her eyes.

"Your turn," she said.

Nathaniel smiled. "Maybe later. Go use the bathroom. Wash

yourself. When you are done, you will join me on the bed."

Kira's eyes widened. "*On* the bed?"

"Yes, pet."

He could tell she wanted more information, but she seemed to think better of asking. Even *he* hadn't decided what he would do to her. He only knew he needed to feel her.

He watched, transfixed, as Kira walked into the bathroom. He had a perfect view of her backside—toned brown skin, round ass, wide hips and muscled shoulders. Her legs were muscled and shapely, but he was pleased to see the slight pudginess of her thighs. He wanted to see those curves compress as she sat astride his cock.

If only.

He'd caught a glimpse of the delicate dark hair on her mound, and it left him breathless as he recalled the feel of the soft hairs on his knuckles as he'd fingered her. It was a shame he had to tame her. Eventually, he would make her shave her pussy, but for now, he savoured its thick wildness. Thoughts of pushing his cock through the nest of hairs and embedding himself inside her made his balls ache painfully.

The bathroom door closed, and he heard the lock click. Smiling, he opened a chest near the window. It was full of treasures—polished leather, soft coils of rope, glittering jewels to adorn her body, and long thick objects of every shape and size. Kira was not the first wolf he'd entertained in his room, but she would be the last.

He hummed as he pulled several items out of the chest and carried them to the bed. The sound of splashing water was audible through the bathroom door. Sooner or later, she would come back out.

And then they would play.

CHAPTER 37

The Vampire's Bed

KIRA

KIRA CREPT TO THE large bed dominating Nathaniel's room. Her skin was damp, her hair trickling water down her back. The bastard hadn't given her a towel.

Nathaniel held one out to her. "Here."

"I'm fine." Kira gave a mock-cheerful smile as she sat on the edge of the bed, making a show of wringing her hair out onto one of his pillows."

"The towel is for your own comfort," Nathaniel explained.

"Are these for my comfort?" Kira asked, gesturing at the bed, where several intimidating objects awaited. Her bravado faltered as she tried to imagine what he intended to do with the mix of chains, ropes, and leathers.

"I'll let you be the judge of that," Nathaniel said, standing before her and nudging her legs apart with his. "But no, they are not intended for your comfort."

He pushed her back onto the mattress.

The black satin sheets were cool on her skin, the mattress luxurious and soft. Without warning, Nathaniel seized her legs and lifted them high onto his shoulders.

"What are you doing?" she cried in alarm, her face flushing with heat.

"I'm going to teach you a lesson."

To her chagrin, he lowered his head, trailing a fang along her inner thigh. She watched him stop to suckle her skin. She'd heard there was an artery in the upper thigh that some vampires favoured during sex—information she wished she hadn't learnt from Victoria.

"Are you going to bite me?" she asked anxiously, conscious of her naked legs sticking up in the air, and of Nathaniel's lips as they grew dangerously close to her pussy.

Nathaniel froze. "No, Kira, I'm not going to bite you." He pressed a soft kiss on her thigh. "Never again."

Something about the way he said it made her feel crestfallen. "Why not?"

He pressed another hot kiss to her thigh. "Because I'm old fashioned. As a general rule, I never feed from the same person twice. The first bite is merely for feeding purposes—or in this case, I claimed you."

Kira felt a jolt as he said 'I claimed you'.

"So, to feed from a person once is a necessity to maintain vitality," he continued. "But to feed from the same person *twice*, well...that means something to me." Nathaniel stopped kissing her.

"What does it mean?"

"It depends on the vampire," he murmured, his eyes twinkling as he ran his tongue along her sensitive wet slit, drawing a gasp from her.

"What does it mean for *you*?" she asked shakily.

His voice was rough as he spoke. "Love."

An awkward silence ensued.

She was stunned, and more unsettled by the word 'love' than everything else combined. "So..." She searched for a change of subject, but only managed to say, "I suppose you would run out of victims quite quickly if you're choosing someone new each time. Or do you feed on animals?"

Nathaniel shrugged. "I rarely bite wolves or humans. Occasionally, animals. But I supplement in other ways."

"Meaning...?"

"Finding other sources of nutrition. For instance, some vegetables like spinach and kale are a good source of iron—" he cut himself off. "What is so funny?"

"A *vegetarian* vampire?"

Nathaniel lifted his head. "I didn't say that."

"Vegetarian," she repeated gleefully.

"I am *not* a vegetarian."

Kira couldn't stop grinning, and she was so distracted by her own chortling that she was caught off guard when his hot, wet tongue dragged over her pussy. She cried out, her arms flying to the side in search of something to hold—and her right hand closed over a long, thick object. She held it in front of her face, staring at it in confusion and distracted by Nathaniel as he ran his tongue over her again, slowly and intently.

He glanced up. "I see you're eager to move on to something bigger."

Kira's eyes widened as she realised what the toy resembled—a penis.

"No," she exclaimed, flinging the object aside so hastily it flew beyond the bed and bounced along the ground.

Nathaniel chuckled. "I'll be making you fetch that later, you know."

"No," she repeated, more firmly this time, but she squealed as the tip of his tongue slid inside her, delivering slow sensual licks.

She couldn't think, couldn't speak as he pleasured her with his tongue.

"You taste divine," he said.

"Do I?" she asked absently.

"Oh, yes. It's a shame I have to stop."

"Stop?"

"You have a toy to fetch, pet."

Her anger sparked. "If you think I'm going to *fetch* for you, you're out of your mind."

"You *will* fetch for me." Nathaniel licked her one more time before pulling back. "You will get on your knees for me and pick up the toy cock with your mouth..." he slid a finger into her, "And then you will crawl back to me..." He thrust a second finger into her, making her squirm, "And you'll drop it at my feet like a good pet."

"No, I won't," she growled, but the menace in her voice was faint, and her head flopped back onto the cool sheets as Nathaniel moved his long fingers in and out of her, causing pleasure and longing to jolt through her like liquid fire.

"I love it when you say 'no'," he said, shoving his fingers in roughly—once, twice, three times—before pulling them out. He smeared her juices across her face, leaving a wet trail running from her temple down to her cheek. "Feel how wet you are for me, Kira."

He climbed over her so their faces were inches apart, and he caressed her face tenderly.

The wetness on her face bothered her, but Nathaniel's gaze was so intense that she momentarily forgot her discomfort.

"You should say 'no' more often," he said.

"Fuck off."

Nathaniel didn't answer. Instead, he reached for the pile of accessories beside them and held up the leather collar.

"Please," she begged, eyeing the ball gag. "Not again."

"Just the collar, pet," Nathaniel said. "Lift your head."

She obeyed, and he fastened the collar around her neck.

"Is that too tight?"

"No," she snapped, even though it was.

It tightened again—too tight. "How about now?"

She was not game enough to say anything that would make him tighten the collar again, not when the neck of her human form was so fragile. She dropped her gaze. "Yes, sir."

Nathaniel made an approving sound, but he didn't loosen the collar. Instead, he showed her a long thin chain. "I hope you're ready to please me, pet. I'm going to train you how to walk on a leash."

Kira recoiled as he went to clip the leash on the collar, but there was nowhere she could go with her legs around his shoulders and her back pressed into the mattress, and her heart fell when she heard it click.

Nathaniel gave it a small tug. "Excellent. Now, here are your instructions..."

She jumped as he inserted his fingers, curling them inside her.

"Are you listening to me, Kira?" His voice had a dangerous timbre as he pumped her slowly.

"Yes," she choked. The collar was too tight, but it was nothing compared to the haywire of her emotions, and the throbbing ache of her pussy. A part of her wanted to keep going. The rest...the rest was paralysed in anticipation, wondering what he would do next.

"Good." Nathaniel pumped his fingers in and out of her again, stroking her folds with his palm. "Now, we're going to go for a walk around the room. While you are on the leash, you will not speak unless spoken to. Is that understood?"

Kira shut her eyes, whimpering as Nathaniel's hand stroked her, spreading her wetness onto her thighs. "Yes, sir."

"Good girl." He gave the leash another tug, the chain clinking as it snapped taut and caused a light pressure to travel around her neck. "Come down off the bed and get on your knees." He nodded once she'd obeyed. "Good. Now...you will crawl directly beside me, always a step behind. Are you ready?"

Her vision was a blur of tears, her face hot with humiliation, but her heart fluttered with excitement, and her body ached for Nathaniel's fingers to be inside her once more. "Yes, sir," she whispered.

"Good girl. *Heel.*"

She followed Nathaniel's heels, doing her best to stay beside him. Crawling on the floor was uncomfortable, and the prickly carpet was almost worse than the hard floorboards on her knees. They paced around the room several times, with Nathaniel humming under his breath and providing corrections when she was not in the position he wanted.

"You may morph, if you wish," he suggested. "It would be easier on you."

Nice try.

It wasn't an order, and she wouldn't have obeyed him even if it was. She didn't reply, and he didn't ask again as they finished the lap and made their way back to the bed.

Nathaniel perched himself on the edge of the mattress and pointed to the ground by his feet. "Play time is over. Come here and sit, pet."

Once she'd complied, he patted her head. "Well, done. That was a fair effort."

She drew her head away from his touch, even though she felt a burst of pride as he stroked her hair. She was surprised when he removed the leash.

"All right, pet. I think you deserve some time off leash. Go fetch your toy. And remember—use your mouth."

Kira felt a pang of fear in her chest. It was irrational, and yet, after being chained to the bed, held down, and then leashed, the prospect of wandering around the room by herself was daunting. He was giving her a tiny kernel of freedom, and she was almost too scared to take it. It bothered her how quickly he'd gotten to her.

Even so, a part of her didn't want to disappoint him, and with her newfound freedom, she crawled directly to the toy.

It was long and purple, firm but supple to touch. It wasn't as big as she'd thought at first glance—about the length of her finger—but its thickness made it intimidating to behold, and it had several rough knots and bulges along its length.

She licked her lips, glancing back at Nathaniel who hadn't moved from where he stood by the bed.

"I'm waiting, pet."

She lowered her head and tentatively placed her teeth around the toy. Her human teeth weren't much help, and it took her two attempts to pick up the fake cock successfully.

She carried it back to Nathaniel.

"Drop," he commanded.

She opened her mouth, the toy landing between them.

"Good girl." The praise was rich and warm as it flowed over her. He picked up the toy. "Open your mouth."

She obeyed, and he pushed the toy in.

"Suck it how you would suck my cock."

Kira tentatively wrapped her lips around the bulbous tip of the toy, frowning as her mouth adjusted to it. It felt nothing like Nathaniel's cock had, and it left her disappointed. It smelt and tasted of nothing, and sucking it did as little for him as it did for her.

"Where would you like this toy next, slut?"

Kira shuddered. She didn't know. She honestly didn't know.

"Down your throat?" He pushed the toy deeper.

Kira tensed, but the toy was too short to cause her to gag.

"Keep sucking," Nathaniel ordered, his expression hard.

She eyed the toy warily before accepting it back in her mouth. The sloppy sounds of her sucking it soon filled the room.

"Maybe you'd prefer the toy in your pussy?" he mused, pulling the toy out of her mouth and lifting her body off the ground. He set her down beside the bed and bent her over it so she was lying face-down, her bottom to him.

Kira tensed when she felt the toy near her folds, the pressure against her gentle as Nathaniel coaxed the tip into her.

"Wait, what about my virginity—"

"Rest assured, slut, this toy is far too short for that. What do you say?"

Yes. Say yes.

She was throbbing with need so much it was agonising.

"Yes, please, sir."

The toy pushed through her wet swollen folds, and she drew her legs apart, welcoming in the thick pressure as it slowly filled her.

"Yes," she breathed, flexing her hips to try and feel more friction, urging Nathaniel to move the toy the way she needed him to. "More, please."

"So greedy. You should hear all the options first so you can make an informed decision."

Before she could protest, Nathaniel swiftly removed the toy, spread her ass cheeks and pushed the tip against her hole, which still felt sore from the plug she'd worn earlier. "What do you think, slut?"

"No," she said immediately.

"I like it when you say no, but I don't think you've really given this a chance."

The toy pressed against her, straining against her tight asshole, the thick bulk digging in. She breathed heavily, braced for the pain... but nothing happened. That was when she realised that Nathaniel was waiting for her.

"Do you really mean 'no', Kira?"

She swallowed. "No, sir."

"What do you mean then?"

She propped herself up on one elbow and half-turned so she could see his shadowy form standing behind her. He was looking at her intently. It was only then that she appreciated his self-restraint. His erection was obvious from the rod-shaped bulge across his trousers, and though his face was full of desire, he looked concerned as well.

That was when she realised he wasn't going to force her, and that he had a moral compass, a line he wouldn't cross. Sure, it was a dark, twisted, fucked-up line, but it was a boundary, nonetheless.

"It's up to you," he added quietly.

I'm in control. It's my choice.

It was more than a little tempting to embrace this moment for all that it had to offer, to suspend her goals and ambitions, her fears and doubts, and to just experience whatever this was.

She wanted Nathaniel to touch her more than she'd ever wanted anything else. He was powerful, but there was a gentleness to him that made her feel safe, and the rules he set out for her were liberating. For the first time, her mind had shut off, and she felt a kind of peace she'd never known before, not even when she'd lived in the cottage on the edge of Nordokk.

With her body burning with desire, the decision was easy.

"Do it," she said.

Without speaking a word, he shoved the thick object deep into her ass, eliciting a sharp sting of pain.

"You fucker!" she shouted, more from surprise than pain as she twisted around to face him.

Nathaniel forced her back face-down on the edge of the bed. "It's less painful if it's inserted quickly, as you can probably tell."

She scowled. He was right, but she would admit no such thing.

"Enough. Time for your lesson." He stood and pointed to the desk. "Get up and move there."

Kira remained bent over the bed. "*Another* lesson?"

"Yes. I intend to keep you busy and productive—and I expect you to do your homework while you're here. I took the liberty of having your school books brought here whilst you were in the bathroom."

Kira spun around. "You went to my *room*?"

"Your Residential Advisor brought them here at my request."

"Susie wouldn't do that. She wouldn't go in my room."

"I didn't give her a choice. Now, think carefully before you choose to speak. I will not ask again."

Kira walked to the desk sullenly.

"Good. Now, put your school skirt back on, and bend over."

CHAPTER 38

A Hard History Lesson

NATHANIEL

NATHANIEL STOOD BEHIND KIRA, admiring her. Once again, she was bent over his desk, this time with a different toy in her ass. His cock twitched every time she opened her mouth to argue, and he wanted nothing more than to sink it into her dripping wet cunt.

He let out a long breath.

Patience.

He flipped open her history textbook to the page he wanted and placed it in front of her on the desk. He felt her shiver under him as he leant over her to tap the start of a paragraph.

"Here. Read it aloud."

There was a moment of silence as she regarded the book with confusion.

"The...*Revolution?*"

"Yes," he said, straightening. "Do not stop until you have reached the end of the page."

The tension was so thick he could have cut it with a knife. As Kira deliberated, he remained behind her, fighting the urge to take hold of her hips and press himself against her exposed pussy. He was still fully clothed, but that could change.

Kira finally began, her voice resonating as she read the passage out loud.

"Despite persistent attempts at diplomatic reconciliation, the escalating tensions between the vampire coterie and the ever-growing wolf populace soon reached a boiling point." Kira paused. "Why are you making me read this?"

Slap.

She flinched from the impact of his open hand on her ass. He braced himself for her reaction, but she seemed too stunned to speak.

"Continue," he said, stroking the skin where he'd slapped her, the beautiful bronze cheek glowing dark pink.

"However, it wasn't until the Wolf King, Bakker, abducted and married the Vampire Queen..." She stopped again, twisting to look at him. "Abducted? But that's not what happened—"

Slap.

"Do not stop. Continue."

Kira glared at him but faced back and kept reading.

"It wasn't until the Wolf King, Bakker, abducted and married the Vampire Queen, Liddia...making her his second spouse and utilising her to breed mixed progeny, that the vampires went to war...What does it mean by mixed progeny?"

Nathaniel bent over her to whisper in her ear, touching her swollen cunt at the same time. It was so wet it was dripping, waiting for him.

Soon.

She whimpered as he rubbed her.

"You're asking a lot of questions, slut," he said, enjoying the way she groaned beneath his touch. He inserted his fingers, coating them in her fluids, and pumped them several times. "They're the right questions...but I ordered you to keep reading." Without removing his fingers, he spanked her with his other hand, harder this time. "Continue."

"Do I have to?" she asked. "The next part is about the murder of—"

Slap.

She gasped. "The murder of the royal family—"

Slap.

"They're my kin—"

Slap. Slap. Slap.

Kira's indignant voice cut off, panting with her body tense and primed, her ass coloured pink on both sides.

"Finish the passage," Nathaniel said, breathing heavily as his charged body burnt with lust and greed.

"You're a monster for making me read this...and for getting off on it."

Nathaniel squeezed her ass tightly. "You are mistaken, pet. It's *you* who I'm getting off on. The reading material is simply important information you need to know."

"I don't agree with it."

"I didn't ask you to. Now, enough interruptions. Finish the paragraph." And then he could finish himself off. He needed her badly. His balls were taut and aching, his cock rock hard, and he was wound up so tightly with the need to fill her. He rubbed himself through his trousers, feeling his cock whilst his other hand probed her. It felt good to touch himself, but not nearly good enough.

"This audacious transgression," Kira continued breathlessly, "ignited the long-dreaded war, culminating in the bloody night known today as the Revolution."

Slap.

Kira flinched. "What was that for? I was reading, just like you told me to—"

Slap.

She fell silent.

"I didn't say stop," Nathaniel said.

Kira's voice, which had started strong, was shaky now. "The b-bloody night known today as the Rev—"

Slap.

She tensed. "The Revolution."

Slap.

He waited a second before dealing the next blow; light enough not to hurt her, hard enough to sting.

Slap.

Kira was struggling to continue. "There, the Wolf King and his—"

Slap.

Slap.

Slap.

"Keep. Going." Nathaniel panted, working her pussy faster with his fingers as he kept spanking her, admiring the way her ass cheeks jiggled with each strike, and the way she whimpered. He was going to make her come—but she was going to finish the passage for him first.

"There, th-the Wolf King and his subjects were slain by the forces commanded by the Vampire King, Henrikk. It was a decisive victory, leading to the downfall of the Bakkers, the once-mighty royal wolf family, as well as many of their subjects. This outcome placed the vampires to dominion over the Capital and its surrounding territories."

A silence stretched when Kira was done. Her head was bowed, her body quivering, her breathing low.

"Well done, pet." Nathaniel leant forward and stroked her hair as he kept fingering her. "You were such a good girl for me...even if you weren't the best student. Did you absorb any of the reading material?"

Kira gave a small shrug and mumbled, "Not really...sir."

"Then perhaps you better read the passage again. What do you think?"

Kira hesitated.

His hand had gone still, his fingers still embedded in her pussy.

"Yes, sir."

"Very well. Start from the beginning. And this time..." his voice was low and husky as he whispered in her ear. "You have my permission to come at any time. But know this. When you do, my cock will be inside you."

CHAPTER 39

Inside Her

NATHANIEL

NATHANIEL FLIPPED KIRA OVER, so she was sitting on the edge of the desk, her legs on either side of him.

"'*You'll be inside me?*' What the hell does that mean?" Kira asked, trying to buck him off. "You just said before you wouldn't take my virginity!"

"And I won't," he said, trying to reassure her even as he undid his trousers and took out his cock. It was rock solid with the head bulging and glistening with precum, the shaft thick and engorged, his balls excruciatingly tight. "But I never said I wouldn't come inside you."

"Well, maybe you fucking should have."

"I'd prefer to show you," he said, moving closer so his throbbing cock hit the entrance of her pussy.

"What are you doing?" she cried in shock as he glided the smooth head of his cock against her, moving it back and forth.

"Shh. I'm only wetting it for what's to come."

"Nathaniel, wait. You can't—"

"Relax. I will ensure you are still intact. Trust me." He wanted to sink his cock into her pretty little cunt.

And so he would. Just not all the way.

He dipped the head of his cock into her swollen folds, and the ache in his balls intensified. It took every last bit of restraint he had not to blow his load all over her now.

"I want you to take the tip of my cock," he said. "Mark may have the honour of being your first, but I'll be damned if he's the first person to come inside you."

Kira drew a sharp breath but said nothing, not even when he began to play with himself. She watched in fascination, and seemed torn about what to do as the sound of him jerking off filled the room. He let out a low moan as he stroked his cock, wincing at how good it felt to get it slick with her juices.

"Tell me you don't want it, pet. Tell me to 'fuck off' like you so often do."

Kira shook her head.

"Tell me the thought of my cum inside you disgusts you."

There was no answer.

He groaned, one arm on the desk for support, the other stroking his cock in quick movements. He was so close, throbbing and ready to explode all over her, but he wouldn't insert it unless she wanted him to.

He could tell from her wide eyes that she could see how much it was killing him to wait. How he was completely at her mercy. Worse still was the ache in his chest, for no matter how he had Kira's body, he would never have her heart.

"Tell me you hate me," he choked as he stroked his cock. "Tell me all the ways you've planned to kill me."

For all she knew, he deserved it. Once he helped reinstate her in the Poplarin pack, he had no doubt she was coming after him.

But even though she hated him, her desire for release took over and she grabbed his shirt and pulled him closer.

"Do you want me inside you, pet?" he asked, his voice strained from exertion.

"Yes," she whispered, gripping his shoulders.

It was all the answer he needed. He fisted his cock harder, grunting deep and loud. Just as he was about to come, he pushed the head of his bulging cock through her entrance. Being careful not to enter her fully, he rocked back and forth, fucking her with just the tip until she reached the brink.

Kira's claws tightened on him as she began to morph. It was only the first phase—the tips of her fingers, which were now sharp with black claws, her yellow eyes were a darker gold, and there was a light coat of fur at the edges of her face. She didn't shift any further, but it was a sign that the last of her control was slipping away.

"Fuck, you are so beautiful," he exclaimed. It took everything not to sink his cock in further as he pushed the head in and out, enjoying her loud cries as he neared the edge. Her tight cunt clamped down around him, the muscles contracting and squeezing his cock.

"Fuck," he groaned, pleasure erupting inside him as he came as well, filling her with his cum. After the first few generous spurts, he pulled out and aimed his cock at her, spraying her pussy, belly, and breasts with hot jets of cum.

They were panting, their bodies hot and flushed, the air in the room thick. It would have been incredible to push his cock back inside her, thrust it in all the way, and enjoy her tight warmth. Instead, he adjusted his cock to the side and lowered his weight onto her, his eyes half-closed.

The room grew quiet as they half-stood, half lay together on the desk, the seconds stretching into minutes.

Kira peered at him with glazed eyes, her expression almost dreamy, but then reality returned and her eyes widened in panic.

Nathaniel waited for her to push him off, or for the look of revulsion to return to her face, but neither of those things happened.

Instead, she confessed, "I've never felt like this before."

He chuckled and stroked her hair. "Neither have I," he admitted, his breathing still raspy. His heart was racing a thousand miles per hour. He couldn't believe it. She'd let him come inside her, marking her as his, and the thought of it drove him crazy. Her bloodstream would absorb his essence, and everywhere she went for the next few days, the wolves would scent his cum on her. *She* would smell it on herself.

He held Kira in the dim light of his room, cherishing these moments. She was his, at least for a while. And even though Mark was the one she wanted, she'd wanted him as well, however briefly.

It took everything he had not to kiss her then and there.

Mine.

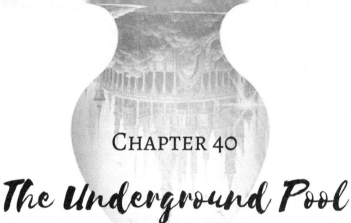

CHAPTER 40

The Underground Pool

KIRA

KIRA SAT STILL AS Nathaniel removed her skirt and cleaned her body with a damp towel. He was gentle, but now that the heat of the moment had passed, she was conscious of herself being naked. A silence stretched between them.

He'd removed the toy from her ass and thankfully hadn't made her wear any others.

"May I shower again?" she asked.

"I have a better idea," Nathaniel said. "Why don't we go swimming?"

"Are you asking me, or telling me?"

"I'm asking."

She raised her eyebrows. "I thought you said I couldn't leave your room all weekend."

"For the most part. But I think some fresh air could do us some good."

"Fresh air? Isn't the pool underground?"

"Yes."

She wasn't sure which of her questions he was agreeing to, but now she was curious.

Nathaniel handed her a woven bag. It contained the clothes she'd bought for herself when Susie had taken her shopping.

"Full disclosure—Susie was adamant about not entering your room and demanded to know where you were. I told her you are safe and with me—"

Kira huffed.

"—and that the alternative is you spend the entire weekend without clothes. It was only then that she agreed to pack you a bag."

"Why are you telling me this?"

"Because I think you have a good friend in her, and I don't want to come between the two of you. I'm sorry if I did."

Kira stared at him. "You're apologising?"

"Yes."

His eyes were so blue, so earnest, that she couldn't look away. It was hard to hate him at that moment—but she gave it a red-hot go. "What about everything else you've put me through?"

"Put you through? You enjoyed everything else, didn't you?"

"Not...everything," she spluttered. "Definitely not everything. Just...maybe some things."

Nathaniel's eyes twinkled with amusement, and she pressed her lips together to stop herself from saying anything more, turning her attention to the bag.

She selected a pair of loose lilac pants in a floral print, and a black short-sleeve blouse. Susie had also packed a brush. Kira seized it gratefully and brushed out her hair until it was smooth and free of knots.

At the bottom of the bag was a bright pink swimsuit in a candy stripe print.

"That one is a gift from Victoria," Nathaniel explained. "She seemed sure you'd like it."

"It's pink," Kira said in dismay.

Hot pink. Fuchsia pink. Eye-gouging, gag-inducing pink.

But, for some reason...it appealed to her. It was wildly different to what she would have worn in the past, but she felt strangely open to trying something new. After all, she was here to reinvent herself, so... Why not?

Nathaniel cleared his throat. "It still has the tags on it if you wish to exchange—"

Kira responded by snapping the tags off. "I like it."

It was a one-piece swimsuit, and she could tell that the form-hugging design with the ruched bodice and cut-out back would be flattering on her figure.

She was right—Nathaniel's reaction when she left the bathroom after changing into the one-piece confirmed it.

He halted in his tracks when he saw her, his eyes flaring. "I'll have to thank Victoria," he muttered.

Kira looked him up and down as well. She'd never seen him in casual clothes; a pair of khaki shorts, sandals, and a pale blue cotton shirt which was unbuttoned at the neck and had the sleeves rolled up. The sight of his straw hat, which had a black silk band that he managed to pull off, made her smile.

She was about to don her pants and blouse to cover the swimsuit, but she hesitated an extra two seconds to give Nathaniel a chance to finish checking her out.

When he didn't break his trance, she cleared her throat loudly. "Ready to go?" she asked, smoothing her blouse and crossing her arms.

"Sure," he said absently, still staring at her. "Why not?"

Or...we could stay, his eyes seemed to suggest, his head canting to one side.

*Nope, nope...*Kira flung the door open and stepped into the corridor, an excited thrill causing her body to tingle with anticipation as they crossed the common room. Why? She wasn't entirely sure.

In the antechamber, Nathaniel led her down a narrow corridor she hadn't noticed before and down a spiral staircase. There wasn't much space, but they walked side-by-side regardless, and Kira was conscious of the many times Nathaniel's arm brushed hers. Her breathing was shallow, the tension thick and dangerous, and she felt they were only heartbeats away from halting in the dark confines of the stairwell and...

And something.

Something she could not bring herself to name, but it involved his smoky scent enveloping her even more than what it was now, his chest pressed against hers, his lips lowering to capture hers.

Very dangerous.

Kira was careful not to look at him, crossing her arms to hug herself, but that only pressed her arms closer to his.

Shit.

Nathaniel's steps slowed, his head angling to look at her.

Nervous energy raised every hair on her head, and she hurried to say something to break the tension. "So..." she began, her voice stuttered as she searched for something to say. "So, err, there's technically *eight* floors to the dorms, not seven. Right?"

"Technically, no. It's still only seven floors."

"That doesn't make sense, aren't we headed for the eighth now?"

Before Nathaniel could answer, the stairwell curved around and bright light blinded her as an archway came into view. It took up the entire stairwell, and the flight of steps ended abruptly at the stone threshold. Knee-high sand was piled up on the other side of the archway, but not a single grain had spilt over. Beyond the sandy landscape was an expanse of water skirted by cliffs topped with palm trees and a sunlit sky. "Is that...the ocean?"

"It is."

Kira stared at the small cove in wonderment. White sand shimmered in the sunlight, and water in rich shades of emerald and turquoise lapped the shore in gentle waves. People swam in the calm water, sunbathed on towels, and a few were sitting on a smooth rocky outcrop.

"I thought it was a swimming pool," Kira queried.

"It is. A coastal one."

"That's misleading."

Nathaniel smiled and took her hand. It felt warm, and not cold like she'd once expected; she didn't protest as his long slender fingers intertwined with hers.

"Come on," he said, a note of eagerness in his voice.

His excitement was infectious as they stepped through the archway together. Kira gasped as the smell of fresh air and saltwater hit her senses. The sun-baked sand was deliciously warm on her bare feet, and the seagulls cried as they soared above.

As they approached the rocky outcrop, she recognised Victoria stretched out on a towel and sunbathing. She raised her head and grinned when she spotted them. "There you both are! Kira, come up here and join me. Nathaniel's been hogging you for far too long. Leave your clothes."

Kira glanced at Nathaniel.

"It's up to you," he offered, releasing her hand. "Do whatever you want to do. We're here to relax."

"I thought I was your 'pet'."

"That hasn't changed," he said. "But we're not playing right now."

She swallowed at the reminder. Less than an hour ago, he'd been inside her. Not all the way, but... enough that she'd had an earth-shattering orgasm. Enough that he'd filled her with his semen. It still coated her insides, making her feel self-conscious.

It also made her feel content in the weirdest way, giving her a sense of belonging on a beach full of relative strangers.

"Oh, yoo-hoo!" Victoria called to her. "Leave lover boy and come hang with us."

Nathaniel gave no sign he'd heard Victoria. He took a step closer and caressed her face as if they were the only two people on the beach, his voice growing deeper. "I want you to enjoy yourself. I *always* want you to enjoy yourself."

She shivered as she met his gaze but couldn't help but give him a teasing smirk. "All right...*lover boy*," she joked.

Nathaniel raised his eyebrows, his lips parting to respond, but he never got a word out. He froze when she stepped back from him, stripped off her blouse, and dropped it at his feet.

"I *will* enjoy myself," she told him, tucking her thumbs into the waistband of her pants and sliding them down.

She straightened, tossing her hair back casually as if examining the rocky outcrop, but in reality, she was spying on Nathaniel from the corner of her eye. He hadn't moved, except for the bob of his Adam's apple as he swallowed hard.

"Bye then," she said in a sultry voice, as she turned and walked away. She might have swayed her hips *slightly* more than usual as she stepped up the flat rocks. Victoria was gathered on the highest platform with her friends—all of whom were male.

"Come join me," Victoria called, shooing Felix away and indicating the towel he'd been sitting on.

Kira sat down, staring at the cove from her new vantage point. It took her a moment to spot Nathaniel, standing some way away with a group of vampires. "This place is amazing."

"Isn't it? Make sure you go for a swim before you leave. The water's warm." Victoria sighed happily as she lay on her stomach on the towel, her head resting on her arms as she faced Kira.

Kira mimicked the posture.

"So? How are you liking Nathaniel?" Victoria asked.

"He's...er...alright." She did not want to commit to an answer when she didn't know herself. She hadn't had a chance to reflect on everything that had happened between them. It felt like days had passed since she'd last sat with Victoria and her friends by the dorm fireplace, but in reality, it had only been last night. "I suppose—"

"Shh, hold that thought. Check out the eye candy." Victoria gestured at a group of male vampires by the shore who were stripping off their shirts and wading into the water. Nathaniel was easily one of the tallest, and his lean, muscled body took her breath away.

"You're drooling," Victoria joked, playfully swiping at Kira's chin with her painted nails—rainbow today.

"I'm not drooling," Kira said, but it was with great difficulty that she dragged her gaze back to Victoria.

"Whatever. But in all seriousness, is he treating you well?"

Kira shrugged. "He's not treating me *badly*. Although..." she pressed her lips together. She hardly knew Victoria, and it didn't seem wise to talk to her about what had gone on in Nathaniel's room. Then again, it would be good to confide in someone to try and make sense of her emotions. She missed Susie.

Victoria gave her a friendly nudge. "It's okay, you can tell me, hun. We girls have to stick together. If he's mistreating you, I'll kill him myself."

Kira laughed. "All right."

"But you're right, we need privacy." Victoria raised her voice. "Anyone who *isn't* Kira, piss off," she said, clapping her hands briskly and dismissing the other vampires, who leapt off the rock and dived into the water below.

"You have my full attention," Victoria smiled, sweeping her dark fringe out of the way. "Go."

"All right, so..." Doing her best to avoid intimate details, Kira recounted the way Nathaniel had made her read about the Revolution. She didn't mention the spanking, or the bulging toy he'd put in her ass, or the way he'd come inside her and then all over her. Even so, she could tell from the glint in Victoria's eyes that the vampiress suspected something more had happened than a simple textbook reading.

Victoria rolled her eyes. "Nathaniel is such a hypocrite to make you read about the Revolution."

"Is he?" Kira could think of many words to describe what Nathaniel had done...*cruel* was one of them. How dare he rub the fall of the wolf monarchy in her face, and then get off on it? But she couldn't see how hypocrisy came into it. "It's part of the school syllabus," she said, unsure why she was defending Nathaniel.

"Listen, sweetie. Nathaniel might have been there when the Revolution took place, but he is nothing like his father. King Henrikk is..." Victoria grew thoughtful. "Incredible. Powerful. Intelligent. An excellent strategist. I know he's not popular with the wolves, but we're lucky to have him as our leader."

Kira disagreed, but she knew better than to argue or disrespect the King, especially in the presence of a vampire. Life may have been better for the vampires now, but it was far worse for wolves.

"Are you saying Nathaniel isn't ruthless or cunning?" Kira asked casually.

Victoria tilted her head. "He is, but not like his father. Nathaniel's a big softie compared to Henrikk."

Great, thought Kira. It made her reluctant to meet the Vampire King.

"Out of curiosity," Victoria asked, "Did Nathaniel tell you about what he did at the Revolution? Or what he *didn't* do, I should say."

"No. What was he supposed to do?"

Victoria glanced around and lowered her voice. "He disappointed his father in a big way. Nathaniel was fourteen years old when they stormed Wintermaw Keep, and he went with his father's men and cornered the Wolf King and his family. It was Nathaniel's chance to prove himself, his father even gave him the honour of killing the King's children himself."

Nausea crept through Kira, and she shifted uncomfortably. She'd never heard the explicit details of what had happened during the Revolution, and she'd certainly never heard it told in such a candid manner.

"And did he?"

"No," Victoria scowled. "And what's worse, Nat didn't kill a single wolf that night. Nobody important, anyway."

Kira was silent. It made her feel strangely touched to think that there was a point in time that Nathaniel had shown her kin mercy... Even if that was no longer the reality now.

Victoria leant closer. "You mustn't tell anyone, Kira. It brought his father so much shame, but it's all in the past now."

"Yeah, sounds like Nathaniel's more than made up for that in his adult life," she snapped.

"Oh, yes," Victoria continued. "Quite a few, in fact. Traitors, usually. And more recently, there were two distant relations of Bakker's line right her at the academy that he took care of...Haley and what's-her-name...Alice."

"Ana," Kira corrected.

Victoria snapped her fingers. "Yes! *Ana*. Now listen, don't get me wrong, Nathaniel is great, but he failed his father during the Revolution. It may be in the past, but there are many of us who remember. That's why the King made his ascension to the throne conditional. It will be Nathaniel's thirtieth birthday soon, that's the age the Crown Prince traditionally takes his father's place. But Henrikk will only step down if Nathaniel has claimed Gloria as his bride. Henrikk thinks Gloria will balance Nathaniel out."

Kira frowned. "How do you know all this?"

Victoria waved dismissively. "I've been friends with Nathaniel for a long time, Kira. And I grew up in Wintermaw Keep. My father's the Royal Treasurer."

This new information made Kira immensely relieved that she hadn't criticised Henrikk before.

"You might be a wolf, Kira, but I'm still your friend, and I'll look out for you." Victoria gave her a tender smile. "And I know what Nathaniel can be like. If he's mistreating you at all..."

"Thanks," Kira said, her attention on Nathaniel, who had finished his swim and emerged from the water.

He looked magnificent, with water droplets running down his muscled body. She watched him towel himself off with wary eyes. Something didn't quite add up.

"*Is* he mistreating you?" Victoria probed.

Kira hesitated, unable to locate the source of her uneasiness, except that she was sure it had nothing to do with Nathaniel. Was he mistreating her? "No," she said firmly, "He isn't." She rose to her feet.

"Where are you going?" Victoria asked.

"I'm going for a swim."

Victoria turned onto her back, shielding her eyes from the sun. "Have fun. Remember, my door is always open. If you're ever concerned or feeling unsafe, you can come talk to me. Nathaniel might be our prince, but I'm not afraid to give him a piece of my mind."

"Thanks."

Kira stood at the edge of the rock ledge, contemplating the dive into the deep pool below. She could feel the wind in her hair and the sun on her skin, and gentle waves murmured as they washed the shore. She shut her eyes to absorb it all. When she opened them, she caught sight of Nathaniel as he approached from the shoreline.

"Will you dive?"

"Maybe," she replied, still eyeing the water below. It was crystal clear, and despite the depth, she could see the sandy bottom.

"Nervous?"

Kira gave her shoulder a small shrug. She was a good swimmer, but she'd never dived before.

Nathaniel climbed up the steep face of the rock with ease and stood beside her.

"You could just pin-drop," he suggested.

"No, I want to dive properly."

He smiled. "Like this," he said, showing her how to hold her arms, his touch gentle as he made corrections.

Kira emulated the posture, her muscles tensed and ready to propel her forward. But she hesitated as fear gripped her.

She was wary of the drop, of the rush of sensations that would follow as she fell, and her body felt more numb with each second she delayed. She liked having both feet—or, preferably, all four paws—on the ground. Not that she wasn't used to taking risks; scaling a treacherous mountain climb or leaping across a narrow ravine? No problem in either human or wolf form. But willingly plummeting vertically down...? Crazy.

"You're overthinking it," Nathaniel whispered, his breath warm as it tickled her ear. "Just do it."

Kira laughed shakily. "Is that an order?"

He kissed her cheek, a soft brush of his lips. "Yes, pet. That's an order."

Something clicked in her mind. Instantly, Nathaniel's order simplified everything, and with the possibility of backing out no longer on the table, her mind grew focused. It wasn't that she was no longer afraid—she was—but her fear wasn't relevant. Instead, there was no choice, and that was surprisingly liberating.

She leapt from the rock, and for a fleeting, terrifying second, she was airborne, her veins surging with exhilaration.

She plunged through the surface, her body enveloped in warm, refreshing water. The underwater world was blurry, the surface above sparkling like magic as sunlight filtered down. Down here, it was peaceful. For several long seconds, she allowed herself to float, her hair swirling around her. The pressure built in her lungs, and she kicked back up, breaking the surface just as Nathaniel dived, plunging through the surface a few feet from her and splashing her with water.

A few seconds later, he emerged, his wet hair covering his face. It made the vampire who had seemed so menacing look adorable, and she giggled as she swam closer and pushed his sopping wet fringe out of his face.

"I did it," she whispered.

"You certainly did," he smiled, his expression more alive and carefree than she'd ever seen him. "Well done. Such a clever girl."

Kira flipped him off, but she grinned happily, wishing he would smile like this more. Suddenly, the gentle swell caused her to drift closer, and she became aware of the small space between them. She licked her lips nervously and tasted salt. What would Nathaniel's lips taste like? It would take so little to close that space between them and find out.

"Want to dive again?" she asked instead.

He nodded slowly. "Whatever you want, Kira."

CHAPTER 41

Sunset

NATHANIEL

NATHANIEL AND KIRA SAT together on a grassy outcrop overlooking the cove, watching the setting sun bathe the sand in a rich orange light. The sky was a midnight blue slashed with red and gold, but its beauty paled in comparison to the woman sitting beside him.

He had one hand around her waist. At first, it had been a sign of possession, a reminder to the others that Kira was his. But now, with everyone else having returned to the dorm, they were alone at the beach, and there were no excuses as to why he held her so close.

Kira didn't shy away from him, and his heart skipped a beat when she rested her head against his shoulder.

"Are you comfortable?" he asked.

"Yes."

He leant in, breathing in her scent and counting her soft breaths and the way they matched his.

They'd spent the afternoon swimming at the cove and throwing a ball around with the others, and it was easily the most fun he'd ever had. He wasn't ready to leave and was content to stay for as long as she was. Her full lips looked just as inviting as her long, elegant neck, and he had to consciously stop himself from rubbing the tip of his tongue against his fangs. He wanted so much to kiss her, to taste her lips, and to feel her in every way. He fantasised about climbing on top of her, spreading her legs, and making love to her as if that was what they were—lovers.

Except they weren't in love.

It was a line he couldn't cross, not when he knew better. He refocused on the sunset, trying to ignore the sentimental emotion tugging at his heartstrings. But he pulled Kira close despite himself.

"So," she said, breaking the silence. "It turns out you didn't kill anyone on the night of the Revolution. 'Nobody important, anyway', were Victoria's words."

Nathaniel flinched. "Victoria has a big mouth."

"You deny it?"

"No. I do not deny that I killed someone. But I disagree that his life was not important."

Kira tilted her head at him, clearly trying to decide if he was genuine. "Who was he? The man that you killed?"

"I wish I knew. He was a wolf shifter, a member of the Royal Guard who'd gotten in the way the night my father and his followers attacked the Keep."

Nathaniel had struck, just as he'd been taught.

And he'd drunk more blood than he needed. Just as he was taught.

He forced himself to unclench his jaws. "It was an accident. That is, I did not mean to kill him. But my father..." He broke off. It was no excuse.

"What is it?" Kira asked.

"My father had kept me famished for a long time. As he did with most of his soldiers." He licked his lips at the memory. "I was young and inexperienced. I drained the guard before I realised I'd taken too much. That night was a wake-up call." His vision had blurred, but he forced himself to meet Kira's gaze. "My personal views aside, my father was disappointed in my lack of kills that evening."

He tensed as she gently traced her hand down his back.

"These scars on your back...did your father do this to you?"

He nodded, shivering beneath her touch.

Kira looked as if she wanted to ask him about it, but he quickly changed the subject.

"Victoria should not speak so openly of these things. My father has done all he can to wipe the details of my incompetence from history. Officially, I slaughtered half the Keeps' residents that night. Contradicting that narrative is dangerous. And speaking about my...*failures*...is punishable by tooth extraction."

"Ouch."

"It's a threat that has proved largely successful." He let out a long sigh. "Victoria likes to behave as if she's above the law. But it is not wise for you to speak about that night."

"Don't worry, I plan on keeping all my teeth."

Kira offered him a wry smile, but he couldn't bring himself to return it.

"Fine, I won't," she said. "But I need to ask. Besides the guard, did you really not kill any wolves that night?"

"Does it matter?"

"It matters to me."

"Why?"

She turned her head to meet his gaze. "Because, I'm starting to think you're not the monster you pretend to be."

His heart was pounding in his chest. It was so loud he was sure she could hear it.

"I've killed plenty of wolves since, and that's all you need to know." He spoke coldly, or as coldly as he could, given how utterly happy and warm he felt with Kira pressed against him.

"You don't look like a killer," she continued.

He made his voice harder. Brittle. Each word enunciated slowly.

"Neither do you."

"Don't underestimate me. I nearly stabbed you in your office, remember?"

"*Nearly* stabbed me?" Nathaniel pointed to the puncture wound on his abdominal muscles. He hadn't realised that the knife had pierced his shirt until after she'd left his office, and it had ruined one of his favourite shirts. The wound had closed over, but the skin was still red and angry. "This is *your* handiwork."

"Oh no," Kira cried, turning so she was kneeling and leaning close to inspect the wound. "I didn't realise I cut you!"

Nathaniel took her by the chin and gently lifted her head to meet his gaze. He smiled. "You're awfully concerned about my health... for a killer."

Her eyes narrowed. "I'm only concerned that it didn't go all the way through."

He barked a laugh, wondering how she'd dispelled his coldness so easily. "That may be, but just so you know... I like the sweet side of you as well."

"Since we're giving out compliments... I like the side of you that isn't an asshole."

"Do you indeed?" He peered at her through half-closed eyes, wondering whether to do it, to lean in all the way.

The last of the sun had melted into the horizon, and Kira's face was half in shadow, half illuminated by the golden glow, and her amber irises glimmered with the captured rays of dying light.

His breathing halted, and he leant in.

He had to.

Just before their lips met, Kira pulled away, her eyes cast down. "It's late. Should we go back?"

"Wait." He scanned her face, noting the worry lines that had appeared and the thin line of her mouth. Why had she averted her eyes so quickly? "What's on your mind, pet?"

He expected her to deflect the question, or to throw an insult at him. But instead, she looked resigned and sad.

"This afternoon with you was nice. Really nice. In fact, I think it's the most fun I've ever had. And for a moment..." She looked down bashfully, twisting her hands, then lifted her chin and met his gaze again. "For a moment, I even thought this thing between us was real."

Nathaniel felt a pang in his chest, and he reached for her, wanting nothing more than to brush her hair behind her ear and tell her that what they felt *was* real. Emotions didn't lie. But his fingers faltered as an aching melancholy seeped into him.

He could never be what she needed.

CHAPTER 42

At His Feet

KIRA

THEY RETURNED TO NATHANIEL'S bedroom in silence, neither of them acknowledging the almost-kiss, and what it might mean. Kira went to the bathroom to change and emerged in her satin pyjama set of singlet and shorts.

Nathaniel was sitting in his armchair, shirtless and wearing loose grey pants. He was reading his book.

"It doesn't look like you've made much progress with your book," she noted.

Nathaniel looked up, his expression roving over her. "No...it hasn't quite captured my attention."

Kira hugged herself to hide the silhouette of her peaked nipples stretching the singlet's lustrous fabric.

"Dinner is by your mat," Nathaniel said, returning his attention to the book.

She moved to the foot of the bed. There was a bowl of water by her mat, and a tray of food—steak, mashed potatoes, and peas. There was cutlery for her to use. She bent her head over the water bowl to drink; it was a rule Nathaniel insisted on.

"Aren't you eating?" she asked him, sitting on the mat and pulling the tray closer.

"I already ate," he replied without looking up from his book. "But you go on ahead. There'll be dessert later, if you're good."

"If I'm good? What's the dessert?"

Nathaniel still didn't look at her. "Chocolate cake."

Kira chewed a piece of steak thoughtfully but didn't reply.

After a minute, Nathaniel lowered his book. "Do you *like* chocolate cake?"

Kira shrugged. "I don't *not* like it. As long as it's not dry."

"It's not."

"We'll see," she quipped, scooping peas into her mouth. "How 'good' do you need me to be for this supposedly moist chocolate cake?"

His lips twitched ever so slightly. "*Very* good."

She could feel him watching her, but she busied herself with her food. "Well, it better be a *very* good chocolate cake, then."

When he didn't reply, she swallowed her mouthful of food and looked up.

Nathaniel's eyes twinkled as he held her gaze. Kira stared back, unperturbed, and after a few minutes, he returned his attention to his book.

After she had eaten, Nathaniel made her kneel at his feet on the fur rug while he read. Kira didn't mind as much as she should have; the fireplace was burning merrily, and she soaked up its warmth. There was also something comforting about being near the vampire. She leant back so that the seat of the armchair was against her back, and Nathaniel's leg warmed her side.

She hated to admit it but...it was nice.

She missed his warmth and presence in the brief moments when Nathaniel rose to stoke the fire. When he sat back down, she settled against him.

Her eyes flew open when she felt his hand on her head. His

fingers weaved through her hair, massaging her scalp and relieving the tension there.

Sighing softly, Kira smiled and shut her eyes. *Fuck it.* Who was she kidding? This *was* nice.

Nathaniel spoke. "Why don't you morph into a wolf, Kira? Would you not be more comfortable?"

"Why don't you give me some chocolate cake?" she countered.

"Because, you have not yet earned it."

To her annoyance, he removed his hand to turn a page before he resumed stroking her hair.

"How do I earn it?"

"By pleasing me."

"Is that an order?"

"Not at all. You may sit quietly, if you prefer."

Sit quietly it is, Kira thought, lying down on her side and placing her head back on her arms to stare at the fire. She was perfectly comfortable as she was. Although, she would have been even more comfortable in her wolf form, but that was something she could never let Nathaniel see. He wouldn't waste time playing with her then—he would kill her on sight if he knew what she really was.

She dismissed the gloomy thought. It would only stress her to think of things that could go wrong. Instead, she adjusted her position to make herself more comfortable.

A wolfish instinct had kicked in, and she found herself staring at Nathaniel's feet, suddenly overcome with the urge to lick them. Not because she had to, but because she could. It was a sign of respect. She wasn't sure if he deserved it, but she felt compelled to do it anyway, if only to see his reaction.

He was wearing socks, but he'd half-rolled them down so they only covered the top halves of his feet. She touched the fabric, tracing the blue zig-zag patterns embroidered on them.

"These are far too cheerful for you," she pointed out.

Nathaniel didn't answer.

She peeled back one of the socks, and when he didn't say anything pulled it off his foot.

"What are you doing, pet?"

"Making sure you're comfortable," she said lightly, pulling off the other one as well. She could have sworn Nathaniel lifted his foot ever so slightly to assist her.

"Are you quite satisfied?"

"Yes, sir," she said, pressing a kiss to the top of his foot. "Quite satisfied."

She heard Nathaniel draw a sharp breath, and wished she was in her wolf form even more now so she could hear his heartbeat. Was it racing, like hers?

"You know I don't like to repeat myself, Kira. What are you doing?"

She felt a jolt to hear her actual name. He so rarely used it.

"Nothing, sir."

"It doesn't feel like nothing."

"Oh?" she asked innocently. "What does it feel like?"

"Like I'm the luckiest man alive."

The sincerity of his words swept her away, and it gave her gesture new meaning as she continued licking the tops of his feet, slowly, patiently, her body shivery despite the fire's warmth.

Smiling to herself, she kissed the top of his foot again, this time with an open mouth, her lower lip dragging along the skin.

Nathaniel's chest rumbled in approval. "No one's ever done this for me before."

"Really? Well..." She ran her tongue around to his ankle, massaging his sole with her fingers. "I suppose you can order your future pets to lick your feet."

Nathaniel didn't answer straight away. "There will be no future pets."

Her chest tightened, trying to decipher his words as she licked the underside of his foot, firmly so it wouldn't tickle. Did he mean she would be his only pet? Or did it mean he would not take another after she left him to join the Poplarins? And why, oh why did she hope he meant the former?

"Besides," he continued. "This does not feel like something I could order you to do... No more than I could ask you to feel love, or hate, or respect."

Her heart fluttered at his words. Nathaniel seemed fully aware of the significance of this seemingly small act, as if he understood that it was not about submission or demeaning herself. It was about... *Well, who the fuck knows. It doesn't matter.*

"I think you're reading too much into it," Kira said quickly.

"Perhaps," Nathaniel replied, "but I hope not."

"I'm just bored," she said, sitting back and kneading his feet.

"Hmm. Have I been neglecting you, pet? Do you wish for me to pay more attention to you?"

"No," she lied, before adding a truth: "I want to give you *my* attention."

She lifted her head to meet his gaze, and felt another jolt as she recognised the hunger in his eyes, and saw the hard outline of his erection against his loose pants.

"Then, by all means..." he murmured, draping his arms over the sides of the chair. "Continue."

He released the book, which hit the floor with a satisfying thud.

Kira shuffled forward to kneel between Nathaniel's legs. She rubbed him through his pants. He was rock hard, and she felt the blood rush to her face as he pulled on his waistband so she could take his cock out.

Her fingers closed over the shaft and she pulled it out, stroking him up and down, revelling in its length and thickness. It twitched to her touch, and as she continued a steady rhythm, running her hand over the sensitive head, he groaned. She cupped his balls as well, and soon the head of his cock was glistening with precum.

"Like this, sir?" she asked.

"Hm-hmm." Nathaniel had shut his eyes, and his knuckles were white from clutching the armrests. "Although I would like to feel your mouth."

He didn't give specifics, and she took full advantage of that. She kept stroking his cock, but she didn't once put it in her mouth. Instead, she licked his balls, just like she'd lick his feet—slowly and methodically, as if they had all the time in the world. Judging by the low sounds he made, he liked it very much.

She continued to run her tongue along his sack, and several more minutes passed before Nathaniel finally realised that was all she intended to do.

"You, my dear, are a tease," he said.

"I don't know what you're talking about," she replied, before adding, "sir."

"Careful, pet, you are straying into dangerous territory."

Goosebumps erupted along her arms at his words, but she continued to tease him. She licked, cupped, and kneaded his balls, stroking his shaft with her other hand and going so far as to press a kiss to the head of his cock. She even feigned taking it in her mouth, breathing hot air onto the tip of his cock before returning to his balls.

He fidgeted, giving low groans of pleasure and frustration.

She smiled, loving the effect she was having on him. It was exciting, and the danger of provoking him turned her on, her clit wet and aching with desire.

"You're driving me insane, pet. I'm still waiting to feel your pretty little mouth."

"You'll be waiting a while," she said cheerfully.

"That is too cruel to tolerate."

Kira shrugged. "Too bad. Deal with it."

"I intend to. Behaviour like this is not in good faith. I fear this is something I must correct."

Without warning, he picked her up and carried her to the bed. She barely had a moment to get her bearings before he dumped her on the mattress.

"Nathaniel? What are you—"

Her voice cut off as he flipped her so she was face-down on the mattress. A rope tightened around her right ankle, binding her to the bedpost.

"Nathan—"

"Quiet."

His voice was sharp as he strode around the bed, his gentleness gone with the return of his sadistic side.

Kira threw her head around to look at him. A heavy cloud of unease shrouded the room. His eyes, which had been soft and tender before, now bore an icy, piercing glare that sent chills down her spine. Each step he took echoed ominously, paralysing her so she could not move.

She came to life when he seized her other ankle. She tried to twist it out of his grasp, but he jerked it towards the corner bedpost and secured it with rope.

"Nathaniel, you're overreacting," she stammered, but the words died as he tied her hands together.

She was lying face-down on the bed, legs forced apart, with her hands bound above her head. She managed to prop herself up on her forearms, but all she could see was the headboard and glimpses of Nathaniel as he moved about the room behind her. "Nathaniel? Come on. This isn't funny. You tease me all the time."

No answer.

"Can't fucking take a joke," she muttered.

She jumped when he spoke from behind her.

"Yes, pet. I *do* like to tease you. And this is one of those times."

She felt the mattress depress as he climbed onto the bed between her spread legs, dragging her tiny shorts up so they rode high and exposed her buttocks.

"Wh-what are you doing?"

"Quiet. I will not warn you again."

"I just want to know what you're—"

His hand came over her mouth, stifling her words, his fingers vice-like on her cheeks and jaw. She tried to bite him, but his hand was clamped tight, and he slapped her ass hard with his other hand, the sound ringing in the room.

She yelped and stopped struggling.

"Push your ass towards me," Nathaniel instructed.

Kira shook her head, her protest muffled.

"Push your ass towards me, *slut*, or the plug is going to hurt going in."

Her eyes flew open in horror as she whipped around to look at him.

"Oh, yes," he whispered, inserting his fingers in her pussy to wet his fingers. He withdrew them and rubbed her asshole, lubricating it. "The special plug I had made for you is going back in."

He pushed a finger through her sphincter, working it in as deep as it could go. Her entire body convulsed from the intrusion.

"You are so fucking tight," Nathaniel said, removing his finger and placing the plug against her sphincter. She heard him spit and felt the splatter of saliva on her ass. He rubbed it on her asshole, making her gasp as he pushed it inside. He spat again, presumably coating the plug as well... "Get ready, pet. Here it comes."

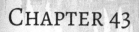

CHAPTER 43

Torture and Gratitude

KIRA

KIRA TENSED, WORRIED THAT Nathaniel was going to shove the plug in quickly like last time. But this time, it was so much worse. He took his time, using the bulging steel plug to expand her sphincter to agonising proportions, stretching her until the toy almost slipped in—*almost*, but not quite—stretching, stretching, stretching her...before pulling it back out again.

"Ffhck," she cried into his hand, her forehead hot and her eyes filling with tears as agony rippled through her. "Plsshe, stpph."

Please stop.

Nathaniel's stern voice held no pity. "Again."

He forced the plug forward, stretching her tight asshole wide and taut before withdrawing it again.

It was torture, and her heart pounded in her chest as she tried to get away.

"Again."

She groaned into his hand each time he repeated the motion. He must have nearly inserted it a dozen times, twisting and shaking the plug before pulling back.

"Fccckc...ghhh."

Fuck. You.

Nathaniel seemed unperturbed by her cussing. "Look at how well you're taking the plug, pet. You should be proud."

Proud?

Because he was pushing a toy into her ass? It was agony and pleasure combined, and she couldn't take much more of it. She was affronted, mortified, embarrassed, humiliated, and she felt sorry for herself.

And, as he stroked her hair and told her what a good girl she was... Pride was another feeling she could add to the list. Pride that he was pleased with her, and pride that she'd returned to this state of mind that was some hellish form of paradise where blissful pleasure and searing flames awaited.

"I wonder how many times I have to do this before you learn your lesson, pet," Nathaniel said, beginning the slow push of the plug into her ass again.

Kira had a new strategy. She pushed her rear closer to him, begging silently for him to insert it fully. At least then, it wouldn't be pressuring her tightest region.

"Tell me, have you learnt your lesson yet, pet?"

She growled, causing saliva to coat his hand.

Taking the hint, Nathaniel removed his hand. But then the fucker wiped her own saliva up across her face, pushing her hair back in the same motion.

"It seems you need more time for the message to *sink* in." He slapped her ass, hard. The strike stung her skin and hit the plug at the same time, forcing it to jolt forward and plunge all the way into her ass.

Kira convulsed in shock, panting and shaking as she tried to adjust to the plug. It was heavy like a lead weight, and she felt so full, so invaded.

At least the torture is over.

She felt a modicum of relief, but she tensed again when Nathaniel climbed off the bed.

What is he doing?

She heard his footsteps in the room. He soon returned and climbed onto the bed in front of her. He still wore his loose pants, lowered at the front to expose his thick heavy member, which he gripped and pointed right at her face.

"We're going to finish what you started before, slut, but there will be no obstructions this time. I'm going to show you how it's done."

That was when she noticed the red object in his hands. It was vaguely circular, resembling large, feminine lips that were spread apart far more than normal. It looked almost comical, but she had the good sense to be afraid.

"Open that pretty mouth, slut."

Kira felt too subdued by the heavy plug weighing down her rear to object. She licked her lips before opening.

"Wider."

She obeyed, but Nathaniel still wasn't satisfied.

"Wider, pet."

Her jaws strained as she opened fully, and Nathaniel placed the circular retractor in her mouth. It was smooth but intrusive, pulling her lips out of the way and covering her teeth as it forced her to stay open. She couldn't have closed them even if she'd wanted to.

Cold reality washed over her. He had reduced her mouth to little more than a hole for him to fuck.

Nathaniel didn't waste time inserting his cock, gripping her tightly by the hair as he eased himself inside her mouth.

He gave a low groan as he hit the back of her throat.

She was defenceless, and she immediately gagged, her muscles contracting around the head of his cock. He withdrew, using her mouth shallower now.

"This is not my favourite toy," Nathaniel said conversationally, pumping in and out of her mouth slowly. "I can't feel your lips on my cock, and it takes the fun out of it for both of us. But I do feel it's necessary for you to receive this lesson. What do you think, pet?"

She nodded weakly, tears forming in the corners of her eyes as Nathaniel held dominion over her, ruling her ass, her mouth, and even reaching down once to fondle the wet, aching folds of her pussy.

"Play with yourself, pet," Nathaniel ordered, sliding his full length into her mouth again. "Make yourself come whilst my cock is down your throat."

Kira's hands were still bound, but she shifted onto her side until she could touch her clit. It was throbbing with need, but she was too distracted by the shield on her lips and teeth to enjoy herself properly.

"Would you like me to remove the retractor, pet?" Nathaniel asked, moving himself in and out of her.

She nodded, attempting to say 'yes sir', but it came out a useless moan.

"I would like that too. Will you be grateful if I do remove it?"

She nodded again.

"Very well. Count to three."

Count to three? What the fuck...

"Ongggh—" she began.

Nathaniel shoved his cock deep, hitting the back of her throat.

She gagged, hard, reeling away as his hands gripped her hair tight.

"Continue," he commanded.

"Twghghh—"

Another hit to the back of the throat.

"Thrrhgh—"

Another smack, and this time, bile rose, stinging her throat and making her retch.

"Good girl. I'm very impressed." Nathaniel removed the retractor from her mouth and tossed it aside. He untied her hands and ankles, freeing her. Only the plug remained.

He patted the spot beside him on the large bed. "Show me how grateful you are, pet." When she hesitated, he added, "unless you'd like to wear the lip retractor again?"

Fine. Grateful it is. Asshole.

Kira crawled close. Nathaniel seized her hips and pulled her onto his face so she was sitting on him, facing away. She gasped as he slid his firm tongue into her clit, exploring her folds hungrily and devouring her.

She moaned, the sound becoming distorted as she bent low and took his erection in her mouth.

They pleasured each other for a long time. Kira tasted, sucked, and savoured every inch of him, her head bobbing up and down on his rigid cock. The intensity made her body burn and her breathing grow heavy, and she didn't stop until Nathaniel grunted like a wild animal and blew his load inside her mouth, washing her mouth out with his cum and filling it to the brim. Without waiting for an order, she swallowed it all, trying not to gag as she felt his thick seed slide down her throat. The taste of him made her come a few seconds later, her aching core shuddering with wave after wave of pleasure as he gripped her hair and told her what a 'good little slut' she was.

When Nathaniel had emptied every last drop onto her tongue, he did not pull out like she expected.

"Keep it warm," he instructed, licking her pussy slowly, tenderly, protecting the low embers of her fading orgasm.

Kira obeyed, shivering in response to his mouth on her clit. She breathed through her nose as she held his cock in her mouth, waiting for it to soften, but it never did. Instead, it hardened, and she was soon sucking it again and taking it so deep that she could swipe his balls with the tip of her tongue.

"Oh, yes," Nathaniel groaned. "Do that again for me, pet. Show me how clever you are."

Kira endeavoured to do just that, choking on his cock as she slid her lips down, further down, his hard length travelling deeper until she gagged. She held there a few extra seconds, lathering his balls with her tongue.

And then she was off, gasping for air.

"Such a clever little slut," Nathaniel said, guiding her back onto his cock. "Touch my balls again with your tongue. Show me how much you want it."

This time, he thrust into her mouth, fast and methodically, pummelling her throat. She welcomed him.

Kira's body was on fire, the perfect blend of discomfort, pain and pleasure as Nathaniel licked her pussy in tantalising ways, and prodded the plug in painful ways, and fucked her face like the ruthless vampire he was.

"You're mine, slut. Do you hear me?" He thrust his cock deep, and she knew he did it to make her gag. "Mine."

He thrust again, and she moaned, swept away by his intensity, and a few minutes later, she was coming on his face as his cock delivered a second load of thick, creamy cum down her throat.

"You know what to do, pet."

She did. She swallowed it all, struggling with his cock still down her throat. Meanwhile, Nathaniel tapped the jewelled end of the plug, causing her to twitch.

Afterwards, he removed the plug and turned her around, pulling her close so her face was pressed against his chest.

"You are such a good pet," he said fondly, stroking her hair. "I'm very proud of you."

They lay there panting until their breathing finally stilled.

Kira felt sleepy, but when she made to rise to go to her mat, Nathaniel's arms tightened around her.

"Stay, pet."

She frowned. "I thought you didn't want me sleeping on the bed."

"That's right, pet," he said, his eyes shut as he stroked her hair.

"But we're not sleeping now."

"We're not?"

"No. We're napping."

He took hold of a black satin sheet shining in the candlelight and pulled it over them.

The last thought that drifted through Kira's mind as she snuggled into Nathaniel's chest was that maybe the 'asshole' side of him wasn't so bad after all.

CHAPTER 44

Awake

KIRA

KIRA WOKE IN THE middle of the night. Nathaniel's arms were wrapped around her, his face buried in her hair, his soft breaths warming her neck. It felt good. Beyond good. Heavenly.

Blinking sleepily, she lifted her head and glanced out the window. Judging by the dark country lane depicted, there were still several hours until dawn...that was assuming the illusion matched reality.

Who had enchanted the frame? And why had they chosen that particular scene? Whilst the birch tree forest was hauntingly beautiful at night, there was something very ordinary about the scene, especially compared to the tropical paradise of the beach cove. Why didn't the frame depict a more interesting place? Lush rainforests with waterfalls? Snow-covered mountains? Picturesque castles perched on clifftops? Kira had seen such breathtaking places in books. The choice of the monotonous country lane felt like a lost opportunity.

Nathaniel stirred.

"Are you awake?" she whispered.

He kissed the top of her head in reply, and she snuggled closer.

"What is that place in the window?" she asked. "It looks so

ordinary."

"It is ordinary. But it's special to me."

"So it's a real place?"

Nathaniel made a sleepy sound of assent.

Before she could ask more about it, he untangled himself from her.

"Back to your mat, pet."

Kira felt a jab of disappointment, but she didn't need to be told twice. Whilst the bed was warm and comfortable, sharing it with the vampire was not a complication she needed. Not when things were already feeling complicated.

After the bed, the mat felt hard and cold, serving as a firm reminder of the reality awaiting her on Monday. But she still had Sunday with Nathaniel, and she felt a glimmer of anticipation at the prospect, wondering what the day would bring. Nothing would top the day at the beach, but she was ready to face whatever challenges Nathaniel threw her way.

And after everything Victoria had said about Nathaniel, she had a plan.

The room grew chilly as the fire burnt low, and she sniffed, pulling her blankets closer. He'd given her an extra blanket, but she still felt cold. Despite herself, she was already missing Nathaniel's warmth.

Gently, Nathaniel draped a warm quilt over her.

"Stay warm," he said, before settling back on the bed.

"Thank you," she whispered into the darkness, wondering if he heard her.

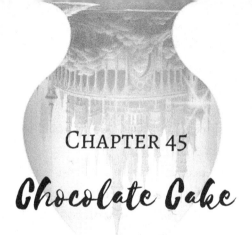

CHAPTER 45

Chocolate Cake

KIRA

"I BELIEVE YOU PROMISED me *good* chocolate cake," Kira said, sitting cross legged on the mat with a plate of frosted cake. "This is dry."

"My apologies," Nathaniel said. "I'm afraid it was sitting on the kitchen bench all night. I can, however, make you something fresh. Bacon and eggs?"

She shook her head, trying to keep a straight face as she ate another spoonful. "You promised me cake. *This* is not acceptable. I feel let down, honestly."

He raised an eyebrow. "I thought you said you didn't like chocolate cake.

"I said I don't *not* like it. And I'd love a coffee, too."

"Anything else?" Nathaniel mused.

"I like foam on my coffee. With sprinkles. Susie treated me to one at the café in the city."

He smiled and rested his chin on interlaced fingers. "Would you like to go to the city, pet? I could take you out for breakfast."

Kira's spirits lifted at that prospect, but she shrugged and looked down at her cake with an exaggerated sigh of disappointment. "Well,

I suppose we'll have to. If *this* is the best you can do."

"Oh no. For you, pet, only *the best* will do."

His tone was sincere, and Kira couldn't help but blush at how special his words made her feel.

"Get dressed. I'll take you out for breakfast in the city," he said.

Kira busied herself with the woven bag of clothes, trying hard to hide her triumphant smile. It had worked—the shopping district was exactly where she needed to go.

It was where the taxidermist's shop that Nathaniel had mentioned was, and it was where she hoped to find answers. After her conversation with Victoria yesterday, she felt like she'd hardly scratched the surface on who Nathaniel really was.

As for how she was going to distract Nathaniel for long enough to find the taxidermist's shop, she did not know. But she was satisfied that she'd successfully manipulated him into taking her shopping.

Kira was still smiling to herself when Nathaniel came up behind her and reached past to place a large jewellery box on the shelf before her. Her smile faltered.

"This is for you, pet."

She looked at the box warily, her skin crawling from Nathaniel's proximity. He was standing so close she could feel his warmth on her back. "What is it?"

"Open it and see."

Kira took one look at the object and snapped the lid shut. "Nah-ah. No way."

Inside was yet another plug. This one was much larger than the first. The jewel was still heart-shaped, but it was blood-red in colour, and the metal base was heavier and bulging so wide that he had to be fucking out of his mind if he thought she was letting it anywhere near her backside.

"I had this one especially made for you," Nathaniel said.

She crossed her arms. "That's what you said about the last metal contraption you made me wear."

"I'm satisfied with your training, so it's time we graduate you."

"Yay, me," she said sarcastically. "And before you get any ideas, I am *not* wearing that to the city, so you can take your perverted fantasies, and the plug, and shove them up *your* ass."

"If you want to go to the city, you *will* wear it," Nathaniel said, tucking a strand of hair behind her ear. "Tell me, pet. How badly do you want that cake?"

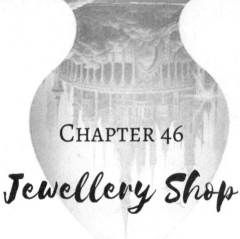

CHAPTER 46

Jewellery Shop

KIRA

THE ONLY REASON KIRA agreed to wear the massive plug was because she didn't want to stay cooped up indoors all day. She wanted to be outside in the fresh air, and to see what dirt she could uncover about Nathaniel and the nine tails scarf he'd commissioned at the taxidermist's shop. Plus, a part of her felt a thrill at the prospect of walking through the city with Nathaniel. Even though he was a vampire, and he'd put her in humiliating situations publicly, she'd never been embarrassed to be seen with him. Instead, she felt a strange sense of pride and belonging.

And a treacherous urge to please him, as if he were her master.

The large toy wedged up her butt, however, was a constant distraction as they left the academy. Kira let out a steady stream of curses as they crossed the school grounds and went out the gate.

"I feel like a fucking duck," she complained. "I can't walk properly with this damn plug!" She walked with her thighs squeezed together, trying hard not to waddle as the bulging toy stretched her sphincter and filled her anal canal and rectum. She was desperate to reach back and take it out. But stronger still was the urge to leap at Nathaniel and tear his throat out or hump his leg until she came—whichever came first. Maybe both.

"You're doing fine," he praised guiding her along the cobbled streets with a hand resting on her lower back.

"You've reduced me to a fucking penguin."

"You look stunning."

Kira huffed. He'd made her wear her school skirt and red socks, the latter of which she regretted not burning in his fireplace when she'd had the chance. She wore a dark long-sleeve shirt, and a scarf to ward out the chilly air. "And I suppose you're getting off on this?"

"Oh yes," he said, his voice dark and smooth like syrup. "You look fucking hot."

Her scowl wavered as her insides melted at the compliment, charging her with throbbing, aching desire.

New plan: Hump his leg first. Rip his throat out later.

Nathaniel halted and pulled her close. Kira blinked up at him breathlessly, bracing herself for his kiss as he leant close.

But his lips stopped short of hers. His eyes were hooded, and he was smirking as his hand slid down her back, travelling lower. She felt his hand on her rear, reaching under her skirt to prod the plug, which shifted and caused a dull ache to radiate inside her. The bastard hadn't even let her wear panties, and now he was making sure she remembered her inferior pet status.

"Can we not do this in public?" she growled.

Nathaniel's hand withdrew. "Just making sure it's in nice and snug."

Kira huffed again. She had a feeling it would take a crowbar to get the giant plug wedged into her ass out, but that was a problem for later. Right now, she desperately needed to scout the area for the taxidermist's shop. The street they were on had several cafés busy with patrons, as well as a grocer, a clockmaker, and a milliner boasting extravagant hats. The sight of the craft shops allowed her to hope that the taxidermist would be somewhere nearby.

Nathaniel led her into a café.

The café was busy, but they managed to secure a small table by the window.

"Sit," he instructed.

She gasped as she sat down. The hard chair surface pushed the flared base of the plug, causing it to burrow deeper. She squirmed, hating the way Nathaniel noticed.

"Wipe that smile off your face," she growled.

Nathaniel laughed. "So feisty."

"Maybe next time *you* can wear the plug and see how *you* like it."

"Maybe," he mused.

His answer caught her off guard. She leant forward and whispered, "Have you worn one before?"

He glanced up from his menu. "Never. But if anyone's ever going to plug me, I have a feeling it will be you."

Damn straight, Kira thought, scanning the menu.

The waiter took their orders, and soon brought them their meals. Nathaniel ordered orange crêpes and black tea. Kira, meanwhile, had a plate of mud cake with cherries and cream, and a mug of foam-topped coffee. The meal was perfect—down to the last sprinkle—but she hardly tasted it. She was scanning the shops outside, including the shopping bags the pedestrians were holding. Some bags were marked with shop names, and she noted the direction the people were coming from, trying to build a rough map in her mind of where each shop was located.

"You seem distracted by more than just the plug," Nathaniel said, sipping from his tea and looking every bit the gentleman with his pinkie raised.

Why was such a simple gesture so attractive? And why was she not as afraid of him as she'd once been?

"I'm just admiring the atmosphere," Kira answered cheerily, taking a hasty sip of her coffee. "There's no place I'd rather be than here with you."

Nathaniel gave her an endearing smile and reached forward to brush foam from her upper lip. "If only that were true, pet. That would make me happy."

"It would?"

His smile turned rueful, and he changed the subject. "Would you like to try my crêpes? They're very good."

"Sure," she said, using the spare seconds she had while he cut her a piece to survey the shops again. A woman wearing a fur coat in the distance was walking down the street. Was it possible she had just purchased it from the taxidermist?

"Open your mouth," Nathaniel murmured.

Kira did as he asked, and she chewed the food without thinking before going still. "Oh my god," she moaned, touching her lips as she chewed slower.

"It's good, isn't it?"

"Oh, my god...is that *alcohol?*"

"An orange liqueur."

"And the crêpe itself...it's so soft, and powdery on the outside, and on the inside it's—"

"Moist," Nathaniel finished, his eyes twinkling. "Would you like another piece?"

"Why not," she said, leaning forward and tearing half his crêpe away. It dripped liqueur across the table between their plates, but Nathaniel seemed unperturbed, and she certainly didn't care for good manners—not now, anyway. Table manners had gone out the window when he'd forced her to wear another fucking butt plug.

I'm going to enjoy my crêpe my way.

"It's actually rather convenient that we've come to the shops," Nathaniel said. "I have a gift for you."

"A gift?" she asked suspiciously. She'd had enough of Nathaniel's so-called-gifts. Especially if it was more jewellery.

"It's at the jewellers. We can go there next to pick it up."

Kira groaned and jabbed a piece of crêpe in his direction. "If it's another plug, it's going straight up your ass."

"It's not another plug, I assure you."

Kira was sceptical, but she hitched a polite smile on her face. "Sure. Let me just freshen up."

In the privacy of the café's washroom, she removed—with some difficulty—the plug. It turned out she didn't need a crowbar after all, but removing it was so intense that it took several attempts, and she nearly chickened out. Finally, she braced herself and wrenched it out, stifling her gasp and cringing as a deep powerful ache left her reeling.

"Fuck you, Nathaniel," she breathed, wrapping the toy in a washcloth and hiding it at the bottom of her purse. There was no way she was going to spend the next few hours waddling around the Capital. She would have to make sure she reinserted it before they returned to the academy. She felt queasy at the prospect, but she didn't want to find out what Nathaniel would do if he noticed she'd removed it.

"Ready?" she asked lightly. She felt less weighed down without the plug in place and was determined not to let Nathaniel think she was up to something.

Thankfully, he was none the wiser as he led her through the shopping district. The jewellery shop was an elegant corner building painted midnight blue with large windows facing both streets. On one side of the jewellery shop was a cobbler, and around the corner on the other was—

Her stomach dropped as she spotted a boutique with fur coats on display in the window and gold lettering that read: *Capital Taxidermy*. She'd never been so pleased to see dead animals before.

"In here," Nathaniel said, leading her into the jewellery shop.

She reluctantly followed him inside. The jeweller was a prim man with a small thin moustache and a large opinion of himself.

"Prince Nathaniel," he greeted, bowing low. He didn't deign to greet Kira, and she didn't appreciate the disapproving way he looked at her. He glanced pointedly at the sign on the wall—*no pets allowed*—but seemed wise enough not to refer to it.

Nathaniel's presence dominated the room as his slow footsteps came to a standstill. He cleared his throat loudly, and it was almost a growl, one that made the wolf in her proud, and caused the jeweller to jump.

"Greetings, miss," he stammered, giving her a quick half bow before glancing fearfully at Nathaniel. "The piece you ordered is ready, Your Royal Highness. If you would care to inspect...?"

While Nathaniel spoke to the jeweller, Kira took note of the escape routes: the front door they'd entered through, the back door behind the counter, and several shuttered windows on the front faces of the shop.

"Here it is, sir," the jeweller said, placing a large, flat case on the glass table. "For your special...*lady*."

Kira would have snapped her teeth at him in warning, but she was enjoying watching Nathaniel defend her honour. Besides her foster parents, who'd rarely accompanied her into Nordokk or the surrounding villages, she'd never had someone to look out for her like that. It was...comforting. Like she wasn't alone in everything.

Nathaniel took the case and presented it to her, opening it as if it were a ring box to reveal its contents.

Despite her apprehension, the beautiful necklace took her breath away. Judging by the short length, it was a collar, but there was nothing demeaning about it. It was an elegant piece, with bright red precious stones that sparkled in the dim light.

"For you," Nathaniel said, and there was a hint of nervousness in the way he waited for her reaction.

Kira touched the collar, tracing the red gems. "This is beautiful," she breathed. "Don't tell me these are real rubies."

"They are indeed, miss," said the jeweller, his enthusiasm seemingly overcoming his bigotry—or perhaps he was just sucking up to Nathaniel. "These are the finest stones—deep pigeon blood red with perfect clarity."

She raised an eyebrow at Nathaniel. "Pigeon blood red?"

"That's just what the colour is called," he smiled. "May I?"

Kira nodded, too startled by the glittering necklace to protest. It seemed too formal to wear during the day. Could she pull off something so elegant?

"You keep buying me jewellery," she murmured as Nathaniel fit the collar around her neck. It was a snug fit.

"Like I said, this one is special," Nathaniel said, his breath soft against her neck as he clipped the clasp into place. "This is from me."

Kira frowned. "The plugs were from you as well."

"Yes, but...this is different."

"Different how?"

Nathaniel didn't answer, and Kira licked her lips in thought. Was this just another way for him to flaunt that he'd claimed her? A red collar to match her red socks and—her heart fluttered—the red jewelled plug? For a brief second, she almost allowed herself to consider that it might mean something more.

"Aren't you worried Gloria will get jealous?"

"No. I'm not."

"Is she not the jealous type? Or do you not care if she becomes jealous?"

"She *is* the jealous type, but I'm not thinking about her right now," Nathaniel answered, still standing behind her.

Kira shivered as he kissed her neck, his lips soft and sensual as they trailed a line down to her collarbone. She all but forgot about the jeweller who was discreetly polishing a glass cabinet on the far side of the room.

Nathaniel's arm wrapped around her and caressed her belly, and his other hand slipped up her skirt.

Kira felt a pang of fear as his fingers slid up the cleft of her ass cheeks, drawing closer to her asshole. She brace herself for his inevitable reaction when he discovered that the plug was gone.

His fingers brushed her asshole, and he stilled. "Oh dear," he said, his voice growing deep and raspy. "Someone's been a very disobedient pet."

"Nathaniel," she began, but he steered her forward until he had her bent over the glass table. Her head turned to the side, her cheek pressed against the cool glass.

"Alonso, give us some privacy," Nathaniel ordered. "I'm afraid I need to discipline my pet."

"Certainly, sir," replied the jeweller.

Nathaniel held her down whilst Alonso locked the front door, shuttered the windows to darken the room further, and disappeared into the back, shutting the door behind him.

They were alone, and a dangerous tension filled the room, pushing the air out.

"Oh, pet," Nathaniel said, his tone full of disappointment, "I had hoped to spend more time preparing your ass for my cock. But it seems you are forgetting who is in charge."

"No, sir, I—"

"Quiet. The time has come for me to claim your ass. And I'm afraid I won't be gentle."

CHAPTER 47

Unplugged

NATHANIEL

KIRA HAD DISOBEYED HIM by removing the plug.

Why am I not surprised? She thought she could circumvent his order without him noticing. He was disappointed, but also excited, because now he would discipline her.

The windows were shuttered, the room dim, the cabinets twinkling with jewel-encrusted accessories, from necklaces and earrings to watches and bracelets. There was even a back cabinet with more interesting items that sparked his imagination.

Alonso had left them alone, although Nathaniel suspected he was eavesdropping. That human was obsessed with climbing the social ladder; he had been brownnosing vampires since the very beginning. Nathaniel was sure the jeweller would have traded his own mother in exchange for an invitation to an exclusive party with the upper class.

It didn't bother him if the human was listening. It mattered not—his focus was Kira.

She looked so beautiful with the sparkling ruby collar around her neck. She looked even better bent over the glass table with the hem of her short tartan skirt barely covering her ass cheeks.

His cock throbbed. Finally, he would take her, rutting her from behind, just like wolves preferred.

Just as I prefer.

He lifted her skirt, exposing her clit, and above it, the tiny pucker of her perfect little asshole. The red jewel of the plug should have been there, marking her as his. Its absence made him feel a twinge of anger.

He inserted two fingers into her damp cunt. She was tight, and he worked her until she was hot and panting. Soon, her folds were swollen and dripping.

"So tight," he murmured, pushing his fingers in and out of her before moving them to her asshole. "But not as tight as your ass." He pushed his fingers in, one at a time, watching Kira shudder under him. "Remember this moment when you're with Mark, Kira. No matter how it feels to have your virginity taken, nothing will ever compare to what I'm about to do to you." He leant over her, stroking himself as he sucked on her earlobe. "No one will ever fuck you like I do. Your hymen might still be intact after this, but you sure as hell won't feel like a virgin once I'm done with you."

"Please, Nathaniel."

"Please what?" he asked, undoing his belt and trousers and pulling out his cock, dipping the head into her dripping pussy. Her folds glistened in the dim light like the diamonds on display in the cabinets, and as he pulled the head of his cock back out, it glistened too.

"I don't want to be punished."

"That's not true," he whispered, dipping the head of his cock into her again, pushing her apart. She felt so good, but it was excruciating to hold back from pushing it into her fully. In one swift moment, he could claim her maidenhead, and feel her blood coat him, just as it should. "I think you like being punished. And you will never forget what I'm about to do to your ass. With his cock head embedded in her folds, he leant forward so he could see her face, taking care not to penetrate her further. "Speechless?"

She swallowed nervously. "You said it would hurt."

"It *will* hurt," he promised, petting her head the way she liked it to reassure her. "But it's nothing you can't handle. The pleasure, I promise, will be worth the discomfort."

Kira nodded, but her voice nearly broke as she whispered, "I'm scared."

He leant closer, sliding another tantalising inch into her.

Fuckkk. Careful.

He cupped her face with one hand and kissed her forehead. "I know. But I'm here with you. I'll never let anything bad happen to you."

The words slipped out before he could stop them. He meant them—he wanted to protect her and shield her from the world's terrors—but the words contradicted the real reason he'd gone to her cottage in the first place.

"You *are* the bad thing that's happened to me," Kira cried, startling him.

"Yes," he admitted thoughtfully, resisting the urge to push his cock in another inch, even though it was killing him, his balls aching as if they were about to explode. "Maybe I am."

Maybe I should stop this.

Doubt crept into his mind, but then Kira nodded, resigning herself to what was about to happen.

Blinding lust took over, and it was all he could do to pull out of her, sliding out of her delicious cunt.

"Ready, pet?" he asked, even though there was no way she could possibly be ready for his cock. At least a plug, once inserted, no longer pushed on her sphincter, but the length and thickness of his cock was another matter entirely. Her sphincter would be stretched wide the entire time he was inside her, rubbing her all along his shaft, and when he moved into her, she would scream.

The prospect excited him to no end.

"I'm ready," she told him, her voice stronger than it was before.

She trusts me.

It was a precious thing, one that he would cherish. One that he did not deserve. But that wouldn't stop him from using her now.

He could see her face reflected in a silver plate behind the table. Their gazes met.

"Eyes on me. Watch what I do to you, pet. Witness your master fuck your ass for the first time."

He pushed the head of his cock against her asshole. It met so much resistance that it was like hitting a wall.

"Fuck," they cried out together.

He pushed harder, and Kira's face contorted as her asshole yielded the tip of his cock.

"You are so fucking tight," he growled, pushing his cock forward. It was an impenetrable wall, but he would not stop until he'd penetrated it.

Kira gasped as he forced his cock into her, this time embedding the broad head, the largest part of him, into her sphincter.

"It's too big," she cried.

"Shh. You can take it."

"Is it nearly all the way in?"

The plea in her voice was almost laughable.

"I'm afraid not, pet. This is just the head of my cock."

She cried out when he pushed another half inch into her.

"Nathaniel, wait! I...I don't think I can do this."

"Let's find out, shall we?" Taking a tight hold of her hips, he thrust himself forward, sheathing himself fully in her perfect round ass.

Kira jerked as he entered her, screaming as his engorged cock speared her. She went quiet and still as he held her in place, listening to her pant as he stroked her back reassuringly. She was impossibly tight, and he was fucking losing his shit waiting for her to adjust to his girth.

"How does it feel, pet?" he asked.

"Too big," she sobbed.

She was crying. Why did that turn him on so much?

"Is it better now that it's in all the way?" he asked.

She nodded feebly. "Yes."

He held her lovingly and kept stroking her back, revelling in her beauty and torturing himself with every second he delayed. Kira was doing well now with him stationary, but it would be a whole different story when he was pounding into her.

"Please," she whimpered.

"Please what, slut?"

"Please...just take me. Get my punishment over with."

"Patience, slut," he said, reaching around to cup her pussy. She was soaking wet. "Your needs will be met first."

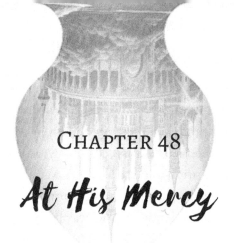

CHAPTER 48

At His Mercy

KIRA

His cock was inside her ass, and it felt colossal in size, torturously stretching her very existence and subduing her until she felt like a shuddering mass of jelly in his arms. At that moment, she was completely his.

Her mind was hazy with lust, her ears buzzing as she lay bent over the table, her ass spread and filled to the brim with *him*. With this dangerous, sinister, complicated vampire. She should have killed him a long time ago. Instead, she had let him mount her like a bitch in heat.

And she was pining for him. She couldn't believe it.

His cock had invaded her ass, that forbidden place, and it had driven her to a state of mind where she was free. She was still afraid of the unknown, but with Nathaniel in charge, she knew everything would be all right. He would take care of her, even if he hurt her. There was no stress, no worry, no decisions she had to make. She simply had to please *him*, because he was her king, her master, her conqueror, and she would succumb to his depravity and let him have all of her.

At least for now.

But right now was all that mattered. The outside world did not exist beyond the dimly lit shop. Expensive jewellery twinkled in the scarce rays of light, and even those were a blur.

She was completely at Nathaniel's mercy, and she ached with longing and anticipation as he stroked her wet folds. His cock was motionless, the head wedged inside her entrance. Even the tiniest movements were pure ecstasy, and the way his balls brushed against her did things to her she would never have imagined.

He knew what he was doing, and he stroked her pussy with determination until she was coming on his hand, shaking and sobbing as wave after wave of hot euphoria swept through her.

She slumped, feeling weak at the knees, but Nathaniel kept her pinned against the table.

"You are so beautiful when you come," he whispered, dragging his fangs along her neck. "I love it when you moan."

"I wasn't moaning...was I? Sir," she added when he didn't reply.

"You moaned like an animal," he said, his rumbling voice causing her hair to stand on end. "Now, look at me, pet."

She met his gaze in the platter's reflection, and felt the air leave her lungs from the cold intensity of his expression.

"Watch me as I fuck your ass."

CHAPTER 49

Plug and Claim

NATHANIEL

NATHANIEL WRAPPED THE END of Kira's thick brown hair around his hand, fisting it like a rein, and gripped her hip with the other as he slowly drew himself back, his thick shaft sliding out of her clenched ass inch by agonising inch until it was just his head stretching her raw and she was whimpering.

She squirmed beneath him, and he soaked in every sound and shudder she made as he pushed his cock back into her again, filling her completely.

She was so fucking perfect.

And she's mine.

As he moved his cock in and out of her, he had to remind her multiple times to look at him in the platter's reflection.

"Eyes on me."

For his part, he couldn't take his eyes off her. Her face was flushed red with exhilaration, her body curved and dipped in all the right places. Her amber eyes were molten; did she regard him with dread or awe?

"Are you enjoying my cock in your ass, slut?" he asked, thrusting in and holding her in place.

"Yes," she gasped, "thank you, sir."

"Thank you?" He held her trapped on his cock for a moment longer, surprised. "Does that mean you're a grateful little slut?"

'Yes, sir."

"And who do you belong to?"

"To you, sir."

"Correct. Remember that."

She'll think of me when the Poplarins initiate her, and it will be me she thinks of during Mark's lazy excuse for a fuck. It will be my cock she'll be craving. And she'll remember this moment and wish she was still mine.

The thought that Kira would soon be taken away from him made him feel anguish, but he pushed that feeling down, choking it with anger as he gripped her hair and fucked her like a savage beast. He no longer held back as he drove in deep, in and out, ramming her with his thick cock. She shrieked with each thrust, just the way he liked it.

"You're mine, slut. Do you understand?"

"Yes, sir," she cried.

He fisted her hair tighter and pounded her, the sound of his balls slapping her pussy filling the room.

"Touch yourself, slut. Make yourself come as I take your ass."

She obeyed, her moans intensifying. Her eyes shut as she neared her climax, and this time, he did not reprimand her for not looking at him.

He was too busy fucking her ass in quick, deep strokes, punishing her for removing the plug and rewarding her for being his.

"That's it, pet, scream for me." He slammed harder, moving faster and faster to cut off Kira mid-scream as he ploughed her ass. "You're mine. Say it."

"I'm yours."

"*Yes.*" He halted for the briefest of moments to drag her up and kiss her. She looked dazed, and if he wasn't mistaken, besotted.

"Nearly there, pet. You feel so fucking good." He pushed her back down. "Take my cock like a good little slut," he said, thrusting into her ass again and again, rough and hard, until he was filling her up with his cum and she was screaming and wailing as she made herself come for him. Made herself come for the vampire who was her enemy.

And even though he had tricked her, and even though he'd won, it hadn't stopped him from falling in love with her.

But that was something he could never confess to her.

As the cum drained out of his cock, so did the brief sliver of hope that he could hold onto her. That she could be his forever.

Kira's legs were shaking as she stood draped over the table. He helped hold her up, his cock still embedded inside her.

Her voice was soft as she spoke. "Can I...can I have a minute to myself?"

"Of course, pet." She could have all the minutes she wanted after how well she'd taken him. But first... "Where is the plug?"

Kira's head whipped round, her eyes widening in horror. "Please...no."

"Where is the plug, pet?" he repeated.

"In m-my purse," she stammered. "But surely you're not going to...?"

Her question trailed off as realisation dawned on her face. She didn't protest as he located the plug, and without lubricating it, pushed it back into her cum-filled ass.

She groaned as it seated fully, and he heard the satisfying squelch as the plug sealed his cum into her tight ass.

"Such a good little cumslut," he whispered, caressing her face and leaving a trail of dampness on her cheek—her fluids, or his, he didn't know.

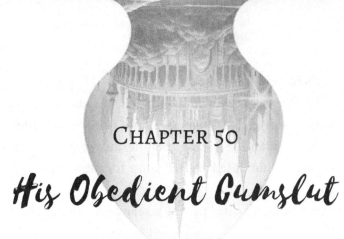

CHAPTER 50

His Obedient Cumslut

NATHANIEL

NATHANIEL WAITED OUTSIDE THE jewellery shop for Kira. She had asked for a moment to compose herself, and he was more than willing to be patient.

He whistled softly, something he hadn't done in a long time. The sun had come out, and he stood with his hands in his pockets and his coat draped over his arm, watching shoppers bustle along the street. He liked the atmosphere of the Capital, especially on the weekend when everyone wore eager smiles as they hurried from one place to another.

The low hum of chatter was accompanied by frequent bursts of laughter, and the aroma of food teased him from a nearby restaurant where diners clinked their glasses.

He was looking forward to showing Kira all that the city had to offer. She deserved to see it all. The botanical gardens were stunning. And if she wished to stay in the city until evening, he would happily take her out to dinner. There was a fine dining restaurant overlooking a lake that he was sure she'd enjoy.

Just like he would enjoy the prospect of knowing that she was filled with his cum, her tight ass stuffed with a girthy plug.

The mere thought was making him harden, and he adjusted his coat to hide his growing erection. He was still spent after taking Kira in the jewellery shop, but he would soon be ready to take her ass again.

A quarter of an hour passed, and Kira still hadn't emerged from the shop. He grew restless, but didn't want to rush her. They were in no hurry. But when ten more minutes passed, he grew concerned, and he knocked before re-entering the jewellery shop.

At least, he tried to—the door was locked.

"Kira?" he called, hammering his fist on the door.

Surely, the jeweller hadn't hurt her? He was only a human, but then again, Kira's guard had been down. His heart raced as he knocked on the door again. "Kira, are you all right?"

No answer.

He didn't hesitate before breaking the door down. It flew off its hinges and landed with a crash inside the shop, shattering a glass cabinet.

Kira was nowhere to be seen.

The only person in the building was the jeweller, and Nathaniel found him cowering in an underground cellar, shaking with fear as he described a dark beast with lashing tails and teeth.

Nathaniel's blood ran cold it dawned on him: Kira had shifted.

Not so obedient after all.

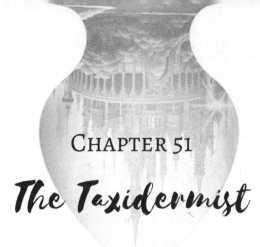

CHAPTER 51

The Taxidermist

KIRA

KIRA REMAINED PANTING OVER the glass table after Nathaniel left. She was shaking after what had happened. The bastard had dominated her, fucked her relentlessly, and plugged her up. She hated him for it, even though she'd secretly wanted him to.

Her core pulsed with satisfaction, her muscles relaxed and limp, but she was also sore. Her anus was raw, and she could still feel the space that Nathaniel had occupied as he claimed her.

He'd kissed her cheek before leaving, the door clicking shut behind him.

The air was still, the room completely silent except for the murmur of the city streets filtering in.

Kira pushed herself off the table. She couldn't afford to waste a second. She took a step towards the door, wincing as the cum inside her rectum squelched.

Ugh.

Ignoring the protests of her body, she moved to the door and locked it, hoping it would slow Nathaniel down. Every step she took caused a squelching sound to come from her rear. It made her feel dirty, and a little satisfied at the same time.

She approached the windows.

Squelch, squelch, squelch.

The windows were shuttered, but she peeked through the slats.

Damn it.

She'd hoped to escape through the windows on this side of the building, but Nathaniel was standing on the corner of the block. She had no chance of making it to the taxidermy shop next door without him noticing—not via the windows anyway.

I'll have to try the back entrance.

She walked behind the shop counter and swung the door open, revealing the jeweller crouching behind it. He startled, and Kira snarled when she realised what he'd been doing: watching her through a peephole.

How long had he been watching?

Had he seen her and Nathaniel have sex?

She felt a jolt. Was he taking pleasure in her helplessness while Nathaniel had his way with her?

She scowled. "You're a sick fuck."

The jeweller, to his credit, stood tall and straightened his jacket indignantly. "I am a voyeur."

"*You* are dead meat," Kira snarled, golden light flooding her vision as she allowed herself to shift. Morphing felt good. She'd been cooped up in human form far too long, and the tension left her body as she grew powerful, furry, and muscled. Her snarl turned deep and harsh, and she only had to gnash her teeth once before the jeweller was fleeing down the hall.

She prowled after him, but he disappeared through a side door. Rather than pursue him, she made her way to the back of the building. The plug was gone for now, but it would reappear when she returned to human form.

She shifted back into her human form as she exited the building. A small yard full of crates adjoined the two shops, and adrenaline rushed through her as she approached the taxidermy shop's door and slipped inside.

The musty smell of furs was strong. The shop was dark and deserted.

"Hello?"

There was no answer, and the sign on the door had the word 'open' facing her, confirming that the shop was closed.

Even better.

The privacy suited her. She only hoped the shop owner was still here.

The shop was larger than the jeweller's had been, with several backrooms full of work benches, sowing equipment, bolts of cloth and mannequins. There was one room that, while clean, smelt of blood and leather. and the skinning knives and flaying tools left her in no doubt of what its purpose was. Disgusted, she began to retreat—and nearly missed the faint scent of magic emanating from a narrow staircase in the back of the room. The sharp tang had been hidden beneath the smell of death.

But not as well hidden as it had been in Nathaniel's office. The smell was stronger here, and she'd detected it even in her human form.

She followed the source up a rickety staircase to the next landing.

Each step creaked loudly, causing her to tense and become hyperaware of every detail, including the discomfort the plug was causing her as she climbed the stairs.

"Hello?" she called.

"Go away please, I'm closed!" an old woman's voice responded.

Kira continued up anyway, crossing the landing to an open door. "I'm not a customer. I'm here to ask you something."

"Come back another time" the woman responded, her voice edged with fear.

"I mean you no harm," Kira said, peering tentatively into the room.

It was filled to the brim with shelves and bookcases teeming with plants, books, scrolls, melted candles, and glassware. The centre of the room did not exist, occupied instead by towers of what looked like junk, and there was a small single bed squeezed in by the window as if it was an afterthought. An elderly woman was lying there with the covers pulled up to her chin, and her face was pallid as she clutched a curved dagger in her trembling hands.

"I'm sorry for the intrusion," Kira said quickly, keeping one eye on the woman as she took in the room's clutter. Everything reeked of magic, to the point that she could taste it on her tongue, like sweet, sour, and bitter, and there was an earthy undertone as if the room were alive. Glancing upwards, she saw fungi growing on a wooden chandelier that was covered in cobwebs and missing most of its candles. She forced her attention back on the woman, moderating her voice to be gentle. "Truly, I mean you no harm. I only wanted to ask you about some furs I found at Volmasque Academy."

Recognition dawned on the woman's face, and she lowered her dagger. "It's you."

"Er, yes." *I guess?* "It's me."

"Kirabelle. The lost daughter."

"Actually, it's just Kira. I was never lost."

The woman's eyes narrowed shrewdly. "No, not to us. But you were hidden, and now, you are found."

Kira hesitated, wondering whether it was worth asking the old woman to clarify her meaning, or whether it would only result in more cryptic nonsense. "Who are you?"

"My dear, you of all people should know who I am."

"You're a witch," Kira said. *And you're batshit crazy.* She wasn't sure whether to be fearful of the woman, or to fear *for* her. Witches were outlawed, a seemingly useless law given that they'd been wiped out. Or so the public was told.

"I'm Barbara," the woman said, her gnarled hand shaking as she dropped the dagger into an open bedside drawer.

"What's wrong with you, Barbara?"

"So blunt and direct. Such a wolfish quality. Don't worry, I mean it as a compliment, dear." The woman sighed and settled back onto her pillow. "I'm dying, as you can see. But I won't suffer much longer. He will come for me soon."

Kira tensed. "*Who* will come for you?"

The old woman opened her mouth to speak, but then a creak sounded from downstairs. She held a finger to her lips.

The creaking of footsteps on the stairs made Kira's stomach knot, and she contemplated whether to shift.

"Speak of the devil," the witch breathed, her head flopping back on the pillow. She shut her eyes. "He's here. I didn't think he would come so soon."

"Who's here?" Kira asked, backing away from the bedroom door as the dreaded footsteps crossed the landing.

She realised who it was a second before the dark figure appeared in the shadowy doorway.

"Nathaniel," she blurted, trying to think of how to explain what she was doing here.

Before she could say anything, however, Nathaniel's gaze slid from her to Barbara.

Does he know she's a witch?

"She's not well," Kira began, but her voice cut off, horrified.

Nathaniel's demeanour stiffened the moment he laid eyes on the witch. His eyes glinted red and his lip curled back, revealing sharp canines that had lengthened.

"No," Kira breathed, her muscles tensing as she realised what he was about to do.

A fraction of a second later, Nathaniel rushed towards the witch, teeth bared and ready to feed.

CHAPTER 52

The Witch

NATHANIEL

NATHANIEL WAS SURPRISED TO see Kira in Barbara's room, but he took one look at the witch's weakened state and rushed to her bedside, his fangs elongating.

At the last second, Kira stepped in between him and Barbara protectively and shoved him full in the chest.

"Kira, what are you—?"

"Fuck off, Nathaniel," ," Kira snarled, her golden eyes flashing dangerously.

He frowned. "What are you—?"

"Leave her alone."

"I only need a minute or two," he said, trying to step past her, but she shoved him again.

"I mean it. If you think I'm letting you sink your fangs into this poor woman, you've got another thing coming."

Realisation crept in. Kira thought he was going to kill the witch, and even though she was mistaken, he felt a surge of pride for her as she faced him.

"It's not what you think," he began, keeping his voice calm and measured. He lifted his hands in a gesture of reassurance. "I promise,

I'm not here to hurt Barbara." Slowly, so as not to startle Kira, he unbuttoned the cuff of his sleeve and turned it to expose his wrist. "I'm here to help her."

Kira did not budge, her gaze tracking his every move. "How? And why would *you* help a witch?"

"Why? Because she's the last witch in existence. And as for the how..." he lifted the underside of his wrist to his mouth and sunk his fangs in, piercing the flesh. Crimson blood trickled down his wrist and dripped onto the floor.

He held Kira's gaze as she regarded him with surprise, apprehension, and something he couldn't quite decipher.

He took a step forward, and this time, she let him pass as he went to Barbara's side. The witch was weaker than he'd ever seen her, with a face etched with deep lines, and her blonde hair turned grey. Her chest was rising and falling in shallow breaths, and she looked barely conscious as she still peered at him through pale eyelashes.

"Nathaniel," she whispered. "You're here."

"Barbara, what have you done to yourself?" he asked, holding his wrist to her lips.

"I got a little carried away."

As Barbara drank his blood, vitality returned to her body, and with it, the ageing effects of magic reversed. The slack muscles and wrinkles of her face smoothed, and her gnarled hands became smooth and youthful, the strength returning as she clutched his hand and drank deeper. Dry, brittle hair became a glossy, vibrant blonde, and when she finally pulled away, the focus had returned to her forest-green eyes.

It had only taken a few minutes, but Barbara was back to full health and now looked to be in her mid-thirties.

"I took too much," she said with a click of her tongue.

"Not at all." He ran his tongue over his wrist, his saliva helping the wound clot faster to stem the bleeding.

Kira, meanwhile, was gaping at him. He knew she could see the way his eyes glowed red, as they always did when he bit someone. Except this time, it hadn't been him doing the feeding, and he felt weak.

Kira was watching him in confusion. "I don't understand."

"Witches can live a very long time," Nathaniel explained. "Indefinitely, some would say. And in order to conjure magic, witches sacrifice their own life essence. If they cast too many spells, it leads to depletion, ageing them, and can even result in death. Vampire blood has regenerative properties that can—"

"You make it sound so clinical, Nat," Barbara complained.

"*Nat?*" Kira repeated.

If he didn't know any better, she was jealous. But she had no reason to be. He'd never felt any romantic inclination towards the witch, and besides, she was several generations older than him. After living a few centuries, most witches and wizards became silly and struggled to string two sensible words together, as if the magic had addled their brain.

Barbara swung her legs out of bed and turned to Kira, her voice bubbly. "Listen, deary. It is the reciprocal nature of things. Using magic is terribly draining, as I'm sure you can imagine. Once upon a time, witches, vampires and wolves all lived closely together. We witches relied on vampires for their blood to restore us. Contrary to what you may think, the vampires of olden days were not our enemies. First and foremost, they were healers."

Kira, who had been listening patiently, scoffed. "Vampires were healers?"

"Oh, yes. Before King Henrikk led this generation astray, and I suppose the generation before that wasn't much to boast about, either...the world was very different. We had balance. Although, Nathaniel's father isn't solely to blame for the state of things. The Wolf King started it all by invading the vampire's ancestral lands, and the two factions have been at each other's throats ever since. Actually, I remember a time—"

"Are you really the last witch?" Kira asked.

Barbara nodded sadly. "As far as I know, I'm the last witch in the world. Nathaniel has protected me all these years."

"Has he now?" Kira asked, looking at him quizzically.

"Oh, yes, indeed. It was his idea for me to live in the Capital. Rather genius, in my opinion, although I wasn't keen on the idea at first. But really, who would suspect an illegal witch to be hiding amongst the thick of things? Good thing vampires can't smell shit—it's the wolves I worry about. There is a reward for turning in illegals, as you know, and while most wolves wouldn't ever think to do such a thing..."

"I won't tell anyone," Kira said.

Barbara smiled. "I know."

"May I ask, how old *are* you, exactly?"

"I have no age as you would measure it, dear."

"I don't understand," Kira said, confused.

"Witches are ageless," Nathaniel explained. "Forever young, rendering them almost immortal—except when they're stupid enough to use magic recklessly," he added, raising his voice pointedly for Barbara's sake.

"I wasn't being reckless," Barbara said, hopping out of bed.

"We've talked about this, Barb. I can't help you if you're dead."

Kira sank down to perch on the edge of an overturned cauldron. *"Barb?"*

"Oh shush," Barbara said to him. "Just wait until you see what I've made for you."

She began pottering around a teetering tower made of hodgepodge items. It was a fascinating collection featuring several rusty cauldrons, beaded jewellery, animal skulls, mouldy tapestries, and, amongst other things, a lute with broken strings, all held together by a mesh of green brambles.

Barbara plucked a blackberry from a branch and popped it into her mouth as she disappeared behind the tower in search of something. "Ah, here it is."

She reappeared on the other side of the tower hauling a heavy coat of white fur.

Kira flinched as Barbara threw it down at their feet, a cloud of dust swirling into the air, causing them to cough.

"What is that?" Kira asked, squinting her eyes.

"For Nathaniel and his bride," Barbara said, hopping over a ship anchor and dusting her hands off. "A thirtieth birthday and wedding gift in one. I dyed the fur white, as you can see."

He went to pick up the fur but hesitated. Kira staring at it looking sick.

"It's not real fur," he murmured.

She shook her head and rolled her eyes. "I know. I was just thinking that maybe I need to get you a wedding present, too."

Her words rendered him speechless, and he suddenly lacked the words to calm the sparks of hurt in her eyes. She smiled and shrugged before turning away, and it was like watching a door close.

"Well? What do you think, Nat?" Barbara asked. "Will that woman of yours be satisfied?"

He tore his eyes from Kira and stooped to pick up the coat. The imitation fur was flawless, a black undercoat topped with soft snow-white hairs that shimmered and glowed like sunlight on snow. The coat was floor-length, with long elegant sleeves and deep pockets, and it was a fashion statement that would be adored by almost any vampiress. "Truly, you've outdone yourself, Barb. But I cannot comment as to whether Gloria will be satisfied, I'm afraid."

Barbara snorted. "S'ppose not. Will you take it now?"

Nathaniel nodded. "Yes. My father will be here at the end of this week." He glanced at Kira, who was watching him closely, before adding, "I may as well show him the coat."

"That was my thinking too," Barbara said. "Let Henrikk think that Nathaniel killed something—the big bad wolf." She chortled. "It's why I was rushing to complete it. Your birthday is just around the corner, and we can't afford for anything to go wrong with your coronation."

"But this isn't real fur," Kira said. "I can smell the magic on it. And before either of you say anything, I know that most of the furs in Nathaniel's office aren't real, either." Her eyes searched his, seeking confirmation.

"Got a good sense of smell, this one," Barbara said approvingly, "And a sharp wit. Are you sure she isn't half-witch?"

Nathaniel gritted his teeth in warning. "Quite sure." He turned to Kira. "You are correct. Most of the furs aren't real. But my father won't know the difference."

A tense silence stretched as the words hung between them.

"You're lying to your father...to protect real wolves?"

"Yes."

"So...what about Haley and Ana?"

He hesitated. "They are alive and well."

Kira's eyes widened. Now she was the one who seemed at a loss for words.

"It sounds like the two of you have a lot to talk about," Barbara commented, ushering them to the door. "And *I* have a lot of work to do. Why don't you both show yourselves out?"

"Wait," Kira said as they reached the corridor, turning back to face Barbara, "What did you mean when you said—"

Slam.

Kira blinked as the door shut in her face.

"Barb has a one-track mind," Nathaniel apologised. "Once she gets an idea in her head, she prefers to be left alone to work."

He led Kira downstairs and back out onto the street.

"I thought you were going to kill her," Kira admitted as they stood outside the shops. "You're the so-called hunter, and yet you're friends with a witch." She sighed and turned away. "I feel like I don't know you at all. And the more time I spend with you, the less this all makes sense..."

Nathaniel's chest grew tight. "I know. It's my fault for not confiding in you."

Kira gave a bitter laugh, the sound ringing oddly. "You have no reason to confide in me. Not when you think so little of me."

"That's not true. Not in the slightest. The opposite, in fact. I think very highly of you."

Kira's gaze flickered at him for the briefest of moments, and she looked as if she wanted to say something, but then she gave her head a small shake. "Let's go back."

They walked in silence, ignoring the shops as they made their way back towards the academy.

"Barb and I have been friends for a long time," Nathaniel said, holding the coat under one arm as they walked. "I admire that you came to her defence, even if you thought I was going to kill her."

"What else was I to think when you brought the fangs out?"

Nathaniel licked his lips. "What I'm trying to say, Kira, is that I admire you."

"Oh."

They passed through the school gates and made their way across the grounds. It was early afternoon, and there were a few students enjoying the sunlit grounds. He took Kira's hand and guided her off the path and into a secluded courtyard.

"We should talk," he said, sinking down on a low stone wall. He felt unusually tired, a result of more than just the blood loss. He was tired of this charade.

Kira remained standing, and before he could think of how to begin, she spoke.

"Tell me a truth, Nathaniel," she implored, emotion creeping into her voice. "Tell me something about you."

Just one truth? When there were so many weighing him down?

"I care about you, Kira," he said hoarsely. "More than you know."

Her lips parted in surprise, and tentative hope blossomed on her features.

"Then why pretend you're a monster?"

"Because, this is so much bigger than the two of us."

"The two of us?" she asked.

His heart skipped a beat, and he reached for her hand and pressed a kiss to it. "Yes, the two of us. You said you wanted something more, something real. Well, so do I."

He held her gaze, trying to convey the sincerity of his words, even as he wondered what the hell he was doing. Nothing good could come of this, and yet, nothing bad had ever come from listening to his heart.

The hint of a shy smile played at the corners of her lips, and he offered a tender smile, drawing her closer. He yearned to kiss her, to feel the warmth of her lips against his own, and, if the stars aligned, she would kiss him back.

His breathing stilled as he cradled her face, savouring the moment and the delicate flutter of her eyelashes. Time stood still as their lips drew near, his heart thundering in his chest. Never had anything felt so right as this moment.

Suddenly, a scream pierced the air.

CHAPTER 53

His Blood

KIRA

"SOMEONE, ANYONE, PLEASE HELP!" shrieked a woman's voice from the direction of the academy.

Kira hurried out of the courtyard towards the cries, Nathaniel a few steps behind her.

They found Chloe, a member of Susie's pack, at the top of the front steps to the school entrance. She was a thin girl with red hair and round glasses, her face collapsed in relief when she saw Kira.

"Chloe, what happened?" Kira asked.

"It's Susie," Chloe cried, sobbing hysterically as she clutched at Kira's hand. "Please, you have to come, quick. I don't know how much longer she has..."

"What do you mean?" Kira asked in alarm, letting Chloe drag her inside and across the foyer.

"She's been attacked. One of the vampires has bitten her. She was so pale when I found her, and—" Chloe's voice choked, and the rest of her words were intelligible.

Kira exchanged an alarmed look with Nathaniel as they rushed to follow Chloe to the library where a crowd of students was gathered outside. They were chattering loudly over the top of the librarian,

Mrs. Andra, who had transformed into a wolf and was snapping her teeth at anyone who tried to enter the library.

She took one look at Nathaniel, however, and let them pass.

They found Susie in a back corner of the library, lying unconscious on the floor.

"No," Kira gasped, her insides clenching with dread at the sight of her friend. "Susie!" She rushed forward to kneel beside her, pushing her strawberry blonde hair out of the way. She was pale—too pale, her skin clammy and cool, and tinged with greyness. A streak of blood trailed down her throat and matted her hair. The sight of two puncture wounds, which had torn the skin of her throat in horizontal gashes, made her sick. Whoever had bitten her had not been gentle.

"Susie, can you hear me?" Kira whimpered, too stricken to cry as she turned Susie's face towards her. *"Susie!"*

A moment later, Nathaniel was by her side, biting his wrist and pressing it to Susie's mouth where blood pooled on her lips and chin. He tipped her head back, talking to her, encouraging her to drink.

Kira watched helplessly, hoping and praying with every fibre of her being that she would survive.

"Just the taste should wake her," Nathaniel said. His voice was reassuring, but he wore a haunted expression. "If it's not too late."

Please, let it not be too late, Kira thought, sitting behind Susie and supporting her head in her lap. *Please.*

A long minute passed where nothing happened. Nathaniel's blood just trickled out of Susie's mouth.

And then out of nowhere, Susie's eyes fluttered open, and she drew a half-breath, choking and spluttering.

"There, there, everything is all right," Nathaniel said, his soothing tone a comfort to Kira as well. "Drink, and you'll feel a lot better."

Susie recoiled, staring at Nathaniel in horror. "N-no. Get away from me!"

"Susie, it's all right," Kira said, leaning forward so Susie could see her.

"Kira?" Susie clutched at Kira's arm, leaning as far away from Nathaniel as she could as she spoke in a high-pitched voice. "Someone attacked me, and..."

"Did you see who?"

Susie breathed heavily, her eyes darting around them at the bookshelves before settling back on Nathaniel. "A vampire," she finally confirmed. "But I don't know who. I stayed after the sleepover to clean up. I heard someone come in, but I had my back turned, and I didn't get a good look at who it was."

"It wasn't Nathaniel," Kira said firmly. "He's been with me all day."

And all night.

"It's going to be all right, Susie," Chloe chimed in, nodding exaggeratedly as if to reassure herself.

Susie hugged herself and shivered violently. "I'm cold."

"Let Nathaniel help you," Kira urged. "It will help, I promise."

Nathaniel, who had sat back patiently on his heels, held his wrist out in offer.

Susie wrinkled her nose and reluctantly accepted his blood.

"So gross," Chloe whispered to Kira.

Kira gave a tight smile. She had a feeling Nathaniel had heard what Chloe had said.

Meanwhile, the disgust on Susie's face had faded, and she lapped at Nathaniel's wrist eagerly, the colour returning to her face.

"It's like he's healing her," Chloe whispered.

"It is like that," Kira agreed quietly. Nathaniel? A healer? Who'd have thought?

"Can you imagine what would have happened if I hadn't come back to get my pencil case?" Chloe whispered fearfully to Kira.

Kira's stomach turned. Susie would probably be dead. No one

would have come into this room on a Sunday, not even the librarian. Come Monday morning... she did not want to imagine that at all.

Meanwhile, Susie had latched on to Nathaniel's wrist and was feeding hungrily, her increasing strength obvious.

Nathaniel swayed where he crouched. Alarmed, Kira leapt forward to intervene.

"Enough, Susie," she said, prying her friend away from Nathaniel.

"Just a little more—"

"Enough."

Nathaniel rose to his feet unsteadily, and Kira stooped to pick up the fur coat they'd discarded and handed it to him.

"You're white as a sheet," she said with concern. There were deep shadows under his eyes, as if he hadn't slept in days; he looked as if a breeze could have blown him over. Nathaniel had always presented as strong, healthy, and in top physical shape, so to see him unwell made her worry. "What do you need?"

"I'm fine," he said. "I just need to sleep this off." He kissed her on top of her head. "Stay with Susie. Ensure she goes to the sick bay—she feels stronger than what she is, but she needs bed rest and plenty of fluids."

Kira hesitated. It was not the appropriate time, but... When was there an appropriate time? She leant close to his ear, which was easy with his posture stooped as he clutched at a bookshelf.

"And the..." she licked her lips. "Plug?"

"Ah." Nathaniel gave a tiny smile, as if he'd only just remembered. "I'll leave that up to you..."

"Easy choice," Kira muttered.

"Do me a favour," he continued. "See if you can convince Susie and Chloe not to tell anyone that I gave blood. It is best my father does not find out."

"I'll try," Kira said doubtfully.

Even if Chloe managed to keep a secret, it wouldn't take much for the students to put two and two together. And with Susie beaming happily at Chloe as she wriggled her feet back and forth, Kira was far more concerned about Nathaniel.

"*You* need to feed," she said, steeling herself for the offer she was about to make. "Do you want to drink my b—"

"No," Nathaniel said, shaking his head. "But thank you."

He ducked in to kiss her cheek, and before she could stop him, he left.

Kira touched her cheek, a pang of disappointment filling her chest. She was torn between going after him and staying with Susie. It was two edges of the same sword. Should she go after the man who maybe kind of wasn't as bad as she'd thought? Or look after her own kind?

If Susie was truly weaker than she seemed, then she should help her. After all, Susie had been there for her from the moment they'd met.

I can't abandon her now.

Convincing Susie to stand was more difficult than she'd expected. She kept giggling, her knees buckling, as if she were delirious with euphoria. It reminded Kira of the laughing potion.

As she coaxed Susie towards the library's exit, her mind wandered to Nathaniel. All this time, she'd thought him cruel and selfish, but today, he'd given so much of himself in order to save two people—a witch and wolf. Two people that most vampires wouldn't have lifted a finger for. The deed had cost him, too. He'd already been weak from giving blood to Barbara, and yet, he hadn't hesitated before helping Susie.

His compassion made her see him in a new light, and she wanted to run after him and thank him. But Susie needed her more.

With Chloe's help, she escorted Susie to the sick bay, dodging questions from the curious students.

"I really can't talk about it," Chloe said, pushing her glasses onto the bridge of her nose. "Top secret."

If Kira hadn't been doing most of the work supporting Susie's weight, she would have facepalmed.

Despite her best efforts, the students had deduced what 'Prince Nathaniel' had done and were telling their own colourful version of what had happened.

"Nathaniel's father will be disappointed," Victoria said matter-of-factly, trailing after them. "But I'm glad Susie is all right, Kira. That's the important thing. If I find out who did it, I'll nail them up."

"Me too," Felix said, who'd offered to help support Susie—which Kira appreciated, especially since Chloe hadn't been much help in lifting.

"I'm worried about Nathaniel," Kira said in a low voice.

Victoria waved dismissively. "He'll be fine," she said. "I guarantee he's already passed out on his bed, assuming he made it that far."

This did nothing to reassure Kira.

"She's exaggerating," Felix said to her in a low voice. "But I'll check on him, I promise."

"Thanks," Kira said gratefully.

"You're such a softie," Victoria said to Felix as they waved goodbye, her tone sounding both fond and disparaging.

Kira stayed by Susie's bedside in the sick bay all afternoon, torn between being there for her friend and finding Nathaniel.

Would he even want her there when he was ill?

Come dinner time, Susie was stable but still not entirely herself. She was woozy on her feet when Kira helped her to the bathroom, and at times became exuberant and said slightly odd things. Chloe left soon after helping Susie eat her strawberry mousse and jelly. By the time ten o'clock rolled around, Susie was sound asleep.

Kira was dozing when she was woken by Mrs. Bur, the warden.

"Still here?" Mrs. Bur asked. "It's past midnight. Get to bed."

"But, what about Susie?" Kira asked.

"I expect to discharge Miss Susanna at noon if she is feeling better," Mrs. Bur said. "But I promise to keep a close eye on her, and I am confident she will be fully recovered come morning. Vampire blood is an extraordinary thing."

Kira winced. Even the warden knew—or assumed—that Nathaniel had given Susie his blood.

"Off you go now," Mrs. Bur said. "You can come back at twelve tomorrow."

Kira was reluctant to leave, but Mrs. Bur briskly shooed her out.

Standing alone in the dark corridor, Kira rubbed her eyes and suppressed a yawn. She didn't feel like returning to her own bed. Her heart drew her to Nathaniel. The mere thought of him feeling unwell had kept her on edge.

She was halfway up the corridor when she made up her mind, and she broke into a run. Her footsteps rang across the foyer and down the dorm staircase, continuing past the fifth floor until she reached the vampire dorm.

Her conversation with Nathaniel and Barbara was at the forefront of her mind. The reciprocal relationship between vampires and witches had come as a shock, but it was only now that she realised they'd left an important piece of information out. As she'd sat by Susie's bed, the missing puzzle piece had clicked into place.

It was not a two-way relationship. It was a triangular nexus that included wolves as well. Someone had to be the lifeblood of the vampires, and who better than the wolf shifters, who were of the earth and of magic? Except somewhere along the way, vampires had forgotten about their side of the bargain. They couldn't simply take what they wanted—they had to remember to give as well.

Nathaniel clearly knew that and had given his blood freely even though it had made him vulnerable. Her heart swelled. He was not at all who she'd pictured him to be, and while there was still so much mystery surrounding him, she was starting to learn that the biggest secret he was hiding was his kindness.

The dorm was dark and empty when she arrived. She didn't stop until she reached his door. He needed her.

And for better or for worse, she needed him.

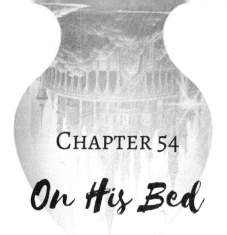

CHAPTER 54

On His Bed

NATHANIEL

NATHANIEL DRAGGED HIMSELF OUT of bed and across the dim room. His body felt heavy and lethargic. Whoever had disturbed him was about to witness the wrathful side of him.

His heart leapt as he swung the door open and saw Kira standing there, her thick hair highlighted by the magical lamps of the corridor, her eyes burning with intention as she stared at him. Her face was flushed and her breathing ragged as if she'd run here.

"Kira, what's the matter—?'

"I want you to feed from me," she said, stepping into the room and placing a hand on his chest.

He froze. "No. Out of the question."

"Yes, you need to regain your strength."

"No, I can't."

"Why not?" she demanded. "You've fed from me before."

A flicker of hurt crossed her features, rendering him speechless.

"I know you said you were old-fashioned," Kira continued, "and that biting someone a second time meant that you loved—" she faltered. "That it means more to you than just feeding. But I want to help you. Please, let me."

Nathaniel pressed a finger to his lips and glanced down the quiet corridor.

"Come inside," he said, drawing her into the room and swinging the door shut, plunging them into darkness.

His vision allowed him to make out her features in the faint light emanating from the hearth's burning coals and the red glow of the lamps. Her gaze was locked on his, her brown eyes glimmering with gold and shadowed by thick lashes, her strong jaw set with that fiery determination he'd fallen in love with.

If only he'd given her the chance to get to know him, then maybe, he could accept her offer.

"I don't deserve your blood," he explained.

She shook her head in disbelief. "How could you not? After everything you did for Barb and Susie today. You were selfless."

"You don't know everything about me."

"I know enough. I know you hide behind a mask, pretending to be someone you're not. I know you're thoughtful and generous. And I know you need my blood."

"I'm touched by your offer," he said sincerely, taking her hand and lifting it to his mouth. At the last moment, he turned it, kissing the underside of her wrist instead, his body thrumming with the pulsing rhythm of the blood-filled arteries flowing there. His fangs extended in anticipation, grazing her skin. Kira made a soft husky sound that didn't make it any easier to resist the hunger aches building in him. It was a testament to how much he needed to feed that he could sense the way her heartbeat sped up. The silence stretched as he held her hand, his body trembling on the precipice of temptation.

"Why are you fighting it?" she whispered. "I'm giving it to you freely."

He laughed weakly. "It's an attractive offer."

"And yet you're declining it. Look, I know I'm not the one you want, Nathaniel, but I thought that maybe..." her words trailed off, the tremble in her voice caused a protective instinct in him to roar to life.

He cupped her face, surprised to feel damp cheeks. She was crying. "Kira, listen to me. *You* are the one that I want. There is no one else for me but you."

Except we can never be together.

He pushed that thought away, finally allowing himself to do what he'd been craving to do ever since he'd gone to the cottage a few weeks ago. When he'd been struck by what a strong and beautiful woman she'd become after all these years. When her defiance had caused hot lightning to crackle through him and made him yearn to be someone other than the son of the Vampire King. To instead be someone who could whisk her away to a different life, away from the clutches of fate that had sunk its talons into both of them before they were even born.

In the quiet peace of his bedroom, he could imagine that such a future was possible, and he leant down, closing the distance between them and taking what he needed, something he desired more than food and life itself. Something he craved more than her blood.

To kiss the woman he had fallen for.

He captured her mouth. A wonderful shiver rippled through him as his lips met hers, and time stood still, allowing them this secret moment in the safety of darkness. She was warm in his arms, her lips soft and sensual. He inhaled her scent, a fragrance reminding him of wildflowers and hidden forests.

He waited for the moment she would pull away.

And then she returned the kiss. His soul came to life, flooding with light as she melted into his embrace. Each brush of her lips was a gift that made him question everything he'd ever known, and when the kiss turned heated, it sent powerful ripples through his being that set his heart ablaze.

When they drew apart, Kira remained in his arms, and neither of them spoke for the longest time. Their breaths mingled, a perfect moment that consumed him with its sweetness. Her kiss had imprinted on him, and he pulled her close, touching her, wanting her.

"What does this mean?" Kira asked. "For us," she added, making him hold her tighter.

"That depends."

"On what?"

"There's so much I need to tell you."

Kira laughed low.

"What?" He asked.

"It can wait," she said, ripping his shirt and sending buttons flying.

"What are you doing, Kira?"

She pushed him towards the bed. "I want you."

He let out a weak laugh. "Now? I'm not sure if I can."

"You can and you will—after you feed from me." She stripped her clothes off and pushed him onto the bed, landing on top of him with her hair cascading down to brush his face. Her eyes gleamed with mischief as she said his own words back to him: "I wouldn't ask if I didn't think you were capable."

"I'm glad you have so much faith in me."

"Quiet," she said, unbuckling his belt and undoing the fastening of his pants.

Even in his weakened state, his body redirected what little blood he had to his cock, which was hard and ready for her, even if he didn't have the energy to do anything with it.

Kira straddled him, lifting her hips and guiding his length so it pressed at her rear entrance.

"It might interest you to know that I'm still wearing the plug," she said.

A lead weight dropped into his stomach, his voice strained as he replied, "Is that so?"

"Yes."

"All this time?"

She took hold of his wrists and pinned them above his head. "Yes. Feel it and see."

"I can't. You've pinned my hands."

She grinned. "That's too bad."

He chuckled, and with significant effort, was able to pull his wrist free of her grasp. He reached around, squeezing her ass before trailing his fingers until he felt the smooth surface of the plug sealing her asshole. His cock twitched. "My, my...Aren't you sore from wearing it all evening?"

"Shh," she said, lowering her weight onto him.

He groaned as her tight pussy encompassed him, forcing his cock to spread her apart as it began the slow deep slide into her.

Except it never got that far. She stopped herself, hovering above him so he was only an inch inside her.

That was the moment he realised she was still saving herself for Mark. He tried not to let himself dwell on that. And with Kira's hot wet folds swallowing his cock head, it was easy to lose himself in the moment and just be thankful for just how lucky he was that she was here.

"Fuck," he said, his voice trembling from more than just fatigue. "You feel so good."

"It's about to feel better," she said with a sly smile. She reached behind, cringing as she pulled the plug out, and threw it across the room.

They both flinched at the sound of shattered glass.

"Was that the mirror?" she whispered.

"Indeed. Did you know that breaking a mirror will bring you seven years of bad fucks?"

Kira snorted. "I hope not." Her eyes narrowed at him, her delicious lips curving in a smile as her pussy clenched around him.

"But maybe you can save me from that fate?"

His entire body tensed as her muscles tightened around his cock. "I'll see what I can do," he said hoarsely.

Suddenly, she raised her body so his cock slipped out, lowering her body so she was lying on top of him. The skin-to-skin contact was incredible. Her body was hot and smooth, her breasts soft and perfect, her stomach plump against his abs where his cock was wetting her skin. He wanted her so badly, and it was heaven and hell at the same time as she wriggled up so they were face to face, his hard cock lying happily between her thighs. She moved her hair aside so her neck was bare and within biting distance of his mouth.

Fuck.

"Bite me," she instructed.

He blinked at her through his haze of pleasure. "Kira..."

"Please, just take what you need. I want you to."

Double fuck.

Her amber eyes were soft, and the way she was begging him to feed from her nearly made him lose his load then and there.

He was starving for blood, and he was starving for her. It was the ultimate test of his integrity on whether he could resist biting her. It wasn't a matter of whether he loved her or not, because he did, heart wrenchingly so. But he could not give her the love she deserved, and so he held back...even if he was holding back by a mere thread.

His fangs were sharp and aching, her body soft and willing as she pressed against him, and he wanted to take her in every way. To have and to hold. To tease, bite, fuck, and claim her. To steal her breaths and feel her heartbeat as her warm blood coated his tongue and he thrust into her again and again until she cried his name.

"Nathaniel," she pleaded, her graceful neck exposed.

"Sit on me," he rasped. "Let me feel your ass."

Kira blinked at him. "Then, will you feed on me?"

His lips twitched. "Then, my dear, you will receive further

instructions."

He watched, enthralled, as she did as he said, sitting back and guiding his cock to her entrance.

He let out a throaty breath as she lowered herself onto it, looking every bit the stunning conqueress that he'd known her to be when he'd met her. Her face scrunched up as she slid down, inch by glorious inch, champion of his cock and victor of his heart as her ass spread to take his thick, raging girth.

They moaned in unison as he bottomed out inside her. With her ass full of his cock, she leant back, her breasts rising up as her hair tumbled back down, her face lifted to the ceiling as she adjusted to his size.

He ran his hands along her body, worshiping her with kisses as he traced her slender curves and took handfuls of her breasts, squeezing them. "Such a good girl. Now, show me what you can do."

He loved the whimpers she made as she lifted her hips up, sliding up the length of his cock until it was just the head inside her, pushing on her sphincter, threatening to drag it apart. Then she eased back down onto his cock, blinking and moaning before repeating the motion.

"That's it," he said, enjoying the tight feel of her. "Show me what a good slut you are."

Her movements were slow, her obvious discomfort riddled with pleasure as she took what she wanted from him. He could tell she was close, and it caused his balls to tighten as he prepared to shoot her full of cum.

"I have this fantasy," Kira began as she rode him, her long hair brushing his chest, "that you suck my blood during sex."

Fuck.

He had fantasies like that too, and they involved filling every hole in her body while he feasted on her.

Kira stopped moving. She tilted her head ever so slightly to expose her throat. Was she doing that on purpose?

Nathaniel groaned, dragging a fang along her skin, sharp enough to scratch, gentle enough not to break the skin. That tiny action made his balls squeeze and his cock tense, and he was ready to sink his fangs into her and fuck the life out of her.

With a harsh, animalistic growl, he grabbed her shoulders and rolled her so she was on her back. Her naked body was so fucking beautiful against the black satin sheets. He wanted her here with him, now and forever.

Kira arched her neck again. She was definitely doing it on purpose.

His voice was harsh and ragged, his mouth inches from her throat. "Don't. Tempt. Me."

He flipped her so she was face-down and dragged her close by the hips. He'd pulled his cock out as he changed positions, but that was easily rectified, and he paused for only a second to admire her tiny pink asshole before he forced his cock back into her ass, savouring the way she squealed as it impaled her. He thrust into her again, punishing his tired body just as much as he was punishing her.

He gripped her hair and tugged her head back whilst covering her mouth with his other hand, silencing her moans as he fucked her.

"Take my cock, slut."

She was everything he wanted, but he couldn't bring himself to bite her, not for a second time.

Even though he loved her. He couldn't burden her with that confession, because love represented trust, and he'd squandered the opportunity to earn hers by not being honest with her.

By keeping secrets.

Starting tomorrow morning, he would tell her everything. And then maybe, if she forgave him, they could build a bond that was stronger. She could have all of him, if she wanted.

In the meantime, she would take his cock.

I'm sorry, he thought, fucking her harder until she was screaming, until he knew he was hurting her just as much as he was making her feel pleasure. He pounded away the guilt as he pounded her ass, relishing the sound of his balls slapping against her cunt and the way she screamed his name as she came on his cock.

He roared with all his might as he slammed into her, filling her with his seed, pumping her full until it was spilling out everywhere onto the bed. Even then, he didn't stop until she'd come a second time, because this was all for her.

He would make her dreams come true, even if he had to break her heart along the way.

By the time he was done, there was no need for a plug, because she and the mattress were covered in his cum and lying in it.

She eventually sat up, but he was too spent to move.

"Are you all right?" Kira asked as she poured them both a glass of water.

It was almost funny that she was the one asking *him*, but she wasn't the one wheezing with shaking muscles.

"I'm fine," he said, draining the glass before pulling her close. "Stay and sleep with me."

"Up here? On your bed?" she asked coyly.

"On *our* bed."

His vision danced with stars as Kira nestled against him, her warmth and fragrance bringing him solace. Their breaths mingled, as if the universe held its breath as he deliberated ruining this moment and telling her everything.

He had to. Kira deserved honesty.

But she was fast asleep, her face serene; her trust in him implicit. It would be cruel to wake her only to hurt her.

He brushed a hair from her face.

Soon, when she wakes up.

Nathaniel stayed awake, stroking Kira's hair long. He loved that she smiled in her sleep, and he cherished the feel of her nestled against him. As soon as she woke, he would tell her.

He dozed, catching a few minutes of sleep here and there, but he felt too agitated to sleep properly.

When the dawn light grazed the tops of the birch trees outside the window, he kissed Kira's forehead.

She murmured happily, her smile widening as she rotated onto her back, stretching and snuggling closer. She snored softly, looking content.

Suddenly, bright golden light appeared around her, and he watched in awe as she began to morph.

Chapter 55

His Two Loves

<u>Nathaniel</u>

Kira shifted, not partially, but completely, until a wolf that was more than just a wolf lay beside him.

His breathing stilled.

Her elegant fur was midnight black, its softness tickling his forearm which draped over her body. Her nose was damp and cool against his hand, and long curved fangs protruded from her delicate snout even with her jaw shut. She may have only been half vampire, but her teeth would have put any vampire's to shame. What would they feel like on his neck? His body tingled. It was something he'd like to find out.

Kira murmured in her sleep, flicking the tips of her nine tails. They did not resemble the furry plumes of a nine tails wolf, but they were equally magnificent. Instead of fur, each tail resembled a whip: black and glossy like polished leather, thick and sinewy at the base, and tapering to sharp, fine points that mirrored her deadly claws, each one hidden amongst tufts of fur.

She was more beautiful than he could have imagined. He'd already known she was something special, a rarity in their world: half nine-tails wolf, half vampire.

Some people called them hybrids, but that term could describe the offspring of any wolf shifter and vampire—not that such children were common either. His father had outlawed marriage and reproduction between vampires and wolves, and had often told him that 'it matters not how many wolves you fuck, provided it is meaningless'.

Except Nathaniel's relationship with Kira was far from meaningless, and now that he'd met her, he couldn't have walled off his heart if he'd tried. He remained perfectly still, hyperaware of every breath she took.

Kira was a true hybrid, a cross between royal lineages, with a vampire queen for a mother, and a pure blood wolf, a nine tails, for a father. She held more power than his own father, King Henrikk. It was why he'd been so hellbent on wiping out the royal wolf family and their children, and it was also why, after many years of reflection, Henrikk had suddenly become obsessed with finding such a wolf of his own.

Nathaniel noticed Kira's muscles tensing, and his arms tightened around her. He swallowed his anger and forced his breathing to calm as he pushed thoughts of his father away and focused on her.

She was the most beautiful creature in the world.

Both of them were.

Because in her wolf form, there wasn't just one of her. There were two, almost like twins, lying side by side. One slept sleepily on its back, just as she had in human form, with its paws tucked above her, her furry tummy exposed. It may have been her upside-down position, but her upper lips had rolled down in a smile, exposing the full impressive length of her fangs. The second wolf was curled up between him and Kira, its whip-like tails curled around itself protectively around all three of them the leathery texture smooth on his skin.

Two breathtakingly gorgeous wolves. It made him sad to think there should have been nine. One person, but with nine wolf selves when she transformed, each with an impressive set of tails. The rest of her wolf selves had been slain when they were cubs, all seven in quick succession, but two had gotten away, bundled up and rescued.

He knew. He remembered.

He was there.

As Nathaniel beheld Kira's true form, he vowed to do all he could to become the person she needed him to be, even if they could never be together.

Even if she went back to hating me. Maybe, she'd never truly stopped.

But first, a painful truth. One she might not forgive.

Kira stirred, still half asleep as she leant past him, bypassing his lips to nuzzle the side of his neck.

The air left him. A kiss was a kiss, but for her to nuzzle him left him in awe. It was an intimate act for a wolf, a gesture of devotion usually reserved for husband and wife.

He was humbled. Not only had she felt comfortable enough around him, at least on a subconscious level, to transform into her natural form, but she'd honoured him with the affectionate caress of her face and muzzle against his.

His chest tightened. *Oh, how little I deserve her.*

Being careful not to wake her, he shut his eyes and nestled his face in her fur, inhaling deep and holding her close, wishing circumstances were different.

Even though he hadn't done half the horrible things credited to him, in some ways, the secret he was keeping from Kira was worse than all of them combined.

CHAPTER 56

Sleeping with the Enemy

KIRA

THE DAWN LIGHT AWOKE Kira, and she tensed as she realised where she was: in Nathaniel's arms. It was warm and safe here, where she was content to stay for as long as he was. She peeked an eye open and felt momentarily confused to realise her head was resting on her paws—and for her other wolf, the paws suspended in the air in a relaxed, trusting posture.

Horror swept through her.

I've morphed. I've fucking morphed in front of the prince of bloody vampires.

Her head snapped up, her gaze darting to Nathaniel, but somehow, miraculously, the vampire was still asleep; his face smooth and his breathing soft and even.

He hadn't seen her, not yet.

Don't panic.

But she was panicking. He had one arm wrapped around one of her wolf selves—the one that was fierce and wary—whilst his face rested on the soft fluffy belly of the other, the one who was more passive and amenable. Both of them had submitted to Nathaniel, in the end.

She watched him sleep from two sets of eyes, fear coursing through her as her mind raced. The urge to flee, to fight, to strike before he struck her, was high.

But she couldn't do it. She could not hurt him. And yet she was in far greater danger than he. It was as if she were caught in a spider's web, where the tiniest movement would alert the predator of her existence. And yet, she *had* to change back into human form—right now, before he saw her.

Right now, Kira! she screamed internally, her heart thundering in her chest as she forced the transformation to begin. Golden light shimmered around her, long black claws and fur receding, face flattening, tails vanishing, and her bodies merging into one. She returned to human form, praying the vampire would not wake.

Had it been a mistake to change back? In her human form, she was more vulnerable than ever. Fear made skin crawl and she couldn't breathe.

She forced herself to turn her head to look at her enemy's face, dreading that his eyes would be open, the irises bright crimson.

Nathaniel didn't stir for several more minutes, during which she lay beside him, stiff and paralysed, trying to decide whether to stay or flee.

I'm safe, I'm safe, I'm safe. He didn't see. She tensed when he spoke.

"Good morning," he greeted, stretching and yawning before he'd even opened his eyes.

She relaxed a little, forcing her tone to be cheerful as she clambered off the bed. "Good morning!"

"Is everything all right?"

"Of course. Just fine." She went to the window, pretending to look out at the forest, but she didn't see any of it. She was all too conscious of the vampire's intense gaze on her back.

She startled when he appeared behind her and placed his hands on her shoulders, massaging the muscles as if he hoped to relieve the tension there.

"Kira, I need to tell you something. Can you come to my office?"

"Your office? N-now?"

"Yes. It's a better place for the conversation we need to have."

Kira didn't ask why that was the case. Instead, she got dressed and followed him upstairs, glancing at him worriedly. She had the horrible feeling she was making a mistake, but she was too anxious to do anything but follow him up the steps.

Nathaniel looked as if he hadn't slept at all, and they walked at a slow pace up the stairs.

"Do you want to stop and rest?" she asked when they reached the foyer, her fear momentarily forgotten. He was weak and slow. If it came to a fight, she could finish him and run. Or, if she didn't have the heart to kill him... She could just run.

"No need," he said lightly, but his smile was strained.

It made her heart clench, and her fear dissipated, leaving her worried for his wellbeing.

Don't be a coward. He needs to feed

She opened her mouth to offer him her blood again, but shut her mouth at the last second. While she believed in the good side of him, she still needed to be cautious. He was still her enemy until proven otherwise, their cooperation a temporary thing. His refusal to drink from her last night may have been a saving grace.

She couldn't afford to forget that, even if she felt for him now. What scared her the most was the fact that she'd been comfortable enough around him to subconsciously morph into her wolf forms. It was almost as terrifying as the feelings coursing through her—the way her heart beat faster whenever his hand brushed hers. The way she couldn't bear the thought of leaving his side, and the way her instincts to protect him kicked in.

Because he was her mate. Whether she'd chosen him or not.

Whether it was fate, or simply that he'd claimed her. But she was irrevocably his.

Or so it felt as she followed him into the forbidden corridor. The cramped narrow space filled her with dread, and as they approached his office door, every one of her hairs stood on end. Something was wrong, but she couldn't grasp what it was, only that she felt like she was walking into a trap.

The door was slightly open. Frowning, Nathaniel swung it open, and they entered cautiously.

Nathaniel stopped dead in his tracks, and she nearly collided with him. Sliding past, she froze when she saw the fear etched on his face, and she followed his gaze to the tall armchair behind his desk.

It swivelled around, revealing a man whose face she'd only ever seen on banners and tapestries.

A chill ran down her spine.

King Henrikk was even more formidable than his son. He had the same ice-blond hair, but he radiated cold hostility like Nathaniel never had; the chill seeping into her until her body felt rigid. Instead of Nathaniel's square jaw, his chin was long and pointed, and he had a thin, sharp moustache that reminded her of a curved blade. His eyes were different too: the irises pale and colourless as if the life had been sucked out of them, blending with the milky-white of his eyes to emphasise the stark blacks of his pupils.

King Henrikk did not speak, but he gave a small smile as his sharp gaze studied them. Kira sensed whoever spoke first would lose.

Nathaniel lost.

"Father? What are you doing here?" There was a note of fear in his voice. "I wasn't expecting you so soon."

"And yet, here I am," Henrikk replied, his voice smooth and sticky like treacle, dangerous enough to entrap them both. "A little bird told me you gave your blood to a female wolf, and I came to see if it was true."

His unspoken question hung in the air, his pupils darting with interest between Nathaniel and Kira. His tiny erratic movements giving her the impression that he was only a heartbeat away from either chortling in good humour or committing murder.

"It's true," Nathaniel said, lifting his chin. "She was injured and close to dying."

"She was injured and close to dying," Henrikk repeated softly, interlacing his hands. 'How noble. And wasteful."

"One of our kind bit her," Nathaniel continued matter-of-factly, and Kira felt a surge of pride at how calm he was. "A wolf murder by our kind, especially of a school student, would only shake people's confidence in the Crown."

"Your sympathy for the wolves is far more damaging to the Crown, as is your apparent weakness." Henrikk said, his voice turning jagged like a knife's edge. He gestured at Nathaniel. "You look worse than I feared. You gave far too much blood."

Nathaniel's lips pressed into a flat line, and Kira knew he was thinking of Barbara. He'd given blood to not only one person, but two.

"I'll be fine in a day or two." Nathaniel said. "I just need to feed."

"See that you do. Yesterday, you were my son, the prince. Today, you are a disappointment."

Nathaniel winced, and Kira opened her mouth to speak in his defence, but he gave his head a quick shake.

"Leave," Nathaniel said to her in an undertone.

"Ah," said Henrikk, rising from his chair and acting as if he'd only just noticed Kira. "Is this the wolf you've been training? Well, well, well...I've heard a few things about *her*."

Kira's blood curdled as the Vampire King rounded the desk, but to her relief, he merely perched himself on the edge.

"Tell me, Nathaniel, is she tractable?"

Nathaniel did not answer, and Kira growled on instinct,

suppressing the urge to morph so she could snarl properly.

"She's got a nasty growl." Henrikk shook his head in disappointment, but his lips curved in a smile as he eyed her. As she stared into his lifeless eyes, she realised that Nathaniel's eyes weren't anywhere near as cold as his father's, which held neither warmth nor empathy. "I see she is not yet domesticated."

Nathaniel spoke through gritted teeth. "She is still in training."

"Indeed? Well. Let us see how effective of a teacher my son is." Henrikk did not take his eyes off Kira. His smile vanished as he pointed to the pelt-covered ground at his feet. "Come and kneel here, girl."

"Wh-what?" Kira stammered, looking to Nathaniel for help.

Nathaniel's face darkened, but he didn't say anything, only turned sad eyes to her.

"Do you require me to repeat myself?" Henrikk barked, his voice making her flinch. *"Come!"*

Her wolf instinct, which so often told her to be bold and attack, or to at least hold her ground, now told her to cower. Nathaniel had never raised his voice with her. She whined as she looked between father and son, her gaze settling on Nathaniel.

Help me, she begged silently with her eyes. *Please, do something.*

"Ah, I see the problem," said Henrikk, his voice softening. "My son has not told you, has he, my dear?"

"Told me what?" she asked, her nausea surging.

He slid off the desk and strode slowly towards her, his presence like a dark cloud that expanded to choke the light from the room.

"Father, don't," Nathaniel said, his voice harsh as he stepped in front of her.

Henrikk placed his hands on Nathaniel and threw him aside with ease.

"Weak." Henrikk sniffed, his attention returning to Kira.

He loomed near, the tan-coloured wolf tails swinging from his scarf sickeningly, the smell of them overpowering. Her insides curled as she realised the scarf of eighteen tails Nathaniel had gifted his father, the one he'd reportedly made from Haley and Ana's tails, were not fake. They were very real.

She flinched when Henrikk seized her chin. He tilted her face up so abruptly it strained her neck muscles.

He smiled fondly at her. "What is your name, wolf creature?"

"Kira," she said, the word sounding strange from the way his cruel fingers dug into her cheeks.

"Wrong. That is not your name...*slut.*"

"What?" she spluttered.

He cackled. "So clueless. So in the dark. Perhaps, it is not so terrible that your training is delayed. It will allow me to better appreciate your compliance later."

She was too afraid to speak, her chest emptying as Henrikk's sharp stare clawed out her soul.

Nathaniel came out of nowhere, leaping at his father with teeth bared and arms poised to strike. But Henrikk was ready for him, hitting Nathaniel's face with the heel of his palm so hard his head snapped back.

Henrikk's gaze darted briefly to Nathaniel, who was struggling to get to his feet, before turning his empty eyes to her.

"My darling Kirabelle, it is my deep pleasure to inform you that *I* am your master. My ever-obedient son has been grooming you to serve me."

It took a moment for the words to sink in.

When they did, Kira's body seized in fear and shock as an icy hand clamped over her heart, just as Henrikk's hand was clamped on her jaw, his fingernails biting her cheeks.

No, no, no.

She felt detached from her body, as if the ground had crumbled away and she was suspended above an abyss. She swallowed hard, her eyes watering as she blinked up at Nathaniel's father in disbelief. "Wh-what?"

Henrikk continued as if she hadn't spoken. "Now, your king gave you an order," he said, his fangs extending in sharp points as he stared down at her with contempt. "Kneel for me, slut. Let us see what you're good for."

Well done, pet. Halfway there. Now brace yourself – it's a long story, and I expect you to take it all.

Visit linktr.ee/darcyfayton for:
Newsletter Sign-up | Amazon | Goodreads | Bookbub | Patreon | Kickstarter

To Be Continued...

Thank you for reading my debut novel, *Plug and Claim.* This was Book 1 of the *Plug and Claim Duology.*

The adventure continues with *Plug and Tame,* the steamy and satisfying conclusion to the duology.

COMING SOON: PLUG AND TAME (BOOK 2)...

DARCY FAYTON

PLUG *and* Tame

THE STEAMY CONCLUSION TO *PLUG AND CLAIM*

"NO MATTER WHERE YOU GO, NO MATTER HOW MANY YEARS PASS, YOU WILL ALWAYS BE MINE. I WILL FIND YOU, AND WHEN I DO, I WILL BEND YOU OVER AND CLAIM YOU AS MANY TIMES AS IT TAKES TO CURE THIS HEARTACHE."

Plug and Tame is the steamy and satisfying conclusion of the paranormal dark romance duology, *Plug and Claim,* and contains more spice, including praise, degradation and punishment.

Kira's newfound perception of the Vampire Prince, Nathaniel, shatters when she uncovers his sinister ploy: to groom her to become his father's play thing.

Forced into a frantic escape, Kira flees the academy, desperate to distance herself from Nathaniel and his malevolent father.

Except Nathaniel will not let her get away so easily. His ambitions for her are vast, and he is determined to help her rise to become the leader she was destined to become. But first, he will make her crawl.

Satisfy your darkest desires with *Plug and Tame*, the

steamy sequel that will deliver heart-pounding action, spice, adventure, and a highly-anticipated happily ever after.

ORDER NOW ON AMAZON:
linktr.ee/darcyfayton

WANT TO READ PLUG AND TAME RIGHT NOW?

Patrons are already reading it. Join my Patreon to receive:

- Early access to my stories as I write them

- Early digital copies of my books

- Early access to ARCs

- Bonus content and Exclusive Polls

- My heartfelt appreciation for your support of my writing career

Check it out: https://www.patreon.com/darcyfayton

BONUS OFFER

- Sign up to my newsletter and receive the first 5 chapters of *Plug and Tame*

Both books are available to order on paperback and hardcover.

TEASER SCENE FROM: *PLUG AND TAME (BOOK 2)*

The darkness of the cave swallowed them whole, dousing Kira's rage until the only emotion she had left was stark fear. Nathaniel took her deeper into its depths until the bright entrance was out of sight.

Kira stopped screaming, partly because the cave amplified her voice in a terrifying echo, and also because she was too busy trying to suck in air past the gag. But she fought Nathaniel every step of the way, and his laboured breathing made her cling to the hope that she could overpower him in his weakened state.

She tried to morph, but he yanked her hair painfully, interrupting the process.

"Not now, pet," he said in a ragged voice. "Not now."

They came to a standstill in the pitch-black, her entire body clammy and paralysed with dread as her heart thumped sickeningly in her chest.

"I just want to talk," Nathaniel whispered in her ear, loosening the gag. "Be a good girl and show me how quiet you can be."

She gasped for breath as the collar and gag fell away, wheezing and spitting excess saliva out. Her body was shaking, but she froze as he gently brushed her hair off her shoulder.

"Please," she whimpered. The word sounded small and useless in the dark void where the only one who heard her was *him*. The quiet, meek wolf of her personality took over as the strong one receded. "Please, Nathaniel," she repeated, "you said you wouldn't bite me again."

Darcy Fayton's Books

PROMISING YOU DARK FANTASY ROMANCE WITH HOT SPICY SLOW BURN ROMANCE. ALWAYS.

Photo by @tata.lifepages

PLUG AND CLAIM

She was ready to fight. She was ready to resist capture. But she was not ready for *him*, nor the collar he placed around her neck.

The complete Plug and Claim Duology featuring Kira and Nathaniel. A dark fantasy romance with BDSM themes including 'on your knees' vibes, pet play, and a quest for revolution.

PLUG AND DRAIN

Vampires crave more than blood when they visit students' beds. Refusing a vampire student is dangerous. Refusing the headmaster? Impossible.

A spicy duology featuring a forbidden romance between wolf shifter student Susie and Headmaster Arken. It is also the gripping prequel to the Plug and Claim Duology.

Book 1 Release Date: Mar 31st 2024

PLUGGED AT THE GATES

It is forbidden for vampires to fall in love with their pet wolf. Public displays of rutting, however, are not only acceptable, but encouraged, especially in the context of punishment.

A spicy short story featuring Kira and Nathaniel. It's a standalone that can be read by itself. It also serves as a bonus spicy chapter in Plug and Tame.

Available on Amazon, Patreon & my Newsletter

Acknowledgements and Praise

PATRONS:

A very special thank you to all my Patrons. Your support is hugely appreciated and has helped make this story possible!

To my **Good Pets**, thank you for being so good to me.

And as for my **Bad Pets**, you've been especially bad. Yes, you know who you are, and now the rest of the world does, too:

bookish.adventures.of.p
Christine Powell
Carla
Danielle Coon-Davis
gloriaoxford
Shauni Breen
Katie
Melissa

KICKSTARTER BACKERS:

A huge thank you to everyone who backed the Kickstarter for *Plug and Claim*. It was such an awesome thing for me to experience as a debut author.

Ruthenia (Ruth) Dillon
Sarah Freedman
redfishguy
Adriane
MCC
Danielle Williams
Karla V.
Christine L. Powell
Jessica Michalski
Diane Wagoner
Elisha Bryant
valen grimes
Maike ten Dam
Cherelle Hopper
Bianca Tatjana Višić Ritorto
Alexandra Varin Thiel
Zyra Kenzi Bosa
Vicky Salas
Cyynder
David Riedinger
Ltz
Brittany Szwaczkowski
Keema
phoenix_17
Amy Wendt

Kimmer Ann
Leticia Henriksen
Abby Adams
Nekia T
Morby
Kara Sanders
Tionna
Alana
chester

EARLY READERS WHO HELPED PROOFREAD THIS DUOLOGY:

This series has benefited from not only two professional editors, but also a group of wonderful readers who took the time to help polish the story and pick-up last-minute typos and errors. As an indie author, I'm so grateful to every single one of you. I did my best to reach out to everyone I could, so if you don't see your name on this list, please know how much I appreciate you.

- **Charlie Foley-Friend (The Book Hangover)**
- **Aisha Prentice @the_bookish_cave_of_wonders**
- **Schuyler Marina**
- **Ellie Greenslade @ellies_littlelibrary**
- **Taylor Wittman**
- **Kez Marie**
- **Tabitha Orr**
- **Stacey's Bookcorner**
- **Tallulah @lulahisreading**

And finally, a huge thank you to everyone who has read my books and encouraged me to continue writing! I love creating stories so much and I hope you'll join me on my next adventure.

~ SUPPORT MY WRITING ~
JOIN MY PATREON FOR EARLY ACCESS TO CHAPTERS AND BONUS CONTENT:
WWW.PATREON.COM/DARCYFAYTON

Made in the USA
Las Vegas, NV
24 February 2024

86253084R00236